FRATERNITY

Fraternity

John Galsworthy

Carroll & Graf Publishers, Inc.
New York

Originally published in the United States in 1909 by
G. P. Putnam's Sons, New York.

First Carroll & Graf edition 1995.

Carroll & Graf Publishers, Inc.
260 Fifth Avenue
New York, NY 10001

ISBN 0-7867-0212-5

Library of Congress Cataloging-in-Publication Data is available.

Manufactured in the United States of America

10 9 8 7 6 5 4 3 2 1

CONTENTS

Brother, brother, on some far shore
Hast thou a city, is there a door
That knows thy footfall, Wandering One?

Murray's *Electra of Euripides*

Chapter 1
THE SHADOW

ON the afternoon of the last day of April, 190—, a billowy sea of little broken clouds crowned the thin air above High Street, Kensington. This soft tumult of vapours, covering nearly all the firmament, was in onslaught round a patch of blue sky, shaped somewhat like a star, which still gleamed—a single gentian flower amongst innumerable grass. Each of these small clouds seemed fitted with a pair of unseen wings, and, as insects fly on their too constant journeys, they were setting forth all ways round this starry blossom which burned so clear with the colour of its far fixity. On one side they were massed in fleecy congeries, so crowding each other that no edge or outline was preserved; on the other, higher, stronger, emergent from their fellow-clouds, they seemed leading the attack on that surviving gleam of the ineffable. Infinite was the variety of those million separate vapours, infinite the unchanging unity of that fixed blue star.

Down in the street beneath this eternal warring of the various soft-winged clouds on the unmisted ether, men, women, children, and their familiars—horses, dogs, and cats—were pursuing their occupations with the sweet zest of the Spring. They streamed along, and the noise of their frequenting rose in an unbroken roar: 'I, I—I, I!'

The crowd was perhaps thickest outside the premises of Messrs Rose and Thorn. Every kind of being, from the highest to the lowest, passed in front of the hundred doors of this establishment; and before the costume window a rather tall, slight, graceful woman stood thinking: 'It really is gentian blue! But I don't know whether I ought to buy it, with all this distress about!'

Her eyes, which were greenish-grey, and often ironical lest they should reveal her soul, seemed probing a blue gown displayed in that window, to the very heart of its desirability.

'And suppose Stephen doesn't like me in it!' This doubt set her gloved fingers pleating the bosom of her frock. Into that little pleat she folded the essence of herself, the wish to have and the fear of having, the wish to be and the fear of being, and her veil, falling from the edge of her hat, three inches from her face, shrouded with its tissue her half-decided little features, her rather too high cheek-bones, her cheeks that were slightly hollowed, as though Time had kissed them just a bit too much.

The old man, with a long face, eyes rimmed like a parrot's, and discoloured nose, who, so long as he did not sit down, was permitted to frequent the pavement just there and sell the *Westminster Gazette*, marked her, and took his empty pipe out of his mouth.

It was his business to know all the passers-by, and his pleasure too; his mind was thus distracted from the condition of his feet. He knew this particular lady with the delicate face, and found her puzzling; she sometimes bought the paper which Fate condemned him, against his politics, to sell. The Tory journals were undoubtedly those which her class of person ought to purchase. He knew a lady when he saw one. In fact, before Life threw him into the streets, by giving him a disease in curing which his savings had disappeared, he had been a butler, and for the gentry had a respect as incurable as was his distrust of 'all that class of people' who bought their things at 'these 'ere large establishments', and attended 'these 'ere subscription dances at the Town 'All over there'. He watched her with special interest, not, indeed, attempting to attract attention, though conscious in every fibre that he had only sold five copies of his early issues. And he was sorry and surprised when she passed from his sight through one of the hundred doors.

The thought which spurred her into Messrs Rose and Thorn's was this: 'I am thirty-eight; I have a daughter of seventeen! I cannot afford to lose my husband's admiration. The time is on me when I really must make myself look nice!'

Before a long mirror, in whose bright pool there yearly bathed hundreds of women's bodies, divested of skirts and bodices, whose unruffled surface reflected daily a dozen women's souls divested of everything, her eyes became as bright as steel; but having ascertained the need of taking two inches off the chest of the gentian frock, one off its waist, three off its hips, and of adding one to its skirt, they clouded again with doubt, as though prepared to fly from the decision she had come to. Resuming her bodice, she asked:

'When could you let me have it?'

'At the end of the week, madam.'

'Not till then?'

'We are very pressed, madam.'

'Oh, but you *must* let me have it by Thursday at the latest, please.'

The fitter sighed: 'I will do my best.'

'I shall rely on you. Mrs Stephen Dallison, 76, The Old Square.'

Going downstairs she thought: 'That poor girl looked very tired; it's a shame they give them such long hours!' and she passed into the street.

A voice said timidly behind her: '*Westminster*, marm?'

'That's the poor old creature,' thought Cecilia Dallison, 'whose nose is so unpleasant. I don't really think I——' and she felt for a penny in her little bag. Standing beside the 'poor old creature' was a woman clothed in worn but neat black clothes, and an ancient toque that had once known a better head. The wan remains of a little bit of fur lay round her throat. She had a thin face, not without refinement, mild, very clear brown eyes, and a twist of smooth black hair. Beside her was a skimpy little boy, and in her arms a baby. Mrs Dallison held out twopence for the paper, but it was at the woman that she looked.

'Oh, Mrs Hughs,' she said, 'we've been expecting you to hem the curtains!'

The woman slightly pressed the baby.

'I am very sorry, ma'am. I knew I was expected, but I've had such trouble.'

Cecilia winced. 'Oh, really?'

'Yes, m'm; it's my husband.'

'Oh, dear!' Cecilia murmured. 'But why didn't you come to us?'

'I didn't feel up to it, ma'am; I didn't really——'

A tear ran down her cheek, and was caught in a furrow near the mouth.

Mrs Dallison said hurriedly: 'Yes, yes; I'm very sorry.'

'This old gentleman, Mr Creed, lives in the same house with us, and he is going to speak to my husband.'

The old man wagged his head on its lean stalk of neck.

'He ought to know better than be'ave 'imself so disrespectable,' he said.

Cecilia looked at him, and murmured: 'I hope he won't turn on *you*!'

The old man shuffled his feet.

'I likes to live at peace with everybody. I shall have the police to 'im if he misdemeans hisself with me! . . . *Westminster*, sir?' And, screening his mouth from Mrs Dallison, he added in a loud whisper: 'Execution of the Shoreditch murderer!'

Cecilia felt suddenly as though the world were listening to her conversation with these two rather seedy persons.

'I don't really know what I can do for you, Mrs Hughs. I'll speak to Mr Dallison, and to Mr Hilary too.'

'Yes, ma'am; thank you, ma'am.'

With a smile that seemed to deprecate its own appearance, Cecilia grasped her skirts and crossed the road. 'I hope I wasn't unsympathetic,' she thought, looking back at the three figures on the edge of the pavement—the old man with his papers, and his discoloured nose thrust upwards under iron-rimmed spectacles; the seamstress in her black dress; the skimpy little boy. Neither speaking nor moving, they were looking out before them at the traffic; and something in Cecilia revolted at this sight. It was lifeless, hopeless, unaesthetic.

'What can one do,' she thought, 'for women like Mrs Hughs, who always look like that? And that poor old man! I suppose I oughtn't to have bought that dress, but Stephen *is* tired of this.'

She turned out of the main street into a road preserved from commoner forms of traffic, and stopped at a long low house half hidden behind the trees of its front garden.

It was the residence of Hilary Dallison, her husband's brother, and himself the husband of Bianca, her own sister.

The queer conceit came to Cecilia that it resembled Hilary. Its look was kindly and uncertain; its colour a palish tan; the eyebrows of its windows rather straight than arched, and those deep-set eyes, the windows, twinkled hospitably; it had, as it were, a sparse moustache and beard of creepers, and dark marks here and there, like the lines and shadows on the faces of those who think too much. Beside it, and apart, though connected by a passage, a studio stood, and about that studio—of white rough-cast, with a black oak door, and peacock-blue paint—was something a little hard and fugitive, well suited to Bianca, who used it, indeed, to paint in. It seemed to stand, with its eyes on the house, shrinking defiantly from too close company, as though it could not entirely give itself to anything. Cecilia, who often worried over the relations between her sister and her brother-in-law, suddenly felt how fitting and symbolical this was.

But, mistrusting inspirations, which, experience told her, committed one too much, she walked quickly up the stone-flagged pathway to the door. Lying in the porch was a little moonlight-coloured lady bulldog, of toy breed, who gazed up with eyes like agates, delicately waving her bell-rope tail, as it was her habit to do towards everyone, for she had been handed down clearer and paler with each generation, till she had at last lost all the peculiar virtues of dogs that bait the bull.

Speaking the word 'Miranda!' Mrs Stephen Dallison tried to pat this daughter of the house. The little bulldog withdrew from her caress, being also unaccustomed to commit herself. . . .

Mondays were Bianca's 'days', and Cecilia made her way towards the studio. It was a large high room, full of people.

Motionless, by himself, close to the door, stood an old man, very thin and rather bent, with silvery hair, and a thin silvery beard grasped in his transparent fingers. He was dressed in a suit of smoke-grey cottage tweed, which smelt of peat, and an Oxford shirt, whose collar, ceasing prematurely, exposed a lean brown neck; his trousers, too, ended very soon, and showed light socks. In his attitude there was something suggestive of the patience and determination of a mule. At Cecilia's approach he raised his eyes. It was at once apparent why, in so full a room, he was standing alone. Those blue eyes looked as if he were about to utter a prophetic statement.

'They have been speaking to me of an execution,' he said.

Cecilia made a nervous movement.

'Yes, Father?'

'To take life,' went on the old man in a voice which, though charged with strong emotion, seemed to be speaking to itself, 'was the chief mark of the insensate barbarism still prevailing in those days. It sprang from the most irreligious fetish, the belief in the permanence of the individual ego after death. From the worship of that fetish had come all the sorrows of the human race.'

Cecilia, with an involuntary quiver of her little bag, said:

'Father, how can you?'

'They did not stop to love each other in this life; they were so sure they had all eternity to do it in. The doctrine was an invention to enable men to act like dogs with clear consciences. Love could never come to full fruition till it was destroyed.'

Cecilia looked hastily round; no one had heard. She moved a little sideways, and became merged in another group. Her father's lips continued moving. He had resumed the patient attitude that so slightly suggested mules. A voice behind her said: 'I do think your father is such an interesting man, Mrs Dallison.'

Cecilia turned and saw a woman of middle height, with her hair done in the early Italian fashion, and very small, dark, lively eyes, which looked as though her love of living would keep her busy each minute of her day and all the minutes that she could occupy of everybody else's days.

'Mrs Tallents Smallpeace? Oh! how do you do? I've been meaning to come and see you for quite a long time, but I know you're always so busy.'

With doubting eyes, half friendly and half defensive, as though chaffing to prevent herself from being chaffed, Cecilia looked at Mrs Tallents Smallpeace, whom she had met several times at Bianca's house. The widow of a somewhat famous connoisseur, she was now secretary of the League for Educating Orphans who have Lost both Parents, vice-president of the Forlorn Hope for Maids in Peril, and treasurer to Thursday Hops for Working Girls. She seemed to know every man and woman who was worth knowing, and some besides; to see all picture-shows; to hear every new musician; and attend the opening performance of every play. With regard to literature, she would say that authors bored her; but she was always doing them good turns, inviting them to meet their critics or editors, and sometimes—though this was not generally known—pulling them out of the holes they were prone to get into, by lending them a sum of money—after which, as she would plaintively remark, she rarely saw them more.

She had a peculiar spiritual significance to Mrs Stephen Dallison, being just on the border-line between those of Bianca's friends whom Cecilia did not wish and those whom she did wish to come to her own house, for Stephen, a barrister in an official position, had a keen sense of the ridiculous. Since Hilary wrote books and was a poet, and Bianca painted, their friends would naturally be either interesting or queer; and though for Stephen's sake it was important to establish which was which, they were so very often both. Such people stimulated, taken in small doses, but neither on her husband's account nor on her daughter's did Cecilia desire that they should come to her in swarms. Her attitude of mind towards them was, in fact, similar—a sort of pleasurable dread—to that in which she purchased the *Westminster Gazette* to feel the pulse of social progress.

Mrs Tallents Smallpeace's dark little eyes twinkled.

'I hear that Mr Stone—that *is* your father's name, I think—is writing a book which will create quite a sensation when it comes out.'

Cecilia bit her lips. 'I hope it never will come out,' she was on the point of saying.

'What will it be called?' asked Mrs Tallents Smallpeace. 'I

gather that it's a book of Universal Brotherhood. That's so nice!'

Cecilia made a movement of annoyance. 'Who told you?'

'Ah!' said Mrs Tallents Smallpeace, 'I do think your sister gets such attractive people at her At Homes. They all take *such* interest in things.'

A little surprised at herself, Cecilia answered: 'Too much for me!'

Mrs Tallents Smallpeace smiled. 'I mean in art and social questions. Surely one can't be too interested in them?'

Cecilia said rather hastily:

'Oh no, of course not.' And both ladies looked around them. A buzz of conversation fell on Cecilia's ears.

'Have you seen the "Aftermath"? It's really quite wonderful!'

'Poor old chap! he's so rococo. . . .'

'There's a new man. . . .'

'She's very sympathetic. . . .'

'But the condition of the poor. . . . ?'

'Is that Mr Balladyce? Oh, really. . . .'

'It gives you such a feeling of life. . . .'

'Bourgeois! . . .'

The voice of Mrs Tallents Smallpeace broke through: 'But do please tell me who is that young girl with the young man looking at the picture over there. She's quite charming!'

Cecilia's cheeks went a very pretty pink.

'Oh, that's my little daughter.'

'Really! Have you a daughter as big as that? Why, she must be seventeen!'

'Nearly eighteen!'

'What is her name?'

'Thyme,' said Cecilia, with a little smile. She felt that Mrs Tallents Smallpeace was about to say: 'How charming!'

Mrs Tallents Smallpeace saw her smile and paused. 'Who is the young man with her?'

'My nephew, Martin Stone.'

'The son of your brother who was killed with his wife in that dreadful Alpine accident? He looks a very decided sort of young man. He's got that new look. What is he?'

'He's very nearly a doctor. I never know whether he's quite finished or not.'

'I thought perhaps he might have something to do with Art.'

'Oh no, he despises Art.'

'And does your daughter despise it, too?'

'No; she's studying it.'

'Oh, really! How interesting! I do think the rising generation amusing don't you? They're so independent.'

Cecilia looked uneasily at the rising generation. They were standing side by side before the picture, curiously observant and detached, exchanging short remarks and glances. They seemed to watch all these circling, chatting, bending, smiling people with a sort of youthful, matter-of-fact, half-hostile curiosity. The young man had a pale face, clean-shaven, with a strong jaw, a long, straight nose, a rather bumpy forehead which did not recede, and clear grey eyes. His sarcastic lips were firm and quick, and he looked at people with disconcerting straightness. The young girl wore a blue-green frock. Her face was charming, with eager, hazel-grey eyes, a bright colour, and fluffy hair the colour of ripe nuts.

'That's your sister's picture, "The Shadow", they're looking at, isn't it?' asked Mrs Tallents Smallpeace. 'I remember seeing it on Christmas Day, and the little model who was sitting for it—an attractive type! Your brother-in-law told me how interested you all were in her. Quite a romantic story, wasn't it, about her fainting from want of food when she first came to sit?'

Cecilia murmured something. Her hands were moving nervously; she looked ill at ease.

These signs passed unperceived by Mrs Tallents Smallpeace, whose eyes were busy.

'In the F.H.M.P., of course, I see a lot of young girls placed in delicate positions, just on the borders, don't you know? You should really join the F.H.M.P., Mrs Dallison. It's a first-rate thing—most absorbing work.'

The doubting deepened in Cecilia's eyes.

'Oh, it must be!' she said. 'I've so little time.'

Mrs Tallents Smallpeace went on at once.

'Don't you think that we live in the most interesting days? There are such a lot of movements going on. It's quite exciting. We all feel that we can't shut our eyes any longer to social questions. I mean the condition of the people alone is enough to give one nightmares!'

'Yes, yes,' said Cecilia; 'it is dreadful, of course.'

'Politicians and officials are so hopeless, one can't look for anything from them.'

Cecilia drew herself up. 'Oh, do you think so?' she said.

'I was just talking to Mr Balladyce. He says that Art and Literature must be put on a new basis altogether.'

'Yes,' said Cecilia; 'really? Is he that funny little man?'

'I think he's so monstrously clever.'

Cecilia answered quickly: 'I know—I know. Of course, *something* must be done.'

'Yes,' said Mrs Tallents Smallpeace absently, 'I think we all feel that. Oh, do tell me! I've been talking to such a delightful person—just the type you see when you go into the City—thousands of them, all in such good black coats. It's so unusual to really meet one nowadays; and they're so refreshing, they have such nice simple views. There he is, standing just behind your sister.'

Cecilia by a nervous gesture indicated that she recognised the personality alluded to. 'Oh yes,' she said; 'Mr Purcey. I don't know why he comes to see us.'

'I think he's so delicious!' said Mrs Tallents Smallpeace dreamily. Her little dark eyes, like bees, had flown to sip honey from the flower in question—a man of broad build and medium height, dressed with accuracy, who seemed just a little out of his proper bed. His mustachioed mouth wore a set smile; his cheerful face was rather red, with a forehead of no extravagant height or breadth, and a conspicuous jaw; his hair was thick and light in colour, and his eyes were small, grey, and shrewd. He was looking at a picture.

'He's so delightfully unconscious,' murmured Mrs Tallents Smallpeace. 'He didn't even seem to know that there was a problem of the lower classes.'

'Did he tell you that he had a picture?' asked Cecilia gloomily.

'Oh yes, by Harpignies, with the accent on the "pig". It's worth three times what he gave for it. It's nice to be made to feel that there is still all that mass of people just simply measuring everything by what they gave for it.'

'And did he tell you my grandfather Carfax's dictum in the Banstock case?' muttered Cecilia.

'Oh yes: "The man who does not know his own mind should be made an Irishman by Act of Parliament." He said it was so awfully good.'

'He would,' replied Cecilia.

'He seems to depress you, rather!'

'Oh no; I believe he's quite a nice sort of person. One can't be rude to him; he really did what he thought a very kind thing to my father. That's how we came to know him. Only it's rather trying when he will come to call regularly. He gets a little on one's nerves.'

'Ah, that's just what I feel is so jolly about him; no one would ever get on his nerves. I do think we've got too many nerves, don't you? Here's your brother-in-law. He's such an uncommon-looking man; I want to have a talk with him about that little model. A country girl, wasn't she?'

She had turned her head towards a tall man with a very slight stoop and a brown, thin, bearded face, who was approaching from the door. She did not see that Cecilia had flushed, and was looking at her almost angrily. The tall thin man put his hand on Cecilia's arm, saying gently: 'Hello, Cis! Stephen here yet?'

Cecilia shook her head.

'You know Mrs Tallents Smallpeace, Hilary?'

The tall man bowed. His hazel-coloured eyes were shy, gentle, and deep-set; his eyebrows, hardly ever still, gave him a look of austere whimsicality. His dark brown hair was very lightly touched with grey, and a frequent kindly smile played on his lips. His unmannerismed manner was quiet to the point of extinction. He had long, thin, brown hands, and nothing peculiar about his dress.

'I'll leave you to talk to Mrs Tallents Smallpeace,' Cecilia said.

A knot of people round Mr Balladyce prevented her from moving far, however, and the voice of Mrs Smallpeace travelled to her ears.

'I was talking about that little model. It was so good of you to take such interest in the girl. I wondered whether *we* could do anything for her.'

Cecilia's hearing was too excellent to miss the tone of Hilary's reply:

'Oh, thank you; I don't think so.'

'I fancied perhaps you might feel that our Society—hers is an unsatisfactory profession for young girls!'

Cecilia saw the back of Hilary's neck turn red. She turned her head away.

'Of course, there are many very nice models indeed,' said the voice of Mrs Tallents Smallpeace. 'I don't mean that they are necessarily at all—if they're girls of strong character; and especially if they don't sit for the—the altogether.'

Hilary's dry, staccato answer came to Cecilia's ears: 'Thank you; it's very kind of you.'

'Oh, of course, if it's not necessary. Your wife's picture was so clever, Mr Dallison—such an interesting type.'

Without intention Cecilia found herself before that picture. It stood with its face a little turned towards the wall, as though somewhat in disgrace, portraying the full-length figure of a girl standing in deep shadow, with her arms half outstretched, as if asking for something. Her eyes were fixed on Cecilia, and through her parted lips breath almost seemed to come. The only colour in the picture was the pale blue of those eyes, the pallid red of those parted lips, the still paler brown of the hair; the rest was shadow. In the foreground light was falling as though from a street-lamp.

Cecilia thought: 'That girl's eyes and mouth haunt me. Whatever made Bianca choose such a subject? It is clever, of course—for her.'

Chapter 2

A FAMILY DISCUSSION

THE marriage of Sylvanus Stone, Professor of the Natural Sciences, to Anne, daughter of Mr Justice Carfax, of the well-known county family—the Carfaxes of Spring Deans, Hants—was recorded in the sixties. The baptisms of Martin, Cecilia, and Bianca, son and daughters of Sylvanus and Anne Stone, were to be discovered registered in Kensington in the three consecutive years following, as though some single-minded person had been connected with their births. After this the baptisms of no more offspring were to be found anywhere, as if that single mind had encountered opposition. But in the eighties there was noted in the register of the same church the burial of 'Anne, *née* Carfax, wife of Sylvanus Stone'. In that '*née* Carfax' there was, to those who knew, something more than met the eye. It summed up the mother of Cecilia and Bianca, and, in more subtle fashions, Cecilia and Bianca too. It summed up that fugitive, barricading look in their bright eyes, which, though spoken of in the family as 'the Carfax eyes', were in reality far from coming from old Mr Justice Carfax. They had been his wife's in turn, and had much annoyed a man of his decided character. He himself had always known his mind, and had let others know it, too; reminding his wife that she was an impracticable woman, who knew not her own mind; and devoting his lawful gains to securing the future of his progeny. It would have disturbed him if he had lived to see his grand-daughters and their times. Like so many able men of his generation, far-seeing enough in practical affairs, he had never considered the possibility that the descendants of those who, like himself, had laid up treasure for their children's children might acquire the quality of taking time, balancing pros and cons, looking ahead, and not putting one foot down before picking the other up. He had not foreseen, indeed, that to wobble might become an art, in order that, before anything was done, people might know the full necessity for doing something, and how impossible it would be to do—indeed, foolish to attempt to do—that which would fully meet the case. He, who had been a man of action all his life, had not perceived how it would grow to be matter of common instinct that to act was to commit oneself, and that, while what one had was not precisely what one wanted, what one had not (if one had it) would be as bad. He had never been self-conscious—it was not the custom of his generation—and, having but little imagination, had never suspected that he was laying up that quality for his descendants, together with a competence that secured them a comfortable leisure.

Of all the persons in his grand-daughter's studio that afternoon, that stray sheep Mr Purcey would have been, perhaps, the only one whose judgments he would have considered sound. No one had laid up a competence for Mr Purcey, who had been in business from the age of twenty.

It is is uncertain whether the mere fact that he was not in his own fold kept this visitor lingering in the studio when all other guests were gone; or whether it was simply the feeling that the longer he stayed in contact with really artistic people the more distinguished he was becoming. Probably the latter, for the possession of that Harpignies, a good specimen, which he had bought by accident, and subsequently by accident discovered to have a peculiar value, had become a factor in his life, marking him out from all his friends, who went in more for a neat type of Royal Academy landscape, together with reproductions of young ladies in eighteenth-century costumes seated on horseback, or in Scotch gardens. A junior partner in a banking-house of some importance, he lived at Wimbledon, whence he passed up and down daily in his car. To this he owed his acquaintance with the family of Dallison. For one day, after telling his chauffeur to await him at the gate of the Broad Walk, he had set out to stroll down Rotten Row, as he often did on the way home, designing to nod to anybody that he knew. It had turned out a somewhat barren expedition. No one of any consequence had met his eye; and it was with a certain, almost fretful longing for distraction that in Kensington Gardens he came on an old man feeding birds out of a paper bag. The birds having flown away on seeing him, he approached the feeder to apologise.

'I'm afraid I frightened your birds, sir,' he began.

This old man, who was dressed in smoke-grey tweeds which exhaled a poignant scent of peat, looked at him without answering.

'I'm afraid your birds saw me coming,' Mr Purcey said again.

'In those days,' said the aged stranger, 'birds were afraid of men.'

Mr Purcey's shrewd grey eyes perceived at once that he had a character to deal with.

'Ah, yes!' he said; 'I see—you allude to the present time. That's very nice. Ha, ha!'

The old man answered: 'The emotion of fear is inseparably connected with a primitive state of fratricidal rivalry.'

This sentence put Mr Purcey on his guard.

'The old chap,' he thought, 'is touched. He evidently oughtn't to be out here by himself.' He debated, therefore, whether he should hasten away towards his car, or stand by in case his assistance should be needed. Being a kind-hearted man, who believed in his capacity for putting things to rights, and noticing a certain, delicacy—a 'sort of something rather distinguished', as he phrased it afterwards—in the old fellow's face and figure, he decided to see if he could be of any service. They walked along together, Mr Purcey watching his new friend askance, and directing the march to where he had ordered his chauffeur to await him.

'You are very fond of birds, I suppose,' he said cautiously.

'The birds are our brothers.'

The answer was of a nature to determine Mr Purcey in his diagnosis of the case.

'I've got my car here,' he said. 'Let me give you a lift home.'

This new but aged acquaintance did not seem to hear; his lips moved as though he were following out some thought.

'In those days,' Mr Purcey heard him say, 'the congeries of men were known as rookeries. The expression was hardly just towards that handsome bird.'

Mr Purcey touched him hastily on the arm.

'I've got my car here, sir,' he said. 'Do let me put you down!'

Telling the story afterwards, he had spoken thus:

'The old chap knew where he lived right enough; but dash me if I believe he noticed that I was taking him there in my car—I had the A.1. Damyer out. That's how I came to make the acquaintance of these Dallisons. He's the writer, you know; and she paints—rather the new school—she admires Harpignies. Well, when I got there in the car I found Dallison in the garden. Of course I was careful not to put my foot into it. I told him: "I found this old gentleman wandering about. I've just brought him back in my car." Who should the old chap turn out to be but her father! They were awfully obliged to me. Charmin' people, but very what d'you call it—*fin de siècle*—like these professors, these artistic pigs—seem to know rather a queer set, advanced people, and all that sort of cuckoo, always talkin' about the poor, and societies, and new religions, and that kind of thing.'

Though he had since been to see them several times, the Dallisons had never robbed him of the virtuous feeling of that good action—they had never let him know that he had brought home, not, as he imagined, a lunatic, but merely a philosopher.

It had been somewhat of a quiet shock to him to find Mr Stone close to the doorway when he entered Bianca's studio that afternoon; for though he had seen him since the encounter in Kensington Gardens, and knew that he was writing a book, he still felt that he was not quite the sort of old man that one ought to meet about. He had at once begun to tell him of the hanging of the Shoreditch murderer, as recorded in the evening papers. Mr Stone's reception of that news had still further confirmed his original views. When all the guests were gone—with the exception of Mr and Mrs Stephen Dallison and Miss Dallison, 'that awfully pretty girl', and the young man 'who was always hangin' about her'—he had approached his hostess for some quiet talk. She stood listening to him, very well bred, with just that habitual spice of mockery in her smile, which to Mr Purcey's eyes made her 'a very strikin'-lookin' woman, but rather——' There he would stop, for it required a greater psychologist than he to describe a secret disharmony which a little marred her beauty. Due to some too violent cross of blood, to an environment too unsuited, to what not—it was branded on her. Those who knew Bianca Dallison better than Mr Purcey were but too well aware of this fugitive, proud spirit permeating one whose beauty would otherwise have passed unquestioned.

She was a little taller than Cecilia, her figure rather fuller and more graceful, her hair darker, her eyes, too, darker and more deeply set, her cheek-bones higher, her colouring richer. That spirit of the age, Disharmony, must have presided when a child so vivid and dark-coloured was christened Bianca.

Mr Purcey, however, was not a man who allowed the finest shades of feeling to interfere with his enjoyments. She was a 'strikin'-lookin' woman', and there was, thanks to Harpignies, a link between them.

'Your father and I, Mrs Dallison, can't quite understand each other,' he began. 'Our views of life don't seem to hit it off exactly.'

'Really,' murmured Bianca; 'I should have thought that you'd have got on so well.'

'He's a little bit too—er—scriptural for me, perhaps,' said Mr Purcey, with some delicacy.

'Did we never tell you,' Bianca answered softly, 'that my father was a rather well-known man of science before his illness?'

'Ah!' replied Mr Purcey, a little puzzled; 'that, of course. D'you know, of all your pictures, Mrs Dallison, I think that one you call "The Shadow" is the most rippin'. There's a something about it that gets hold of you. That was the original, wasn't it, at your Christmas party—attractive girl—it's an awf'ly good likeness.'

Bianca's face had changed, but Mr Purcey was not a man to notice a little thing like that.

'If ever you want to part with it,' he said, 'I hope you'll give me a chance. I mean it'd be a pleasure to me to have it. I think it'll be worth a lot of money some day.'

Bianca did not answer, and Mr Purcey, feeling suddenly a little awkward, said: 'I've got my car waiting. I must be off—really.' Shaking hands with all of them, he went away.

When the door had closed behind his back, a universal sigh went up. It was followed by a silence, which Hilary broke.

'We'll smoke, Stevie, if Cis doesn't mind.'

Stephen Dallison placed a cigarette between his moustacheless lips, always rather screwed up, and ready to nip with a smile anything that might make him feel ridiculous.

'Phew!' he said. 'Our friend Purcey becomes a little tedious. He seems to take the whole of Philistia about with him.'

'He's a very decent fellow,' murmured Hilary.

'A bit heavy, surely!' Stephen Dallison's face, though also long and narrow, was not much like his brother's. His eyes, though not unkind, were far more scrutinising, inquisitive, and practical; his hair darker, smoother.

Letting a puff of smoke escape, he added:

'Now, that's the sort of man to give you a good sound opinion. You should have asked *him*, Cis.'

Cecilia answered with a frown:

'Don't chaff, Stephen; I'm perfectly serious about Mrs Hughs.'

'Well, I don't see what I can do for the good woman, my dear. One can't interfere in these domestic matters.'

'But it seems dreadful that we who employ her should be able to do nothing for her. Don't you think so, B.?'

'I suppose we could do something for her if we wanted to badly enough.'

Bianca's voice, which had the self-distrustful ring of modern music, suited her personality.

A glance passed between Stephen and his wife.

'That's B. all over!' it seemed to say.

'Hound Street, where they live, is a horrid place.'

It was Thyme who spoke, and everybody looked round at her.

'How do you know that?' asked Cecilia.

'I went to see.'

'With whom?'

'Martin.'

The lips of the young man whose name she mentioned curled sarcastically.

Hilary asked gently:

'Well, my dear, what *did* you see?'

'Most of the doors are open——'

Bianca murmured: 'That doesn't tell us much.'

'On the contrary,' said Martin suddenly, in a deep bass voice, 'it tells you everything. Go on.'

'The Hughs live on the top floor at No. 1. It's the best house in the street. On the ground-floor are some people called Budgen; he's a labourer, and she's lame. They've got one son. The Hughs have let off the first-floor front-room to an old man named Creed——'

'Yes, I know,' Cecilia muttered.

'He makes about one and tenpence a day by selling papers. The back-room on that floor they let, of course, to your little model Aunt B.'

'She is not my model now.'

There was a silence such as falls when no one knows how far the matter mentioned is safe to touch on. Thyme proceeded with her report.

'Her room's much the best in the house; it's airy, and it looks out over someone's garden. I suppose she stays there because it's so cheap. The Hugh's rooms are——' She stopped, wrinkling her straight nose.

'So that's the household,' said Hilary. 'Two married couples, one young man, one young girl'—his eyes travelled from one to another of the two married couples, the young man, and the young girl, collected in this room—'and one old man,' he added softly.

'Not quite the sort of place for you to go poking about in, Thyme,' Stephen said ironically. 'Do you think so, Martin?'

'Why not?'

Stephen raised his brows, and glanced towards his wife. Her face was dubious, a little scared. There was a silence. Then Bianca spoke:

'Well?' That word, like nearly all her speeches, seemed rather to disconcert her hearers.

'So Hughs ill-treats her?' said Hilary.

'She says so,' replied Cecilia—'at least, that's what I understood. Of course, I don't know any details.'

'She had better get rid of him, I should think,' Bianca murmured.

Out of the silence that followed Thyme's clear voice was heard saying:

'She can't get a divorce; she could get a separation.'

Cecilia rose uneasily. These words concreted suddenly a wealth of half-acknowledged doubts about her little daughter. This came of letting her hear people talk, and go about with Martin! She might even have been listening to her grandfather—such a thought was most disturbing. And, afraid, on the one hand, of gainsaying the liberty of speech, and, on the other, of seeming to approve her daughter's knowledge of the world, she looked at her husband.

But Stephen did not speak, feeling, no doubt, that to pursue the subject would be either to court an ethical, even an abstract, disquisition, and this one did not do in anybody's presence, much less one's wife and daughter's; or to touch on sordid facts of doubtful character, which was equally distasteful in the circumstances. He, too, however, was uneasy that Thyme should know so much.

The dusk was gathering outside; the fire threw a flickering light, fitfully outlining their figures, making those faces, so familiar to each other, a little mysterious.

At last Stephen broke the silence. 'Of course, I'm very sorry for her, but you'd better let it alone—you can't tell with those sort of people; you never can make out what they want—it's safer not to meddle. At all events, it's a matter for a Society to look into first!'

Cecilia answered: 'But she's on my conscience, Stephen.'
'They're all on *my* conscience,' muttered Hilary.
Bianca looked at him for the first time; then, turning to her nephew, said: 'What do you say, Martin?'
The young man, whose face was stained by the firelight the colour of pale cheese, made no answer.
But suddenly through the stillness came a voice:
'I have thought of something.'
Everyone turned round. Mr Stone was seen emerging from behind 'The Shadow'; his frail figure, in its grey tweeds, his silvery hair and beard, were outlined sharply against the wall.
'Why, Father,' Cecilia said, 'we didn't know that you were here!'
Mr Stone looked round bewildered; it seemed as if he, too, had been ignorant of that fact.
'What is it that you've thought of?'
The firelight leaped suddenly on to Mr Stone's thin yellow hand.
'Each of us,' he said, 'has a shadow in those places—in those streets.'
There was a vague rustling, as of people not taking a remark too seriously, and the sound of a closing door.

Chapter 3

HILARY'S BROWN STUDY

'WHAT do you really think, Uncle Hilary?'
Turning at his writing-table to look at the face of his young niece, Hilary Dallison answered:
'My dear, we have had the same state of affairs since the beginning of the world. There is no chemical process, as far as my knowledge goes, that does not make waste products. What your grandfather calls our "shadows" are the waste products of the social process. That there is a submerged tenth is as certain as that there is an emerged fiftieth like ourselves; exactly who they are and how they come, whether they can ever be improved away, is, I think, as uncertain as anything can be.'
The figure of the girl seated in the big armchair did not stir. Her lips pouted contemptuously, a frown wrinkled her forehead.
'Martin says that a thing is only impossible when we think it so.'

'Faith and the mountain, I'm afraid.'

Thyme's foot shot forth; it nearly came into contact with Miranda, the little bulldog.

'Oh, duckie!'

But the little moonlight bulldog backed away.

'I hate these slums, uncle; they're so disgusting!'

Hilary leaned his face on his thin hand; it was his characteristic attitude.

'They are hateful, disgusting, and heartrending. That does not make the problem any the less difficult, does it?'

'I believe we simply make the difficulties ourselves by seeing them.'

Hilary smiled. 'Does Martin say that too?'

'Of course he does.'

'Speaking broadly,' murmured Hilary, 'I see only one difficulty—human nature.'

Thyme rose. 'I think it horrible to have a low opinion of human nature.'

'My dear,' said Hilary, 'don't you think perhaps that people who have what is called a low opinion of human nature are really more tolerant of it, more in love with it, in fact, than those who, looking to what human nature might be, are bound to hate what human nature is.'

The look which Thyme directed at her uncle's amiable, attractive face, with its pointed beard, high forehead, and peculiar little smile, seemed to alarm Hilary.

'I don't want you to have an unnecessarily low opinion of me, my dear. I'm not one of those people who tell you that everything's all right because the rich have their troubles as well as the poor. A certain modicum of decency and comfort is obviously necessary to man before we can begin to do anything but pity him; but that doesn't make it any easier to know how you're going to insure him that modicum of decency and comfort, does it?'

'We've got to do it,' said Thyme; 'it won't wait any longer.'

'My dear,' said Hilary, 'think of Mr Purcey! What proportion of the upper classes do you imagine is even conscious of that necessity? We, who have got what I call the social conscience, rise from the platform of Mr Purcey; we're just a gang of a few thousands to Mr Purcey's tens of thousands, and how many even of us are prepared, or, for the matter of that, fitted, to act on our consciousness? In spite of your grandfather's ideas, I'm afraid we're all too much divided into classes; man acts, and always has acted, in classes.'

'Oh—classes!' answered Thyme—'that's the old superstition, uncle.'

'Is it? I thought one's class, perhaps, was only oneself exaggerated—not to be shaken off. For instance, what are you and I, with our particular prejudices, going to do?'

Thyme gave him the cruel look of youth, which seemed to say: 'You are my very good uncle, and a dear; but you are more than twice my age. That, I think, is conclusive!'

'Has something been settled about Mrs Hughs?' she asked abruptly.

'What does your father say this morning?'

Thyme picked up her portfolio of drawings, and moved towards the door.

'Father's hopeless. He hasn't an idea beyond referring her to the S.P.B.'

She was gone; and Hilary, with a sigh, took his pen up, but he wrote nothing down. . . .

Hilary and Stephen Dallison were grandsons of that Canon Dallison, well known as friend, and sometime adviser, of a certain Victorian novelist. The Canon, who came of an old Oxfordshire family, which for three hundred years at least had served the Church or State, was himself the author of two volumes of 'Socratic Dialogues'. He had bequeathed to his son—a permanent official in the Foreign Office—if not his literary talent, the tradition at all events of culture. This tradition had in turn been handed on to Hilary and Stephen.

Educated at a public school and Cambridge, blessed with competent, though not large, independent incomes, and brought up never to allude to money if it could possibly be helped, the two young men had been turned out of the mint with something of the same outward stamp on them. Both were kindly, both fond of open-air pursuits, and neither of them lazy. Both, too, were very civilised, with that bone-deep decency, that dislike of violence, nowhere so prevalent as in the upper classes of a country whose settled institutions are as old as its roads, or the walls that insulate its parks. But as time went on, the one great quality which heredity and education, environment and means, had bred in both of them—self-consciousness—acted in these two brothers very differently. To Stephen it was preservative, keeping him, as it were, in ice throughout hot-weather seasons, enabling him to know exactly when he was in danger of decomposition, so that he might nip the process in the bud; it was with him a healthy, perhaps slightly chemical, ingredient, binding his component parts, causing them to work together safely, homogeneously. In Hilary the effect seemed to have been otherwise; like some slow and subtle poison, this great quality, self-consciousness, had soaked his system through and through; permeated every cranny of his spirit, so that to think a definite thought, or do a definite deed, was obviously becoming difficult to him. It took in the main the form of a sort of gentle desiccating humour.

'It's a remarkable thing,' he had one day said to Stephen, 'that by the process of assimilating little bits of chopped-up cattle one should be able to form the speculation of how remarkable a thing it is.'

Stephen had paused a second before answering—they were lunching off roast beef in the Law Courts—he had then said:

'You're surely not going to eschew the higher mammals, like our respected father-in-law?'

'On the contrary,' said Hilary, 'to chew them; but it *is* remarkable, for all that; you missed my point.'

It was clear that a man who could see anything remarkable in such a thing was far gone, and Stephen had murmured:

'My dear old chap, you're getting too introspective.'

Hilary, having given his brother the peculiar retiring smile, which seemed not only to say, 'Don't let me bore you,' but also, 'Well, perhaps you *had* better wait outside,' the conversation closed.

That smile of Hilary's, which jibbed away from things, though disconcerting and apt to put an end to intercourse, was natural enough. A sensitive man, who had passed his life amongst cultivated people in the making of books, guarded from real wants by modest, not vulgar, affluence, had not reached the age of forty-two without finding his delicacy sharpened to the point of fastidiousness. Even his dog could see the sort of man he was. She knew that he would take no liberties, either with her ears or with her tail. She knew that he would never hold her mouth ajar, and watch her teeth, as some men do; that when she was lying on her back he would gently rub her chest without giving her the feeling that she was doing wrong, as women will; and if she sat, as she was sitting now, with her eyes fixed on his study fire, he would never, she knew, even from afar, prevent her thinking of the nothing she loved to think on.

In his study, which smelt of a special mild tobacco warranted to suit the nerves of any literary man, there was a bust of Socrates, which always seemed to have a strange attraction for its owner. He had once described to a fellow-writer the impression produced on him by that plaster face, so capaciously ugly, as though comprehending the whole of human life, sharing all man's gluttony and lust, his violence and rapacity, but sharing also his strivings towards love and reason and serenity.

'He's telling us,' said Hilary, 'to drink deep, to dive down and live with mermaids, to lie out on the hills under the sun, to sweat with helots, to know all things and all men. No seat, he says, among the Wise, unless we've been through it all before we climb! That's how he strikes me—not too cheering for people of our sort!'

Under the shadow of this bust Hilary rested his forehead on his hand. In front of him were three open books and a pile of manuscript, and pushed to one side a little sheaf of pieces of green-white paper, press-cuttings of his latest book.

The exact position occupied by his work in the life of such a man is not too easy to define. He earned an income by it, but he was not dependent on that income. As poet, critic, writer of essays, he had made himself a certain name—not a great name, but enough to swear by. Whether his fastidiousness could have stood the conditions of literary existence without private means was now and then debated by his friends; it could probably have done so better than was supposed, for he sometimes startled those who set him down as a dilettante by a horny way of retiring into his shell for the finish of a piece of work.

Try as he would that morning to keep his thoughts concentrated on his literary labour, they wandered to his conversation with his niece and to the discussion on Mrs Hughs, the family seamstress, in his wife's studio the day before. Stephen had lingered behind Cecilia and Thyme when they went away after dinner, to deliver a last counsel to his brother at the garden gate.

'Never meddle between man and wife—you know what the lower classes are!'

And across the dark garden he had looked back towards the house. One room on the ground-floor alone was lighted. Through its open window the head and shoulders of Mr Stone could be seen close to a small green reading-lamp. Stephen shook his head, murmuring:

'But, I say, our old friend, eh? "In those places—in those

streets!" It's worse than simple crankiness—the poor old chap is getting almost——' And, touching his forehead lightly with two fingers, he had hurried off with the ever-springy step of one whose regularity habitually controls his imagination.

Pausing a minute amongst the bushes, Hilary too had looked at the lighted window that broke the dark front of his house, and his little moonlight bulldog, peering round his legs, had gazed up also. Mr Stone was still standing, pen in hand, presumably deep in thought. His silvered head and beard moved slightly to the efforts of his brain. He came over to the window, and, evidently not seeing his son-in-law, faced out into the night.

In that darkness were all the shapes and lights and shadows of a London night in spring: the trees in dark bloom; the wan yellow of the gas-lamps, pale emblems of the self-consciousness of towns; the clustered shades of the tiny leaves, spilled, purple, on the surface of the road, like bunches of black grapes squeezed down into the earth by the feet of the passers-by. There, too, were shapes of men and women hurrying home, and the great blocked shapes of the houses where they lived. A halo hovered above the City—a high haze of yellow light, dimming the stars. The black, slow figure of a policeman moved noiselessly along the railings opposite.

From then till eleven o'clock, when he would make himself some cocoa on a little spirit-lamp, the writer of the 'Book of Universal Brotherhood' would alternate between his bent posture above his manuscript and his blank consideration of the night. . . .

With a jerk, Hilary came back to his reflections beneath the bust of Socrates.

'Each of us has a shadow in those places—in those streets!'

There certainly was a virus in that notion. One must either take it as a jest, like Stephen; or, what must one do? How far was it one's business to identify oneself with other people, especially the helpless—how far to preserve oneself intact—*integer vitae?* Hilary was no young person, like his niece or Martin, to whom everything seemed simple; nor was he an old person like their grandfather, for whom life had lost its complications.

And, very conscious of his natural disabilities for a decision on a like, or indeed on any, subject except, perhaps, a point of literary technique, he got up from his writing-table, and, taking his little bulldog, went out. His intention was to visit Mrs Hughs in Hound Street, and see with his own eyes the state of things. But he had another reason, too, for wishing to go there. . . .

Chapter 4

THE LITTLE MODEL

WHEN in the preceding autumn Bianca began her picture called 'The Shadow', nobody was more surprised than Hilary that she asked him to find her a model for the figure. Not knowing the nature of the picture, nor having been for many years—perhaps never—admitted into the workings of his wife's spirit, he said:

'Why don't you ask Thyme to sit for you?'

Bianca answered: 'She's not the type at all—too matter-of-fact. Besides, I don't want a lady; the figure's to be half draped.'

Hilary smiled.

Bianca knew quite well that he was smiling at this distinction between ladies and other women, and understood that he was smiling, not so much at her, but at himself, for secretly agreeing with the distinction she had made.

And suddenly she smiled too.

There was the whole history of their married life in those two smiles. They meant so much: so many thousand hours of suppressed irritation, so many baffled longings and earnest efforts to bring their natures together. They were the supreme, quiet evidence of the divergence of two lives—that slow divergence which had been far from being wilful, and was the more hopeless in that it had been so gradual and so gentle. They had never really had a quarrel, having enlightened views of marriage; but they had smiled. They had smiled so often through so many years that no two people in the world could very well be further from each other. Their smiles had banned the revelation even to themselves of the tragedy of their wedded state. It is certain that neither could help those smiles, which were not intended to wound, but came on their faces as naturally as moonlight falls on water, out of their inimically constituted souls.

Hilary spent two afternoons among his artist friends, trying, by means of the indications he had gathered, to find a model for 'The Shadow'. He had found one at last. Her name, Barton, and address had been given him by a painter of still life, called French.

'She's never sat to me,' he said; 'my sister discovered her in the West Country somewhere. She's got a story of some sort. I don't know what. She came up about three months ago, I think.'

'She's not sitting to your sister now?' Hilary asked.

'No,' said the painter of still life; 'my sister's married and gone out to India. I don't know whether she'd sit for the half-draped, but I should think so. She'll have to, sooner or later; she may as well begin, especially as your wife's a woman. There's a something about her that's attractive—you might try her!' And with these words he resumed the painting of still life which he had broken off to talk to Hilary.

Hilary had written to this girl to come and see him. She had come just before dinner the same day.

He found her standing in the middle of his study, not daring, as it seemed, to go near the furniture, and as there was very little light, he could hardly see her face. She was resting a foot, very patient, very still, in an old brown skirt, an ill-shaped blouse, and a blue-green tam-o'-shanter cap. Hilary turned up the light. He saw a round little face with broad cheek-bones, flower-blue eyes, short lamp-black lashes, and slightly parted lips. It was difficult to judge of her figure in those old clothes, but she was neither short nor tall; her neck was white and well set on, her hair pale brown and abundant. Hilary noted that her chin, though not receding, was too soft and small; but what he noted chiefly was her look of patient expectancy, as though beyond the present she were seeing something, not necessarily pleasant, which had to come. If he had not known from the painter of still life that she was from the country, he would have thought her a town-bred girl, she looked so pale. Her appearance, at all events, was not 'too matter-of-fact'. Her speech, however, with its slight West-Country burr, was matter-of-fact enough, concerned entirely with how long she would have to sit, and the pay she was to get for it. In the middle of their conversation she sank down on the floor, and Hilary was driven to restore her with biscuits and liqueur, which in his haste he took for brandy. It seemed she had not eaten since her breakfast the day before, which had consisted of a cup of tea. In answer to his remonstrance, she made this matter-of-fact remark:

'If you haven't money, you can't buy things. . . . There's no one I can ask up here; I'm a stranger.'

'Then you haven't been getting work?'

'No,' the little model answered sullenly; 'I don't want to sit as most of them want me to till I'm obliged.' The blood rushed up in her face with startling vividness, then left it white again.

'Ah!' thought Hilary, 'she has had experience already.'

Both he and his wife were accessible to cases of distress, but the nature of their charity was different. Hilary was constitutionally unable to refuse his aid to anything that held out a hand for it. Bianca (whose sociology was sounder), while affirming that charity was wrong, since in a properly constituted State no one should need help, referred her cases, like Stephen, to the 'Society for the Prevention of Begging', which took much time and many pains to ascertain the worst.

But in this case what was of importance was that the poor girl should have a meal, and after that to find out if she were living in a decent house; and since she appeared not to be, to recommend her somewhere better. And as in charity it is always well to kill two birds with one expenditure of force, it was found that Mrs Hughs, the seamstress, had a single room to let unfurnished, and would be more than glad of four shillings, or even three and six, a week for it. Furniture was also found for her: a bed that creaked, a washstand, table, and chest of drawers; a carpet, two chairs, and certain things to cook with; some of those old photographs and prints that hide in cupboards, and a peculiar little clock, which frequently forgot the time of day. All these and some elementary articles of dress were sent round in a little van, with three ferns whose time had nearly come, and a piece of the plant called 'honesty'. Soon after this she came to 'sit'. She was a very quiet and passive little model, and was not required to pose half-draped, Bianca having decided that, after all, 'The Shadow' was better represented fully clothed; for, though she discussed the nude, and looked on it with freedom, when it came to painting unclothed people, she felt a sort of physical aversion.

Hilary, who was curious, as a man naturally would be, about anyone who had fainted from hunger at his feet, came every now and then to see, and would sit watching this little half-starved girl with kindly and screwed-up eyes. About his personality there was all the evidence of that saying current among those who knew him: 'Hilary would walk a mile sooner than tread on an ant.' The little model, from the moment when he poured liqueur between her teeth, seemed to feel he had a claim on her, for she reserved her small, matter-of-fact confessions for his ears. She made them in the garden, coming in or going out; or outside, and, now and then, inside his study, like a child who comes and shows you a sore finger. Thus, quite suddenly: 'I've four shillings left over this week, Mr Dallison,' or, 'Old Mr Creed's gone to the hospital today, Mr Dallison.'

Her face soon became less bloodless than on that first evening, but it was still pale, inclined to colour in wrong places on cold days, with little blue veins about the temples and shadows under the eyes. The lips were still always a trifle parted, and she still seemed to be looking out for what was coming, like a little Madonna, or Venus, in a Botticelli picture. This look of hers, coupled with the matter-of-factness of her speech, gave its flavour to her personality. . . .

On Christmas Day the picture was on view to Mr Purcey, who had chanced to 'give his car a run', and to other connoisseurs. Bianca had invited her model to be present at this function, intending to get her work. But, slipping at once into a corner, the girl had stood as far as possible behind a canvas. People, seeing her standing there and noting her likeness to the picture, looked at her with curiosity, and passed on, murmuring that she was an interesting type. They did not talk to her, either because they were afraid she could not talk of the things they could talk of, or that they could not talk of the things she could talk of, or because they were anxious not to seem to patronise her. She talked to no one, therefore. This occasioned Hilary some distress. He kept coming up and smiling at her, or making tentative remarks or jests, to which she would reply, 'Yes, Mr Dallison', or 'No, Mr Dallison', as the case might be.

Seeing him return from one of these little visits, an Art Critic standing before the picture had smiled, and his round, clean-shaven, sensual face had assumed a greenish tint in eyes and cheeks, as of the fat in turtle soup.

The only two other people who had noticed her particularly were those old acquaintances Mr Purcey and Mr Stone. Mr Purcey had thought, 'Rather a good-lookin' girl', and his eyes strayed somewhat continually in her direction. There was something piquant and, as it were, unlawfully enticing to him in the fact that she was a real artist's model.

Mr Stone's way of noticing her had been different. He had approached in his slightly inconvenient way, as though seeing but one thing in the whole world.

'You are living by yourself?' he had said. 'I shall come and see you.'

Made by the Art Critic or by Mr Purcey, that somewhat strange remark would have had one meaning; made by Mr Stone it obviously had another. Having finished what he had to say, the author of the book of 'Universal Brotherhood' had bowed and turned to go. Perceiving that he saw before him the door and nothing else, everybody made way for him at once. The remarks that usually arose behind his back began to be heard—'Extraordinary old man!' 'You know, he bathes in the Serpentine all the year round?' 'And he cooks his food himself, and does his own room, they say; and all the rest of his time he writes a book!' 'A perfect crank!'

Chapter 5

THE COMEDY BEGINS

THE Art Critic who had smiled was—like all men—a subject for pity rather than for blame. An Irishman of real ability, he had started life with high ideals and a belief that he could live with them. He had hoped to serve Art, to keep his service pure; but, having one day let his acid temperament out of hand to revel in an orgy of personal retaliation, he had since never known when she would slip her chain and come home smothered in mire. Moreover, he no longer chastised her when she came. His ideals had left him, one by one; he now lived alone, immune from dignity and shame, soothing himself with whisky. A man of rancour, meet for pity, and, in his cups, contented.

He had lunched freely before coming to Bianca's Christmas function, but by four o'clock the gases which had made him feel the world a pleasant place had nearly all evaporated, and he was suffering from a wish to drink again. Or it may have been that this girl, with her soft look, gave him the feeling that she ought to have belonged to him; and as she did not, he felt, perhaps, a natural irritation that she belonged, or might belong, to somebody else. Or, again, it was possibly his natural male distaste for the works of women painters that induced an awkward frame of mind.

Two days later in a daily paper, over no signature, appeared this little paragraph: 'We learn that "The Shadow", painted by Bianca Stone, who is not generally known to be the wife of the writer, Mr Hilary Dallison, will soon be exhibited at the Bencox Gallery. This very *fin-de-siècle* creation, with its unpleasant subject, representing a woman (presumably of the streets) standing beneath a gas-lamp, is a somewhat anaemic piece of painting. If Mr Dallison, who finds the type an interesting one, embodies her in one of his very charming poems, we trust the result will be less bloodless.'

The little piece of green-white paper containing this information was handed to Hilary by his wife at breakfast. The blood mounted slowly in his cheeks. Bianca's eyes fastened themselves on that flush. Whether or no—as philosophers say—little things are all big with the past, of whose chain they are the latest links, they frequently produce what apparently are great results.

The marital relations of Hilary and his wife, which till then had been those of, at all events, formal conjugality, changed from that moment. After ten o'clock at night their lives became as separate as though they lived in different houses. And this change came about without expostulations, reproach, or explanation, just by the turning of a key; and even this was the merest symbol, employed once only, to save the ungracefulness of words. Such a hint was quite enough for a man like Hilary, whose delicacy, sense of the ridiculous, and peculiar faculty of starting back and retiring into himself, put the need of anything further out of the question. Both must have felt, too, that there was nothing that could be explained. An anonymous *double entendre* was not precisely evidence on which to found a rupture of the marital tie. The trouble was so much deeper than that—the throbbing of a woman's wounded self-esteem, of the feeling that she was no longer loved, which had long cried out for revenge.

One morning in the middle of the week after this incident the innocent author of it presented herself in Hilary's study, and, standing in her peculiar patient attitude, made her little statements. As usual, they were very little ones; as usual, she seemed helpless, and suggested a child with a sore finger. She had no other work; she owed the week's rent; she did not know what would happen to her; Mrs Dallison did not want her any more; she could not tell what she had done! The picture was finished, she knew, but Mrs Dallison had said she was going to paint her again in another picture. . . .

Hilary did not reply.

'. . . That old gentleman, Mr—Mr Stone, had been to see her. He wanted her to come and copy out his book for two hours a day, from four to six, at a shilling an hour. Ought she to come, please? He said his book would take him years.'

Before answering her Hilary stood for a full minute staring at the fire. The little model stole a look at him. He suddenly turned and faced her. His glance was evidently disconcerting to the girl. It was, indeed, a critical and dubious look, such as he might have bent on a folio of doubtful origin.

'Don't you think,' he said at last, 'that it would be much better for you to go back into the country?'

The little model shook her head vehemently.

'Oh no!'

'Well, but why not? This is a most unsatisfactory sort of life.'

The girl stole another look at him, then said sullenly:

'I can't go back there.'

'What is it? Aren't your people nice to you?'

She grew red.

'No; and I don't want to go;' then, evidently seeing from Hilary's face that his delicacy forbade his questioning her further, she brightened up, and murmured: 'The old gentleman said it would make me independent.'

'Well,' replied Hilary, with a shrug, 'you'd better take his offer.'

She kept turning her face back as she went down the path, as though to show her gratitude. And presently, looking up from his manuscript, he saw her face still at the railings, peering through a lilac bush. Suddenly she skipped, like a child let out of school. Hilary got up, perturbed. The sight of that skipping was like the rays of a lantern turned on the dark street of another human being's life. It revealed, as in a flash, the loneliness of this child, without money and without friends, in the midst of this great town.

The months of January, February, March passed, and the little model came daily to copy the 'Book of Universal Brotherhood'.

Mr Stone's room, for which he insisted on paying rent, was never entered by a servant. It was on the ground-floor, and anyone passing the door between the hours of four and six could hear him dictating slowly, pausing now and then to spell a word. In these two hours it appeared to be his custom to read out, for fair copying, the labours of the other seven.

At five o'clock there was invariably a sound of plates and cups, and out of it the little model's voice would rise, matter-of-fact, soft, monotoned, making little statements; and in turn Mr Stone's, also making statements that clearly lacked cohesion with those of his young friend. On one occasion, the door being open, Hilary heard distinctly the following conversation:

The LITTLE MODEL: 'Mr Creed says he was a butler. He's got an ugly nose.' (A pause.)

Mr STONE: 'In those days men were absorbed in thinking of their individualities. Their occupations seemed to them important——'

The LITTLE MODEL: 'Mr Creed says his savings were all swallowed up by illness.'

Mr STONE: '—it was not so.'

The LITTLE MODEL: 'Mr Creed says he was always brought up to go to church.'

Mr STONE (suddenly): 'There has been no church worth going to since A.D. 700.'

The LITTLE MODEL: 'But he doesn't go.'

And with a flying glance through the just open door Hilary saw her holding bread-and-butter with inky fingers, her lips a little parted, expecting the next bite, and her eyes fixed curiously on Mr Stone, whose transparent hand held a teacup, and whose eyes were immovably fixed on distance.

It was one day in April that Mr Stone, heralded by the scent of Harris tweed and baked potatoes which habitually encircled him, appeared at five o'clock in Hilary's study doorway.

'She has not come,' he said.

Hilary laid down his pen. It was the first real Spring day.

'Will you come for a walk with me, sir, instead?' he asked.

'Yes,' said Mr Stone.

They walked out into Kensington Gardens, Hilary with his head rather bent towards the ground, and Mr Stone, with eyes fixed on his far thoughts, slightly poking forward his silver beard.

In their favourite firmaments the stars of crocuses and daffodils were shining. Almost every tree had its pigeon cooing, every bush its blackbird in full song. And on the paths were babies in perambulators. These were their happy hunting-grounds, and here they came each day to watch from a safe distance the little dirty girls sitting on the grass nursing little dirty boys, to listen to the ceaseless chatter of these common urchins, and learn to deal with the great problem of the lowest classes. They sat there in their perambulators, thinking and sucking indiarubber tubes. Dogs went before them, and nursemaids followed after.

The spirit of colour was flying in the distant trees, swathing them with brownish-purple haze; the sky was saffroned by dying sunlight. It was such a day as brings a longing to the heart, like that which the moon brings to the hearts of children.

Mr Stone and Hilary sat down in the Broad Walk.

'Elm-trees!' said Mr Stone. 'It is not known when they assumed their present shape. They have one universal soul. It is the same with man.' He ceased, and Hilary looked round uneasily. They were alone on the bench.

Mr Stone's voice rose again. 'Their form and balance is their single soul; they have preserved it from century to century. This is all they live for. In those days'—his voice sank; he had plainly forgotten that he was not alone—'when men had no universal conceptions, they would have done well to look at the trees. Instead of fostering a number of little souls on the pabulum of varying theories of future life, they should have been concerned to improve their present shapes, and thus to dignify man's single soul.'

'Elms were always considered dangerous trees, I believe,' said Hilary.

Mr Stone turned, and, seeing his son-in-law beside him, asked:

'You spoke to me, I think?'

'Yes, sir.'

Mr Stone said wistfully:

'Shall we walk?'

They rose from the bench and walked on. . . .

The explanation of the little model's absence was thus stated by herself to Hilary: 'I had an appointment.'

'More work?'

'A friend of Mr French.'

'Yes—who?'

'Mr Lennard. He's a sculptor; he's got a studio in Chelsea. He wants me to pose to him.'

'Ah!'

She stole a glance at Hilary, and hung her head.

Hilary turned to the window. 'You know what posing to a sculptor means, of course?'

The little model's voice sounded behind him, matter-of-fact as ever: 'He said I was just the figure he was looking for.'

Hilary continued to stare through the window. 'I thought you didn't mean to begin standing for the nude.'

'I don't want to stay poor always.'

Hilary turned round at the strange tone of these unexpected words.

The girl was in a streak of sunlight; her pale cheeks flushed; her pale, half-opened lips red; her eyes, in their setting of short black lashes, wide and mutinous; her young round bosom heaving as if she had been running.

'I don't want to go on copying books all my life.'

'Oh, very well.'

'Mr Dallison! I didn't mean that—I didn't, really! I want to do what you tell me to do—I do!'

Hilary stood contemplating her with the dubious, critical look, as though asking: 'What is there behind you? Are you really a genuine edition, or what?' which had so disconcerted her before. At last he said: 'You must do just as you like. I never advise anybody.'

'But you don't want me to—I know you don't. Of course, if *you* don't want me to, then it'll be a pleasure not to!'

Hilary smiled.

'Don't you like copying for Mr Stone?'

The little model made a face. 'I like Mr Stone—he's such a funny old gentleman.'

'That *is* the general opinion,' answered Hilary. 'But Mr Stone, you know, thinks that *we* are funny.'

The little model smiled faintly, too; the streak of sunlight had slanted past her, and, standing there behind its glamour and million floating specks of gold-dust, she looked for the moment like the young Shade of Spring, watching with expectancy for what the year would bring her.

With the words 'I am ready', spoken from the doorway, Mr Stone interrupted further colloquy. . . .

But though the girl's position in the household had, to all seeming, become established, now and then some little incident—straws blowing down the wind—showed feelings at work beneath the family's apparent friendliness, beneath that tentative and almost apologetic manner towards the poor or helpless, which marks out those who own what Hilary had called the 'social conscience'. Only three days, indeed, before he sat in his brown study, meditating beneath the bust of Socrates, Cecilia, coming to lunch, had let fall this remark:

'Of course, I know nobody can read his handwriting; but I can't think why father doesn't dictate to a typist, instead of to that little girl. She could go twice the pace!'

Bianca's answer, deferred for a few seconds, was:

'Hilary perhaps knows.'

'Do you dislike her coming here?' asked Hilary.

'Not particularly. Why?'

'I thought from your tone you did.'

'I don't dislike her coming here for that purpose.'

'Does she come for any other?'

Cecilia, dropping her quick glance to her fork, said just a little hastily: 'Father *is* extraordinary, of course.'

But the next three days Hilary was out in the afternoon when the little model came.

This, then, was the other reason, on the morning of the first of

May, that made him not averse to go and visit Mrs Hughs in Hound Street, Kensington.

Chapter 6

FIRST PILGRIMAGE TO HOUND STREET

HILARY and his little bulldog entered Hound Street from its eastern end. It was a grey street of three-storied houses, all in one style of architecture. Nearly all their doors were open, and on the doorsteps babes and children were enjoying Easter holidays. They sat in apathy, varied by sudden little slaps and bursts of noise. Nearly all were dirty; some had whole boots, some half boots, and two or three had none. In the gutters more children were at play; their shrill tongues and febrile movements gave Hilary the feeling that their 'caste' exacted of them a profession of this faith: 'To-day we live; to-morrow—if there be one—will be like to-day.'

He had unconsciously chosen the very centre of the street to walk in, and Miranda, who had never in her life demeaned herself to this extent, ran at his heels, turning up her eyes, as though to say: 'One thing I make a point of—no dog must speak to me!'

Fortunately, there were no dogs; but there were many cats, and these cats were thin.

Through the upper windows of the houses Hilary had glimpses of women in poor habiliments doing various kinds of work, but stopping now and then to gaze into the street. He walked to the end, where a wall stopped him, and, still in the centre of the road, he walked the whole length back. The children stared at his tall figure with indifference; they evidently felt that he was not of those who, like themselves, had no to-morrow.

No. 1, Hound Street, abutting on the garden of a house of better class, was distinctly the show building of the street. The door, however, was not closed, and pulling the remnant of a bell, Hilary walked in.

The first thing that he noticed was a smell; it was not precisely bad, but it might have been better. It was a smell of walls and washing, varied rather vaguely by red herrings. The second thing he noticed was his moonlight bulldog, who stood on the doorstep eyeing a tiny sandy cat. This very little cat, whose back was arched with fury, he was obliged to chase away before his bulldog would come in. The third thing he noticed was a lame woman of short stature, standing in the doorway of a room. Her face, with big cheek-bones, and wide-open, light grey, dark-lashed eyes, was broad and patient; she rested her lame leg by holding to the handle of the door.

'I dunno if you'll find anyone upstairs. I'd go and ask, but my leg's lame.'

'So I see,' said Hilary; 'I'm sorry.'

The woman sighed: 'Been like that for five years;' and turned back into her room.

'Is there nothing to be done for it?'

'Well, I did think so once,' replied the woman, 'but they say the bone's diseased; I neglected it at the the start.'

'Oh dear!'

'We hadn't the time to give to it,' the woman said defensively, retiring into a room so full of china cups, photographs, coloured prints, waxwork fruits, and other ornaments, that there seemed no room for the enormous bed.

Wishing her good-morning, Hilary began to mount the stairs. On the first floor he paused. Here, in the back room, the little model lived.

He looked around him. The paper on the passage walls was of a dingy orange colour, the blind of the window torn, and still pursuing him, pervading everything, was the scent of walls and washing and red herrings. There came on him a sickness, a sort of spiritual revolt. To live here, to pass up these stairs, between these dingy, bilious walls, on this dirty carpet, with this—ugh! every day; twice, four times, six times, who knew how many times a day! And that sense, the first to be attracted or revolted, the first to become fastidious with the culture of the body, the last to be expelled from the temple of the pure spirit; that sense to whose refinement all breeding and all education is devoted; that sense which, ever an inch at least in front of man, is able to retard the development of nations, and paralyse all social schemes—this Sense of Smell awakened within him the centuries of his gentility, the ghosts of all those Dallisons who, for three hundred years and more, had served Church or State. It revived the souls of scents he was accustomed to, and with them, subtly mingled, the whole live fabric of aestheticism, woven in fresh air and laid in lavender. It roused the simple, non-extravagant demand of perfect cleanliness. And though he knew that chemists would have certified the composition of his blood to be the same as that of the dwellers in this house, and that this smell, composed of walls and washing and red herrings, was really rather healthy, he stood frowning fixedly at the girl's door, and the memory of his young niece's delicately wrinkled nose as she described the house rose before him. He went on upstairs, followed by his moonlight bulldog.

Hilary's tall thin figure appearing in the open doorway of the top-floor front, his kind and worried face, and the pale agate eyes of the little bulldog peeping through his legs, were witnessed by nothing but a baby, who was sitting in a wooden box in the centre of the room. This baby, who was very like a piece of putty to which Nature had by some accident fitted two movable black eyes, was clothed in a woman's knitted undervest, spreading beyond his feet and hands, so that nothing but his head was visible. This vest divided him from the wooden shavings on which he sat, and, since he had not yet attained the art of rising to his feet, the box divided him from contacts of all other kinds. As completely isolated from his kingdom as the Czar of all the Russias, he was doing nothing. In this realm there was a dingy bed, two chairs, and a washstand, with one lame leg, supported by an aged foot-stool. Clothes and garments were hanging on nails, pans lay about the hearth, a sewing-machine stood on a bare deal table. Over the bed was hung an oleograph, from a Christmas supplement, of the birth of Jesus, and above it a bayonet, under which was printed in an illiterate hand on a rough scroll of paper: 'Gave three of em what for at Elandslaagte. S. Hughs.' Some photographs adorned the walls, and two drooping ferns stood on the window-ledge. The room withal had a sort of desperate tidiness; in a large cupboard, slightly open, could be seen stowed all that must not see the light of day. The window of the baby's kingdom was tightly closed; the scent was the scent of walls and washing and red herrings, and—of other things.

Hilary looked at the baby, and the baby looked at him. The eyes of that tiny scrap of grey humanity seemed saying:

'You are not my mother, I believe?'

He stooped down and touched its cheek. The baby blinked its black eyes once.

'No,' it seemed to say again, 'you are *not* my mother.'

A lump rose in Hilary's throat; he turned and went downstairs. Pausing outside the little model's door, he knocked, and, receiving no answer, turned the handle. The little square room was empty; it was neat and clean enough, with a pink-flowered paper of comparatively modern date. Through its open window could be seen a pear-tree in full bloom. Hilary shut the door again with care, ashamed of having opened it.

On the half-landing, staring up at him with black eyes like the baby's, was a man of medium height and active build, whose short face, with broad cheek-bones, cropped dark hair, straight nose, and little black moustache, was burnt a dark dun colour. He was dressed in the uniform of those who sweep the streets—a loose blue blouse, and trousers tucked into boots reaching half-way up his calves; he held a peaked cap in his hand.

After some seconds of mutual admiration, Hilary said:

'Mr Hughs, I believe?'

'Yes.'

'I've been up to see your wife.'

'Have you?'

'You know me, I suppose?'

'Yes, I know you.'

'Unfortunately, there's only your baby at home.'

Hughs motioned with his cap towards the little model's room. 'I thought perhaps you'd been to see *her*,' he said. His black eyes smouldered; there was more than class resentment in the expression of his face.

Flushing slightly and giving him a keen look, Hilary passed down the stairs without replying. But Miranda had not followed. She stood, with one paw delicately held up above the topmost step.

'I don't know this man,' she seemed to say, 'and I don't like his looks.'

Hughs grinned. 'I never hurt a dumb animal,' he said; 'come on, tykie!'

Stimulated by a word she had never thought to hear, Miranda descended rapidly.

'He meant that for impudence,' thought Hilary as he walked away.

'*Westminster*, sir? Oh dear!'

A skinny trembling hand was offering him a greenish newspaper.

'Terrible cold wind for the time o' year!'

A very aged man in black-rimmed spectacles, with a distended nose and long upper lip and chin, was tentatively fumbling out change for sixpence.

'I seem to know your face,' said Hilary.

'Oh dear, yes. You deals with this 'ere shop—the tobacco department. I've often seen you when you've a-been a-goin' in. Sometimes you has the *Pell Mell* off o' this man here.' He jerked his head a trifle to the left, where a younger man was standing armed with a sheaf of whiter papers. In that gesture were years of envy, heart-burning, and sense of wrong. 'That's my paper,' it seemed to say, 'by all the rights of man; and that low-class fellow sellin' it, takin' away my profits!'

'I sells this 'ere *Westminster*. I reads it on Sundays—it's a gentleman's paper, 'igh-class paper—notwithstandin' of its politics. But, Lor', sir, with this 'ere man a-sellin' the *Pell Mell*'—lowering his voice, he invited Hilary to confidence—'so many o' the gentry takes that; an' there ain't too many o' the gentry about 'ere—I mean, not o' the *real* gentry—that I can afford to 'ave 'em took away from me.'

Hilary, who had stopped to listen out of delicacy, had a flash of recollection. 'You live in Hound Street?'

The old man answered eagerly: 'Oh dear! Yes, sir—No. 1, name of Creed. You're the gentleman where the young person goes for to copy of a book!'

'It's not my book she copies.'

'Oh no; it's an old gentleman; I know 'im. He come an' see me once. He come in one Sunday morning. "Here's a pound o' tobacca for you!" 'e says. "You was a butler," 'e says. "Butlers!" 'e says, "there'll be no butlers in fifty years." An' out 'e goes. Not quite'—he put a shaky hand up to his head—'not quite—oh dear!'

'Some people called Hughs live in your house, I think?'

'I rents my room off o' them. A lady was a-speakin' to me yesterday about 'em; that's not your lady, I suppose, sir?'

His eyes seemed to apostrophise Hilary's hat, which was of soft felt: 'Yes, yes—I've seen your sort a-stayin' about in the best houses. They has you down because of your learnin'; and quite the manners of a gentleman you've got.'

'My wife's sister, I expect.'

'Oh dear! She often has a paper off o' me. A real lady—not one o' these'—again he invited Hilary to confidence—'you know what I mean, sir—that buys their things a' ready-made at these 'ere large establishments. Oh, I know her well.'

'The old gentleman that visited you is her father.'

'Is he? Oh dear!' The old butler was silent, evidently puzzled.

Hilary's eyebrows began to execute those intricate manoeuvres which always indicated that he was about to tax his delicacy.

'How—how does Hughs treat the little girl who lives in the next room to you?'

The old butler replied in a rather gloomy tone:

'She takes my advice, and don't 'ave nothin' to say to 'im.

Dreadful foreign-lookin' man 'e is. Wherever 'e was brought up I can't think!'

'A soldier, wasn't he?'

'So he says. He's one o' these that works for the Vestry; an' then 'e'll go an' get upon the drink, an' when that sets 'im off, it seems as if there wasn't no respect for nothing in 'im; he goes on against the gentry, and the Church, and every sort of institution. I never met no soldiers like *him*. Dreadful foreign—Welsh, they tell me.'

'What do you think of the street you're living in?'

'I keeps myself to myself; low class o' street it is; dreadful low class o' person there—no self-respect about 'em.'

'Ah!' said Hilary.

'These little 'ouses, they get into the hands o' little men, and *they* don't care so long as they makes their rent out o' them. They can't help themselves—low class o' man like that; 'e's got to do the best 'e can for 'imself. They say there's thousands o' these 'ouses all over London. There's some that's for pullin' of 'em down, but that's talkin' rubbish; where are you goin' to get the money for to do it? These 'ere little men, they can't afford not even to put a paper on the walls, and the big ground landlords—you can't expect *them* to know what's happenin' behind their backs. There's some ignorant fellers like this Hughs talks a lot o' wild nonsense about the duty o' ground landlords; but you can't expect the real gentry to look into these sort o' things. They've got their estates down in the country. I've lived with them, and of course I know.'

The little bulldog, incommoded by the passers-by, now took the opportunity of beating with her tail against the old butler's legs.

'Oh dear! what's this? He don't bite, do 'e? Good Sambo!'

Miranda sought her master's eye at once. 'You see what happens to her if a lady loiters in the streets,' she seemed to say.

'It must be hard standing about here all day, after the life you've led,' said Hilary.

'I mustn't complain; it's been the salvation o' me.'

'Do you get shelter?'

Again the old butler seemed to take him into confidence.

'Sometimes of a wet night they lets me stand up in the archway there; they know I'm respectable. 'Twouldn't never do for that man'—he nodded at his rival—'or any of them boys to get standin' there, obstructin' of the traffic.'

'I wanted to ask you, Mr Creed, is there anything to be done for Mrs Hughs?'

The frail old body quivered with the vindictive force of his answer.

'Accordin' to what she says, if I'm a-to believe 'er, I'd have him up before the magistrate, sure as my name's Creed, an' get a separation, an' I wouldn't never live with 'im again: that's what she ought to do. An' if he come to go for her after that, I'd have 'im in prison, if 'e killed me first! I've no patience with a low class o' man like that! He insulted of me this morning.'

'Prison's a dreadful remedy,' murmured Hilary.

The old butler answered stoutly: 'There ain't but one way o' treatin' them low fellers—ketch hold o' them until they holler!'

Hilary was about to reply when he found himself alone. At the edge of the pavement some yards away, Creed, his face upraised to heaven, was embracing with all his force the second edition of the *Westminster Gazette*, which had been thrown him from a cart.

'Well,' thought Hilary, walking on, '*you* know your own mind, anyway!'

And trotting by his side, with her jaw set very firm, his little bulldog looked above her eyes, and seemed to say: 'It was time we left that man of action!'

Chapter 7

CECILIA'S SCATTERED THOUGHTS

IN her morning room Mrs Stephen Dallison sat at an old oak bureau collecting her scattered thoughts. They lay about on pieces of stamped notepaper, beginning 'Dear Cecilia', or 'Mrs Tallents Smallpeace requests', or on bits of pasteboard headed by the names of theatres, galleries, or concert-halls; or, again, on paper of not quite so good a quality, commencing, 'Dear Friend', and ending with a single well-known name like 'Wessex', so that no suspicion should attach to the appeal contained between the two. She had before her also sheets of her own writing-paper, headed '76, The Old Square, Kensington', and two little books. One of these was bound in marbleised paper, and on it written: 'Please keep this book in safety'; across the other, cased in the skin of some small animal deceased, was inscribed the solitary word 'Engagements'.

Cecilia had on a Persian-green silk blouse with sleeves that would have hidden her slim hands, but for silver buttons made in the likeness of little roses at her wrists; on her brow was a faint frown, as though she were wondering what her thoughts were all about.

She sat there every morning catching those thoughts, and placing them in one or other of her little books. Only by thus working hard could she keep herself, her husband, and daughter, in due touch with all the different movements going on. And that the touch might be as due as possible, she had a little headache nearly every day. For the dread of letting slip one movement, or of being too much taken with another, was very real to her; there were so many people who were interesting, so many sympathies of hers and Stephen's which she desired to cultivate, that it was a matter of the utmost import not to cultivate any single one too much. Then, too, the duty of remaining feminine with all this going forward taxed her constitution. She sometimes thought enviously of the splendid isolation now enjoyed by Bianca, of which some subtle instinct, rather than definite knowledge, had informed her; but not often, for she was a loyal little person, to whom Stephen and his comforts were of the first moment. And though she worried somewhat because her thoughts *would* come by every post, she did not worry very much—hardly more than the Persian kitten on her lap, who also sat for hours trying to catch her tail, with a line between her eyes, and two small hollows in her cheeks.

When she had at last decided what concerts she would be obliged to miss, paid her subscription to the League for the Suppression of Tinned Milk, and accepted an invitation to watch a man fall from a balloon, she paused. Then, dipping her pen in ink, she wrote as follows:

'Mrs Stephen Dallison would be glad to have the blue dress ordered by her yesterday sent home at once without alteration.—Messrs Rose and Thorn, High Street, Kensington.'

Ringing the bell, she thought: 'It will be a job for Mrs Hughs, poor thing: I believe she'll do it quite as well as Rose and Thorn.—Would you please ask Mrs Hughs to come to me?—Oh, is that you, Mrs Hughs? Come in.'

The seamstress, who had advanced into the middle of the room, stood with her worn hands against her sides, and no sign of life but the liquid patience in her large brown eyes. She was an enigmatic figure. Her presence always roused a sort of irritation in Cecilia, as if she had been suddenly confronted with what might possibly have been herself if certain little accidents had omitted to occur. She was so conscious that she ought to sympathise, so anxious to show that there was no barrier between them, so eager to be all she ought to be, that her voice almost purred.

'Are you getting on with the curtains, Mrs Hughs?'

'Yes, m'm, thank you, m'm.'

'I shall have another job for you to-morrow—altering a dress. Can you come?'

'Yes, m'm, thank you, m'm.'

'Is the baby well?'

'Yes, m'm, thank you, m'm.'

There was a silence.

'It's no good talking of her domestic matters,' thought Cecilia; 'not that I don't care!' But the silence getting on her nerves, she said quickly: 'Is your husband behaving himself better?'

There was no answer; Cecilia saw a tear trickle slowly down the woman's cheek.

'Oh dear, oh dear,' she thought; 'poor thing! I'm in for it!'

Mrs Hughs' whispering voice began: 'He's behaving himself dreadful, m'm. I was going to speak to you. It's ever since that young girl'—her face hardened—'come to live down in my room there; he seem to—he seem to—just do nothing but neglect me.'

Cecilia's heart gave the little pleasurable flutter which the heart must feel at the love dramas of other people, however painful.

'You mean the little model?' she said.

The seamstress answered in an agitated voice: 'I don't want to speak against her, but she's put a spell on him, that's what she has; he don't seem able to do nothing but talk of her, and hang about her room. It was that troubling me when I saw you the other day. And ever since yesterday midday, when Mr Hilary came—he's been talking that wild—and he pushed me—and—and ——' Her lips ceased to form articulate words, but, since it was not etiquette to cry before her superiors, she used them to swallow down her tears, and something in her lean throat moved up and down.

At the mention of Hilary's name the pleasurable sensation in Cecilia had undergone a change. She felt curiosity, fear, offence.

'I don't quite understand you,' she said.

The seamstress plaited at her frock. 'Of course, I can't help the way he talks, m'm. I'm sure I don't like to repeat the wicked things he says about Mr Hilary. It seems as if he were out of his mind when he gets talkin' about *that young girl*.'

The tone of those last three words was almost fierce.

Cecilia was on the point of saying: 'That will do, please; I want to hear no more.' But her curiosity and queer subtle fear forced her instead to repeat: 'I don't understand. Do you mean he insinuates that Mr Hilary has anything to do with—with this girl, or what?' And she thought: 'I'll stop that, at any rate.'

The seamstress's face was distorted by her efforts to control her voice.

'I tell him he's wicked to say such things, m'm, and Mr Hilary such a kind gentleman. And what business is it of his, I say, that's got a wife and children of his own? I've seen him in the street, I've watched him hanging about Mrs Hilary's house when I've been working there—waiting for that girl, and following her—home ——' Again her lips refused to do service, except in the swallowing of her tears.

Cecilia thought: 'I must tell Stephen at once. That man is dangerous.' A spasm gripped her heart, usually so warm and snug; vague feelings she had already entertained presented themselves now with startling force; she seemed to see the face of sordid life staring at the family of Dallison. Mrs Hughs' voice, which did not dare to break, resumed:

'I've said to him: "Whatever are you thinking of? And after Mrs Hilary's been so kind to me!" But he's like a madman when he's in liquor, and he says he'll go to Mrs Hilary——'

'Go to my sister? What about? The ruffian!'

At hearing her husband being called a ruffian by another woman the shadow of resentment passed across Mrs Hughs' face, leaving it quivering and red. The conversation had already made a strange difference in the manner of these two women to each other. It was as though each now knew exactly how much sympathy and confidence could be expected of the other, as though life had suddenly sucked up the mist, and shown them standing one on either side of a deep trench. In Mrs Hughs' eyes there was the look of those who have long discovered that they must not answer back for fear of losing what little ground they have to stand on; and Cecilia's eyes were cold and watchful. 'I sympathise,' they seemed to say, 'I sympathise; but you must please understand that you cannot expect sympathy if your affairs compromise the members of my family.' Her chief thought now was to be relieved of the company of this woman, who had been betrayed into showing what lay beneath her dumb, stubborn patience. It was not callousness, but the natural result of being fluttered. Her heart was like a bird agitated in its gilt-wire cage by the contemplation of a distant cat. She did not, however, lose her sense of what was practical, but said calmly: 'Your husband was wounded in South Africa, you told me? It looks as if he wasn't quite . . . I think you should have a doctor!'

The seamstress's answer, slow and matter-of-fact, was worse than her emotion.

'No, m'm, he isn't mad.'

Crossing to the hearth—whose Persian-blue tiling had taken her so long to find—Cecilia stood beneath a reproduction of Botticelli's 'Primavera', and looked doubtfully at Mrs Hughs. The Persian kitten, sleepy and disturbed on the bosom of her blouse, gazed up into her face. 'Consider me,' it seemed to say; 'I am worth consideration; I am of a piece with you, and everything round you. We are both elegant and rather slender; we both love warmth and kittens; we both dislike interference with our fur. You took a long time to buy me, so as to get me perfect. You see that woman over there! I sat on her lap this morning while she was sewing your curtains. She has no right in here; she's not what she seems; she can bite and scratch, I know; her lap is skinny; she drops water from her eyes. She made me wet all down my back. Be careful what you're doing, or she'll make you wet down yours!'

All that was like the little Persian kitten within Cecilia—cosiness and love of pretty things, attachment to her own abode with its high-art lining, love for her mate and her own kitten, Thyme, dread of disturbance—all made her long to push this woman from the room; this woman with the skimpy figure, and eyes that, for all their patience, had in them something virago-like; this woman who carried about with her an atmosphere of sordid grief, of squalid menaces, and scandal. She longed all the more because it could well be seen from the seamstress's helpless attitude that she too would have liked an easy life. To dwell on things like this was to feel more than thirty-eight!

Cecilia had no pocket, Providence having removed it now for some time past, but from her little bag she drew forth the two essentials of gentility. Taking her nose, which she feared was shining, gently within one, she fumbled in the other. And again she looked doubtfully at Mrs Hughs. Her heart said: 'Give the poor woman half a sovereign; it might comfort her!' But her brain said: 'I owe her four-and-six; after what she's just been saying about her husband and that girl and Hilary, it mayn't be safe to give her more.' She held out two half-crowns, and had an inspiration: 'I shall mention to my sister what you've said; you can tell your husband that!'

No sooner had she said this, however, than she saw, from a little smile devoid of merriment and quickly extinguished, that Mrs Hughs did not believe she would do anything of the kind; from which she concluded that the seamstress was convinced of Hilary's interest in the little model. She said hastily:

'You can go now, Mrs Hughs.'

Mrs Hughs went, making no noise or sign of any sort.

Cecilia returned to her scattered thoughts. They lay there still, with a gleam of sun from the low window smearing their importance; she felt somehow that it did not now matter very much whether she and Stephen, in the interests of science, saw that man fall from his balloon, or, in the interests of art, heard Herr von Kraaffe sing his Polish songs; she experienced, too, almost a revulsion in favour of tinned milk. After meditatively tearing up her note to Messrs Rose and Thorn, she lowered the bureau lid and left the room.

Mounting the stairs, whose old oak banisters on either side were a real joy, she felt she was stupid to let vague, sordid rumours, which, after all, affected her but indirectly, disturb her morning's work. And entering Stephen's dressing-room, she stood looking at his boots.

Inside each one of them was a wooden soul; none had any creases, none had any holes. The moment they wore out, their wooden souls were taken from them and their bodies given to the poor, whilst—in accordance with that theory, to hear a course of lectures on which a scattered thought was even now inviting her —the wooden souls migrated instantly to other leathern bodies.

Looking at that polished row of boots, Cecilia felt lonely and unsatisfied. Stephen worked in the Law Courts, Thyme worked at Art; both were doing something definite. She alone, it seemed, had to wait at home, and order dinner, answer letters, shop, pay calls, and do a dozen things that failed to stop her thoughts from dwelling on that woman's tale. She was not often conscious of the nature of her life, so like the lives of many hundred women in this London, which she said she could not stand, but which she stood very well. As a rule, with practical good sense, she kept her doubting eyes fixed friendlily on every little phase in turn, enjoying well enough the Chinese puzzle of her scattered thoughts, setting out on each small adventure with a certain cautious zest, and taking Stephen with her as far as he allowed. This last year or so, now that Thyme was a grown girl, she had felt at once a loss of purpose and a gain of liberty. She hardly knew whether to be glad or sorry. It freed her for the tasting of more things, more people, and more Stephen; but it left a little void in her heart, a little soreness round it. What would Thyme think if she heard this story about her uncle? The thought started a whole train of doubts that had of late beset her. Was her little daughter going to turn out like herself? If not, why not? Stephen joked about his daughter's skirts, her hockey, her friendship with young men. He joked about the way Thyme refused to let him joke about her art or about her interest in 'the people'. His joking was a source of irritation to Cecilia. For, by woman's instinct rather than by any reasoning process, she was conscious of a disconcerting change. Amongst the people she knew, young men were not now attracted by girls as they had been in her young days. There was a kind of cool and friendly matter-of-factness in the way they treated them, a sort of almost scientific playfulness. And Cecilia felt uneasy as to how far this was to go. She seemed left behind. If young people were really becoming serious, if youths no longer cared about the colour of Thyme's eyes, or dress, or hair, what would there be left to care for—that is, up to the point of definite relationship? Not that she wanted her daughter to be married. It would be time enough to think of that when she was twenty-five. But her own experiences had been so different. She had spent so many youthful hours in wondering about men, had seen so many men cast furtive looks at her; and now there did not seem in men or girls anything left worth the other's while to wonder or look furtive about. She was not of a philosophic turn of mind, and had attached no deep meaning to Stephen's jest—'If young people will reveal their ankles, they'll soon have no ankles to reveal.'

To Cecilia the extinction of the race seemed threatened; in reality her species of the race alone was vanishing, which to her, of course, was very much the same disaster. With her eyes on Stephen's boots she thought: 'How shall I prevent what I've heard from coming to Bianca's ears? I know how she would take it! How shall I prevent Thyme's hearing? I'm sure I don't know what the effect would be on her! I must speak to Stephen. He's so fond of Hilary.'

And, turning away from Stephen's boots, she mused: 'Of course it's nonsense. Hilary's much too—too nice, too fastidious, to be more than just interested; but he's so kind he might easily put himself in a false position. And—it's ugly nonsense! B. can be so disagreeable; even now she's not—on terms with him!' And suddenly the thought of Mr Purcey leaped into her mind—Mr Purcey, who, as Mrs Tallents Smallpeace had declared, was not even conscious that there was a problem of the poor. To think of him seemed somehow at that moment comforting, like rolling oneself in a blanket against a draught. Passing into her room, she opened her wardrobe door.

'Bother the woman!' she thought. 'I do want that gentian dress got ready, but now I simply *can't* give it to her to do.'

Chapter 8

THE SINGLE MIND OF MR STONE

SINCE in the flutter of her spirit caused by the words of Mrs Hughs, Cecilia felt she must do something, she decided to change her dress.

The furniture of the pretty room she shared with Stephen had not been hastily assembled. Conscious, even fifteen years ago, when they moved into this house, of the grave Philistinism of the upper classes, she and Stephen had ever kept their duty to aestheticism green; and, in the matter of their bed, had lain for two years on two little white affairs, comfortable, but purely temporary, that they might give themselves a chance. The chance had come at last —a bed in real keeping with the period they had settled on, and going for twelve pounds. They had not let it go, and now slept in it—not quite so comfortable, perhaps, but comfortable enough, and conscious of duty done.

For fifteen years Cecilia had been furnishing her house; the process approached completion. The only things remaining on her mind—apart, that is, from Thyme's development and the condition of the people—were: item, a copper lantern that would allow some light to pass its framework; item, an old oak washstand not going back to Cromwell's time. And now this third anxiety had come!

She was rather touching, as she stood before the wardrobe glass divested of her bodice, with dimples of exertion in her thin white arms as she hooked her skirt behind, and her greenish eyes troubled, so anxious to do their best for everyone, and save risk of any sort. Having put on a bramble-coloured frock, which laced across her breast with silver lattice-work, and a hat (without feathers, so as to encourage birds) fastened to her head with pins (bought to aid a novel school of metal-work), she went to see what sort of day it was.

The window looked out at the back over some dreary streets, where the wind was flinging light drifts of smoke athwart the sunlight. They had chosen this room, not indeed for its view over the condition of the people, but because of the sky effects at sunset, which were extremely fine. For the first time, perhaps, Cecilia was conscious that a sample of the class she was so interested in was exposed to view beneath her nose. 'The Hughs live somewhere there,' she thought. 'After all, I think B. ought to know about that man. She might speak to father, and get him to give up having the girl to copy for him—the whole thing's so worrying.'

In pursuance of this thought, she lunched hastily, and went out, making her way to Hilary's. With every step she became more uncertain. The fear of meddling too much, of not meddling enough, of seeming meddlesome; timidity at touching anything so awkward; distrust, even ignorance, of her sister's character, which was like, yet so very unlike, her own; a real itch to get the matter settled, so that nothing whatever should come of it—all this she felt. She first hurried, then dawdled, finished the adventure at a run, then told the servant not to announce her. The vision of Bianca's eyes, as she listened to this tale, was suddenly too much for Cecilia. She decided to pay a visit to her father first.

Mr Stone was writing, attired in his working dress—a thick brown woollen gown, revealing his thin neck above the line of a blue shirt, and tightly gathered round the waist with tasselled cord; the lower portions of grey trousers were visible above woollen-slippered feet. His hair straggled over his thin long ears. The window, wide open, admitted an east wind; there was no fire. Cecilia shivered.

'Come in quickly,' said Mr Stone. Turning to a big high desk of stained deal which occupied the middle of one wall, he began methodically to place the inkstand, a heavy paper-knife, a book, and stones of several sizes, on his fluttering sheets of manuscript.

Cecilia looked about her; she had not been inside her father's room for several months. There was nothing in it but that desk, a camp bed in the far corner (with blankets, but no sheets), a folding washstand, and a narrow bookcase, the books in which Cecilia unconsciously told off on the fingers of her memory. They never varied. On the top shelf the Bible and the works of Plautus and Diderot; on the second from the top the plays of Shakespeare in a blue edition; on the third from the bottom Don Quixote, in four volumes, covered with brown paper; a green Milton; the 'Comedies of Aristophanes'; a leather book, partially burned, comparing the philosophy of Epicurus with the philosophy of Spinoza; and in a yellow binding Mark Twain's 'Huckleberry Finn'. On the second from the bottom was lighter literature: 'The Iliad'; a 'Life of Francis of Assisi'; Speke's 'Discovery of the Sources of the Nile'; the 'Pickwick Papers'; 'Mr Midshipman Easy'; The Verses of Theocritus, in a very old translation; Renan's 'Life of Christ'; and the 'Autobiography of Benvenuto Cellini'. The bottom shelf of all was full of books on natural science.

The walls were whitewashed, and, as Cecilia knew, came off on anybody who leaned against them. The floor was stained, and had no carpet. There was a little gas cooking-stove, with cooking things ranged on it; a small bare table; and one large cupboard. No draperies, no pictures, no ornaments of any kind; but by the window an ancient golden leather chair. Cecilia could never bear to sit in that oasis; its colour in this wilderness was too precious to her spirit.

'It's an east wind, father; aren't you terribly cold without a fire?'

Mr Stone came from his writing-desk, and stood so that light might fall on a sheet of paper in his hand. Cecilia noted the scent that went about with him of peat and baked potatoes. He spoke:

'Listen to this: "In the condition of society, dignified in those days with the name of civilisation, the only source of hope was the persistence of the quality of courage. Amongst a thousand nerve-destroying habits, amongst the dram-shops, patent medicines, the undigested chaos of inventions and discoveries, while hundreds were prating in their pulpits of things believed in by a negligible fraction of the population, and thousands writing down to-day what nobody would want to read in two days' time; while men shut animals in cages, and make bears jig to please their children, and all were striving one against the other; while, in a word, like gnats above a stagnant pool on a summer's evening, man danced up and down without the faintest notion why—in this condition of affairs the quality of courage was alive. It was the only fire within that gloomy valley." ' He stopped, though evidently anxious to go on, because he had read the last word on that sheet of paper. He moved towards the writing-desk. Cecilia said hastily:

'Do you mind if I shut the window, father?'

Mr Stone made a movement of his head, and Cecilia saw that he held a second sheet of paper in his hand. She rose, and going towards him, said:

'I want to talk to you, Dad!' Taking up the cord of his dressing-gown, she pulled it by its tassel.

'Don't!' said Mr Stone; 'it secures my trousers.'

Cecilia dropped the cord. 'Father is really terrible!' she thought.

Mr Stone, lifting the second sheet of paper, began again:

'"The reason, however, was not far to seek——"'

Cecilia said desperately:

'It's about that girl who comes to copy for you.'

Mr Stone lowered the sheet of paper, and stood, slightly curved from head to foot; his ears moved as though he were about to lay them back; his blue eyes, with little white spots of light alongside the tiny black pupils, stared at his daughter.

Cecilia thought: 'He's listening now.'

She made haste. '*Must* you have her here? Can't you do without her?'

'Without whom?' said Mr Stone.

'Without the girl who comes to copy for you.'

'Why?'

'For this very good reason——'

Mr Stone dropped his eyes, and Cecilia saw that he had moved the sheet of paper up as far as his waist.

'Does she copy better than any other girl could?' she asked hastily.

'No,' said Mr Stone.

'Then, Father, I do wish, to please me, you'd get someone else. I know what I'm talking about, and I——' Cecilia stopped; her father's lips and eyes were moving; he was obviously reading to himself. 'I've no patience with him,' she thought; 'he thinks of nothing but his wretched book.'

Aware of his daughter's silence, Mr Stone let the sheet of paper sink, and waited patiently again.

'What do you want, my dear?' he said.

'Oh, Father, do listen just a minute!'

'Yes, yes.'

'It's about that girl who comes to copy for you. Is there any reason why she should come instead of any other girl?'

'Yes,' said Mr Stone.

'What reason?'

'Because she has no friends.'

So awkward a reply was not expected by Cecilia; she looked at the floor, forced to search within her soul. Silence lasted several seconds; then Mr Stone's voice rose above a whisper:

'"The reason was not far to seek. Man, differentiated from the other apes by his desire to *know*, was from the first obliged to steel himself against the penalties of knowledge. Like animals subjected to the rigors of an Arctic climate, and putting forth more fur with each reduction in the temperature, man's hide of courage thickened automatically to resist the spear-thrusts dealt him by his own insatiate curiosity. In those days of which we speak, when undigested knowledge, in a great invading horde, had swarmed all his defences, man, suffering from a foul dyspepsia, with a nervous system in the latest stages of exhaustion, and a reeling brain, survived by reason of his power to go on making courage. Little heroic as (in the then general state of petty competition) his deeds appeared to be, there never had yet been a time when man in bulk was more courageous, for there never had yet been a time when he had more need to be. Signs were not wanting that this desperate state of things had caught the eyes of the community. A little sect——"' Mr Stone stopped; his eyes had again tumbled over the bottom edge; he moved hurriedly towards the desk. Just as his hand removed a stone and took up a third sheet, Cecilia cried out:

'Father!'

Mr Stone stopped, and turned towards her. His daughter saw that he had gone quite pink; her annoyance vanished.

'Father! About that girl——'

Mr Stone seemed to reflect. 'Yes, yes,' he said.

'I don't think Bianca likes her coming here.'

Mr Stone passed his hand across his brow.

'Forgive me for reading to you, my dear,' he said; 'it's a great relief to me at times.'

Cecilia went close to him, and refrained with difficulty from taking up the tasselled cord.

'Of course, dear,' she said; 'I quite understand that.'

Mr Stone looked full in her face, and before a gaze which seemed to go through her and see things the other side, Cecilia dropped her eyes.

'It's strange,' he said, 'how you came to be my daughter!'

To Cecilia, too, this had often seemed a problem.

'There is a great deal in atavism,' said Mr Stone, 'that we know nothing of at present.'

Cecilia cried with heat, 'I do wish you would attend a minute, Father; it's really an important matter,' and she turned towards the window, tears being very near her eyes.

The voice of Mr Stone said humbly: 'I will try, my dear.'

But Cecilia thought: 'I must give him a good lesson. He really is too self-absorbed;' and she did not move, conveying by the posture of her shoulders how gravely she was vexed.

She could see nursemaids wheeling babies towards the Gardens, and noted their faces gazing, not at the babies, but, uppishly, at other nursemaids, or, with a sort of cautious longing, at men who passed. How selfish they looked! She felt a little glow of satisfaction that she was making this thin and bent old man behind her conscious of his egoism.

'He will know better another time,' she thought. Suddenly she heard a whistling, squeaking sound—it was Mr Stone whispering the third page of his manuscript:

' "—animated by some admirable sentiments, but whose doctrines—riddled by the fact that life is but the change of form to form—were too constricted for the evils they designed to remedy; this little sect, who had as yet to learn the meaning of universal love, were making the most strenuous efforts, in advance of the community at large, to understand themselves. The necessary movement which they voiced—reaction against the high-tide of the fratricidal system then prevailing—was young, and had the freshness and honesty of youth. . . ." '

Without a word Cecilia turned round and hurried to the door. She saw her father drop the sheet of paper; she saw his face, all pink and silver, stooping after it; and remorse visited her anger.

In the corridor outside she was arrested by a noise. The uncertain light of London halls fell there; on close inspection the sufferer was seen to be Miranda, who, unable to decide whether she wanted to be in the garden or the house, was seated beneath the hat-rack snuffling to herself. On seeing Cecilia she came out.

'What do you want, you little beast?'

Peering at her over the tops of her eyes, Miranda vaguely lifted a white foot. 'Why ask me that?' she seemed to say. 'How am I to know? Are we not all like this?'

Her conduct, coming at that moment, overtried Cecilia's nerves. She threw open Hilary's study-door, saying sharply: 'Go in and find your master!'

Miranda did not move, but Hilary came out instead. He had been correcting proofs to catch the post, and wore the look of a man abstracted, faintly contemptuous of other forms of life.

Cecilia, once more saved from the necessity of approaching her sister, the mistress of the house, so fugitive, haunting, and unseen, yet so much the centre of this situation, said:

'Can I speak to you a minute, Hilary?'

They went into his study, and Miranda came creeping in behind.

To Cecilia her brother-in-law always seemed an amiable and more or less pathetic figure. In his literary preoccupations he allowed people to impose on him. He looked unsubstantial beside the bust of Socrates, which moved Cecilia strangely—it was so very massive and so very ugly! She decided not to beat about the bush.

'I've been hearing some odd things from Mrs Hughs about that little model, Hilary.'

Hilary's smile faded from his eyes, but remained clinging to his lips.

'Indeed!'

Cecilia went on nervously: 'Mrs Hughs says it's because of her that Hughs behaves so badly. I don't want to say anything against the girl, but she seems—she seems to have——'

'Yes?' said Hilary.

'To have cast a spell on Hughs, as the woman puts it.'

'On Hughs!' repeated Hilary.

Cecilia found her eyes resting on the bust of Socrates, and hastily proceeded:

'She says he follows her about, and comes down here to lie in wait for her. It's a most strange business altogether. You went to see them, didn't you?'

Hilary nodded.

'I've been speaking to Father,' Cecilia murmured; 'but he's hopeless—I couldn't get him to pay the least attention.'

Hilary seemed thinking deeply.

'I wanted him,' she went on, 'to get some other girl instead to come and copy for him.'

'Why?'

Under the seeming impossibility of ever getting any farther, without saying what she had come to say, Cecilia blurted out:

'Mrs Hughs says that Hughs has threatened *you*.'

Hilary's face became ironical.

'Really!' he said. 'That's good of him! What for?'

The frightful indelicacy of her situation at this moment, the feeling of unfairness that she should be placed in it, almost overwhelmed Cecilia. 'Goodness knows I don't want to meddle. I never meddle in anything—it's horrible!'

Hilary took her hand.

'My dear Cis,' he said, 'of course! But we'd better have this out!'

Grateful for the pressure of his hand, she gave it a convulsive squeeze.

'It's so sordid, Hilary!'

'Sordid! H'm! Let's get it over, then.'

Cecilia had grown crimson. 'Do you want me to tell you everything?'

'Certainly.'

'Well, Hughs evidently thinks you're interested in the girl. You can't keep anything from servants and people who work about your house; they always think the worst of everything—and, of course, they know that you and B. don't—aren't——'

Hilary nodded.

'Mrs Hughs actually said the man meant to go to B.!'

Again the vision of her sister seemed to float into the room, and she went on desperately: 'And, Hilary, I can see Mrs Hughs really thinks you are interested. Of course, she wants to, for if you were, it would mean that a man like her husband could have no chance.'

Astonished at this flash of cynical inspiration, and ashamed of such plain speaking, she checked herself. Hilary had turned away.

Cecilia touched his arm. 'Hilary, dear,' she said, 'isn't there any chance of you and B——?'

Hilary's lips twitched. 'I should say not.'

Cecilia looked sadly at the floor. Not since Stephen was bad with pleurisy had she felt so worried. The sight of Hilary's face brought back her doubts with all their force. It might, of course, be only anger at the man's impudence, but it might be—she hardly liked to frame her thought—a more personal feeling.

'Don't you think,' she said, 'that, anyway, she had better not come here again?'

Hilary paced the room.

'It's her only safe and certain piece of work; it keeps her independent. It's much more satisfactory than this sitting. I can't have any hand in taking it away from her.'

Cecilia had never seen him moved like this. Was it possible that he was not incorrigibly gentle, but had in him some of that animality which she, in a sense, admired? This uncertainty terribly increased the difficulties of the situation.

'But, Hilary,' she said at last, 'are you satisfied about the girl—I mean, are you satisfied that she really is worth helping?'

'I don't understand.'

'I mean,' murmured Cecilia, 'that we don't know anything about her past.' And, seeing from the movement of his eyebrows that she was touching on what had evidently been a doubt with him, she went on with great courage: 'Where are her friends and relations? I mean, she may have had a—adventures.'

Hilary withdrew into himself.

'You can hardly expect me,' he said, 'to go into that with her.'

His reply made Cecilia feel ridiculous.

'Well,' she said in a hard little voice, 'if this is what comes of helping the poor, I don't see the use of it.'

The outburst evoked no reply from Hilary; she felt more tremulous than ever. The whole thing was so confused, so unnatural. What with the dark, malignant Hughs and that haunting vision of Bianca, the matter seemed almost Italian. That a man of Hughs' class might be affected by the passion of love had somehow never come into her head. She thought of the back streets she had looked out on from her bedroom window. Could anything like passion spring up in those dismal alleys? The people who lived there, poor down-trodden things, had enough to do to keep themselves alive. She knew all about them; they were in the air; their condition was deplorable! Could a person whose condition was deplorable find time or strength for any sort of lurid exhibition such as this? It was incredible.

She became aware that Hilary was speaking.

'I daresay the man is dangerous!'

Hearing her fears confirmed, and in accordance with the secret vein of hardness which kept her living, amid all her sympathies and hesitations, Cecilia felt suddenly that she had gone as far as it was in her to go.

'I shall have no more to do with them,' she said; 'I've tried my best for Mrs Hughs. I know quite as good a needlewoman, who'll be only too glad to come instead. Any other girl will do as well to copy father's book. If you take my advice, Hilary, you'll give up trying to help them too.'

Hilary's smile puzzled and annoyed her. If she had known, this was the smile that stood between him and her sister.

'You may be right,' he said, and shrugged his shoulders.

'Very well,' said Cecilia, 'I've done all I can. I must go now. Good-bye.'

During her progress to the door she gave one look behind. Hilary was standing by the bust of Socrates. Her heart smote her to leave him thus embarrassed. But again the vision of Bianca—fugitive in her own house, and with something tragic in her mocking immobility—came to her, and she hastened away.

A voice said: 'How are you, Mrs Dallison? Your sister at home?'

Cecilia saw before her Mr Purcey, rising and falling a little with the oscillation of his A.1. Damyer as he prepared to alight.

A sense as of having just left a house visited by sickness or misfortune made Cecilia murmur:

'I'm afraid she's not.'

'Bad luck!' said Mr Purcey. His face fell as far as so red and square a face could fall. 'I was hoping perhaps I might be allowed to take them for a run. She's wanting exercise.' Mr Purcey laid his hand on the flank of his palpitating car. 'Know these A.1. Damyers, Mrs Dallison? Best value you can get, simply rippin' little cars. Wish you'd try her.'

The A.1. Damyer, diffusing an aroma of the finest petrol, leaped and trembled, as though conscious of her master's praise. Cecilia looked at her.

'Yes,' she said. 'she's very sweet.'

'Now do!' said Mr Purcey. 'Let me give you a run—just to please me, I mean. I'm sure you'll like her.'

A little compunction, a little curiosity, a sudden revolt against all the discomfiture and sordid doubts she had been suffering from, made Cecilia glance softly at Mr Purcey's figure; almost before she knew it, she was seated in the A.1. Damyer. It trembled, emitted two small sounds, one large scent, and glided forward. Mr Purcey said:

'That's rippin' of you!'

A postman, dog, and baker's cart, all hurrying at top speed, seemed to stand still; Cecilia felt the wind beating her cheeks. She gave a little laugh.

'You must just take me home, please.'

Mr Purcey touched the chauffeur's elbow.

'Round the park,' he said. 'Let her have it.'

The A.1. Damyer uttered a tiny shriek. Cecilia, leaning back in her padded corner, glanced askance at Mr Purcey leaning back in his; an unholy, astonished little smile played on her lips.

'What am I doing?' it seemed to say. 'The way he got me here—really! And now I am here I'm just going to enjoy it!'

There were no Hughes, no little model—all that sordid life had vanished; there was nothing but the wind beating her cheeks and the A.1. Damyer leaping under her.

Mr Purcey said: 'It just makes all the difference to me; keeps my nerves in order.'

'Oh,' Cecilia murmured, 'have *you* got nerves?'

Mr Purcey smiled. When he smiled his cheeks formed two hard red blocks, his trim moustache stood out, and many little wrinkles ran from his light eyes.

'Chock full of them,' he said; 'least thing upsets me. Can't bear to see a hungry-lookin' child, or anything.'

A strange feeling of admiration for this man had come upon Cecilia. Why could not she, and Thyme, and Hilary, and Stephen, and all the people they knew and mixed with, be like him, so sound and healthy, so unravaged by disturbing sympathies, so innocent of 'social conscience', so content?

As though jealous of these thoughts about her master, the A.1. Damyer stopped of her own accord.

'Hallo,' said Mr Purcey, 'hallo, I say! Don't you get out; she'll be all right directly.'

'Oh,' said Cecilia, 'thanks but I must go in here, anyhow; I think I'll say good-bye. Thank you so much. I *have* enjoyed it.'

From the threshold of a shop she looked back. Mr Purcey, on foot, was leaning forward from the waist, staring at his A.1. Damyer with profound concentration.

Chapter 9

HILARY GIVES CHASE

THE ethics of a man like Hilary were not those of the million purebred Purceys of this life, founded on a sense of property in this world and the next; nor were they precisely the morals and religion of the aristocracy, who, though aestheticised in parts, quietly used, in bulk, their fortified position to graft on Mr Purcey's ethics the principle of 'You be damned!' In the eyes of the majority he was probably an immoral and irreligious man; but in fact his morals and religion were those of his special section of society—the cultivated classes, 'the professors, the artistic pigs, advanced people, and all that sort of cuckoo,' as Mr Purcey called them—a section of society supplemented by persons, placed beyond the realms of want, who speculated in ideas.

Had he been required to make a profession of his creed he would probably have framed it in some such way as this: 'I disbelieve in all Church dogmas, and do not go to church; I have no definite ideas about a future state, and do not want to have; but in a private way I try to identify myself as much as possible with what I see about me, feeling that if I could ever really be at one with the world I live in I should be happy. I think it foolish not to trust my senses and my reason; as for what my senses and my reason will not tell me, I assume that all is as it had to be, for if one could get to know the why of everything, one would be the Universe. I do not believe that chastity is a virtue in itself, but only so far as it ministers to the health and happiness of the community. I do not believe that marriage confers the rights of ownership, and I loathe all public wrangling on such matters; but I am temperamentally averse to the harming of my neighbours, if in reason it can be avoided. As to manners, I think that to repeat a bit of scandal, and circulate backbiting stories, are worse offences than the actions that gave rise to them. If I mentally condemn a person, I feel guilty of moral lapse. I hate self-assertion; I am ashamed of self-advertisement. I dislike loudness of any kind. Probably I have too much tendency to negation of all sorts. Small-talk bores me to extinction, but I will discuss a point of ethics or psychology half the night. To make capital out of a person's weakness is repugnant to me. I want to be a decent man, but—I really can't take myself too seriously.'

Though he had preserved his politeness towards Cecilia, he was in truth angry, and grew angrier every minute. He was angry with her, himself, and the man Hughs; and suffered from this anger as only they can who are not accustomed to the rough-and-tumble of things.

Such a retiring man as Hilary was seldom given the opportunity for an obvious display of chivalry. The tenor of his life removed him from those situations. Such chivalry as he displayed was of a negative order. And confronted suddenly with the conduct of Hughs, who, it seemed, knocked his wife about, and dogged the footsteps of the helpless girl, he took it seriously to heart.

When the little model came walking up the garden on her usual visit, he fancied her face looked scared. Quieting the growling of Miranda, who from the first had stubbornly refused to know this girl, he sat down with a book to wait for her to go away. After sitting an hour or more, turning over pages, and knowing little of their sense, he saw a man peer over his garden gate. He was there for half a minute, then lounged across the road, and stood hidden by some railings.

'So?' thought Hilary. 'Shall I go out and warn the fellow to clear off, or shall I wait to see what happens when she goes away?'

He determined on the latter course. Presently she came out, walking with her peculiar gait, youthful and pretty, but too matter-of-fact, and yet, as it were, too purposeless to be a lady's. She looked back at Hilary's window, and turned uphill.

Hilary took his hat and stick and waited. In half a minute Hughs came out from under cover of the railings and followed. Then Hilary, too, set forth.

There is left in every man something of the primeval love of stalking. The delicate Hilary, in cooler blood, would have revolted at the notion of dogging people's footsteps. He now experienced the holy pleasures of the chase. Certain that Hughs was really following the girl, he had but to keep him in sight and remain unseen. This was not hard for a man given to mountain-climbing, almost the only sport left to one who thought it immoral to hurt anybody but himself.

Taking advantage of shop-windows, omnibuses, passers-by, and other bits of cover, he prosecuted the chase up the steepy heights of Campden Hill. But soon a nearly fatal check occurred; for, chancing to take his eyes off Hughs, he saw the little model returning on her tracks. Ready enough in physical emergencies, Hilary sprang into a passing omnibus. He saw her stopping before the window of a picture-shop. From the expression of her face and figure, she evidently had no idea that she was being followed, but stood with a sort of slack-lipped wonder, lost in admiration of a well-known print. Hilary had often wondered who could possibly admire that picture—he now knew. It was obvious that the girl's aesthetic sense was deeply touched.

While this was passing through his mind, he caught sight of Hughs lurking outside a public-house. The dark man's face was sullen and dejected, and looked as if he suffered. Hilary felt a sort of pity for him.

The omnibus leaped forward, and he sat down smartly almost on a lady's lap. This was the lap of Mrs Tallents Smallpeace, who greeted him with a warm, quiet smile, and made a little room.

'Your sister-in-law has just been to see me, Mr Dallison. She's such a dear—so interested in everything. I tried to get her to come on to my meeting with me.'

Raising his hat, Hilary frowned. For once his delicacy was at fault. He said:

'Ah, yes! Excuse me!' and got out.

Mrs Tallents Smallpeace looked after him, and then glanced round the omnibus. His conduct was very like the conduct of a man who had got in to keep an assignation with a lady, and found that lady sitting next his aunt. She was unable to see a soul who seemed to foster this view, and sat thinking that he was 'rather attractive'. Suddenly her dark busy eyes lighted on the figure of the little model strolling along again.

'Oh!' she thought. 'Ah! Yes, really! How very interesting!'

Hilary, to avoid meeting the girl point-blank, had turned up a by-street, and, finding a convenient corner waited. He was puzzled. If this man were persecuting her with his attentions, why had he not gone across when she was standing at the picture-shop?

She passed across the opening of the by-street, still walking in the slack way of one who takes the pleasures of the streets. She passed from view; Hilary strained his eyes to see if Hughs were following. He waited several minutes. The man did not appear. The chase was over! And suddenly it flashed across him that Hughs had merely dogged her to see that she had no assignation with anybody. They had both been playing the same game! He flushed up in that shady little street, in which he was the only person to be seen. Cecilia was right! It was a sordid business. A man more in touch with facts than Hilary would have had some mental pigeon-hole into which to put an incident like this; but, being by profession concerned mainly with ideas and thoughts, he did not quite know where he was. The habit of his mind precluded him from thinking very definitely on any subject except his literary work—precluded him especially in a matter of this sort, so inextricably entwined with that delicate, dim question, the impact of class on class.

Pondering deeply, he ascended the leafy lane that leads between high railings from Notting Hill to Kensington.

It was so far from traffic that every tree on either side was loud with the Spring songs of birds; the scent of running sap came forth shyly as the sun sank low. Strange peace, strange feeling of old Mother Earth up there above the town; wild tunes, and the quiet sight of clouds. Man in this lane might rest his troubled thoughts, and for a while trust the goodness of the Scheme that gave him birth, the beauty of each day, that laughs or broods itself into night. Some budding lilacs exhaled a scent of lemons; a sandy cat on the coping of a garden wall basking in the setting sun.

In the centre of the lane a row of elm-trees displayed their gnarled, knotted roots. Human beings were seated there, whose matted hair clung round their tired faces. Their gaunt limbs were clothed in rags; each had a stick, and some sort of dirty bundle tied to it. They were asleep. On a bench beyond, two toothless old women sat, moving their eyes from side to side, and a crimson-faced woman was snoring. Under the next tree a Cockney youth and his girl were sitting side by side—pale young things with loose mouths, and hollow cheeks, and restless eyes. Their arms were enlaced; they were silent. A little farther on two young men in working clothes were looking straight before them, with desperately tired faces. They, too, were silent.

On the last bench of all Hilary came on the little model, seated slackly by herself.

Chapter 10

THE TROUSSEAU

THIS, the first time these two had met each other at large, was clearly not a comfortable event for either of them. The girl blushed, and hastily got off her seat. Hilary, who raised his hat and frowned, sat down on it.

'Don't get up,' he said; 'I want to talk to you.'

The little model obediently resumed her seat. A silence followed. She had on the old brown skirt and knitted jersey, the old blue-green tam-o'-shanter cap, and there were marks of weariness beneath her eyes.

At last Hilary remarked: 'How are you getting on?'

The little model looked at her feet.

'Pretty well, thank you, Mr Dallison.'

'I came to see you yesterday.'

She slid a look at him which might have meant nothing or meant much, so perfect its shy stolidity.

'I was out,' she said, 'sitting to Miss Boyle.'

'So you have some work?'

'It's finished now.'

'Then you're only getting the two shillings a day from Mr Stone?'

She nodded.

'H'm!'

The unexpected fervour of this grunt seemed to animate the little model.

'Three and sixpence for my rent, and breakfast costs threepence nearly—only bread-and-butter—that's five and two; and washing's always at least tenpence—that's six; and little things last week was a shilling—even when I don't take buses—seven; that leaves five shillings for my dinners. Mr Stone always gives me tea. It's my clothes worries me.' She tucked her feet farther beneath the seat, and Hilary refrained from looking down. 'My hat is awful, and I do want some——' She looked Hilary in the face for the first time. 'I do wish I was rich.'

'I don't wonder.'

The little model gritted her teeth, and, twisting at her dirty gloves, said: 'Mr Dallison, d'you know the first thing I'd buy if I was rich?'

'No.'

'I'd buy everything new on me from top to toe, and I wouldn't ever wear any of these old things again.'

Hilary got up: 'Come with me now, and buy everything new from top to toe.'

'Oh!'

Hilary had already perceived that he had made an awkward, even dangerous, proposal; short, however, of giving her money, the idea of which offended his sense of delicacy, there was no way out of it. He said brusquely: 'Come along!'

The little model rose obediently. Hilary noticed that her boots were split, and this—as though he had seen someone strike a child—so moved his indignation that he felt no more qualms, but rather a sort of pleasant glow, such as will come to the most studious man when he levels a blow at the conventions.

He looked down at his companion—her eyes were lowered; he could not tell at all what she was thinking of.

'This is what I was going to speak to you about,' he said: 'I don't like that house you're in; I think you ought to be somewhere else. What do you say?'

'Yes, Mr Dallison.'

'You'd better make a change, I think; you could find another room, couldn't you?'

The little model answered as before: 'Yes, Mr Dallison.'

'I'm afraid that Hughs is—a dangerous sort of fellow.'

'He's a funny man.'

'Does he annoy you?'

Her expression baffled Hilary; there seemed a sort of slow enjoyment in it. She looked up knowingly.

'I don't mind him—he won't hurt me. Mr Dallison, do you think blue or green?'

Hilary answered shortly: 'Bluey-green.'

She clasped her hands, changed her feet with a hop, and went on walking as before.

'Listen to me,' said Hilary; 'has Mrs Hughs been talking to you about her husband?'

The little model smiled again.

'She goes on,' she said.

Hilary bit his lips.

'Mr Dallison, please—about my hat?'

'What about your hat?'

'Would you like me to get a large one or a small one?'

'For God's sake,' answered Hilary, 'a small one—no feathers.'

'Oh!'

'Can you attend to me a minute? Have either Hughs or Mrs Hughs spoken to you about—coming to my house, about—me?'

The little model's face remained impassive, but by the movement of her fingers Hilary saw that she was attending now.

'I don't care what they say.'

Hilary looked away; an angry flush slowly mounted in his face.

With surprising suddenness the little model said:

'Of course, if I was a lady, I might mind!'

'Don't talk like that!' said Hilary; 'every woman is a lady.'

The stolidity of the girl's face, more mocking far than any smile, warned him of the cheapness of this verbiage.

'If I was a lady,' she repeated simply, 'I shouldn't be livin' there, should I?'

'No,' said Hilary; 'and you had better not go on living there, anyway.'

The little model making no answer, Hilary did not quite know what to say. It was becoming apparent to him that she viewed the situation with a very different outlook from himself, and that he did not understand that outlook.

He felt thoroughly at sea, conscious that this girl's life contained a thousand things he did not know, a thousand points of view he did not share.

Their two figures attracted some attention in the crowded street, for Hilary—tall and slight, with his thin, bearded face and soft felt hat—was what is known as 'a distinguished-looking man'; and the little model, though not 'distinguished-looking' in her old brown skirt and tam-o'-shanter cap, had the sort of face which made men and even women turn to look at her. To men she was a little bit of strangely interesting, not too usual, flesh and blood; to women, she was that which made men turn to look at her. Yet now and again there would rise in some passer-by a feeling more impersonal, as though the God of Pity had shaken wings overhead, and dropped a tiny feather.

So walking, and exciting vague interest, they reached the first of the hundred doors of Messrs Rose and Thorn.

Hilary had determined on this end door, for, as the adventure grew warmer, he was more alive to its dangers. To take this child into the very shop frequented by his wife and friends seemed a little mad; but that same reason which caused them to frequent it—the fact that there was no other shop of the sort half so handy—was the reason which caused Hilary to go there now. He had acted on impulse; he knew that if he let his impulse cool he would not act at all. The bold course was the wise one; this was why he chose the end door round the corner. Standing aside for her to go in first, he noticed the girl's brightened eyes and cheeks; she had never looked so pretty. He glanced hastily round; the department was barren for their purposes, filled entirely with pyjamas. He felt a touch on his arm. The little model, rather pink, was looking up at him.

'Mr Dallison, am I to get more than one set of—underthings?'

'Three—three,' muttered Hilary; and suddenly he saw that they were on the threshold of that sanctuary. 'Buy them,' he said, 'and bring me the bill.'

He waited close beside a man with a pink face, a moustache, and an almost perfect figure, who was standing very still, dressed from head to foot in blue-and-white stripes. He seemed the apotheosis of what a man should be, his face composed in a deathless simper: 'Long, long have been the struggles of man, but civilisation has produced me at last. Further than this it cannot go. Nothing shall make me continue my line. In me the end is reached. See my back: "The Amateur. This perfect style, 8s. 11d. Great reduction." '

He would not talk to Hilary, and the latter was compelled to watch the shopmen. It was but half an hour to closing time; the youths were moving languidly, bickering a little, in the absence of their customers—like flies on a pane, that cannot get out into the sun. Two of them came and asked him what they might serve him with, they were so refined and pleasant that Hilary was on the point of buying what he did not want. The reappearance of the little model saved him.

'It's thirty shillings; five and eleven was the cheapest, and stockings, and I bought some sta——'

Hilary produced the money hastily.

'This is a very dear shop,' she said.

When she had paid the bill, and Hilary had taken from her a large brown-paper parcel, they journeyed on together. He had armoured his face now in a slightly startled quizzicality, as though, himself detached, he were watching the adventure from a distance.

On the central velvet seat of the boot and shoe department, a lady, with an egret in her hat, was stretching out a slim silk-stockinged foot, waiting for a boot. She looked with negligent amusement at this common little girl and her singular companion. This look of hers seemed to affect the woman serving, for none came near the little model. Hilary saw them eyeing her boots, and, suddenly forgetting his rôle of looker-on, he became very angry. Taking out his watch, he went up to the eldest woman.

'If somebody,' he said, 'does not attend this young lady within a minute, I shall make a personal complaint to Mr Thorn.'

The hand of the watch, however, had not completed its round before a woman was at the little model's side. Hilary saw her taking off her boot, and by a sudden impulse he placed himself between her and the lady. In doing this, he so far forgot his delicacy as to fix his eyes on the little model's foot. The sense of physical discomfort which first attacked him became a sort of aching in his heart. That brown, dingy stocking was darned till no stocking, only darning, and one toe and two little white bits of foot were seen, where the threads refused to hold together any longer.

The little model wagged the toe uneasily—she had hoped, no doubt, that it would not protrude—then concealed it with her skirt. Hilary moved hastily away; when he looked again, it was not at her, but at the lady.

Her face had changed; it was no longer amused and negligent, but stamped with an expression of offence. 'Intolerable,' it seemed to say, 'to bring a girl like that into a shop like this! I shall never come here again!' The expression was but the outward sign of that inner physical discomfort Hilary himself had felt when he first saw the little model's stocking. This naturally did not serve to lessen his anger, especially as he saw her animus mechanically reproduced on the faces of the serving women.

He went back to the little model, and sat down by her side.

'Does it fit? You'd better walk in it and see.'

The little model walked.

'It squeezes me,' she said.

'Try another, then,' said Hilary.

The lady rose, stood for a second with her eyebrows raised and her nostrils slightly distended, then went away, and left a peculiarly pleasant scent of violets behind.

The second pair of boots not 'squeezing' her, the little model was soon ready to go down. She had all her trousseau now, except the dress—selected and, indeed, paid for, but which, as she told Hilary, she was coming back to try on to-morrow, when—when—— She had obviously meant to say when she was all new underneath. She was laden with one large and two small parcels, and in her eyes there was a holy look.

Outside the shop she gazed up in his face.

'Well, you are happy now?' asked Hilary.

Between the short black lashes were seen two very bright, wet shining eyes; her parted lips began to quiver.

'Good-night, then,' he said abruptly, and walked away.

But looking round, he saw her still standing there, half buried in parcels, gazing after him. Raising his hat, he turned into the High Street towards home. . . .

The old man, known to that low class of fellow with whom he was now condemned to associate as '*Westminster*', was taking a whiff or two out of his old clay pipe, and trying to forget his feet. He saw Hilary coming, and carefully extended a copy of the last edition.

'Good-evenin', sir! Quite seasonable to-day for the time of year! Ho yes! *Westminster!*'

His eyes followed Hilary's retreat. He thought:

'Oh dear! He's a-given me an 'arf-a-crown. He does look well—I like to see 'im look as well as that—quite young! Oh dear!'

The sun—that smokey, flaring ball, which in its time had seen so many last editions of the *Westminster Gazette*—was dropping down to pass the night in Shepherd's Bush. It made the old butler's eyelids blink when he turned to see if the coin really was a half-crown, or too good to be true.

And all the spires and house-roofs, and the spaces up above and underneath them, glittered and swam, and little men and horses looked as if they had been powdered with golden dust.

Chapter 11

PEAR BLOSSOM

WEIGHED down by her three parcels, the little model pursued her way to Hound Street. At the door of No. 1 the son of the lame woman, a tall weedy youth with a white face, was resting his legs alternately, and smoking a cigarette. Closing one eye, he addressed her thus:

''Allo, miss! Kerry your parcels for you?'

The little model gave him a look. 'Mind your own business!' it said; but there was that in the flicker of her eyelashes which more than nullified this snub.

Entering her room, she deposited the parcels on her bed, and untied the strings with quick, pink fingers. When she had freed the garments from wrappings and spread them out, she knelt down, and began to touch them, putting her nose down once or twice to sniff the linen and feel its texture. There were little frills attached here and there, and to these she paid particular attention, ruffling their edges with the palms of her hands, while the holy look came back to her face. Rising at length, she locked the door, drew down the blind, undressed from head to foot, and put on the new garments. Letting her hair down, she turned herself luxuriously round and round before the too-small looking-glass. There was utter satisfaction in each gesture of that whole operation, as if her spirit, long starved, were having a good meal. In this rapt contemplation of herself, all childish vanity and expectancy, and all that wonderful quality found in simple unspiritual natures of delighting in the present moment, were perfectly displayed. So, motionless, with her hair loose on her neck, she was like one of those half-hours of Spring that have lost their restlessness and are content just to *be*.

Presently, however, as though suddenly remembering that her happiness was not utterly complete, she went to a drawer, took out a packet of pear-drops, and put one in her mouth.

The sun, near to setting, had found its way through a hole in the blind, and touched her neck. She turned as though she had received a kiss, and, raising a corner of the blind, peered out. The pear-tree, which, to the annoyance of its proprietor, was placed so close to the back court of this low-class house as almost to seem to belong to it, was bathed in slanting sunlight. No tree in all the world could have looked more fair than it did just then in its garb of gilded bloom. With her hand up to her bare neck, and her cheeks indrawn from sucking the sweet, the little model fixed her eyes on the tree. Her expression did not change; she showed no signs of admiration. Her gaze passed on to the back windows of the house that really owned the pear-tree, spying out whether anyone could see her—hoping, perhaps, someone *would* see her while she was feeling so nice and new. Then, dropping the blind, she went back to the glass and began to pin her hair up. When this was done she stood for a long minute looking at her old brown skirt and blouse, hesitating to defile her new-found purity. At last she put them on and drew up the blind. The sunlight had passed off the pear-tree; its bloom was now white, and almost as still as snow. The little model put another sweet into her mouth, and producing from her pocket an ancient leather purse, counted out her money. Evidently discovering that it was no more than she expected, she sighed, and rummaged out of a top drawer an old illustrated magazine.

She sat down on the bed, and turning the leaves rapidly till she reached a certain page, rested the paper in her lap. Her eyes were fixed on a photograph in the left-hand corner—one of those effigies of writers that appear occasionally in the public press. Under it were printed the words: 'Mr Hilary Dallison'. And suddenly she heaved a sigh.

The room grew darker; the wind, getting up as the sun went down, blew a few dropped petals of the pear-tree against the window-pane.

Chapter 12

SHIPS IN SAIL

IN due accord with the old butler's comment on his looks, Hilary had felt so young that, instead of going home, he mounted an omnibus, and went down to his club—the 'Pen and Ink', so called because the man who founded it could not think at the moment of any other words. This literary person had left the club soon after its initiation, having conceived for it a sudden dislike. It had indeed a certain reputation for bad cooking, and all its members complained bitterly at times that you never could go in without meeting someone you knew. It stood in Dover Street. Unlike other clubs, it was mainly used to talk in, and had special arrangements for the safety of umbrellas and such books as had not yet vanished from the library; not, of course, owing to any peculative tendency among its members, but because, after interchanging their ideas, those members would depart, in a long row, each grasping some material object in his hand. Its maroon-coloured curtains, too, were never drawn, because, in the heat of their discussions, the members were always drawing them. On the whole, those members did not like each other much; wondering a little, one by one, why the others wrote; and when the printed reasons were detailed to them, reading them with irritation. If really compelled to hazard an opinion about each other's merits, they used to say that, no doubt 'So-and-so' was 'very good', but they had never read him! For it had early been established as the principle underlying membership not to read the writings of another man, unless you could be certain he was dead, lest you might have to tell him to his face that you disliked his work. For they were very jealous of the purity of their literary consciences. Exception was made, however, in the case of those who lived by written criticism, the opinions of such persons being read by all, with a varying smile, and a certain cerebral excitement. Now and then, however, some member, violating every sense of decency, would take a violent liking for another member's books. This he would express in words, to the discomfort of his fellows, who, with a sudden chilly feeling in the stomach, would wonder why it was not their books that he was praising.

Almost every year, and generally in March, certain aspirations would pass into the club; members would ask each other why there was no Academy of British Letters; why there was no concerted movement to limit the production of other authors' books; why there was no prize given for the best work of the year. For a little time it almost seemed as if their individualism were in danger; but, the windows having been opened wider than usual some morning, the aspirations would pass out, and all would feel secretly as a man feels when he has swallowed the mosquito that has been worrying him all night—relieved, but just a little bit embarrassed. Socially sympathetic in their dealings with each other—they were mostly quite nice fellows—each kept a little fame-machine, on which he might be seen sitting every morning about the time the papers and his correspondence came, wondering if his fame were going up.

Hilary stayed in the club till half-past nine; then, avoiding a discussion which was just setting in, he took his own umbrella, and bent his steps towards home.

It was the moment of suspense in Piccadilly; the tide had flowed up to the theatres, and had not yet begun to ebb. The tranquil trees, still feathery, draped their branches along the farther bank of that broad river, resting from their watch over the tragi-comedies played on its surface by men, their small companions. The gentle sighs which distilled from their plume-like boughs seemed utterances of the softest wisdom. Not far beyond their trunks it was all dark velvet, into which separate shapes, adventuring, were lost, as wild birds vanishing in space, or the souls of men received into their Mother's heart.

Hilary walked, hearing no sighs of wisdom, noting no smooth darkness, wrapped in thought. The mere fact of having given pleasure was enough to produce a warm sensation in a man so naturally kind. But, as with all self-conscious, self-distrustful, natures, that sensation had not lasted. He was left with a feeling of emptiness and disillusionment, as of having given himself a good mark without reason.

While walking, he was a target for the eyes of many women, who passed him rapidly, like ships in sail. The peculiar fastidious shyness of his face attracted those accustomed to another kind of face. And though he did not precisely look at them, they in turn inspired in him the compassionate, morbid curiosity which persons who live desperate lives necessarily inspire in the leisured, speculative mind. One of them deliberately approached him from a side-street. Though taller and fuller, with heightened colour, frizzy hair, and a hat with feathers, she was the image of the little model—the same shape of face, broad cheek-bones, mouth a little open; the same flower-coloured eyes and short black lashes, all coarsened and accentuated as Art coarsens and accentuates the lines of life. Looking boldly into Hilary's startled face, she laughed. Hilary winced and walked on quickly.

He reached home at half-past ten. The lamp was burning in Mr Stone's room, and his window was, as usual, open; that which was not usual, however, was a light in Hilary's own bedroom. He went gently up. Through the door—ajar—he saw, to his surprise, the figure of his wife. She was reclining in a chair, her elbows on its arms, the tips of her fingers pressed together. Her face, with its dark hair, vivid colouring, and sharp lines, was touched with shadows; her head turned as though towards somebody beside her; her neck gleamed white. So—motionless, dimly seen—she was like a woman sitting alongside her own life, scrutinising, criticising, watching it live, taking no part in it. Hilary wondered whether to go in or slip away from his strange visitor.

'Ah! it's you,' she said.

Hilary approached her. For all her mocking of her own charms, this wife of his was strangely graceful. After nineteen years in which to learn every line of her face and body, every secret of her nature, she still eluded him; that elusiveness, which had begun by being such a charm, had got on his nerves, and extinguished the flame it had once lighted. He had so often tried to see, and never seen, the essence of her soul. Why was she made like this? Why was she for ever mocking herself, himself, and every other thing? Why was she so hard to her own life, so bitter a foe to her own happiness? Leonardo da Vinci might have painted her, less sensual and cruel than his women, more restless and disharmonic, but physically, spiritually enticing, and, by her refusals to surrender either to her spirit or her senses, baffling her own enticements.

'I don't know why I came,' she said.

Hilary found no better answer than: 'I am sorry I was out to dinner.'

'Has the wind gone round? My room is cold.'

'Yes, north-east. Stay here.'

Her hand touched his; that warm and restless clasp was agitating.

'It's good of you to ask me; but we'd better not begin what we can't keep up.'

'Stay here,' said Hilary again, kneeling down beside her chair.

And suddenly he began to kiss her face and neck. He felt her answering kisses; for a moment they were clasped together in a fierce embrace. Then, as though by mutual consent, their arms relaxed; their eyes grew furtive, like the eyes of children who have egged each other on to steal; and on their lips appeared the faintest of faint smiles. It was as though those lips were saying: 'Yes, but we are not quite animals!'

Hilary got up and sat down on his bed. Bianca stayed in the chair, looking straight before her, utterly inert, her head thrown back, her white throat gleaming, on her lips and in her eyes that flickering smile. Not a word more, nor a look, passed between them.

Then rising, without noise, she passed behind him and went out.

Hilary had a feeling in his mouth as though he had been chewing ashes. And a phrase—as phrases sometimes fill the spirit of a man without rhyme or reason—kept forming on his lips: 'The house of harmony!'

Presently he went to her door, and stood there listening. He could hear no sound whatever. If she had been crying—if she had been laughing—it would have been better than this silence. He put his hands up to his ears and ran downstairs.

Chapter 13

SOUND IN THE NIGHT

PASSING his study door, he halted at Mr Stone's; the thought of the old man, so steady and absorbed in the face of all external things, refreshed him.

Still in his brown woollen gown, Mr Stone was sitting with his eyes fixed on something in the corner, whence a little perfumed steam was rising.

'Shut the door,' he said; 'I am making cocoa; will you have a cup?'

'Am I disturbing you?' asked Hilary.

Mr Stone looked at him steadily before answering:

'If I work after cocoa, I find it clogs the liver.'

'Then, if you'll let me, sir, I'll stay a little.'

'It is boiling,' said Mr Stone. He took the saucepan off the flame, and, distending his frail cheeks, blew. Then, while the steam mingled with his frosty beard, he brought two cups from a cupboard, filled one of them, and looked at Hilary.

'I should like you,' he said, 'to hear three or four pages I have just completed; you may perhaps be able to suggest a word or two.'

He placed the saucepan back on the stove, and grasped the cup he had filled.

'I will drink my cocoa, and read them to you.'

Going to the desk, he stood, blowing at the cup.

Hilary turned up the collar of his coat against the night wind which was visiting the room, and glanced at the empty cup, for he was rather hungry. He heard a curious sound: Mr Stone was blowing his own tongue. In his haste to read, he had drunk too soon and deeply of the cocoa.

'I have burnt my mouth,' he said.

Hilary moved hastily towards him: 'Badly? Try cold milk, sir.'

Mr Stone lifted the cup.

'There is none,' he said, and drank again.

'What would I not give,' thought Hilary, 'to have his singleness of heart!'

There was the sharp sound of a cup set down. Then, out of a rustling of papers, a sort of droning rose:

' "The Proletariat—with a cynicism natural to those who really are in want, and even amongst their leaders only veiled when these attained a certain position in the public eye—desired indeed the wealth and leisure of their richer neighbours, but in their long night of struggle with existence they had only found the energy to formulate their pressing needs from day to day. They were a heaving, surging sea of creatures, slowly, without consciousness or real guidance, rising in long tidal movements to set the limits of the shore a little farther back, and cast afresh the form of social life; and on its pea-green bosom——" ' Mr Stone paused. 'She has copied it wrong,' he said; 'the word is "sea-green". "And on its sea-green bosom sailed a fleet of silver cockle-shells, wafted by the breath of those not in themselves driven by the wind of need. The voyage of these silver cockle-shells, all heading across each other's bows, was, in fact, the advanced movement of that time. In the stern of each of these little craft, blowing at the sails, was seated a by-product of the accepted system. These by-products we should now examine." '

Mr Stone paused, and looked into his cup. There were some grounds in it. He drank them, and went on:

' "The fratricidal principal of the survival of the fittest, which in those days was England's moral teaching, had made the country one huge butcher's shop. Amongst the carcasses of countless victims there had fattened and grown purple many butchers, physically strengthened by the smell of blood and sawdust. These had begotten many children. Following out the laws of Nature providing against surfeit, a proportion of these children were born with a feeling of distaste for blood and sawdust; many of them, compelled for the purpose of making money to follow in their father's practices, did so unwillingly; some, thanks to their fathers' butchery, were in a position to abstain from practising; but whether in practice or at leisure, distaste for the scent of blood and sawdust was the common feature that distinguished them. Qualities hitherto but little known, and generally despised—not, as we shall see, without some reason—were developed in them. Self-consciousness, aestheticism, a dislike for waste, a hatred of injustice; these—or some one of these, when coupled with that desire natural to men throughout all ages to accomplish something—constituted the motive forces which enabled them to work their bellows. In practical affairs those who were under the necessity of labouring were driven, under the then machinery of social life, to the humaner and less exacting kinds of butchery, such as the Arts, Education, the practice of Religions and Medicine, and the paid representation of their fellow-creatures. Those not so driven occupied themselves in observing and complaining of the existing state of things. Each year saw more of their silver cockle-shells putting out from port, and the cheeks of those who blew the sails more violently distended. Looking back on that pretty voyage, we see the reason why those ships were doomed never to move, but, seated on the sea-green bosom of that sea, to heave up and down, heading across each other's bows in the self-same place for ever. That reason, in a few words, was this: 'The man who blew should have been in the sea, not on the ship.'"'

The droning ceased. Hilary saw that Mr Stone was staring fixedly at his sheet of paper, as though the merits of this last sentence were surprising him. The droning instantly began again: '"In social effort, as in the physical processes of Nature, there had ever been a single fertilising agent—the mysterious and wonderful attraction known as Love. To this—that merging of one being in another—had been due all the progressive variance of form, known by man under the name of Life. It was this merger, this mysterious, unconscious Love, which was lacking to the windy efforts of those who tried to sail that fleet. They were full of reason, conscience, horror, full of impatience, contempt, revolt; but they did not *love* the masses of their fellow-men: They could not fling themselves into the sea. Their hearts were glowing; but the wind that made them glow was not the salt and universal zephyr: it was the desert wind of scorn. As with the flowering of the aloe-tree—so long awaited, so strange and swift when once it comes—man had yet to wait for his delirious impulse to Universal Brotherhood, and the forgetfulness of Self."'

Mr Stone had finished, and stood gazing at his visitor with eyes that clearly saw beyond him. Hilary could not meet those eyes; he kept his own fixed on the empty cocoa cup. It was not, in fact, usual for those who heard Mr Stone read his manuscript to look him in the face. He stood thus absorbed so long that Hilary rose at last, and glanced into the saucepan. There was no cocoa in it. Mr Stone had only made enough for one. He had meant it for his visitor, but self-forgetfulness had supervened.

'You know what happens to the aloe, sir, when it has flowered?' asked Hilary, with malice.

Mr Stone moved, but did not answer.

'It dies,' said Hilary.

'No,' said Mr Stone; 'it is at peace.'

'When is self at peace, sir? The individual is surely as immortal as the universal. That is the eternal comedy of life.'

'What is?' said Mr Stone.

'The fight between the two.'

Mr Stone stood a moment looking wistfully at his son-in-law. He laid down the sheets of manuscript. 'It is time for me to do my exercises.' So saying, he undid the tasselled cord tied round the middle of his gown.

Hilary hastened to the door. From that point of vantage he looked back.

Divested of his gown and turned towards the window, Mr Stone was already rising on his toes, his arms were extended, his palms pressed hard together in the attitude of prayer, his trousers slowly slipping down.

'One, two, three, four, five!' There was a sudden sound of breath escaping. . . .

In the corridor upstairs, flooded with moonlight from a window at the end, Hilary stood listening again. The only sound that came to him was the light snoring of Miranda, who slept in the bathroom, not caring to lie too near to anyone. He went to his room, and for a long time sat buried in thought; then, opening the side window, he leaned out. On the trees of the next garden, and the sloping roofs of stables and out-houses, the moonlight had come down like a flight of milk-white pigeons; with outspread wings, vibrating faintly as though yet in motion, they covered everything. Nothing stirred. A clock was striking two. Past that flight of milk-white pigeons were black walls as yet unvisited. Then, in the stillness, Hilary seemed to hear, deep and very faint, the sound as of some monster breathing, or the far beating of muffled drums. From every side of the pale sleeping town it seemed to come, under the moon's cold glamour. It rose, and fell, and rose, with a weird, creepy rhythm, like a groaning of the hopeless and hungry. A hansom cab rattled down the High Street; Hilary strained his ears after the failing clatter of hoofs and bell. They died; there was silence. Creeping nearer, drumming, throbbing, he heard again the beating of that vast heart. It grew and grew. His own heart began thumping. Then, emerging from that sinister dumb groan, he distinguished a crunching sound, and knew that it was no muttering echo of men's struggles, but only the waggons coming into Covent Garden Market.

Chapter 14

A WALK ABROAD

THYME DALLISON, in the midst of her busy life, found leisure to record her recollections and ideas in the pages of old school note-books. She had no definite purpose in so doing, nor did she desire the solace of luxuriating in her private feelings—this she would have scorned as out of date and silly. It was done from the fulness of youthful energy, and from the desire to express oneself what was 'in the air'. It was everywhere, that desire: among her fellow-students, among her young men friends, in her mother's drawing-room, and her aunt's studio. Like sentiment and marriage to the Victorian miss, so was this duty to express herself to Thyme; and, going hand-in-hand with it, the duty to have a good and jolly youth. She never read again the thoughts which she recorded, she took no care to lock them up, knowing that her liberty, development, and pleasure were sacred things which no one would dream of touching—she kept them stuffed down in a drawer among her handkerchiefs and ties and blouses, together with the indelible fragment of a pencil.

This journal, naïve and slipshod, recorded without order the current impression of things on her mind.

In the early morning of the 4th of May she sat, nightgowned, on the foot of her white bed, with chestnut hair all fluffy about her neck, eyes bright and cheeks still rosy with sleep, scribbling away and rubbing one bare foot against the other in the ecstasy of self-expression. Now and then, in the middle of a sentence, she would stop and look out of the window, or stretch herself deliciously, as though life were too full of joy for her to finish anything.

'I went into grandfather's room yesterday, and stayed while he was dictating to the little model. I do think grandfather's so splendid. Martin says an enthusiast is worse than useless; people, he says, can't afford to dabble in ideas or dreams. He calls grandfather's idea palaeolithic. I hate him to be laughed at. Martin's so cocksure. I don't think he'd find many men of eighty who'd bathe in the Serpentine all the year round, and do his own room, cook his own food, and live on about ninety pounds a year out of his pension of three hundred, and give all the rest away. Martin says that's unsound, and the "Book of Universal Brotherhood" rot. I don't care if it is; it's fine to go on writing it as he does all day. Martin admits that. That's the worst of him: he's so cool, you can't score him off; he seems to be always criticising you; it makes me wild. . . . That little model is a hopeless duffer. I could have taken it all down in half the time. She kept stopping and looking up with that mouth of hers half open, as if she had all day before her. Grandfather's so absorbed he doesn't notice; he likes to read the thing over and over, to hear how the words sound. That girl would be no good at any sort of work, except "sitting", I suppose. Aunt B. used to say she sat well. There's something queer about her face; it reminds me a little of that Botticelli Madonna in the National Gallery, the full-face one; not so much in the shape as in the expression—almost stupid, and yet as if things were going to happen to her. Her hands and arms are pretty, and her feet are smaller than mine. She's two years older than me. I asked her why she went in for being a model, which is beastly work. She said she was glad to get anything! I asked her why she didn't go into a shop or into service. She didn't answer at once, and then said she hadn't had any recommendations—didn't know where to try; then, all of a sudden, she grew quite sulky, and said she didn't want to. . . .'

Thyme paused to pencil in a sketch of the little model's profile. . . .

'She had on a really pretty frock, quite simple and well made—it must have cost three or four pounds. She can't be so very badly off, or somebody gave it her. . . .'

And again Thyme paused.

'She looked ever so much prettier in it than she used to in her old brown skirt, I thought. . . . Uncle Hilary came to dinner last night. We talked of social questions; we always discuss things when he comes. I can't help liking Uncle Hilary; he has such kind eyes, and he's so gentle that you never lose your temper with him. Martin calls him weak and unsatisfactory because he's not in touch with life. I should say it was more as if he couldn't bear to force anyone to do anything; he seems to see both sides of every question, and he's not good at making up his mind, of course. He's rather like Hamlet might have been, only nobody seems to know now what Hamlet was really like. I told him what I thought about the lower classes. One can talk to him. I hate father's way of making feeble little jokes, as if nothing were serious. I said I didn't think it was any use to dabble; we ought to go to the root of everything. I said that money and class distinctions are two bogeys we have got to lay. Martin says, when it comes to real dealing with social questions and the poor, all the people we know are amateurs. He says that we have got to shake ourselves free of all the old sentimental notions, and just work at putting everything to the test of Health. Father calls Martin a "Sanitist"; and Uncle Hilary says that if you wash people by *law* they'll all be as dirty again to-morrow. . . .'

Thyme paused again. A blackbird in the garden of the Square was uttering a long, low, chuckling trill. She ran to the window and peeped out. The bird was on a plane-tree, and, with throat uplifted, was letting through his yellow beak that delicious piece of self-expression. All things he seemed to praise—the sky, the sun, the trees, the dewy grass, himself!

'You darling!' thought Thyme. With a shudder of delight she dropped her notebook back into the drawer, flung off her night-gown, and flew into her bath.

That same morning she slipped quietly out at ten o'clock. Her Saturdays were free of classes, but she had to run the gauntlet of her mother's liking for her company and her father's wish for her to go with him to Richmond and play golf. For on Saturdays Stephen almost always left the precincts of the Courts before three o'clock. Then, if he could induce his wife or daughter to accompany him, he liked to get a round or two in preparation for Sunday, when he always started off at half-past ten and played all day. If Cecilia and Thyme failed him, he would go to his club, and keep himself in touch with every kind of social movement by reading the reviews.

Thyme walked along with her head up and a wrinkle in her brow, as though she were absorbed in serious reflection; if admiring glances were flung at her, she did not seem aware of them. Passing not far from Hilary's, she entered the Broad Walk, and crossed it to the farther end.

On a railing, stretching out his long legs and observing the passers-by, sat her cousin, Martin Stone. He got down as she came up.

'Late again,' he said. 'Come on!'

'Where are we going first?' Thyme asked.

'The Notting Hill district's all we can do to-day if we're to go again to Mrs Hughs'. I must be down at the hospital this afternoon.'

Thyme frowned. 'I do envy you living by yourself, Martin. It's silly having to live at home.'

Martin did not answer, but one nostril of his long nose was seen to curve, and Thyme acquiesced in this without remark. They walked for some minutes between tall houses, looking about them calmly. Then Martin said: 'All Purceys round here.'

Thyme nodded. Again there was silence; but in these pauses there was no embarrassment, no consciousness apparently that it was silence, and their eyes—those young, impatient, interested eyes—were for ever busy observing.

'Boundary line. We shall be in a patch directly.'

'Black?' asked Thyme.

'Dark blue—black farther on.'

They were passing down a long, grey, curving road, whose narrow houses, hopelessly unpainted, showed marks of grinding poverty. The Spring wind was ruffling straw and little bits of paper in the gutters; under the bright sunlight a bleak and bitter struggle seemed raging. Thyme said:

'This street gives me a hollow feeling.'

Martin nodded. 'Worse than the real article. There's half a mile of this. Here it's all grim fighting. Farther on they've given it up.'

And still they went on up the curving street, with its few pinched shops and its unending narrow grimness.

At the corner of a by-street Martin said: 'We'll go down here.'

Thyme stood still, wrinkling her nose. Martin eyed her.

'Don't funk!'

'I'm not funking, Martin, only I can't stand the smells.'

'You'll have to get used to them.'

'Yes, I know; but—but I forgot my eucalyptus.'

The young man took out a handkerchief which had not yet been unfolded.

'Here, take mine.'

'They do make me feel so—it's a shame to take yours,' and she took the handkerchief.

'That's all right,' said Martin. 'Come on!'

The houses of this narrow street, inside and out, seemed full of women. Many of them had babies in their arms; they were working or looking out of windows or gossiping on doorsteps. And all stopped to stare as the young couple passed. Thyme stole a look at her companion. His long stride had not varied; there was the usual pale, observant, sarcastic expression on his face. Clenching the handkerchief in readiness, and trying to imitate his callous air, she looked at a group of five women on the nearest doorstep. Three were seated and two were standing. One of these, a young woman with a round, open face, was clearly very soon to have a child; the other, with a short, dark face and iron-grey, straggling hair, was smoking a clay pipe. Of the three seated, one, quite young, had a face as grey-white as a dirty sheet, and a blackened eye; the second, with her ragged dress disarranged, was nursing a baby; the third, in the centre, on the top step, with red arms akimbo, her face scored with drink, was shouting friendly obscenities to a neighbour in the window opposite. In Thyme's heart rose the passionate feeling, 'How disgusting! how *disgusting!*' and since she did not dare to give expression to it, she bit her lips and turned her head from them, resenting, with all a young girl's horror, that her sex had given her away. The women stared at her, and in those faces, according to their different temperaments, could be seen first the same vague, hard interest that had been Thyme's when she first looked at them, then the same secret hostility and criticism, as though they too felt that by this young girl's untouched modesty, by her flushed cheeks and unsoiled clothes, their sex had given *them* away. With contemptuous movements of their lips and bodies, on that doorstep they proclaimed their emphatic belief in the virtue and reality of their own existences and in the vice and unreality of her intruding presence.

'Give the doll to Bill; 'e'd make 'er work for once, the ——' In a burst of laughter the epithet was lost.

Martin's lips curled.

'Purple just here,' he said.

Thyme's cheeks were crimson.

At the end of the little street he stopped before a shop.

'Come on,' he said, 'you'll see the sort of place where they buy their grub.'

In the doorway were standing a thin brown spaniel, a small fair woman with a high, bald forehead, from which the hair was gleaned into curl-papers, and a little girl with some affection of the skin.

Nodding coolly, Martin motioned them aside. The shop was ten feet square; its counters, running parallel to two of the walls, were covered with plates of cake, sausages, old ham-bones, peppermint sweets, and household soap; there was also bread, margarine, suet in bowls, sugar, bloaters—many bloaters—Captain's biscuits, and other things besides. Two or three dead rabbits hung against the wall. All was uncovered, so that what flies there were sat feeding socialistically. Behind the counter a girl of seventeen was serving a thin-faced woman with portions of a cheese which she was holding down with her strong, dirty hand, while she sawed it with a knife. On the counter, next the cheese, sat a quiet-looking cat.

They all glanced round at the two young people, who stood and waited.

'Finish what you're at,' said Martin, 'then give me three pennyworth of bull's-eyes.'

The girl, with a violent effort, finished severing the cheese. The thin-faced woman took it, and, coughing above it, went away. The girl, who could not take her eyes off Thyme, now served them with three pennyworth of bull's-eyes, which she took out with her fingers, for they had stuck. Putting them in a screw of newspaper, she handed them to Martin. The young man, who had been observing negligently, touched Thyme's elbow. She, who had stood with eyes cast down, now turned. They went out, Martin handing the bull's-eyes to the little girl with an affection of the skin.

The street now ended in a wide road formed of little low houses.

'Black,' said Martin, 'here; all down this road—casual labour, criminals, loafers, drunkards, consumps. Look at the faces!'

Thyme raised her eyes obediently. In this main thoroughfare it was not as in the by-street, and only dull or sullen glances, or none at all, were bent on her. Some of the houses had ragged plants on the window-sills; in one window a canary was singing. Then, at a bend, they came into a blacker reach of human river. Here were out-buildings, houses with broken windows, houses with windows boarded up, fried-fish shops, low public-houses, houses without doors. There were more men here than women, and those men were wheeling barrows full of rags and bottles, or not even full of rags and bottles; or they were standing by the public-houses gossiping or quarrelling in groups of three or four; or very slowly walking in the gutters, or on the pavements, as though trying to remember if they were alive. Then suddenly some young man with gaunt violence in his face would pass, pushing his barrow desperately, striding fiercely by. And every now and then, from a fried-fish or hardware shop, would come out a man in a dirty apron to take the sun and contemplate the scene, not finding in it, seemingly, anything that in any way depressed his spirit. Amongst the constant, crawling, shifting stream of passengers were seen women carrying food wrapped up in newspaper, or with bundles beneath their shawls. The faces of these women were generally either very red and coarse or of a sort of bluish-white; they wore the expression of such as know themselves to be existing in the way that Providence has arranged they should exist. No surprise, revolt, dismay, or shame was ever to be seen on those faces; in place of these emotions a drab and brutish acquiescence or mechanical coarse jocularity. To pass like this about their business was their occupation each morning of the year; it was needful to accept it. Not having any hope of ever being different, not being able to imagine any other life, they were not so wasteful of their strength as to attempt either to hope or to imagine. Here and there, too, very slowly passed old men and women, crawling along, like winter bees who, in some strange and evil moment, had forgotten to die in the sunlight of their toil, and, too old to be of use, had been chivied forth from their hive to perish slowly in the cold twilight of their days.

Down the centre of the street Thyme saw a brewer's dray creeping its way due south under the sun. Three horses drew it, with braided tails and beribboned manes, the brass glittering on their harness. High up, like a god, sat the drayman, his little slits of eyes above huge red cheeks fixed immovably on his horses' crests. Behind him, with slow, unceasing crunch, the dray rolled, piled up with hogsheads, whereon the drayman's mate lay sleeping. Like the slumbrous image of some mighty unrelenting Power, it passed, proud that its monstrous bulk contained all the joy and blessing those shadows on the pavement had ever known.

The two young people emerged on to the high road running east and west.

'Cross here,' said Martin, 'and cut down into Kensington. Nothing more of interest now till we get to Hound Street. Purceys and Purceys all round about this part.'

Thyme shook herself.

'O Martin, let's go down a road where there's some air. I feel so dirty.' She put her hand up to her chest.

'There's one here,' said Martin.

They turned to the left into a road that had many trees. Now that she could breathe and look about her, Thyme once more held her head erect and began to swing her arms.

'Martin, something must be done!'

The young doctor did not reply; his face still wore its pale, sarcastic, observant look. He gave her arm a squeeze with a half-contemptuous smile.

Chapter 15

SECOND PILGRIMAGE TO HOUND STREET

ARRIVING in Hound Street, Martin Stone and his companion went straight up to Mrs Hughs' front room. They found her doing the week's washing, and hanging out before a scanty fire part of the little that the week had been suffered to soil. Her arms were bare, her face and eyes red; the steam of soapsuds had congealed on them.

Attached to the bolster by a towel, under his father's bayonet and the oleograph depicting the Nativity, sat the baby. In the air there was the scent of him, or walls, and washing, and red herrings. The two young people took their seat on the window-sill.

'May we open the window, Mrs Hughs?' said Thyme. 'Or will it hurt the baby?'

'No, miss.'

'What's the matter with your wrists?' asked Martin.

The seamstress, muffling her arms with the garment she was dipping in soapy water, did not answer.

'Don't do that. Let me have a look.'

Mrs Hughs held out her arms; the wrists were swollen and discoloured.

'The brute!' cried Thyme.

The young doctor muttered: 'Done last night. Got any arnica?'

'No, sir.'

'Of course not.' He laid a sixpence on the sill. 'Get some and rub it in. Mind you don't break the skin.'

Thyme suddenly burst out: 'Why don't you leave him, Mrs Hughs? Why do you live with a brute like that?'

Martin frowned.

'Any particular row,' he said, 'or only just the ordinary?'

Mrs Hughs turned her face to the scanty fire. Her shoulders heaved spasmodically.

Thus passed three minutes, then she again began rubbing the soapy garment.

'If you don't mind, I'll smoke,' said Martin. 'What's your baby's name? Bill? Here, Bill!' He placed his little finger in the baby's hand. 'Feeding him yourself?'

'Yes, sir.'

'What's his number?'

'I've lost three, sir; there's only his brother Stanley now.'

'One a year?'

'No, sir. I missed two years in the war, of course.'

'Hughs wounded out there?'

'Yes, sir—in the head.'

'Ah! And fever?'

'Yes, sir.'

Martin tapped his pipe against his forehead. 'Least drop of liquor goes to it, I suppose?'

Mrs Hughs paused in the dipping of a cloth; her tear-stained face expressed resentment, as though she had detected an attempt to find excuses for her husband.

'He didn't ought to treat me as he does,' she said.

All three now stood round the bed, over which the baby presided with solemn gaze.

Thyme said: 'I wouldn't care what he did, Mrs Hughs; I wouldn't stay another day if I were you. It's your duty as a woman.'

To hear her duty as a woman Mrs Hughs turned; slow vindictiveness gathered on her thin face.

'Yes, miss?' she said. 'I don't know what to do.'

'Take the children and go. What's the good of waiting? We'll give you money if you haven't got enough.'

But Mrs Hughs did not answer.

'Well?' said Martin, blowing out a cloud of smoke.

Thyme burst out again; 'Just go, the very minute your little boy comes back from school. Hughs'll never find you. It'll serve him right. No woman ought to put up with what you have; it's simply weakness, Mrs Hughs.'

As though that word had forced its way into her very heart and set the blood free suddenly, Mrs Hughs' face turned the colour of tomatoes. She poured forth words:

'And leave him to that young girl—and leave him to his wickedness! After I've been his wife eight years and borne him five! After I've done what I have for him! I never want no better husband than what he used to be, till *she* came with her pale face and her prinky manners, and—and her mouth that you can tell she's bad by. Let her keep to her profession—sitting naked's what she's fit for—coming here to decent folk——' And holding out her wrists to Thyme, who had shrunk back, she cried: 'He's never struck me before. I got these all because of her new clothes!'

Hearing his mother speak with such strange passion, the baby howled. Mrs Hughs stopped, and took him up. Pressing him close to her thin bosom, she looked above his little dingy head at the two young people.

'I got my wrists like this last night, wrestling with him. He swore he'd go and leave me, but I held him, I did. And don't you ever think that I'll let him go to that young girl—not if he kills me first!'

With those words the passion in her face died down. She was again a meek, mute woman.

During this outbreak, Thyme, shrinking, stood by the doorway with lowered eyes. She now looked up at Martin, clearly asking him to come away. The latter had kept his gaze fixed on Mrs Hughs, smoking silently. He took his pipe out of his mouth, and pointed with it at the baby.

'This gentleman,' he said, 'can't stand too much of that.'

In silence all three bent their eyes on the baby. His little fists, and nose, and forehead, even his little naked, crinkled feet, were thrust with all his feeble strength against his mother's bosom, as though he were striving to creep into some hole away from life. There was a sort of dumb despair in that tiny pushing of his way back to the place whence he had come. His head, covered with dingy down, quivered with his effort to escape. He had been alive so little; that little had sufficed. Martin put his pipe back into his mouth.

'This won't do, you know,' he said. 'He can't stand it. And look here! If you stop feeding him, I wouldn't give that for him to-morrow!' He held up the circle of his thumb and finger. 'You're the best judge of what sort of chance you've got of going on in your present state of mind!' Then, motioning to Thyme, he went down the stairs.

Chapter 16

BENEATH THE ELMS

SPRING was in the hearts of men, and their tall companions, trees. Their troubles, the stiflings of each other's growth, and all such things, seemed of little moment. Spring had them by the throat. It turned old men round, and made them stare at women younger than themselves. It made young men and women walking side by side touch each other, and every bird on the branches tune his pipe. Flying sunlight speckled the fluttered leaves, and flushed the cheeks of crippled boys who limped into the Gardens, till their pale Cockney faces shone with a strange glow.

In the Broad Walk, beneath those dangerous trees, the elms, people sat and took the sun—cheek by jowl, generals and nurse-maids, parsons and the unemployed. Above, in that Spring wind, the elm-tree boughs were swaying, rustling, creaking ever so gently, carrying on the innumerable talk of trees—their sapient, wordless conversation over the affairs of men. It was pleasant, too, to see and hear the myriad movement of the million little separate leaves, each shaped differently, flighting never twice alike, yet all obedient to the single spirit of their tree.

Thyme and Martin were sitting on a seat beneath the largest of all the elms. Their manner lacked the unconcern and dignity of the moment, when, two hours before, they had started forth on their discovery from the other end of the Broad Walk. Martin spoke:

'It's given you the hump! First sight of blood, and you're like all the rest of them!'

'I'm not, Martin. How perfectly beastly of you!'

'Oh yes, you are. There's plenty of aestheticism about you and your people—plenty of good intentions—but not an ounce of real business!'

'Don't abuse my people; they're just as kind as you!'

'Oh, they're kind enough, and they can see what's wrong. It's not that which stops them. But your dad's a regular official. He's got so much sense of what he ought not to do that he never does anything; just as Hilary's got so much consciousness of what he *ought* to do that *he* never does anything. You went to that woman's this morning with your ideas of helping her all cut and dried, and now that you find the facts aren't what you thought, you're stumped!'

'One can't believe anything they say. That's what I hate. I thought Hughs simply knocked her about. I didn't know it was her jealousy——'

'Of course you didn't. Do you imagine those people give anything away to our sort unless they're forced? They know better.'

'Well, I hate the whole thing—it's all so sordid!'

'O Lord!'

'Well, it is! I don't feel that I want to help a woman who can say and feel such horrid things, or the girl, or any of them.'

'Who cares what they say or feel? That's not the point. It's simply a case of common sense. Your people put that girl there, and they must get her to clear out again sharp. It's just a question of what's healthy.'

'Well, I know it's not healthy for me to have anything to do with, and I won't! I don't believe you can help people unless they want to be helped.'

Martin whistled.

'You're rather a brute, I think,' said Thyme.

'*A* brute, not rather a brute. That's all the difference.'

'For the worse!'

'I don't think so. Thyme!'

There was no answer.

'Look at me.'

Very slowly Thyme turned her eyes.

'Well?'

'Are you one of us, or are you not?'

'Of course I am.'

'You're not!'

'I am.'

'Well, don't let's fight about it. Give me your hand.'

He dropped his hand on hers. Her face had flushed rose colour. Suddenly she freed herself. 'Here's Uncle Hilary!'

It was indeed Hilary, with Miranda trotting in advance. His hands were crossed behind him, his face bent towards the ground. The two young people on the bench sat looking at him.

'Buried in self-contemplation,' murmured Martin; 'that's the way he always walks. I shall tell him about this!'

The colour of Thyme's face deepened from rose to crimson.

'No!'

'Why not?'

'Well—those new——' She could not bring out that word 'clothes'. It would have given her thoughts away.

Hilary seemed making for their seat, but Miranda, aware of Martin, stopped 'A man of action!' she appeared to say. 'The one who pulls my ears.' And turning, as though unconscious, she endeavoured to lead Hilary away. Her master, however, had already seen his niece. He came and sat down on the bench beside her.

'We wanted *you!*' said Martin, eyeing him slowly, as a young dog will eye another of a different age and breed. 'Thyme and I have been to see the Hughs in Hound Street. Things are blowing up for a mess. You, or whoever put the girl there, ought to get her away again as quick as possible.'

Hilary seemed at once to withdraw into himself.

'Well,' he said, 'let us hear all about it.'

'The woman's jealous of her: that's all the trouble!'

'Oh!' said Hilary; 'that's all the trouble?'

Thyme murmured: 'I don't see a bit why Uncle Hilary should bother. If they will be so horrid—I didn't think the poor were like that. I didn't think they had it in them. I'm sure the girl isn't worth it, or the woman either!'

'I didn't say they were,' growled Martin. 'It's a question of what's healthy.'

Hilary looked from one of his young companions to the other.

'I see,' he said. 'I thought perhaps the matter was more delicate.'

Martin's lip curled.

'Ah, your precious delicacy! What's the good of that? What did it ever do? It's the curse that you're all suffering from. Why don't you act? You could think about it afterwards.'

A flush came into Hilary's sallow cheeks.

'Do you never think before you act, Martin?'

Martin got up and stood looking down on Hilary.

'Look here!' he said; 'I don't go in for your subtleties. I use my eyes and nose. I can see that the woman will never be able to go on feeding the baby in the neurotic state she's in. It's a matter of health for both of them.'

'Is everything a matter of health with you?'

'It is. Take any subject that you like. Take the poor themselves—what's wanted? Health. Nothing on earth but health! The discoveries and inventions of the last century have knocked the floor out of the old order; we've got to put a new one in, and we're going to put it in, too—the floor of health. The crowd doesn't yet see what it wants, but *they're looking for it*, and when we show them they'll catch on fast enough.'

'But who are "you"?' murmured Hilary.

'Who are we? I'll tell you one thing. While all the reformers are pecking at each other we shall quietly come along and swallow up the lot. We've simply grasped this elementary fact, that theories are no basis for reform. We go on the evidence of our eyes and noses; what we see and smell is wrong we correct by practical and scientific means.'

'Will you apply that to human nature?'

'It's human nature to want health.'

'I wonder! It doesn't look much like it at present.'

'Take the case of this woman.'

'Yes,' said Hilary, 'take her case. You can't make this too clear to me, Martin.'

'She's no use—poor sort altogether. The man's no use. A man who's been wounded in the head, and isn't a teetotaller, is done for. The girl's no use—regular pleasure-loving type!'

Thyme flushed crimson, and, seeing that flood of colour in his niece's face, Hilary bit his lips.

'The only things worth considering are the children. There's this baby—well, as I said, the important thing is that the mother should be able to look after it properly. Get hold of that, and let the other facts go hang.'

'Forgive me, but my difficulty is to isolate this question of the baby's health from all the other circumstances of the case.'

Martin grinned.

'And you'll make that an excuse, I'm certain, for doing nothing.'

Thyme slipped her hand into Hilary's.

'You *are* a brute, Martin,' she murmured.

The young man turned on her a look that said: 'It's no use calling me a brute; I'm proud of being one. Besides, you know you don't dislike it.'

'It's better to be a brute than an amateur,' he said.

Thyme, pressing close to Hilary, as though he needed her protection, cried out:

'Martin, you really are a Goth!'

Hilary was still smiling, but his face quivered.

'Not at all,' he said. 'Martin's powers of diagnosis do him credit.' And, raising his hat, he walked away.

The two young people, both on their feet now, looked after him. Martin's face was a queer study of contemptuous compunction; Thyme's was startled, softened, almost tearful.

'It won't do him any harm,' muttered the young man. 'It'll shake him up.'

Thyme flashed a vicious look at him.

'I hate you sometimes,' she said. 'You're so coarse-grained—your skin's just like leather.'

Martin's hand descended on her wrist.

'And yours,' he said, 'is tissue-paper. You're all the same, you amateurs.'

'I'd rather be an amateur than a—than a bounder!'

Martin made a queer movement of his jaw, then smiled. That smile seemed to madden Thyme. She wrenched her wrist away and darted after Hilary.

Martin impassively looked after her. Taking out his pipe, he filled it with tobacco, slowly pressing the golden threads down into the bowl with his little finger.

Chapter 17

TWO BROTHERS

IT has been said that Stephen Dallison, when unable to get his golf on Saturdays, went to his club and read reviews. The two forms of exercise, in fact, were very similar: in playing golf you went round and round; in reading reviews you did the same, for in course of time you were assured of coming to articles that nullified articles already read. In both forms of sport the balance was preserved which keeps a man both sound and young.

And to be both sound and young was to Stephen an everyday necessity. He was essentially a Cambridge man, springy and undemonstrative, with just that air of taking a continual pinch of peculiarly perfect snuff. Underneath this manner he was a good worker, a good husband, a good father, and nothing could be urged against him except his regularity and the fact that he was never in the wrong. Where he worked, and indeed in other places, many men were like him. In one respect he resembled them, perhaps, too much—he disliked leaving the ground unless he knew precisely where he was coming down again.

He and Cecilia had 'got on' from the first. They had both desired to have one child—no more; they had both desired to keep up with the times—no more; they now both considered Hilary's position awkward—no more; and when Cecilia, in the special Jacobean bed, and taking care to let him have his sleep out first, had told him of this matter of the Hughs, they had both turned it over carefully, lying on their backs, and speaking in grave tones. Stephen was of opinion that poor old Hilary must look out what he was doing. Beyond this he did not go, keeping even from his wife the more unpleasant of what seemed to him the possibilities.

Then, in the words she had used to Hilary, Cecilia spoke:

'It's so sordid, Stephen.'

He looked at her, and almost with one accord they both said:

'But it's all nonsense!'

These speeches, so simultaneous, stimulated them to a robuster view. What was this affair, if real, but the sort of episode that they read of in their papers? What was it, if true, but a duplicate of some bit of fiction or drama which they daily saw described by that word 'sordid'? Cecilia, indeed, had used this word instinctively. It had come into her mind at once. The whole affair disturbed her ideals of virtue and good taste—that particular mental atmosphere mysteriously, inevitably woven round the soul by the conditions of special breeding and special life. If, then, this affair were real it was sordid, and if it were sordid it was repellent to suppose that her family could be mixed up in it; but her people *were* mixed up in it, therefore it must be—nonsense!

So the matter rested until Thyme came back from her visit to her grandfather, and told them of the little model's new pretty clothes. When she detailed this news they were all sitting at dinner, over the ordering of which Cecilia's loyalty had been taxed till her little headache came, so that there might be nothing too conventional to overnourish Stephen or so essentially aesthetic as not to nourish him at all. The manservant being in the room, they neither of them raised their eyes. But when he was gone to fetch the bird, each found the other looking furtively across the table. By some queer misfortune the word 'sordid' had leaped into their minds again. Who had given her those clothes? But feeling that it was sordid to pursue this thought, they looked away, and, eating hastily, began pursuing it. Being man and woman, they naturally took a different line of chase, Cecilia hunting in one grove and Stephen in another.

Thus ran Stephen's pack of meditations:

'If old Hilary has been giving her money and clothes and that sort of thing, he's either a greater duffer than I took him for, or there's something in it. B.'s got herself to thank, but that won't help to keep Hughs quiet. He wants money, I expect. Oh, damn!'

Cecilia's pack ran other ways:

'I know the girl can't have bought those things out of her proper earnings. I believe she's a really bad lot. I don't like to think it, but it must be so. Hilary can't have been so stupid after what I said to him. If she really *is* bad, it simplifies things very much; but Hilary is just the sort of man who will never believe it. Oh dear!'

It was, to be quite fair, immensely difficult for Stephen and his wife—or any of their class and circle—in spite of genuinely good intentions, to really feel the existence of their 'shadows', except in so far as they saw them on the pavements. They knew that these people lived, because they saw them, but they did not *feel* it—with such extraordinary care had the web of social life been spun. They were, and were bound to be, as utterly divorced from understanding of, or faith in, all that shadowy life, as those 'shadows' in their by-streets were from knowledge or belief that gentlefolk really existed except in so far as they had money from them.

Stephen and Cecilia, and their thousands, knew these 'shadows' as 'the people', knew them as slums, as districts, as sweated industries, or different sorts of workers, knew them in the capacity of persons performing odd jobs for them; but as human beings possessing the same faculties and passions with themselves, they did not, could not, know them. The reason, the long reason, extending back through generations, was so plain, so very simple, that it was never mentioned—in their heart of hearts, where there was no room for cant, they knew it to be just a little matter of the senses. They knew that whatever money they might give, or time devote, their hearts could never open, unless—unless they closed their ears, and eyes, and noses. This little fact, more potent than all the teaching of philosophers, than every Act of Parliament, and all the sermons ever preached, reigned paramount, supreme. It divided class from class, man from his shadow—as the Great Underlying Law had set dark apart from light.

On this little fact, too gross to mention, they and their kind had in secret built and built, till it was not too much to say that laws, worship, trade, and every art were based on it, if not in theory, then in fact. For it must not be thought that those eyes were dull or that nose plain—no, no, those eyes could put two and two together; that nose, of myriad fancy, could imagine countless things unsmelled which must lie behind a state of life not quite its own. It could create, as from the scent of an old slipper dogs create their masters.

So Stephen and Cecilia sat, and their butler brought in the bird. It was a nice one, nourished down in Surrey, and as he cut it into portions the butler's soul turned sick within him—not because he wanted some himself, or was a vegetarian, or for any sort of principle, but because he was by natural gifts an engineer, and deadly tired of cutting up and handing birds to other people and watching while they ate them. Without a glimmer of expression on his face he put the portions down before the persons who, having paid him to do so, could not tell his thoughts.

That same night, after working at a Report on the present Laws of Bankruptcy, which he was then drawing up, Stephen entered the joint apartment with excessive caution, having first made all his dispositions, and, stealing to the bed, slipped into it. He lay there, offering himself congratulations that he had not awakened Cecilia, and Cecilia, who was wide awake, knew by his unwonted carefulness that he had come to some conclusion which he did not wish to impart to her. Devoured, therefore, by disquiet, she lay sleepless till the clock struck two.

The conclusion to which Stephen had come was this: Having twice gone through the facts—Hilary's corporeal separation from Bianca (communicated to him by Cecilia), cause unknowable; Hilary's interest in the little model, cause unknown; her known poverty; her employment by Mr Stone; her tenancy of Mrs Hughs' room; the latter's outburst to Cecilia; Hughs' threat; and, finally, the girl's pretty clothes—he had summed it up as just a common 'plant', to which his brother's possibly innocent, but in any case imprudent, conduct had laid him open. It was a man's affair. He resolutely tried to look on the whole thing as unworthy of attention, to feel that nothing would occur. He failed dismally, for three reasons. First, his inherent love of regularity, of having everything in proper order; secondly, his ingrained mistrust of and aversion from Bianca; thirdly, his unavowed conviction, for all his wish to be sympathetic to them, that the lower classes always wanted something out of you. It was a question of how much they would want, and whether it were wise to give them anything. He decided that it would not be wise at all. What then? Impossible to say. It worried him. He had a natural horror of any sort of scandal, and he was very fond of Hilary. If only he knew the attitude Bianca would take up! He could not even guess it.

Thus, on that Saturday afternoon, the 4th of May, he felt for once such a positive aversion from the reading of reviews, as men will feel from their usual occupations when their nerves have been disturbed. He stayed late at Chambers, and came straight home outside an omnibus.

The tide of life was flowing in the town. The streets were awash with wave on wave of humanity, sucked into a thousand crossing currents. Here men and women were streaming out from the meeting of a religious congress, there streaming in at the gates of some social function; like bright water confined within long shelves of rock and dyed with myriad scales of shifting colour, they thronged Rotten Row, and along the closed shop-fronts were woven into an inextricable network of little human runlets. And everywhere amongst this sea of men and women could be seen their shadows, meandering like streaks of grey slime stirred up from the lower depths by some huge, never-ceasing finger. The innumerable roar of that human sea climbed out above the roofs and trees, and somewhere in illimitable space blended, and slowly reached the meeting-point of sound and silence—that Heart where Life, leaving its little forms and barriers, clasps Death, and from that clasp springs forth new-formed, within new barriers.

Above this crowd of his fellow-creatures Stephen drove, and the same Spring wind that had made the elm-trees talk, whispered to him, and tried to tell him of the million flowers it had fertilised, the million leaves uncurled, the million ripples it had awakened on the sea, of the million flying shadows flung by it across the Downs, and how into men's hearts its scent had driven a million longings and sweet pains.

It was but moderately successful, for Stephen, like all men of culture and neat habits, took Nature only at those moments when he had gone out to take her, and of her wild heart he had a secret fear.

On his own doorstep he encountered Hilary coming out.

'I ran across Thyme and Martin in the Gardens,' the latter said. 'Thyme brought me back to lunch, and here I've been ever since.'

'Did she bring our young Sanitist in too?' asked Stephen dubiously.

'No,' said Hilary.

'Good! That young man gets on my nerves.'

Taking his elder brother by the arm, he added: 'Will you come in again, old boy, or shall we go for a stroll?'

'A stroll,' said Hilary.

Though different enough, perhaps because they were so different, these two brothers had the real affection for each other which depends on something deeper and more elementary than a similarity of sentiments, and is permanent because unconnected with the reasoning powers. It depended on the countless times they had kissed and wrestled as tiny boys, slept in small beds alongside, refused to 'tell' about each other, and even now and then taken up the burden of each other's peccadilloes. They might get irritated or tired of being in each other's company, but it would have been impossible for either to have been disloyal to the other in any circumstances, because of that traditional loyalty which went back to their cribs.

Preceded by Miranda, they walked along the flower walk towards the Park, talking of indifferent things, though in his heart each knew well enough what was in the other's.

Stephen broke through the hedge.

'Cis has been telling me,' he said, 'that this man Hughs is making trouble of some sort.'

Hilary nodded.

Stephen glanced a little anxiously at his brother's face; it struck him as looking different, neither so gentle nor so impersonal as usual.

'He's a ruffian, isn't he?'

'I can't tell you,' Hilary answered. 'Probably not.'

'He must be, old chap,' murmured Stephen. Then, with a friendly pressure of his brother's arm, he added: 'Look here old boy, can I be of any use?'

'In what?' asked Hilary.

Stephen took a hasty mental view of his position; he had been in danger of letting Hilary see that he suspected him. Frowning slightly, and with some colour in his clean-shaven face, he said:

'Of course, there's nothing in it.'

'In what?' said Hilary again.

'In what this ruffian says.'

'No,' said Hilary, 'there's nothing in it, though what there may be if people give me credit for what there isn't, is another thing.'

Stephen digested this remark, which hurt him. He saw that his suspicions had been fathomed, and this injured his opinion of his own diplomacy.

'You mustn't lose your head, old man,' he said at last.

They were crossing the bridge over the Serpentine. On the bright waters below, young clerks were sculling their inamoratas up and down; the ripples set free by their oars gleamed beneath the sun, and ducks swam lazily along the banks. Hilary leaned over.

'Look here, Stephen, I take an interest in this child—she's a helpless sort of little creature, and she seems to have put herself under my protection. I can't help that. But that's all. Do you understand?'

This speech produced a queer turmoil in Stephen, as though his brother had accused him of a petty view of things. Feeling that he must justify himself somehow, he began:

'Oh, of course I understand, old boy! But don't think, anyway, that I should care a damn—I mean as far as I'm concerned—even if you had gone as far as ever you liked, considering what you have to put up with. What I'm thinking of is the general situation.'

By this clear statement of his point of view Stephen felt he had put things back on a broad basis, and recovered his position as a man of liberal thought. He too leaned over, looking at the ducks. There was a silence. Then Hilary said:

'If Bianca won't get that child into some fresh place, I shall.'

Stephen looked at his brother in surprise, amounting almost to dismay; he had spoken with such unwonted resolution.

'My dear old chap,' he said. 'I wouldn't go to B. Women are so funny.'

Hilary smiled. Stephen took this for a sign of restored impersonality.

'I'll tell you exactly how the thing appeals to me. It'll be much better for you to chuck it altogether. Let Cis see to it.'

Hilary's eyes became bright with angry humour.

'Many thanks,' he said, 'but this is entirely our affair.'

Stephen answered hastily:

'That's exactly what makes it difficult for you to look at it all round. That fellow Hughs could make himself quite nasty. I wouldn't give him any sort of chance. I mean to say—giving the girl clothes and that kind of thing——'

'I see,' said Hilary.

'You know, old man,' Stephen went on hastily, 'I don't think you'll get Bianca to look at things in your light. If you were on—terms, of course it would be different. I mean the girl, you know, is rather attractive in her way.'

Hilary roused himself from contemplation of the ducks, and they moved on towards the Powder Magazine. Stephen carefully abstained from looking at his brother; the respect he had for Hilary—result, perhaps, of the latter's seniority, perhaps of the feeling that Hilary knew more of him than he of Hilary—was beginning to assert itself in a way he did not like. With every word, too, of this talk, the ground, instead of growing firmer, felt less and less secure. Hilary spoke:

'You mistrust my powers of action?'

'No, no,' said Stephen. 'I don't want you to act at all.'

Hilary laughed. Hearing that rather bitter laugh, Stephen felt a little ache about his heart.

'Come, old boy,' he said, 'we can trust each other, anyway.'

Hilary gave his brother's arm a squeeze.

Moved by that pressure, Stephen spoke:

'I hate you to be worried over such a rotten business.'

The whizz of a motor-car rapidly approaching them became a sort of roar, and out of it a voice shouted: 'How are you?' A hand was seen to rise in salute. It was Mr Purcey driving his A.1. Damyer back to Wimbledon. Before him in the sunlight a little shadow fled; behind him the reek of petrol seemed to darken the road.

'There's a symbol for you,' muttered Hilary.

'How do you mean?' said Stephen dryly. The word 'symbol' was distasteful to him.

'The machine in the middle moving on its business; shadows like you and me skipping in front; oil and used-up stuff dropping behind. Society—body, beak, and bones.'

Stephen took time to answer. 'That's rather far-fetched,' he said. 'You mean these Hughs and people are the droppings?'

'Quite so,' was Hilary's sardonic answer. 'There's the body of that fellow and his car between our sort and them—and no getting over it, Stevie.'

'Well, who wants to? If you're thinking of our old friend's Fraternity, I'm not taking any.' And Stephen suddenly added: 'Look here, I believe this affair is all "a plant".'

'You see that Powder Magazine?' said Hilary. 'Well, this business that you call a "plant" is more like that. I don't want to alarm you, but I think you, as well as our young friend Martin, are inclined to under-rate the emotional capacity of human nature.'

Disquietude broke up the customary mask on Stephen's face. 'I don't understand,' he stammered.

'Well, we're none of us machines, not even amateurs like me—not even under-dogs like Hughs. I fancy you may find a certain warmth, not to say violence, about this business. I tell you frankly that I don't live in married celibacy quite with impunity. I can't answer for anything, in fact. You had better stand clear, Stephen—that's all.'

Stephen marked his thin hands quivering, and this alarmed him as nothing else had done.

They walked on beside the water. Stephen spoke quietly, looking at the ground. 'How can I stand clear, old man, if you are going to get into a mess? That's impossible.'

He saw at once that this shot, which indeed was from his heart, had gone right home to Hilary's. He sought within him how to deepen the impression.

'You mean a lot to us,' he said. 'Cis and Thyme would feel it awfully if you and B.——' He stopped.

Hilary was looking at him; that faintly smiling glance, searching him through and through, suddenly made Stephen feel inferior. He had been detected trying to extract capital from the effect of his little piece of brotherly love. He was irritated at his brother's insight.

'I have no right to give advice, I suppose,' he said; 'but in my opinion you should drop it—drop it dead. The girl is not worth your looking after. Turn her over to that Society—Mrs Tallents Smallpeace's thing—whatever it's called.'

At a sound as of mirth Stephen, who was not accustomed to hear his brother laugh, looked round.

'Martin,' said Hilary, 'also wants the case to be treated on strictly hygienic grounds.'

Nettled by this, Stephen answered:

'Don't confound me with our young Sanitist, please; I simply think there are probably a hundred things you don't know about the girl which ought to be cleared up.'

'And then?'

'Then,' said Stephen, 'they could—er—deal with her accordingly.'

Hilary shrank so palpably at this remark that he added rather hastily:

'You call that cold-blooded, I suppose; but I think, you know, old chap, that you're too sensitive.'

Hilary stopped rather abruptly.

'If you don't mind, Stevie,' he said, 'we'll part here. I want to think it over.' So saying, he turned back, and sat down on a seat that faced the sun.

Chapter 18

THE PERFECT DOG

HILARY sat long in the sun, watching the pale bright waters and many well-bred ducks circling about the shrubs, searching with their round, bright eyes for worms. Between the bench where he was sitting and the spiked iron railings people passed continually—men, women, children of all kinds. Every now and then a duck would stop and cast her knowing glance at these creatures, as though comparing the condition of their forms and plumage with her own. 'If I had had the breeding of you,' she seemed to say, 'I could have made a better fist of it than that. A worse-looking lot of ducks, take you all round, I never wish to see!' And with a quick but heavy movement of her shoulders, she would turn away and join her fellows.

Hilary, however, got small distraction from the ducks. The situation gradually developing was something of a dilemma to a man better acquainted with ideas than facts, with the trimming of words than with the shaping of events. He turned a queer, perplexed, almost quizzical eye on it. Stephen had irritated him profoundly. He had such a way of pettifying things! Yet, in truth, the affair would seem ridiculous enough to an ordinary observer. What would a man of sound common sense, like Mr Purcey, think of it? Why not, as Stephen had suggested, drop it? Here, however, Hilary approached the marshy ground of feeling.

To give up befriending a helpless girl the moment he found himself personally menaced was exceedingly distasteful. But would she be friendless? Were there not, in Stephen's words, a hundred things he did not know about her? Had she not other resources? Had she not a story? But here, too, he was hampered by his delicacy: one did not pry into the private lives of others!

The matter, too, was hopelessly complicated by the domestic troubles of the Hughs family. No conscientious man—and whatever Hilary lacked, no one ever accused him of a lack of conscience —could put aside that aspect of the case.

Wandering among these reflections were his thoughts about Bianca. She was his wife. However he might feel towards her now, whatever their relations, he must not put her in a false position. Far from wishing to hurt her, he desired to preserve her, and everyone, from trouble and annoyance. He had told Stephen that his interest in the girl was purely protective. But since the night when, leaning out into the moonlight, he heard the waggons coming in to Covent Garden Market, a strange feeling had possessed him—the sensation of a man who lies, with a touch of fever on him, listening to the thrum of distant music—sensuous, not unpleasurable.

Those who saw him sitting there so quietly, with his face resting on his hand, imagined, no doubt, that he was wrestling with some deep, abstract proposition, some great thought to be given to mankind; for there was that about Hilary which forced everyone to connect him instantly with the humaner arts.

The sun began to leave the long pale waters.

A nursemaid and two children came and sat down beside him. Then it was that, underneath his seat, Miranda found what she had been looking for all her life. It had no smell, made no movement, was pale-grey in colour, like herself. It had no hair that she could find; its tail was like her own; it took no liberties, was silent, had no passions, committed her to nothing. Standing a few inches from its head, closer than she had ever been of her free will to any dog, she smelt its smell-lessness with a long, delicious snuffling, wrinkling up the skin on her forehead, and through her upturned eyes her little moonlight soul looked forth. 'How unlike you are,' she seemed to say, 'to all the other dogs I know! I would love to live with you. Shall I ever find a dog like you again? "The latest—sterilised cloth—see white label underneath: 4s. 3d.!"' Suddenly she slithered out her slender grey-pink tongue and licked its nose. The creature moved a little way and stopped. Miranda saw that it had wheels. She lay down close to it, for she knew it was the perfect dog.

Hilary watched the little moonlight lady lying vigilant, affectionate, beside this perfect dog, who could not hurt her. She panted slightly, and her tongue showed between her lips.

Presently behind his seat he saw another idyll. A thin white spaniel had come running up. She lay down in the grass quite close, and three other dogs who followed, sat and looked at her. A poor, dirty little thing she was, who seemed as if she had not seen a home for days. Her tongue lolled out, she panted piteously, and had no collar. Every now and then she turned her eyes, but though they were so tired and desperate, there was a gleam in them. 'For all its thirst and hunger and exhaustion, this is life!' they seemed to say. The three dogs, panting too, and watching till it should be her pleasure to begin to run again, seemed with their moist, loving eyes to echo: 'This is life!'

Because of this idyll, people near were moving on.

And suddenly the thin white spaniel rose, and, like a little harried ghost, slipped on amongst the trees, and the three dogs followed her.

Chapter 19

BIANCA

IN her studio that afternoon Bianca stood before her picture of the little model—the figure with parted pale-red lips and haunting, pale-blue eyes, gazing out of shadow into lamplight.

She was frowning, as though resentful of a piece of work which had the power to kill her other pictures. What force had moved her to paint like that? What had she felt while the girl was standing before her, still as some pale flower placed in a cup of water? Not love—there was no love in the presentment of that twilight figure; not hate—there was no hate in the painting of her dim appeal. Yet in the picture of this shadow girl, between the gloom and glimmer, was visible a spirit, driving the artist on to create that which had the power to haunt the mind.

Bianca turned away and went up to a portrait of her husband, painted ten years before. She looked from one picture to the other, with eyes as hard and stabbing as the points of daggers.

In the more poignant relationships of human life there is a point beyond which men and women do not quite truthfully analyse their feelings—they *feel* too much. It was Bianca's fortune, too, to be endowed to excess with that quality which, of all others, most obscures the real significance of human issues. Her pride had kept her back from Hilary, till she had felt herself a failure. Her pride had so revolted at that failure that she had led the way to utter estrangement. Her pride had forced her to the attitude of one who says: 'Live your own life; I should be ashamed to let you see that I care what happens between us.' Her pride had concealed from her the fact that beneath her veil of mocking liberality there was an essential woman tenacious of her dues, avid of affection and esteem. Her pride prevented the world from guessing that there was anything amiss. Her pride even prevented Hilary from really knowing what had spoiled his married life—this ungovernable itch to be appreciated, governed by ungovernable pride. Hundreds of times he had been baffled by the hedge round that disharmonic nature. With each failure something had shrivelled in him, till the very roots of his affection had dried up. She had worn out a man who, to judge from his actions and appearance, was naturally long-suffering to a fault. Beneath all manner of kindness and consideration for each other—for their good taste, at all events, had never given way—this tragedy of a woman, who wanted to be loved, slowly killing the power of loving her in the man, had gone on year after year. It had ceased to be tragedy, as far as Hilary was concerned; the nerve of his love for her was quite dead, slowly frozen out of him. It was still active tragedy with Bianca, the nerve of whose jealous desire for his appreciation was not dead. Her instinct, too, ironically informed her that, had he been a man with some brutality, a man who had set himself to ride and master her, instead of one too delicate, he might have trampled down the hedge. This gave her a secret grudge against him, a feeling that it was not she who was to blame.

Pride was Bianca's fate, her flavour, and her charm. Like a shadowy hill-side behind glamorous bars of waning sunlight, she was enveloped in smiling pride—mysterious, one thinks, even to herself. This pride of hers took part even in her many generous impulses, kind actions which she did rather secretly and scoffed at herself for doing. She scoffed at herself continually, even for putting on dresses of colours which Hilary was fond of. She would not admit her longing to attract him.

Standing between those two pictures, pressing her mahl-stick against her bosom, she suggested somewhat the image of an Italian saint forcing the dagger of martyrdom into her heart.

That other person, who had once brought the thought of Italy into Cecilia's mind—the man Hughs—had been for the last eight hours or so walking the streets, placing in a cart the refuses of Life; nor had he at all suggested the aspect of one tortured by the passions of love and hate. For the first two hours he had led the horse without expression of any sort on his dark face, his neat soldier's figure garbed in the costume which had made 'Westminister' describe him as a 'dreadful foreign-lookin' man'. Now and then he had spoken to the horse; save for those speeches, of no great importance, he had been silent. For the next two hours, following the cart, he had used a shovel, and still his square, short face, with little black moustache and still blacker eyes, had given no sign of conflict in his breast. So he had passed the day. Apart from the fact, indeed, that men of any kind are not too given to expose private passions to public gaze, the circumstances of a life devoted from the age of twenty onwards to the service of his country, first as a soldier, now in the more defensive part of Vestry scavenger, had given him a kind of gravity. Life had cloaked him with passivity—the normal look of men whose bread and cheese depends on their not caring much for anything. Had Hughs allowed his inclinations play, or sought to express himself, he could hardly have been a private soldier; still less, on his retirement from that office with an honourable wound, would he have been selected out of many others as a Vestry scavenger. For such an occupation as the lifting from the streets of the refuses of Life—a calling greatly sought after, and, indeed, one of the few open to a man who had served his country—charm of manner, individuality, or the engaging quality of self-expression, were perhaps out of place.

He had never been trained in the voicing of his thoughts, and, ever since he had been wounded, felt at times a kind of desperate looseness in his head. It was not, therefore, remarkable that he should be liable to misconstruction, more especially by those who had nothing in common with him, except that somewhat negligible factor, common humanity. The Dallisons had misconstructed him as much as, but no more than, he had misconstructed them when, as 'Wesminister' had informed Hilary, he 'went on against the gentry'. He was, in fact, a ragged screen, a broken vessel, that let light through its holes. A glass or two of beer, the fumes of which his wounded head no longer dominated, and he at once became 'dreadful foreign'. Unfortunately, it was his custom, on finishing his work, to call at the 'Green Glory'. On this particular afternoon the glass had become three, and in sallying forth he had felt a confused sense of duty urging him to visit the house where this girl for whom he had conceived his strange infatuation 'carried on her games'. The 'no-tale-bearing' tradition of a soldier fought hard with this sense of duty; his feelings were mixed as he rang the bell and asked for Mrs Dallison. Habit, however, masked his face, and he stood before her at 'attention', his black eyes lowered, clutching his peaked cap.

Bianca noted curiously the scar on the left side of his cropped black head.

Whatever Hughs had to say was not said easily.

'I've come,' he began at last in a dogged voice, 'to let you know. I never wanted to come into this house. I never wanted to see no one.'

Bianca could see his lips and eyelids quivering in a way strangely out of keeping with his general stolidity.

'My wife has told you tales of me, I suppose. She's told you I knock her about, I daresay. I don't care what she tells you or any o' the people that she works for. But this I'll say: I never touched her but she touched me first. Look here! that's marks of hers!' and, drawing up his sleeve, he showed a scratch on his sinewy tattooed forearm. 'I've not come here about her; that's no business of anyone's.'

Bianca turned towards her pictures. 'Well?' she said, 'but what *have* you come about, please? You see I'm busy.'

Hughs' face changed. Its stolidity vanished, the eyes became as quick, passionate, and leaping as a dark torrent. He was more violently alive than she had ever seen a man. Had it been a woman she would have felt—as Cecilia had felt with Mrs Hughs—the indecency, the impudence of this exhibition; but from that male violence the feminine in her derived a certain satisfaction. So in Spring, when all seems lowering and grey, the hedges and trees suddenly flare out against the purple clouds, their twigs all in flame. The next moment that white glare is gone, the clouds are no longer purple, fiery light no longer quivers and leaps along the hedgerows. The passion in Hughs' face was gone as soon. Bianca felt a sense of disappointment, as though she could have wished her life held a little more of that. He stole a glance at her out of his dark eyes, which, when narrowed, had a velvety look, like the body of a wild bee, then jerked his thumb at the picture of the little model.

'It's about *her* I come to speak.'

Bianca faced him frigidly.

'I have not the slightest wish to hear.'

Hughs looked round, as though to find something that would help him to proceed; his eyes lighted on Hilary's portrait.

'Ah! I'd put the two together if I was you,' he said.

Bianca walked past him to the door.

'Either you or I must leave the room.'

The man's face was neither sullen now nor passionate, but simply miserable.

'Look here, lady,' he said, 'don't take it hard o' me coming here. I'm not out to do you any harm. I've got a wife of my own, and Gawd knows I've enough to put up with from her about this girl. I'll be going in the water one of these days. It's him giving her them clothes that set me coming here.'

Bianca opened the door. 'Please go,' she said.

'I'll go quiet enough,' he muttered, and, hanging his head, walked out.

Having seen him through the side door out into the street, Bianca went back to where she had been standing before he came. She found some difficulty in swallowing; for once there was no armour on her face. She stood there a long time without moving, then put the pictures back into their places and went down the little passage to the house. Listening outside her father's door, she turned the handle quietly and went in.

Mr Stone, holding some sheets of paper out before him, was dictating to the little model, who was writing laboriously with her face close above her arm. She stopped at Bianca's entrance. Mr Stone did not stop, but, holding up his other hand, said:

'I will take you through the last three pages again. Follow!'

Bianca sat down at the window.

Her father's voice, so thin and slow, with each syllable disjointed from the other, rose like monotony itself.

'"There was tra-cea-able indeed, in those days, certain rudi-mentary at-tempts to f-u-s-e the classes . . ."'

It went on unwavering, neither rising high nor falling low, as though the reader knew he had yet far to go, like a runner that brings great news across mountains, plains and rivers.

To Bianca that thin voice might have been the customary sighing of the wind, her attention was so fast fixed on the girl, who sat following the words down the pages with her pen's point.

Mr Stone paused.

'Have you got the word "insane"?' he asked.

The little model raised her face. 'Yes, Mr Stone.'

'Strike it out.'

With his eyes fixed on the trees he stood breathing audibly. The little model moved her fingers, freeing them from cramp. Bianca's curious, smiling scrutiny never left her, as though trying to fix an indelible image on her mind. There was something terrifying in that stare, cruel to herself, cruel to the girl.

'The precise word,' said Mr Stone, 'eludes me. Leave a blank. Follow! . . . "Neither that sweet fraternal interest of man in man, nor a curiosity in phenomena merely as phenomena . . ."' His voice pursued its tenuous path through spaces, frozen by the calm eternal presence of his beloved idea, which, like a golden moon, far and cold, presided glamorously above the thin track of words. And still the girl's pen-point traced his utterance across the pages. Mr Stone paused again, and looking at his daughter as though surprised to see her sitting there, asked:

'Do you wish to speak to me, my dear?'

Bianca shook her head.

'Follow!' said Mr Stone.

But the little model's glance had stolen round to meet the scrutiny fixed on her.

A look passed across her face which seemed to say: 'What have I done to you, that you should stare at me like this?'

Furtive and fascinated, her eyes remained fixed on Bianca, while her hand moved, mechanically ticking the paragraphs. That silent duel of eyes went on—the woman's fixed, cruel, smiling; the girl's uncertain, resentful. Neither of them heard a word that Mr Stone was reading. They treated it as, from the beginning, Life has treated Philosophy—and to the end will treat it.

Mr Stone paused again, seeming to weigh his last sentences.

'That, I think,' he murmured to himself, 'is true.' And suddenly he addressed his daughter. 'Do you agree with me, my dear?'

He was evidently waiting with anxiety for her answer, and the little silver hairs that straggled on his lean throat beneath his beard were clearly visible.

'Yes, father, I agree.'

'Ah!' said Mr Stone, 'I am glad that you confirm me. I was anxious. Follow!'

Bianca rose. Burning spots of colour had settled in her cheeks. She went towards the door, and the little model pursued her figure with a long look, cringing, mutinous, and wistful.

Chapter 20

THE HUSBAND AND THE WIFE

IT was past six o'clock when Hilary at length reached home, preceded a little by Miranda, who almost felt within her the desire to eat. The lilac bushes, not yet in flower, were giving forth spicy fragrance. The sun still netted their top boughs, as with golden silk, and a blackbird, seated on a low branch of the acacia-tree, was summoning the evening. Mr Stone, accompanied by the little model, dressed in her new clothes, was coming down the path. They were evidently going for a walk, for Mr Stone wore his hat, old and soft and black, with a strong green tinge, and carried a paper parcel, which leaked crumbs of bread at every step.

The girl grew very red. She held her head down, as though afraid of Hilary's inspection of her new clothes. At the gate she suddenly looked up. His face said: 'Yes, you look very nice!' And into her eyes a look leaped such as one may see in dogs' eyes lifted in adoration to their masters' faces. Manifestly disconcerted, Hilary turned to Mr Stone. The old man was standing very still; a thought had evidently struck him.

'I have not, I think,' he said, 'given enough consideration to the question whether force is absolutely, or only relatively, evil. If I saw a man ill-treat a cat, should I be justified in striking him?'

Accustomed to such divagations, Hilary answered: 'I don't know whether you would be justified, but I believe that you would strike him.'

'I am not sure,' said Mr Stone. 'We are going to feed the birds.'

The little model took the paper bag. 'It's all dropping out,' she said. From across the road she turned her head. 'Won't you come, too?' she seemed to say.

But Hilary passed rather hastily into the garden and shut the gate behind him. He sat in his study, with Miranda near him, for fully an hour, without doing anything whatever, sunk in a strange half-pleasurable torpor. At this hour he should have been working at his book; and the fact that his idleness did not trouble him might well have given him uneasiness. Many thoughts passed through his mind, imaginings of things he had thought left behind for ever—sensations and longings which to the normal eye of middle age are but dried forms hung in the museum of memory. They started up at the whip of the still-living youth, and lost wildness at the heart of every man. Like the reviving flame of half-spent fires, longing for discovery leaped and flickered in Hilary—to find out once again what things were like before he went down the hill of age.

No trivial ghost was beckoning him; it was the ghost, with unseen face and rosy finger, that comes to men whose youth has gone.

Miranda, hearing him so silent, rose. At this hour it was her master's habit to scratch paper. She, who seldom scratched anything, because it was not delicate, felt dimly that this was what he should be doing. She held up a slim foot and touched his knee.

Receiving no discouragement, she delicately sprang into his lap, and, forgetting for once her modesty, placed her arms on his chest, and licked his face all over.

It was while receiving this embrace that Hilary saw Mr Stone and the little model returning across the garden. The old man was walking very rapidly, holding out the fragment of a broken stick. He was extremely pink.

Hilary went to meet them.

'What's the matter, sir?' he said.

'I cut him over the legs,' said Mr Stone. 'I do not regret it;' and he walked on to his room.

Hilary turned to the little model.

'It was a little dog. The man kicked it, and Mr Stone hit him. He broke his stick. There were several men; they threatened us.' She looked up at Hilary. 'I—I was frightened. Oh! Mr Dallison, isn't he—funny?'

'All heroes are funny,' murmured Hilary.

'He wanted to hit them again, after his stick was broken. Then a policeman came, and they all ran away.'

'That was quite as it should be,' said Hilary. 'And what did *you* do?'

Perceiving that she had not as yet made much effect, the little model cast down her eyes.

'I shouldn't have been frightened if *you* had been there!'

'Heavens!' muttered Hilary. 'Mr Stone is far more valiant than I.'

'I don't think he is,' she replied stubbornly, and again looked up at him.

'Well, good-night!' said Hilary hastily. 'You must run off. . . .'

That same evening, driving with his wife back from a long, dull dinner, Hilary began:

'I've something to say to you.'

An ironic 'Yes?' came from the other corner of the cab.

'There is some trouble with the little model.'

'Really!'

'This man Hughs has become infatuated with her. He has even said, I believe, that he was coming to see you.'

'What about?'

'Me.'

'And what is he going to say about you?'

'I don't know; some vulgar gossip—nothing true.'

There was a silence, and in the darkness Hilary moistened his dry lips.

Bianca spoke: 'May I ask how you knew of this?'

'Cecilia told me.'

A curious noise, like a little strangled laugh, fell on Hilary's ears.

'I am very sorry,' he muttered.

Presently Bianca said:

'It was good of you to tell me, considering that we go our own ways. What made you?'

'I thought it right.'

'And—of course, the man might have come to me!'

'*That* you need not have said.'

'One does not always say what one ought.'

'I have made the child a present of some clothes which she badly needed. As far as I know, that's all I've done!'

'Of course!'

This wonderful 'of course' acted on Hilary like a tonic. He said dryly:

'What do you wish me to do?'

'I?' No gust of the east wind, making the young leaves curl and shiver, the gas jets flare and die down in their lamps, could so have nipped the flower of amity. Through Hilary's mind flashed Stephen's almost imploring words: 'Oh, I wouldn't go to her! Women are so funny!'

He looked round. A blue gauze scarf was wrapped over his wife's dark head. There, in her corner, as far away from him as she could get, she was smiling. For a moment Hilary had the sensation of being stifled by fold on fold of that blue gauze scarf, as if he were doomed to drive for ever, suffocated, by the side of this woman who had killed his love for her.

'You will do what you like, of course,' she said suddenly.

A desire to laugh seized Hilary. 'What do you wish me to do?' 'You will do what you like, of course!' Could civilised restraint and tolerance go further?

'B.,' he said, with an effort, 'the wife is jealous. We put the girl into that house—we ought to get her out.'

Bianca's reply came slowly.

'From the first,' she said, 'the girl has been your property; do what you like with her. I shall not meddle!'

'I am not in the habit of regarding people as my property.'

'No need to tell me that—I have known you twenty years.'

Doors sometimes slam in the minds of the mildest and most restrained of men.

'Oh, very well! I have told you; you can see Hughs when he comes—or not, as you like.'

'I *have* seen him.'

Hilary smiled.

'Well, was his story very terrible?'

'He told me no story.'

'How was that?'

Bianca suddenly sat forward, and threw back the blue scarf, as though she, too, were stifling. In her flushed face her eyes were bright as stars; her lips quivered.

'Is it likely,' she said, 'that I should listen? That's enough, please, of these people.'

Hilary bowed. The cab, bearing them fast home turned into the last short cut. This narrow street was full of men and women circling round barrows and lighted booths. The sound of coarse talk and laughter floated out into air thick with the reek of paraffin and the scent of frying fish. In every couple of those men and women Hilary seemed to see the Hughs, that other married couple, going home to wedded happiness above the little model's head. The cab turned out of the gay alley.

'Enough, please, of these people!'

That same night, past one o'clock, he was roused from sleep by hearing bolts drawn back. He got up, hastened to the window, and looked out. At first he could distinguish nothing. The moonless night, like a dark bird, had nested in the garden; the sighing of the lilac bushes was the only sound. Then, dimly, just below him, on the steps of the front door, he saw a figure standing.

'Who is that?' he called.

The figure did not move.

'Who are you?' said Hilary again.

The figure raised its face, and by the gleam of his white beard Hilary knew that it was Mr Stone.

'What is it, sir?' he said. 'Can I do anything?'

'No,' answered Mr Stone. 'I am listening to the wind. It has visited everyone to-night.' And lifting his hand, he pointed out into the darkness.

Chapter 21

A DAY OF REST

CECILIA'S house in the Old Square was steeped from roof to basement in the peculiar atmosphere brought by Sunday to houses whose inmates have no need of religion or of rest.

Neither she nor Stephen had been to church since Thyme was christened; they did not expect to go again till she was married, and they felt that even to go on these occasions was against their principles; but for the sake of other people's feelings they had made the sacrifice, and they meant to make it once more, when the time came. Each Sunday, therefore, everything tried to happen exactly as it happened on every other day, with indifferent success. This was because, for all Cecilia's resolutions, a joint of beef and Yorkshire pudding would appear on the luncheon-table, notwithstanding the fact that Mr Stone—who came when he remembered that it was Sunday—did not devour the higher mammals. Every week, when it appeared, Cecilia, who for some reason carved on Sundays, regarded it with a frown. Next week she would really discontinue it; but when next week came, there it was, with its complexion that reminded her so uncomfortably of cabmen. And she would partake of it with unexpected heartiness. Something very old and deep, some horrible whole-hearted appetite, derived, no doubt, from Mr Justice Carfax, rose at that hour precisely every week to master her. Having given Thyme the second helping which she invariably took, Cecilia, who detested carving, would look over the fearful joint at a piece of glass procured by her in Venice, and at the daffodils standing upright in it, apparently without support. Had it not been for this piece of beef, which had made itself smelt all the morning, and would make itself felt all the afternoon, it need never have come into her mind at all that it was Sunday—and she would cut herself another slice.

To have told Cecilia that there was still a strain of the Puritan in her would have been to occasion her some uneasiness, and provoked a strenuous denial; yet her way of observing Sunday furnished indubitable evidence of this peculiar fact. She did more that day than any other. For, in the morning she invariably 'cleared off' her correspondence; at lunch she carved the beef; after lunch she cleared off the novel or book on social questions she was reading; went to a concert, clearing off a call on the way back; and on first

Sundays—a great bore—stayed at home to clear off the friends who came to visit her. In the evening she went to some play or other, produced by Societies for the benefit of persons compelled, like her, to keep a Sunday with which they felt no sympathy.

On this particular 'first Sunday', having made the circuit of her drawing-room, which extended the whole breadth of her house, and through long, low windows cut into leaded panes, looked out both back and front, she took up Mr Balladyce's latest book. She sat, with her paper-knife pressed against the tiny hollow in her flushed cheek, and pretty little bits of lace and real old jewellery nestling close to her. And while she turned the pages of Mr Balladyce's book, Thyme sat opposite in a bright blue frock, and turned the pages of Darwin's work on earth-worms.

Regarding her 'little daughter', who was so much more solid than herself, Cecilia's face wore a very sweet, faintly surprised expression.

'My kitten is a bonny thing,' it seemed to say. 'It is queer that I should have a thing so large.'

Outside in the Square Gardens a shower, the sunlight, and blossoms, were entangled. It was the time of year when all the world had kittens; young things were everywhere—soft, sweet, uncouth. Cecilia felt this in her heart. It brought depth into her bright, quick eyes. What a secret satisfaction it was that she had once so far committed herself as to have borne a child! What a queer vague feeling she sometimes experienced in the Spring—almost amounting to a desire to bear another! So one may mark the warm eye of a staid mare, following with her gaze the first strayings of her foal. 'I must get used to it,' she seems to say. 'I certainly do miss the little creature, though I used to threaten her with my hoofs, to show I couldn't be bullied by anything of that age. And there she goes! Ah, well!'

Remembering suddenly, however, that she was sitting there to clear off Mr Balladyce, because it was so necessary to keep up with what he wrote, Cecilia dropped her gaze to the page before her; and instantly, by uncomfortable chance, not the choice pastures of Mr Balladyce appeared, where women might browse at leisure, but a vision of the little model. She had not thought of her for quite an hour; she had tired herself out with thinking—not, indeed, of her, but of all that hinged on her, ever since Stephen had spoken of his talk with Hilary. Things Hilary had said seemed to Cecilia's delicate and rather timid soul so ominous, so unlike himself. Was there really going to be complete disruption between him and Bianca—

worse, an ugly scandal? She, who knew her sister better, perhaps, than anyone, remembered from schoolroom days Bianca's moody violence when anything had occurred to wound her—remembered, too, the long fits of brooding that followed. This affair, which she had tried to persuade herself was exaggerated, loomed up larger than ever. It was not an isolated squib; it was a lighted match held to a train of gunpowder. This girl of the people, coming from who knew where, destined for who knew what—this young, not very beautiful, not even clever child, with nothing but a sort of queer haunting naïveté to give her charm—might even be a finger used by Fate! Cecilia sat very still before that sudden vision of the girl. There was no staid mare to guard *that* foal with the dark devotion of her eye. There was no wise whinnying to answer back those tiny whinnies; no long look round to watch the little creature nodding to sleep on its thin trembling legs in the hot sunlight; no ears to prick up and hoofs to stamp at the approach of other living things. These thoughts passed through Cecilia's mind and were gone, being too far and pale to stay. Turning the page which she had not been reading, she heaved a sigh. Thyme sighed also.

'These worms are fearfully interesting,' she said. 'Is anybody coming in this afternoon?'

'Mrs Tallents Smallpeace was going to bring a young man in, a Signor Pozzi—Egregio Pozzi, or some such name. She says he is the coming pianist.' Cecilia's face was spiced with faint amusement. Some strain of her breeding (the Carfax strain, no doubt) still heard such names and greeted such proclivities with an inclination to derision.

Thyme snatched up her book. 'Well,' she said, 'I shall be in the attic. If anyone interesting comes you might send up to me.'

She stood, luxuriously stretching, and turning slowly round in a streak of sunlight so as to bathe her body in it. Then, with a long soft yawn, she flung up her chin till the sun streamed on her face. Her eyelashes rested on cheeks already faintly browned; her lips were parted; little shivers of delight ran down her; her chestnut hair glowed, burnished by the kisses of the sun.

'Ah!' Cecilia thought, 'if that other girl were like this, now, I could understand well enough!'

'Oh, Lord!' said Thyme, 'there they are!' She flew towards the door.

'My dear,' murmured Cecilia, 'if you *must* go, do please tell Father.'

A minute later Mrs Tallents Smallpeace came in, followed by a young man with an interesting, pale face and a crop of dusky hair.

Let us consider for a minute the not infrequent case of a youth cursed with an Italian mother and a father of the name of Potts, who had baptised him William. He had emanated from the lower classes, he might with impunity have ground an organ under the name of Bill; but springing from the bourgeoisie, and playing Chopin at the age of four, his friends had been confronted with a problem of no mean difficulty. Heaven, on the threshold of his career, had intervened to solve it. Hovering, as it were, with one leg raised before the gladiatorial arena of musical London, where all were waiting to turn their thumbs down on the figure of the native Potts, he had received a letter from his mother's birthplace. It was inscribed: 'Egregio Signor Pozzi'. He was saved. By the simple inversion of the first two words, the substitution of *z*'s for *t*'s without so fortunately making any difference in the sound, and the retention of that *i*, all London knew him now to be the rising pianist.

He was a quiet, well-mannered youth, invaluable just then to Mrs Tallents Smallpeace, a woman never happy unless slightly leading a genius in strings.

Cecilia, while engaging them to right and left in her half-sympathetic, faintly mocking way—as if doubting whether they really wanted to see her or she them—heard a word of fear.

'Mr Purcey.'

'Oh, Heaven!' she thought.

Mr Purcey, whose A.1. Damyer could be heard outside, advanced in his direct and simple way.

'I thought I'd give my car a run,' he said. 'How's your sister?' And seeing Mrs Tallents Smallpeace, he added: 'How do you do? We met the other day.'

'We did,' said Mrs Tallents Smallpeace, whose little eyes were sparkling. 'We talked about the poor, do you remember?'

Mr Purcey, a sensitive man if you could get through his skin, gave her a shrewd look. 'I don't quite cotton to this woman,' he seemed saying; 'there's a laugh about her I don't like.'

'Ah! yes—you were tellin' me about them.'

'Oh, Mr Purcey, but you had heard of them, you remember!'

Mr Purcey made a movement of his face which caused it to seem all jaw. It was a sort of unconscious declaration of a somewhat formidable character. So one may see bulldogs, those amiable animals, suddenly disclose their tenacity.

'It's rather a blue subject,' he said bluntly.

Something in Cecilia fluttered at those words. It was like the saying of a healthy man looking at a box of pills which he did not mean to open. Why could not she and Stephen keep that lid on, too? And at this moment, to her deep astonishment, Stephen entered. She had sent for him, it is true, but had never expected he would come.

His entrance, indeed, requires explanation.

Feeling, as he said, a little 'off colour', Stephen had not gone to Richmond to play golf. He had spent the day instead in the company of his pipe and those ancient coins, of which he had the best collection of any man he had ever met. His thoughts had wandered from them, more than he thought proper, to Hilary and that girl. He had felt from the beginning that he was so much more the man to deal with an affair like this than poor old Hilary. When, therefore, Thyme put her head into his study and said, 'Father, Mrs Tallents Smallpeace!' he had first thought, 'That busybody!' and then, 'I wonder—perhaps I'd better go and see if I can get anything out of her.'

In considering Stephen's attitude towards a woman so firmly embedded in the various social movements of the day, it must be remembered that he represented that large class of men who, unhappily too cultivated to put aside, like Mr Purcey, all blue subjects, or deny the need for movements to make them less blue, still could not move, for fear of being out of order. He was also temperamentally distrustful of anything too feminine; and Mrs Tallents Smallpeace was undoubtedly extremely feminine. Her merit, in his eyes, consisted of her attachment to Societies. So long as mankind worked through Societies, Stephen, who knew the power of rules and minute books, did not despair of too little progress being made. He sat down beside her, and turned the conversation on her chief work—'the Maids in Peril'.

Searching his face with those eyes so like little black bees sipping honey from all the flowers that grew, Mrs Tallents Smallpeace said:

'Why don't you get your wife to take an interest in our work?'

To Stephen this question was naturally both unexpected and annoying, one's wife being the last person he wished to interest in other people's movements. He kept his head.

'Ah, well!' he said, 'we haven't all got a talent for that sort of thing.'

The voice of Mr Purcey travelled suddenly across the room.

'Do tell me! How do you go to work to worm things out of them?'

Mrs Tallents Smallpeace, prone to laughter, bubbled.

'Oh, that is such a delicious expression, Mr Purcey! I almost think we ought to use it in our Report. Thank you!'

Mr Purcey bowed. 'Not at all!' he said.

Mrs Tallents Smallpeace turned again to Stephen.

'We have our trained inquirers. That is the advantage of Societies such as ours; so that we don't personally have the unpleasantness. Some cases do baffle everybody. It's such very delicate work.'

'You sometimes find you let in a rotter?' said Mr Purcey—'or, I should say, a rotter lets you in! Ha, ha!'

Mrs Tallents Smallpeace's eyes flew deliciously down his figure.

'Not often,' she said; and turning rather markedly once more to Stephen: 'Have you any special case that you are interested in, Mr Dallison?'

Stephen consulted Cecilia with one of those masculine half-glances so discreet that Mrs Tallents Smallpeace intercepted it without looking up. She found it rather harder to catch Cecilia's reply, but she caught it before Stephen did. It was, 'You'd better wait, perhaps,' conveyed by a tiny raising of the left eyebrow and a slight movement to the right of the lower lip. Putting two and two together, she felt within her bones that they were thinking of the little model. And she remembered the interesting moment in the omnibus when that attractive-looking man had got out so hastily.

There was no danger whatever from Mrs Tallents Smallpeace feeling anything. The circle in which she moved did not now talk scandal, or, indeed, allude to matters of that sort without deep sympathy; and in the second place she was really far too good a fellow, with far too dear a love of life, to interfere with anybody else's love of it. At the same time it was interesting.

'That little model, now,' she said, 'what about her?'

'Is that the girl I saw?' broke in Mr Purcey, with his accustomed shrewdness.

Stephen gave him the look with which he was accustomed to curdle the blood of persons who gave evidence before Commissions.

'This fellow is impossible,' he thought.

The little black bees flying below Mrs Tallents Smallpeace's dark hair, done in the Early Italian fashion, tranquilly sucked honey from Stephen's face.

'She seemed to me,' she answered, 'such a very likely type.'

'Ah!' murmured Stephen, 'there would be, I suppose, a danger——' And he looked angrily at Cecilia.

Without ceasing to converse with Mr Purcey and Signor Egregio Pozzi, she moved her left eye upwards. Mrs Tallents Smallpeace understood this to mean: 'Be frank, and guarded!' Stephen, however, interpreted it otherwise. To him it signified: 'What the deuce do you look at me for?' And he felt justly hurt. He therefore said abruptly:

'What would you do in a case like that?'

Mrs Tallents Smallpeace, sliding her face sideways, with a really charming little smile, asked softly:

'In a case like what?'

And her little eyes fled to Thyme, who had slipped into the room, and was whispering to her mother.

Cecilia rose.

'You know my daughter,' she said. 'Will you excuse me just a minute? I'm so very sorry.' She glided towards the door, and threw a flying look back. It was one of those social moments precious to those who are escaping them.

Mrs Tallents Smallpeace was smiling, Stephen frowning at his boots; Mr Purcey stared admiringly at Thyme, and Thyme, sitting very upright, was calmly regarding the unfortunate Egregio Pozzi, who apparently could not bring himself to speak.

When Cecilia found herself outside, she stood still a moment to compose her nerves. Thyme had told her that Hilary was in the dining-room, and wanted specially to see her.

As in most women of her class and bringing-up, Cecilia's qualities of reticence and subtlety, the delicate treading of her spirit, were seen to advantage in a situation such as this. Unlike Stephen, who had shown at once that he had something on his mind, she received Hilary with that exact shade of friendly, intimate, yet cool affection long established by her as the proper manner towards her husband's brother. It was not quite sisterly, but it was very nearly so. It seemed to say: 'We understand each other as far as it is right and fitting that we should; we even sympathise with the difficulties we have each of us experienced in marrying the other's sister or brother, as the case may be. We know the worst. And we like to see each other, too, because there are bars between us, which make it almost piquant.'

Giving him her soft little hand, she began at once to talk of things farthest from her heart. She saw that she was deceiving Hilary, and this feather in the cap of her subtlety gave her pleasure.

But her nerves fluttered at once when he said: 'I want to speak to you, Cis. You know that Stephen and I had a talk yesterday, I suppose?'

Cecilia nodded.

'I have spoken to B.!'

'Oh!' Cecilia murmured. She longed to ask what Bianca had said, but did not dare, for Hilary had his armour on, the retired, ironical look which he always wore when any subject was broached for which he was too sensitive.

She waited.

'The whole thing is distasteful to me,' he said; 'but I must do something for this child. I can't leave her completely in the lurch.'

Cecilia had an inspiration.

'Hilary,' she said softly, 'Mrs Tallents Smallpeace is in the drawing-room. She was just speaking of the girl to Stephen. Won't you come in, and arrange with her quietly?'

Hilary looked at his sister-in-law for a moment without speaking, then said:

'I draw the line there. No, thank you. I'll see this through myself.'

Cecilia fluttered out:

'Oh, but, Hilary, what do you mean?'

'I am going to put an end to it.'

It needed all Cecilia's subtlety to hide her consternation. End to what? Did he mean that he and B. were going to separate?

'I won't have all this vulgar gossip about the poor girl. I shall go and find another room for her.'

Cecilia sighed with relief.

'Would you—would you like me to come too, Hilary?'

'It's very good of you,' said Hilary dryly. 'My actions appear to rouse suspicion.'

Cecilia blushed.

'Oh, that's absurd! Still, no one could think *anything* if I come with you. Hilary, have you thought that if she continues coming to father——'

'I shall tell her that she mustn't!'

Cecilia's heart gave two thumps, the first with pleasure, the second with sympathy.

'It will be horrid for you,' she said. 'You hate doing anything of that sort.'

Hilary nodded.

'But I'm afraid it's the only way,' went on Cecilia, rather hastily.

'And, of course, it will be no good saying anything to Father; one must simply let him suppose that she has got tired of it.'

Again Hilary nodded.

'He will think it very funny,' murmured Cecilia pensively. 'Oh, and have you thought that taking her away from where she is will only make those people talk the more?'

Hilary shrugged his shoulders.

'It may make that man furious,' Cecilia added.

'It will.'

'Oh, but then, of course, if you don't see her afterwards, they will have no—no excuse at all.'

'I shall not see her afterwards,' said Hilary, 'if I can avoid it.'

Cecilia looked at him.

'It's very sweet of you, Hilary.'

'What is sweet?' asked Hilary stonily.

'Why, to take all this trouble. Is it really necessary for you to do anything?' But looking in his face, she went on hastily: 'Yes, yes, it's best. Let's go at once. Oh, those people in the drawing-room! Do wait ten minutes.'

A little later, running up to put her hat on, she wondered why it was that Hilary always made her want to comfort him. Stephen never affected her like this.

Having little or no notion where to go, they walked in the direction of Bayswater. To place the Park between Hound Street and the little model was the first essential. On arriving at the other side of the Broad Walk, they made instinctively away from every sight of green. In a long, grey street of dismally respectable appearance they found what they were looking for, a bed-sitting room furnished, advertised on a card in the window. The door was opened by the landlady, a tall woman of narrow build, with a West-Country accent, and a rather hungry sweetness running through her hardness. They stood talking with her in a passage, whose oilcloth of variegated pattern emitted a faint odour. The staircase could be seen climbing steeply up past walls covered with a shining paper cut by narrow red lines into small yellow squares. An almanack, of so floral a design that nobody would surely want to steal it, hung on the wall; below it was an umbrella stand without umbrellas. The dim little passage led past two grimly closed doors painted rusty red to two half-open doors with dull glass in their panels. Outside, in the street from which they had mounted by stone steps, a shower of sleet had begun to fall.

Hilary shut the door, but the cold spirit of that shower had already slipped into the bleak, narrow house.

'This is the apartment, m'm,' said the landlady, opening the first of the rusty-coloured doors. The room, which had a paper of blue roses on a yellow ground, was separated from another room by double doors.

'I let the rooms together sometimes, but just now that room's taken—a young gentleman in the City; that's why I'm able to let this cheap.'

Cecilia looked at Hilary. 'I hardly think——'

The landlady quickly turned the handles of the doors, showing that they would not open.

'*I* keep the key,' she said. 'There's a bolt on both sides.'

Reassured, Cecilia walked round the room as far as this was possible, for it was practically all furniture. There was the same little wrinkle across her nose as across Thyme's nose when she spoke of Hound Street. Suddenly she caught sight of Hilary. He was standing with his back against the door. On his face was a strange and bitter look, such as a man might have on seeing the face of Ugliness herself, feeling that she was not only without him, but within—a universal spirit; the look of a man who had thought that he was chivalrous, and found that he was not; of a leader about to give an order that he would not himself have executed.

Seeing that look, Cecilia said with some haste:

'It's all very nice and clean; it will do very well, I think. Seven shillings a week, I believe you said. We will take it for a fortnight, at all events.'

The first glimmer of a smile appeared on the landlady's grim face, with its hungry eyes, sweetened by patience.

'When would she be coming in?' she asked.

'When do you think, Hilary?'

'I don't know,' muttered Hilary. 'The sooner the better—if it must be. To-morrow, or the day after.'

And with one look at the bed, covered with a piece of cheap red-and-yellow tasselled tapestry, he went out into the street. The shower was over, but the house faced north, and no sun was shining on it.

Chapter 22

HILARY PUTS AN END TO IT

LIKE flies caught among the impalpable and smoky threads of cobwebs, so men struggle in the webs of their own natures, giving here a start, there a pitiful small jerking, long sustained, and failing into stillness. Enmeshed they were born, enmeshed they die, fighting according to their strength to the end; to fight in the hope of freedom, their joy; to die, not knowing they are beaten, their reward. Nothing, too, is more to be remarked than the manner in which Life devises for each man the particular dilemmas most suited to his nature; that which to the man of gross, decided, or fanatic turn of mind appears a simple sum, to the man of delicate and speculative temper seems to have no answer.

So it was with Hilary in that special web wherein his spirit struggled, sunrise unto sunset, and by moonlight afterward. Inclination, and the circumstances of a life which had never forced him to grips with either men or women, had detached him from the necessity for giving or taking orders. He had almost lost the faculty. Life had been a picture with blurred outlines melting into a softly shaded whole. Not for years had anything seemed to him quite a case for 'Yes' or 'No'. It had been his creed, his delight, his business, too, to try and put himself in everybody's place, so that now there were but few places where he did not, speculatively speaking, feel at home.

Putting himself into the little model's place gave him but small delight. Making due allowance for the sentiment men naturally import into their appreciation of the lives of women, his conception of her place was doubtless not so very wrong.

Here was a child, barely twenty years of age, country bred, neither a lady nor quite a working-girl, without a home or relatives, according to her own account—at all events, without those who were disposed to help her—without apparently any sort of friend; helpless by nature, and whose profession required a more than common wariness—this girl he was proposing to set quite adrift again by cutting through the single slender rope which tethered her. It was like digging up a little rose-tree planted with one's own hands in some poor shelter, just when it had taken root, and setting it where the full winds would beat against it. To do so brusque and, as it seemed to Hilary, so inhumane a thing was foreign to his nature. There was also the little matter of that touch of fever—the distant music he had been hearing since the waggons came in to Covent Garden.

With a feeling that was almost misery, therefore, he waited for her on Monday afternoon, walking to and fro in his study, where all the walls were white, and all the woodwork coloured like the leaf of a cigar; where the books were that colour too, in Hilary's special deerskin binding; where there were no flowers nor any sunlight coming through the windows, but plenty of sheets of paper—a room that youth seemed to have left for ever, the room of middle age!

He called her in with the intention of at once saying what he had to say, and getting it over in the fewest words. But he had not reckoned fully either with his own nature or with woman's instinct. Nor had he allowed—being, for all his learning, perhaps because of it, singularly unable to gauge the effects of simple actions—for the proprietary relations he had established in the girl's mind by giving her those clothes.

As a dog whose master has it in his mind to go away from him, stands gazing up with tragic inquiry in his eyes, scenting to his soul that coming cruelty—as a dog thus soon to be bereaved, so stood the little model.

By the pose of every limb, and a fixed gaze bright as if tears were behind it, and by a sort of trembling, she seemed to say: 'I know why you have sent for me.'

When Hilary saw her stand like that he felt as a man might when told to flog his fellow-creature. To gain time he asked her what she did with herself all day. The little model evidently tried to tell herself that her foreboding had been needless.

Now that the mornings were nice—she said with some animation—she got up much earlier, and did her needlework first thing; she then 'did out' the room. There were mouse-holes in her room, and she had bought a trap. She had caught a mouse last night. She hadn't liked to kill it; she had put it in a tin box, and let it go when she went out. Quick to see that Hilary was interested in this, as well he might be, she told him that she could not bear to see cats hungry or lost dogs, especially lost dogs, and she described to him one that she had seen. She had not liked to tell a policeman; they stared so hard. Those words were of strange omen, and Hilary turned his head away. The little model, perceiving that she had made an effect of some sort, tried to deepen it. She had heard they did all sorts of things to people—but, seeing at once from Hilary's face that she was not improving her effect, she broke off suddenly, and hastily began to tell him of her breakfast, of how comfortable she was now she had got her clothes; how she liked her room; how old Mr Creed was very funny, never taking any notice of her when he met her in the morning. Then followed a minute account of where she had been trying to get work; of an engagement promised; Mr Lennard, too, still wanted her to pose to him. At this she flashed a look at Hilary, then cast down her eyes. She could get plenty of work if she began that way. But she hadn't, because he had told her not, and, of course, she didn't want to; she liked coming to Mr Stone so much. And she got on very well, and she liked London, and she liked the shops. She mentioned neither Hughs nor Mrs Hughs. In all this rigmarole, told with such obvious purpose, stolidity was strangely mingled with almost cunning quickness to see the effect made; but the dog-like devotion was never quite out of her eyes when they were fixed on Hilary.

This look got through the weakest places in what little armour Nature had bestowed on him. It touched one of the least conceited and most amiable of men profoundly. He felt it an honour that anything so young as this should regard him in that way. He had always tried to keep out of his mind that which might have given him the key to her special feeling for himself—those words of the painter of still life: 'She's got a story of some sort.' But it flashed across him suddenly like an inspiration: If her story were the simplest of all stories—the direct, rather brutal, love affair of a village boy and girl—would not she, naturally given to surrender, be forced this time to the very antithesis of that young animal amour which had brought on her such sharp consequences?

But, wherever her devotion came from, it seemed to Hilary the grossest violation of the feelings of a gentleman to treat it ungratefully. Yet it was as if for the purpose of saying, 'You are a nuisance to me, or worse!' that he had asked her to his study. Her presence had hitherto chiefly roused in him the half-amused, half-tender feelings of one who strokes a foal or calf, watching its soft uncouthness; now, about to say good-bye to her, there was the question of whether that was the only feeling.

Miranda, stealing out between her master and his visitor, growled.

The little model, who was stroking a china ash-tray with her ungloved, inky fingers, muttered, with a smile, half pathetic, half cynical: 'She doesn't like me! She knows I don't belong here. She hates me to come. She's jealous!'

Hilary said abruptly:

'Tell me! Have you made any friends since you've been in London?'

The girl flashed a look at him that said:

'Could I make *you* jealous?'

Then, as though guilty of a far too daring thought, drooped her head, and answered:

'No.'

'Not one?'

The little model repeated almost passionately: 'No. I don't want any friends; I only want to be let alone.'

Hilary began speaking rapidly.

'But these Hughs have not left you alone. I told you, I thought you ought to move; I've taken another room for you quite away from them. Leave your furniture with a week's rent, and take your trunk quietly away tomorrow in a cab without saying a word to anyone. This is the new address, and here's the money for your expenses. They're dangerous for you, those people.'

The little model muttered desperately: 'But I don't care what they do!'

Hilary went on: 'Listen! You mustn't come here again, or the man will trace you. We will take care you have what's necessary till you can get other work.'

The little model looked up at him without a word. Now that the thin link which bound her to some sort of household gods had snapped, all the patience and submission bred in her by village life, by the hard facts of her story, and by these last months in London, served her well enough. She made no fuss. Hilary saw a tear roll down her cheek.

He turned his head away, and said: 'Don't cry, my child!'

Quite obediently the little model swallowed the tear. A thought seemed to strike her:

'But I could see you, Mr Dallison, couldn't I, sometimes?'

Seeing from his face that this was not in the programme, she stood silent again, looking up at him.

It was a little difficult for Hilary to say: 'I can't see you because my wife is jealous!' It was cruel to tell her: 'I don't want to see you!'—besides, it was not true.

'You'll soon be making friends,' he said at last, 'and you can always write to me;' and with a queer smile he added: 'You're only just beginning life; you mustn't take these things to heart; you'll find plenty of people better able to advise and help you than ever I shall be!'

The little model answered this by seizing his hand with both of hers. She dropped it again at once, as if guilty of presumption, and stood with her head bent. Hilary, looking down on the little hat which, by his special wish, contained no feathers, felt a lump rise in his throat.

'It's funny,' he said; 'I don't know your Christian name.'

'Ivy,' muttered the little model.

'Ivy! Well, I'll write to you. But you must promise me to do exactly as I said.'

The girl looked up; her face was almost ugly—like a child's in whom a storm of feeling is repressed.

'Promise!' repeated Hilary.

With a bitter droop of her lower lip, she nodded, and suddenly put her hand to her heart. The action, of which she was clearly unconscious, so naïvely, so almost automatically was it done, nearly put an end to Hilary's determination.

'Now you must go,' he said.

The little model choked, grew very red, and then quite white.

'Aren't I even to say good-bye to Mr Stone?'

Hilary shook his head.

'He'll miss me,' she said desperately. 'He will. I know he will!'

'So shall I,' said Hilary. 'We can't help that.'

The little model drew herself up to her full height; her breast heaved beneath the clothes which had made her Hilary's. She was very like 'The Shadow' at that moment, as though whatever Hilary might do there she would be—a little ghost, the spirit of the helpless submerged world, for ever haunting with its dumb appeal the minds of men.

'Give me your hand,' said Hilary.

The little model put out her not too white, small hand. It was soft, clinging, and as hot as fire.

'Good-bye, my dear, and bless you!'

The little model gave him a look with who-knows-what of reproach in it, and, faithful to her training, went submissively away.

Hilary did not look after her, but, standing by the lofty mantelpiece above the ashes of the fire, rested his forehead on his arm. Not even a fly's buzzing broke the stillness. There was sound for all that—not of distant music, but of blood beating in his ears and temples.

Chapter 23

THE 'BOOK OF UNIVERSAL BROTHERHOOD'

IT is fitting that a few words should be said about the writer of the 'Book of Universal Brotherhood'.

Sylvanus Stone, having graduated very highly at the London University, had been appointed at an early age lecturer to more than one Public Institution. He had soon received the professional robes due to a man of his profound learning in the natural sciences, and from that time till he was seventy his life had flowed on in one continual round of lectures, addresses, disquisitions, and arguments on the subjects in which he was a specialist. At the age of seventy, long after his wife's death and the marriages of his three children, he had for some time been living by himself, when a very serious illness—the result of liberties taken with an iron constitution by a single mind—prostrated him.

During the long convalescence following this illness the power of contemplation, which the Professor had up to then given to natural science, began to fix itself on life at large. But the mind which had made of natural science an idea, a passion, was not content with vague reflections on life. Slowly, subtly, with irresistible centrifugal force—with a force which perhaps it would not have acquired but for that illness—the idea, the passion of Universal Brotherhood had sucked into itself all his errant wonderings on the riddle of existence. The single mind of this old man, divorced by illness from his previous existence, pensioned and permanently shelved, began to worship a new star, that with every week and month and year grew brighter, till all other stars had lost their glimmer and died out.

At the age of seventy-four he had begun his book. Under the spell of his subject and of advancing age, his extreme inattention to passing matters became rapidly accentuated. His figure had become almost too publicly conspicuous before Bianca, finding him one day seated on the roof of his lonely little top-storey flat, the better to contemplate his darling Universe, had inveigled him home with her, and installed him in a room in her own house. After the first day or two he had not noticed any change to speak of.

His habits in his new home were soon formed, and once formed, they varied not at all; for he admitted into his life nothing that took him from the writing of his book.

On the afternoon following Hilary's dismissal of the little model, being disappointed of his amanuensis, Mr Stone had waited for an hour, reading his pages over and over to himself. He had then done his exercises. At the usual time for tea he had sat down, and, with his cup and brown bread-and-butter alternately at his lips, had looked long and fixedly at the place where the girl was wont to sit. Having finished, he left the room and went about the house. He found no one but Miranda, who, seated in the passage leading to the studio, was trying to keep one eye on the absence of her master and the other on the absence of her mistress. She joined Mr Stone maintaining a respect-compelling interval behind him when he went before, and before him when he went behind. When they had finished hunting, Mr Stone went down to the garden gate. Here Bianca found him presently, motionless, without a hat, in the full sun, craning his white head in the direction from which he knew the little model habitually came.

The mistress of the house was herself returning from her annual visit to the Royal Academy, where she still went, as dogs, from some perverted sense, will go and sniff round other dogs to whom they have long taken a dislike. A loose-hanging veil depended from her mushroom-shaped and coloured hat. Her eyes were brightened by her visit.

Mr Stone soon seemed to take in who she was, and stood regarding her a minute without speaking. His attitude towards his daughters was rather like that of an old drake towards two swans whom he has inadvertently begotten—there was inquiry in it, disapproval, admiration, and faint surprise.

'Why has she not come?' he said.

Bianca winced behind her veil. 'Have you asked Hilary?'

'I cannot find him,' answered Mr Stone. Something about his patient stooping figure and white head, on which the sunlight was falling, made Bianca slip her hand through his arm.

'Come in, Dad. I'll do your copying.'

Mr Stone looked at her intently, and shook his head.

'It would be against my principles; I cannot take an unpaid service. But if you would come, my dear, I should like to read to you. It is stimulating.'

At that request Bianca's eyes grew dim. Pressing Mr Stone's shaggy arm against her breast, she moved with him towards the house.

'I think I may have written something that will interest you,' Mr Stone said, as they went along.

'I am sure you have,' Bianca murmured.

'It is universal,' said Mr Stone; 'it concerns birth. Sit at the table. I will begin, as usual, where I left off yesterday.'

Bianca took the little model's seat, resting her chin on her hand, as motionless as any of the statues she had just been viewing.

It almost seemed as if Mr Stone were feeling nervous. He twice arranged his papers; cleared his throat; then, lifting a sheet suddenly, took three steps, turned his back on her, and began to read.

' "In that slow, incessant change of form to form, called Life, men, made spasmodic by perpetual action, had seized on a certain moment, no more intrinsically notable than any other moment, and had called it Birth. This habit of honouring one single instant of the universal process to the disadvantage of all the other instants had done more, perhaps, than anything to obfuscate the crystal clearness of the fundamental flux. As well might such as watch the process of the green, unfolding earth, emerging from the brumous arms of winter, isolate a single day and call it Spring. In the tides of rhythm by which the change of form to form was governed" '—Mr Stone's voice, which had till then been but a thin, husky murmur, gradually grew louder and louder, as though he were addressing a great concourse—' "the golden universal haze in which men should have flown like bright wingbeats round the sun gave place to the parasitic halo which every man derived from the glorifying of his own nativity. To this primary mistake could be traced his intensely personal philosophy. Slowly but surely there had dried up in his heart the wish to be his brother." '

He stopped reading suddenly.

'I see him coming in,' he said.

The next minute the door opened, and Hilary entered.

'She has not come,' said Mr Stone; and Bianca murmured:

'We miss her!'

'Her eyes,' said Mr Stone, 'have a peculiar look; they help me to see into the future. I have noticed the same look in the eyes of female dogs.'

With a little laugh, Bianca murmured again:

'That is good!'

'There is one virtue in dogs,' said Hilary, 'which human beings lack—they are incapable of mockery.'

But Bianca's lips, parted, indrawn, seemed saying: 'You ask too much! I no longer attract you. Am I to sympathise in the attraction this common little girl has for you?'

Mr Stone's gaze was fixed intently on the wall.

'The dog,' he said, 'has lost much of its primordial character.'

And, moving to his desk, he took up his quill pen.

Hilary and Bianca made no sound, nor did they look at one another; and in this silence, so much more full of meaning than any talk, the scratching of the quill went on. Mr Stone put it down at last, and, seeing two persons in the room, said:

'Looking back at those days when the doctrine of evolution had reached its pinnacle, one sees how the human mind, by its habit of continual crystallisations, had destroyed all the meaning of the process. Witness, for example, that sterile phenomenon, the pagoda of "caste"! Like this Chinese building, so was Society then formed. Men were living there in layers, as divided from each other, class from class——' He took up the quill, and again began to write.

'You understand, I suppose,' said Hilary in a low voice, 'that she has been told not to come?'

Bianca moved her shoulders.

With a most unwonted look of anger, he added:

'Is it within the scope of your generosity to credit me with the desire to meet your wishes?'

Bianca's answer was a laugh so strangely hard, so cruelly bitter, that Hilary involuntarily turned, as though to retrieve the sound before it reached the old man's ears.

Mr Stone had laid down his pen. 'I shall write no more to-day,' he said; 'I have lost my feeling—I am not myself.' He spoke in a voice unlike his own.

Very tired and worn his old figure looked; as some lean horse, whose sun has set, stands with drooped head, the hollows in his neck showing under his straggling mane. And suddenly, evidently quite oblivious that he had any audience, he spoke:

'O great Universe, I am an old man of a faint spirit, with no singleness of purpose. Help me to write on—help me to write a book such as the world has never seen!'

A dead silence followed that strange prayer; then Bianca, with tears rolling down her face, got up and rushed out of the room.

Mr Stone came to himself. His mute, white face had suddenly grown scared and pink. He looked at Hilary.

'I fear that I forgot myself. Have I said anything peculiar?'

Not feeling certain of his voice, Hilary shook his head, and he, too, moved towards the door.

Chapter 24
SHADOWLAND

'EACH of us has a shadow in those places—in those streets.'

That saying of Mr Stone's, which—like so many of his sayings—had travelled forth to beat the air, might have seemed, even 'in those days', not altogether without meaning to anyone who looked into the room of Mr Joshua Creed in Hound Street.

This aged butler lay in bed waiting for the inevitable striking of a small alarum clock placed in the very centre of his mantelpiece. Flanking that round and ruthless arbiter, which drove him day by day to stand up on feet whose time had come to rest, were the effigies of his past triumphs. On the one hand, in a papier-mâché frame, slightly tinged with smuts, stood a portrait of the 'Honorable Bateson', in the uniform of his peculiar Yeomanry. Creed's former master's face wore that dare-devil look with which he had been wont to say: 'D——n it, Creed! lend me a pound. I've got no money!' On the other hand, in a green frame that had once been plush, and covered by a glass with a crack in the left-hand corner, was a portrait of the Dowager Countess of Glengower, as this former mistress of his appeared, conceived by the local photographer, laying the foundation-stone of the local almshouse. During the wreck of Creed's career, which, following on a lengthy illness, had preceded his salvation by the *Westminster Gazette*, these two household gods had lain at the bottom of an old tin trunk, in the possession of the keeper of a lodging-house, waiting to be bailed out. The 'Honorable Bateson' was now dead, nor had he paid as yet the pounds he had borrowed. Lady Glengower, too, was in heaven, remembering that she had forgotten all her servants in her will. He who had served them was still alive, and his first thought, when he had secured his post on the *Westminster*, was to save enough to rescue them from a dishonourable confinement. It had taken him six months. He had found them keeping company with three pairs of woollen drawers; an old but respectable black tail-coat; a plaid cravat; a Bible; four socks, two of which had toes and two of which had heels; some darning-cotton and a needle; a pair of elastic-sided boots; a comb and a sprig of white heather, wrapped up with a little piece of shaving-soap and two pipe-cleaners in a bit of the *Globe* newspaper; also two collars, whose lofty points, separated by gaps of quite two inches, had been wont to reach their master's gills; the small alarum clock aforesaid; and a tie-pin formed in the likeness of Queen Victoria at the date of her first Jubilee. How many times had he not gone in thought over those stores of treasure while he was parted from them! How many times since they had come back to him had he not pondered with a slow but deathless anger on the absence of a certain shirt, which he could have sworn had been amongst them!

But now he lay in bed waiting to hear the clock go off, with his old bristly chin beneath the bedclothes, and his old discoloured nose above. He was thinking the thoughts which usually came into his mind about this hour—that Mrs Hughs ought not to scrape the butter off his bread for breakfast in the way she did; that she ought to take that sixpence off his rent; that the man who brought his late editions in the cart ought to be earlier, letting 'that man' get his *Pell Mells* off before him, when he himself would be having the one chance of his day; that, sooner than pay the ninepence which the bootmaker had proposed to charge for resoling him, he would wait until the summer came—'low-class o' feller' as he was, he'd be glad enough to sole him then for sixpence!

And the high-souled critic, finding these reflections sordid, would have thought otherwise, perhaps, had it been standing on those feet (now twitching all by themselves beneath the bedclothes) up to eleven o'clock the night before, because there were still twelve numbers of the late edition that nobody would buy. No one knew more surely than Joshua Creed himself that, if he suffered himself to entertain any large and lofty views of life, he would infallibly find himself in that building to keep out of which he was in the habit of addressing to God his only prayer to speak of. Fortunately, from a boy up, together with a lengthy, oblong, square-jawed face, he had been given by Nature a single-minded view of life. In fact, the mysterious, stout tenacity of a soul born in the neighbourhood of Newmarket could not have been done justice to had he constitutionally seen—any more than Mr Stone himself—two things at a time. The one thing he had seen, for the five years that he had now stood outside Messrs Rose and Thorn's, was the workhouse; and, as he was not going there so long as he was living, he attended carefully to all little matters of expense in this somewhat sordid way.

While attending thus, he heard a scream. Having by temperament considerable caution, but little fear, he waited till he heard another, and then got out of bed. Taking the poker in his hand, and putting on his spectacles, he hurried to the door. Many a time and oft in old days had he risen in this fashion to defend the plate of the 'Honorable Bateson' and the Dowager Countess of Glengower from the periodical attacks of his imagination. He stood with his ancient nightgown flapping round his still more ancient legs, slightly shivering; then, pulling the door open, he looked forth. On the stairs just above him Mrs Hughs, clasping her baby with one arm, was holding the other out at full length between herself and Hughs. He heard the latter say: 'You've drove me to it; I'll do a swing for you!' Mrs Hughs' thin body brushed past into his room; blood was dripping from her wrist. Creed saw that Hughs had his bayonet in his hand. With all his might he called out: 'Ye ought to be ashamed of yourself!' raising the poker to a position of defence. At this moment—more really dangerous than any he had ever known—it was remarkable that he instinctively opposed to it his most ordinary turns of speech. It was as though the extravagance of this un-English violence had roused in him the full measure of a native moderation. The sight of the naked steel deeply disgusted him; he uttered a long sentence. What did Hughs call this —disgracin' of the house at this time in the mornin'? Where was he brought up? Call 'imself a soldier, attackin' of old men and women in this way? He ought to be ashamed!

While these words were issuing between the yellow stumps of teeth in that withered mouth, Hughs stood silent, the back of his arm covering his eyes. Voices and a heavy tread were heard. Distinguishing in that tread the advancing footsteps of the Law, Creed said: 'You attack me if you dare!'

Hughs dropped his arm. His short, dark face had a desperate look, as of a caged rat; his eyes were everywhere at once.

'All right, daddy,' he said; 'I won't hurt *you*. She's drove my head all wrong again. Catch hold o' this; I can't trust myself.' He held out the bayonet.

'Westminister' took it gingerly in his shaking hand.

'To use a thing like that!' he said. 'An' call yourself an Englishman! I'll ketch me death standin' here, I will.'

Hughs made no answer, leaning against the wall. The old butler regarded him severely. He did not take a wide or philosophic view of him, as a tortured human being, driven by the whips of passion in his dark blood; a creature whose moral nature was the warped, stunted tree his life had made it; a poor devil half destroyed by drink and by his wound. The old butler took a more single-minded and old-fashioned line. 'Ketch 'old of 'im!' he thought. 'With these low fellers there's nothin' else to be done. Ketch 'old of 'im until he squeals.'

Nodding his ancient head, he said:

'Here's an orficer. I shan't speak for yer; you deserves all you'll get, and more.'

Later, dressed in an old Newmarket coat, given him by some client, and walking towards the police-station alongside Mrs Hughs, he was particularly silent, presenting a front of some austerity, as became a man mixed up in a low class of incident like this. And the seamstress, very thin and scared, with her wounded wrist slung in a muffler of her husband's, and carrying the baby on her other arm, because the morning's incident had upset the little thing, slipped along beside him, glancing now and then into his face.

Only once did he speak, and to himself:

'I don't know what they'll say to me down at the orfice, when I go again—missin' my day like this! Oh dear, what a misfortune! What put it into him to go on like that?'

At this, which was far from being intended as encouragement, the waters of speech broke up and flowed from Mrs Hughs. She had only told Hughs how that young girl had gone, and left a week's rent, with a bit of writing to say she wasn't coming back; it wasn't *her* fault that she was gone—that ought never to have come there at all, a creature that knew no better than to come between husband and wife. She couldn't tell no more than he could where that young girl had gone!

The tears, stealing forth, chased each other down the seamstress's thin cheeks. Her face had now but little likeness to the face with which she had stood confronting Hughs when she informed him of the little model's flight. None of the triumph which had leaped out of her bruised heart, none of the strident malice with which her voice, whether she would or no, strove to avenge her wounded sense of property; none of that unconscious abnegation, so very near to heroism, with which she had rushed and caught up her baby from beneath the bayonet, when, goaded by her malice and triumph, Hughs had rushed to seize that weapon. None of all that, but, instead, a pitiable terror of the ordeal before her—a pitiful, mute, quivering distress, that this man, against whom, two hours before, she had felt such a store of bitter rancour, whose almost murderous assault she had so narrowly escaped, should now be in this plight.

The sight of her emotion penetrated through his spectacles to something lying deep in the old butler.

'Don't you take on,' he said; 'I'll stand by yer. He shan't treat yer with impuniness.'

To his uncomplicated nature the affair was still one of tit for tat. Mrs Hughs became mute again. Her torn heart yearned to cancel the penalty that would fall on all of them, to deliver Hughs from the common enemy—the Law; but a queer feeling of pride and bewilderment, and a knowledge, that, to demand an eye for an eye was expected of all self-respecting persons, kept her silent.

Thus, then, they reached the great consoler, the grey resolver of all human tangles, haven of men and angels, the police court. It was situated in a back street. Like trails of ooze, when the tide, neither ebb nor flow, is leaving and making for some estuary, trails of human beings were moving to and from it. The faces of these shuffling 'shadows' wore a look as though masked with some hard but threadbare stuff—the look of those whom Life has squeezed into a last resort. Within the porches lay a stagnant marsh of suppliants, through whose centre trickled to and fro that stream of ooze. An old policeman, too, like some grey lighthouse, marked the entrance to the port of refuge. Close to that lighthouse the old butler edged his way. The love of regularity, and of an established order of affairs, born in him and fostered by a life passed in the service of the 'Honorable Bateson' and the other gentry, made him cling instinctively to the only person in this crowd whom he could tell for certain to be on the side of law and order. Something in his oblong face and lank, scanty hair parted precisely in the middle, something in that high collar supporting his lean gills, not subservient exactly, but as it were suggesting that he was in league against all this low-class of fellow, made the policeman say to him:

'What's your business, daddy?'

'Oh!' the old butler answered. 'This poor woman. I'm a witness to her battery.'

The policeman cast his not unkindly look over the figure of the seamstress. 'You stand here,' he said; 'I'll pass you in directly.'

And soon by his offices the two were passed into the port of refuge.

They sat down side by side on the edge of a long, hard, wooden bench; Creed fixing his eyes, whose colour had run into a brownish rim round their centres, on the magistrate, as in old days sun-worshippers would sit blinking devoutly at the sun; and Mrs Hughs fixing her eyes on her lap, while tears of agony trickled down her face. On her unwounded arm the baby slept. In front of them, and unregarded, filed one by one those shadows who had drunk the day before too deeply of the waters of forgetfulness. To-day, instead, they were to drink the water of remembrance, poured out for them with no uncertain hand. And somewhere very far away, it may have been that Justice sat with her ironic smile watching men judge their shadows. She had watched them so long about that business. With her elementary idea that hares and tortoises should not be made to start from the same mark, she had a little given up expecting to be asked to come and lend a hand; they had gone so far beyond her. Perhaps she knew, too, that men no longer punished, but now only reformed, their erring brothers, and this made her heart as light as the hearts of those who had been in the prisons where they were no longer punished.

The old butler, however, was not thinking of her; he had thoughts of a simpler order in his mind. He was reflecting that he had once valeted the nephew of the late Lord Justice Hawthorn, and in the midst of this low-class business the reminiscence brought him refreshment. Over and over to himself he conned these words: 'I interpylated in between them, and I says, "Ye ought to be ashamed of yourself; call yourself an Englishman, I says, attackin' of old men and women with cold steel, I says!"' And suddenly he saw that Hughs was in the dock.

The dark man stood with his hands pressed to his sides, as though at attention on parade. A pale profile, broken by a line of black moustache, was all 'Westminister' could see of that impassive face, whose eyes, fixed on the magistrate, alone betrayed the fires within. The violent trembling of the seamstress roused in Joshua Creed a certain irritation, and seeing the baby open his black eyes, he nudged her, whispering: 'Ye've woke the baby!'

Responding to words, which alone perhaps could have moved her at such a moment, Mrs Hughs rocked this dumb spectator of the drama. Again the old butler nudged her.

'They want yer in the box,' he said.

Mrs Hughs rose, and took her place.

He who wished to read the hearts of this husband and wife who stood at right angles, to have their wounds healed by Law, would have needed to have watched the hundred thousand hours of their wedded life, known and heard the million thoughts and words which had passed in the dim spaces of their world, to have been cognisant of the million reasons why they neither of them felt that they could have done other than they had done. Reading their hearts by the light of knowledge such as this, he would not have been surprised that, brought into this place of remedy, they seemed to enter into a sudden league. A look passed between them. It was not friendly, it had no appeal; but it sufficed. There seemed to be expressed in it the knowledge bred by immemorial experience and immemorial time: This Law before which we stand was not made by us! As dogs, when they hear the crack of a far whip, will shrink, and in their whole bearing show wary quietude, so Hughs and Mrs Hughs, confronted by the questionings of Law, made only such answers as could be dragged from them. In a voice hardly above a whisper Mrs Hughs told her tale. They had fallen out. What about? She did not know. Had he attacked her? He had had it in his hand. What then? She had slipped, and hurt her wrist against the point. At this statement Hughs turned his eyes on her, and seemed to say: 'You drove me to it; I've got to suffer, for all your trying to get me out of what I've done. I gave you one, and I don't want your help. But I'm glad you stick to me against this —— Law!' Then, lowering his eyes, he stood motionless during her breathless little outburst. He was her husband; she had borne him five; he had been wounded in the war. She had never wanted him brought here.

No mention of the little model. . . .

The old butler dwelt on this reticence of Mrs Hughs' when, two hours afterwards, in pursuance of his instinctive reliance on the gentry, he called on Hilary.

The latter, surrounded by books and papers—for, since his dismissal of the girl, he had worked with great activity—was partaking of lunch, served to him in his study on a tray.

'There's an old gentleman to see you, sir; he says you know him; his name is Creed.'

'Show him in,' said Hilary.

Appearing suddenly from behind the servant in the doorway, the old butler came in at a stealthy amble; he looked round, and, seeing a chair, placed his hat beneath it, then advanced, with nose and spectacles upturned, to Hilary. Catching sight of the tray, he stopped, checked in an evident desire to communicate his soul.

'Oh dear,' he said, 'I'm intrudin' on your luncheon. I can wait; I'll go and sit in the passage.'

Hilary, however, shook his hand, faded now to skin and bone, and motioned him to a chair.

He sat down on the edge of it, and again said:

'I'm intrudin' on yer.'

'Not at all. Is there anything I can do?'

Creed took off his spectacles, wiped them to help himself to see more clearly what he had to say, and put them on again.

'It's a-concerning of these domestic matters,' he said. 'I come up to tell yer, knowing as you're interested in this family.'

'Well,' said Hilary. 'What has happened?'

'It's along of the young girl's having left them, as you may know.'

'Ah!'

'It's brought things to a crisax,' explained Creed.

'Indeed, how's that?'

The old butler related the facts of the assault. 'I took 'is bayonet away from him,' he ended; 'he didn't frighten *me*.'

'Is he out of his mind?' asked Hilary.

'I've no conscience of it,' replied Creed. 'His wife, she's gone the wrong way to work with him, in my opinion, but that's particular to women. She's a-goaded of him respecting a certain party. I don't say but what that young girl's no better than what she ought to be; look at her profession, and her a country girl, too! She must be what she oughtn't to. But he ain't the sort o' man you can treat like that. You can't get thorns from figs; you can't expect it from the lower orders. They only give him a month, considerin' of him bein' wounded in the war. It'd been more if they'd a-known he was a-hankerin' after that young girl—a married man like him; don't ye think so, sir?'

Hilary's face had assumed its retired expression. 'I cannot go into that with you,' it seemed to say.

Quick to see the change, Creed rose. 'But I'm intrudin' on your dinner,' he said—'your luncheon, I should say. The woman goes on irritatin' of him, but he must expect of that, she bein' his wife. But what a misfortune! He'll be back again in no time, and what'll happen then? It won't improve him, shut up in one of them low prisons!' Then, raising his old face to Hilary: 'Oh dear! It's like a-walkin' on a black night, when ye can't see your 'and before yer.'

Hilary was unable to find a suitable answer to this simile.

The impression made on him by the old butler's recital was queerly twofold; his more fastidious side felt distinct relief that he had severed connection with an episode capable of developments so sordid and conspicuous. But all the side of him—and Hilary was a complicated product—which felt compassion for the helpless, his suppressed chivalry, in fact, had also received its fillip. The old butler's references to the girl showed clearly how the hands of all men and women were against her. She was that pariah, a young girl without property or friends, spiritually soft, physically alluring.

To recompense 'Westminister' for the loss of his day's work, to make a dubious statement that nights were never so black as they appeared to be, was all that he could venture to do. Creed hesitated in the doorway.

'Oh dear,' he said, 'there's a-one thing that the woman was a-saying that I've forgot to tell you. It's a-concernin' of what this 'ere man was boastin' in his rage. "Let them," he says, "as is responsive for the movin' of her look out," he says; "I ain't done with them!" That's conspiracy, I should think!'

Smiling away this diagnosis of Hughs' words, Hilary shook the old man's withered hand, and closed the door. Sitting down again at his writing-table, he buried himself almost angrily in his work. But the queer, half-pleasurable, fevered feeling, which had been his, since the night he walked down Piccadilly, and met the image of the little model, was unfavourable to the austere process of his thoughts.

Chapter 25
MR STONE IN WAITING

THAT same afternoon, while Mr Stone was writing, he heard a voice saying:

'Dad, stop writing just a minute, and talk to me.'

Recognition came into his eyes. It was his younger daughter.

'My dear,' he said, 'are you unwell?'

Keeping his hand, fragile and veined and chill, under her own warm grasp, Bianca answered: 'Lonely.'

Mr Stone looked straight before him.

'Loneliness,' he said, 'is man's chief fault;' and seeing his pen lying on the desk, he tried to lift his hand. Bianca held it down. At that hot clasp something seemed to stir in Mr Stone. His cheeks grew pink.

'Kiss me, Dad.'

Mr Stone hesitated. Then his lips resolutely touched her eye. 'It is wet,' he said. He seemed for a moment struggling to grasp the meaning of moisture in connection with the human eye. Soon his face again became serene. 'The heart,' he said, 'is a dark well; its depth unknown. I have lived eighty years. I am still drawing water.'

'Draw a little for me, Dad.'

This time Mr Stone looked at his daughter anxiously, and suddenly spoke, as if afraid that if he waited he might forget.

'You are unhappy!'

Bianca put her face down to his tweed sleeve. 'How nice your coat smells!' she murmured.

'You are unhappy,' repeated Mr Stone.

Bianca dropped his hand, and moved away.

Mr Stone followed her. 'Why?' he said. Then, grasping his brow, he added: 'If it would do you any good, my dear, to hear a page or two, I could read to you.'

Bianca shook her head.

'No; talk to me!'

Mr Stone answered simply: 'I have forgotten.'

'You talk to that little girl,' murmured Bianca.

Mr Stone seemed to lose himself in reverie.

'If that is true,' he said, following out his thoughts, 'it must be due to the sex instinct not yet quite extinct. It is stated that the blackcock will dance before his females to a great age, though I have never seen it.'

'If you dance before *her*,' said Bianca, with her face averted, 'can't you even talk to me?'

'I do not dance, my dear,' said Mr Stone; 'I will do my best to talk to you.'

There was a silence, and he began to pace the room. Bianca, by the empty fireplace, watched a shower of rain driving past the open window.

'This is the time of year,' said Mr Stone suddenly, 'when lambs leap off the ground with all four legs at a time.' He paused as though for an answer; then, out of the silence, his voice rose again—it sounded different: 'There is nothing in Nature more symptomatic of that principle which should underlie all life. Live in the future; regret nothing; leap! A lamb that has left earth with all four legs at once is the symbol of true life. That she must come down again is but an inevitable accident. "In those days men were living on their pasts. They leaped with one, or, at the most, two legs at a time; they never left the ground, or in leaving, they wished to know the reason why. It was this paralysis" '—Mr Stone did not pause, but, finding himself close beside his desk, took up his pen—' "it was this paralysis of the leaping nerve which undermined their progress. Instead of millions of leaping lambs, ignorant of why they leaped, they were a flock of sheep lifting up one leg and asking whether it was or was not worth their while to lift another." '

The words were followed by a silence, broken only by the scratching of the quill with which Mr Stone was writing.

Having finished, he again began to pace the room, and coming suddenly on his daughter, stopped short. Touching her shoulder timidly, he said: 'I was talking to you, I think, my dear; where were we?'

Bianca rubbed her cheek against his hand.

'In the air, I think.'

'Yes, yes,' said Mr Stone, 'I remember. You must not let me wander from the point again.'

'No, dear.'

'Lambs,' said Mr Stone, 'remind me at times of that young girl who comes to copy for me. I make her skip to promote her circulation before tea. I myself do this exercise.' Leaning against the wall, with his feet twelve inches from it, he rose slowly on his toes. 'Do you know that exercise? It is excellent for the calves of the legs, and for the lumbar regions.' So saying, Mr Stone left the wall, and began again to pace the room; the whitewash had also left the wall, and clung in a large square patch on his shaggy coat.

'I have seen sheep in Spring,' he said, 'actually imitate their lambs in rising from the ground with all four legs at once.' He stood still. A thought had evidently struck him.

'If Life is not all Spring, it is of no value whatsoever; better to die, and to begin again. Life is a tree putting on a new green gown; it is a young moon rising—no, that is not so, we do not see the young moon rising—it is a young moon setting, never younger than when we are about to die——'

Bianca cried out sharply: 'Don't, Father! Don't talk like that; it's so untrue! Life is all autumn, it seems to me!'

Mr Stone's eyes grew very blue.

'That is a foul heresy,' he stammered; 'I cannot listen to it. Life is the cuckoo's song; it is a hill-side bursting into leaf; it is the wind; I feel it in me every day!'

He was trembling like a leaf in the wind he spoke of, and Bianca moved hastily towards him, holding out her arms. Suddenly his lips began to move; she heard him mutter: 'I have lost force; I will boil some milk. I must be ready when she comes.' And at those words her heart felt like a lump of ice.

Always that girl! And without again attracting his attention she went away. As she passed out through the garden she saw him at the window holding a cup of milk, from which the steam was rising.

Chapter 26

THIRD PILGRIMAGE TO HOUND STREET

LIKE water, human character will find its level; and Nature, with her way of fitting men to their environment, had made young Martin Stone what Stephen called a 'Sanitist'. There had been nothing else for her to do with him.

This young man had come into the social scheme at a moment when the conception of existence as a present life corrected by a life to come, was tottering; and the conception of the world as an upper-class preserve somewhat seriously disturbed.

Losing his father and mother at an early age, and brought up till he was fourteen by Mr Stone, he had formed the habit of thinking for himself. This had rendered him unpopular, and added force to the essential single-heartedness transmitted to him through his grandfather. A particular aversion to the sights and scents of suffering, which had caused him as a child to object to killing flies, and to watching rabbits caught in traps, had been regulated by his training as a doctor. His fleshly horror of pain and ugliness was now disciplined, his spiritual dislike of them forced into a philosophy. The peculiar chaos surrounding all young men who live in large towns and think at all, had made him gradually reject all abstract speculation; but a certain fire of aspiration coming, we may suppose, through Mr Stone, had nevertheless impelled him to embrace something with all his might. He had therefore embraced health. And living, as he did, in the Euston Road, to be in touch with things, he had every need of the health which he embraced.

Late in the afternoon of the day when Hughs had committed his assault, having three hours of respite from his hospital, Martin dipped his face and head into cold water, rubbed them with a corrugated towel, put on a hard bowler hat, took a thick stick in his hand, and went by Underground to Kensington.

With his usual cool, high-handed air he entered his aunt's house, and asked for Thyme. Faithful to his definite, if somewhat crude theory, that Stephen and Cecilia and all their sort were amateurs, he never inquired for them, though not unfrequently he would, while waiting, stroll into Cecilia's drawing-room, and let his sarcastic glance sweep over the pretty things she had collected, or, lounging in some luxurious chair, cross his long legs, and fix his eyes on the ceiling.

Thyme soon came down. She wore a blouse of some blue stuff bought by Cecilia for the relief of people in the Balkan States, a skirt of purplish tweed woven by Irish gentlewomen in distress, and held in her hand an open envelope addressed in Cecilia's writing to Mrs Tallents Smallpeace.

'Hallo!' she said.

Martin answered by a look that took her in from head to foot.

'Get on a hat! I haven't got much time. That blue thing's new.'

'It's pure flax. Mother bought it.'

'It's rather decent. Hurry up!'

Thyme raised her chin; that lazy movement showed her round, creamy neck in all its beauty.

'I feel rather slack,' she said; 'besides, I must get back to dinner, Martin.'

'Dinner!'

Thyme turned quickly to the door. 'Oh, well, I'll come,' and ran upstairs.

When they had purchased a postal order for ten shillings, placed it in the envelope addressed to Mrs Tallents Smallpeace, and passed the hundred doors of Messrs Rose and Thorn, Martin said: 'I'm going to see what that precious amateur has done about the baby. If he hasn't moved the girl, I expect to find things in a pretty mess.'

Thyme's face changed at once.

'Just remember,' she said, 'that *I* don't want to go there. I don't see the good, when there's such a tremendous lot waiting to be done.'

'Every other case, except the one in hand!'

'It's not *my* case. You're so disgustingly unfair, Martin. I don't like those people.'

'Oh, you amateur!'

Thyme flushed crimson. 'Look here!' she said, speaking with dignity, 'I don't care what you call *me*, but I won't have you call Uncle Hilary an amateur.'

'What is he, then?'

'I like him.'

'That's conclusive.'

'Yes, it is.'

Martin did not reply, looking sideways at Thyme with his queer, protective smile. They were passing through a street superior to Hound Street in its pretensions to be called a slum.

'Look here!' he said suddenly; 'a man like Hilary's interest in all this sort of thing is simply sentimental. It's on his nerves. He takes philanthropy just as he'd take sulphonal for sleeplessness.'

Thyme looked shrewdly up at him.

'Well,' she said, 'it's just as much on your nerves. You see it from the point of view of health; he sees it from the point of view of sentiment, that's all.'

'Oh! you think so?'

'You just treat all these people as if they were in hospital.'

The young man's nostrils quivered. 'Well, and how should they be treated?'

'How would you like to be looked at as a "case"?' muttered Thyme.

Martin moved his hand in a slow half-circle.

'These houses and these people,' he said, 'are in the way—in the way of you and me, and everyone.'

Thyme's eyes followed that slow, sweeping movement of her cousin's hand. It seemed to fascinate her.

'Yes, of course; I know,' she murmured. 'Something must be done!'

And she reared her head up, looking from side to side, as if to show him that she, too, could sweep away things. Very straight, and solid, fair, and fresh, she looked just then.

Thus, in the hypnotic silence of high thought the two young 'Sanitists' arrived in Hound Street.

In the doorway of No. 1 the son of the lame woman, Mrs Budgen—the thin, white youth as tall as Martin, but not so broad—stood, smoking a dubious-looking cigarette. He turned his lack-lustre, jeering gaze on the visitors.

'Who d'you want?' he said. 'If it's the girl, she's gone away, and left no address.'

'I want Mrs Hughs,' said Martin.

The young man coughed. 'Right-o! You'll find *her*; but for *him*, apply Wormwood Scrubs.'

'Prison! What for?'

'Stickin' her though the wrist with his bayonet;' and the young man let a long, luxurious fume of smoke trickle through his nose.

'How horrible!' said Thyme.

Martin regarded the young man, unmoved. 'That stuff you're smoking's rank,' he said. 'Have some of mine; I'll show you how to make them. It'll save you one and three per pound of baccy, and won't rot your lungs.'

Taking out his pouch, he rolled a cigarette. The white young man bent his dull wink on Thyme, who, wrinkling her nose, was pretending to be far away.

Mounting the narrow stairs that smelt of walls and washing and red herrings, Thyme spoke: 'Now, you see, it wasn't so simple as you thought. I don't want to go up; I don't want to see her. I shall wait for you here.' She took her stand in the open doorway of the little model's empty room. Martin ascended to the second floor.

There, in the front room, Mrs Hughs was seen standing with the baby in her arms beside the bed. She had a frightened and uncertain air. After examining her wrist, and pronouncing it a scratch, Martin looked long at the baby. The little creature's toes were stiffened against its mother's waist, its eyes closed, its tiny fingers crisped against her breast. While Mrs Hughs poured forth her tale, Martin stood with his eyes still fixed on the baby. It could not be gathered from his face what he was thinking, but now and then he moved his jaw, as though he were suffering from toothache. In truth, by the look of Mrs Hughs and her baby, his recipe did not seem to have achieved conspicuous success. He turned away at last from the trembling, nerveless figure of the seamstress, and went to the window. Two pale hyacinth plants stood on the inner edge; their perfume penetrated through the other savours of the room—and very strange they looked, those twin, starved children of the light and air.

'These are new,' he said.

'Yes, sir,' murmured Mrs Hughs. 'I brought them upstairs. I didn't like to see the poor things left to die.'

From the bitter accent of these words Martin understood that they had been the little model's.

'Put them outside,' he said; 'they'll never live in here. They want watering, too. Where are your saucers?'

Mrs Hughs laid the baby down, and, going to the cupboard where all the household gods were kept, brought out two old, dirty saucers. Martin raised the plants, and as he held them, from one close, yellow petal there rose up a tiny caterpillar. It reared a green, transparent body, feeling its way to a new resting-place. The little writhing shape seemed, like the wonder and mystery of life, to mock the young doctor, who watched it with eyebrows raised, having no hand at liberty to remove it from the plant.

'*She* came from the country. There's plenty of men there for her!'

Martin put the plants down, and turned round to the seamstress.

'Look here!' he said, 'it's no good crying over spilt milk. What you've got to do is to set to and get some work.'

'Yes, sir.'

'Don't say it in that sort of way,' said Martin, 'you must rise to the occasion.'

'Yes, sir.'

'You want a tonic. Take this half-crown, and get in a dozen pints of stout, and drink one every day.'

And again Mrs Hughs said, 'Yes, sir.'

'And about that baby.'

Motionless, where it had been placed against the foot-rail of the bed, the baby sat with its black eyes closed. The small grey face was curled down on the bundle of its garments.

'It's a silent gentleman,' Martin muttered.

'It never was a one to cry,' said Mrs Hughs.

'That's lucky, anyway. When did you feed it last?'

Mrs Hughs did not reply at first. 'About half-past six last evening, sir.'

'What?'

'It slept all night; but to-day, of course, I've been all torn to pieces; my milk's gone. I've tried it with the bottle, but it wouldn't take it.'

Martin bent down to the baby's face, and put his finger on its chin; bending lower yet, he raised the eyelid of the tiny eye.

'It's dead,' he said.

At the word 'dead' Mrs Hughs, stooping behind him, snatched the baby to her throat. With its drooping head close to her face, she clutched and rocked it without sound. Full five minutes this desperate mute struggle with eternal silence lasted—the feeling, and warming, and breathing on the little limbs. Then, sitting down, bent almost double over her baby, she moaned. That single sound was followed by utter silence. The tread of footsteps on the creaking stairs broke it. Martin, rising from his crouching posture by the bed, went towards the door.

His grandfather was standing there, with Thyme behind him.

'She has left her room,' said Mr Stone. 'Where has she gone?'

Martin, understanding that he meant the little model, put his finger to his lips, and, pointing to Mrs Hughs, whispered:

'This woman's baby has just died.'

Mr Stone's face underwent the queer discoloration that marked the sudden summoning of his far thoughts. He stepped past Martin, and went up to Mrs Hughs.

He stood there a long time gazing at the baby, and at the dark head bending over it with such despair. At last he spoke:

'Poor woman! He is at peace.'

Mrs Hughs looked up, and, seeing that old face, with its hollows and thin silver hair, she spoke:

'He's dead, sir.'

Mr Stone put out his veined and fragile hand, and touched the baby's toes. 'He is flying; he is everywhere; he is close to the sun—Little brother!' And turning on his heel, he went out.

Thyme followed him as he walked on tiptoe down stairs that seemed to creak the louder for his caution. Tears were rolling down her cheeks.

Martin sat on, with the mother and her baby, in the close, still room, where, like strange visiting spirits, came stealing whiffs of the perfume of hyacinths.

Chapter 27

STEPHEN'S PRIVATE LIFE

MR STONE and Thyme, in coming out, again passed the tall, white young man. He had thrown away the hand-made cigarette, finding that it had not enough saltpetre to make it draw, and was smoking one more suited to the action of his lungs. He directed towards them the same lack-lustre, jeering stare.

Unconscious, seemingly, of where he went, Mr Stone walked with his eyes fixed on space. His head jerked now and then, as a dried flower will shiver in a draught.

Scared at these movements, Thyme took his arm. The touch of that soft young arm squeezing his own brought speech back to Mr Stone.

'In those places . . .' he said, 'in those streets! . . . I shall not see the flowering of the aloe—I shall not see the living peace! "As with dogs, each couched over his proper bone, so men were living then!"' He sank back into silence.

Thyme, watching him askance, pressed still closer to his side, as though to try and warm him back to every day.

'Oh!' went her fluttered thoughts. 'I do wish grandfather would say something one could understand. I wish he would lose that dreadful stare.'

Mr Stone spoke in answer to his grand-daughter's thoughts.

'I have seen a vision of fraternity. A barren hillside in the sun, and on it a man of stone talking to the wind. I have heard an owl hooting in the daytime; a cuckoo singing in the night.'

'Grandfather, grandfather!'

To that appeal Mr Stone responded: 'Yes, what is it?'

But Thyme, thus challenged, knew not what to say, having spoken out of terror.

'If the poor baby had lived,' she stammered out, 'it would have grown up. . . . It's all for the best, isn't it?'

'Everything is for the best,' said Mr Stone. ' "In those days men, possessed by thoughts of individual life, made moan at death, careless of the great truth that the world was one unending song." '

Thyme thought: 'I have never seen him as bad as this!' She drew him on more quickly. With deep relief she saw her father, latchkey in hand, turning into the Old Square.

Stephen, who was still walking with his springy step, though he had come on foot the whole way from the Temple, hailed them with his hat. It was tall and black, and very shiny, neither quite oval nor positively round, and had a little curly brim. In this and his black coat, cut so as to show the front of him and cover the behind, he looked his best. The costume suited his long, rather narrow face, corrugated by two short parallel lines slanting downwards from his eyes and nostrils on either cheek; suited his neat, thin figure and the close-lipped corners of his mouth. His permanent appointment in the world of Law had ousted from his life (together with all uncertainty of income) the need for putting on a wig and taking his moustache off; but he still preferred to go clean-shaved.

'Where have you two sprung from?' he inquired, admitting them into the hall.

Mr Stone gave him no answer, but passed into the drawing-room, and sat down on the verge of the first chair he came across, leaning forward with his hands between his knees.

Stephen, after one dry glance at him, turned to his daughter.

'My child,' he said softly, 'what have you brought the old boy here for? If there happens to be anything of the high mammalian order for dinner, your mother will have a fit.'

Thyme answered: 'Don't chaff, father!'

Stephen, who was very fond of her, saw that for some reason she was not herself. He examined her with unwonted gravity. Thyme turned away from him. He heard, to his alarm, a little gulping sound.

'My dear!' he said.

Conscious of her sentimental weakness, Thyme made a violent effort.

'I've seen a baby dead,' she cried in a quick, hard voice; and, without another word, she ran upstairs.

In Stephen there was a horror of emotion that amounted almost to disease. It would have been difficult to say when he had last shown emotion; perhaps not since Thyme was born, and even then not to anyone except himself, having first locked the door, and then walked up and down, with his teeth almost meeting in the mouthpiece of his favourite pipe. He was unaccustomed, too, to witness this weakness on the part of other people. His looks and speech unconsciously discouraged it, so that if Cecilia had been at all that way inclined, she must long ago have been healed. Fortunately, she never had been, having too much distrust of her own feelings to give way to them completely. And Thyme, that healthy product of them both, at once younger for her age, and older, than they had ever been, with her incapacity for nonsense, her love for open air and facts—that fresh, rising plant, so elastic and so sane—she had never given them a single moment of uneasiness.

Stephen, close to his hat-rack, felt soreness in his heart. Such blows as Fortune had dealt, and meant to deal him, he had borne, and he could bear, so long as there was nothing in his own manner, or in that of others, to show him they *were* blows.

Hurriedly depositing his hat, he ran to Cecilia. He still preserved the habit of knocking on her door before he entered, though she had never, so far, answered, 'Don't come in!' because she knew his knock. The custom gave, in fact, the measure of his idealism. What he feared, or what he thought he feared, after nineteen years of unchecked entrance, could never have been ascertained; but there it was, that flower of something formal and precise, of something reticent, within his soul.

This time, for once, he did not knock, and found Cecilia hooking up her tea-gown and looking very sweet. She glanced at him with mild surprise.

'What's this, Cis,' he said, 'about a baby dead? Thyme's quite upset about it; and your dad's in the drawing-room!'

With the quick instinct that was woven into all her gentle treading, Cecilia's thoughts flew—she could not have told why—first to the little model, then to Mrs Hughs.

'Dead?' she said. 'Oh, poor woman!'

'What woman?' Stephen asked.

'It must be Mrs Hughs.'

The thought passed darkly through Stephen's mind: 'Those people again! What now?' He did not express it, being neither brutal nor lacking in good taste.

A short silence followed, then Cecilia said suddenly: 'Did you say that father was in the drawing-room? There's fillet of beef, Stephen!'

Stephen turned away. 'Go and see Thyme!' he said.

Outside Thyme's door Cecilia paused, and, hearing no sound, tapped gently. Her knock not being answered, she slipped in. On the bed of that white room, with her face pressed into the pillow, her little daughter lay. Cecilia stood aghast. Thyme's whole body was quivering with suppressed sobs.

'My *darling*!' said Cecilia, 'what is it?'

Thymes answer was inarticulate.

Cecilia sat down on the bed and waited, drawing her fingers through the girl's hair, which had fallen loose; and while she sat there she experienced all that sore, strange feeling—as of being skinned—which comes to one who watches the emotion of someone near and dear without knowing the exact cause.

'This is dreadful,' she thought. 'What am I to do?'

To see one's child cry was bad enough, but to see her cry when that child's whole creed of honour and conduct for years past had precluded this relief as unfeminine, was worse than disconcerting.

Thyme raised herself on her elbow, turning her face carefully away.

'I don't know what's the matter with me,' she said, choking. 'It's—it's purely physical.'

'Yes, darling,' murmured Cecilia; 'I know.'

'Oh, Mother!' said Thyme suddenly, 'it looked so tiny.'

'Yes, yes, my sweet.'

Thyme faced round; there was a sort of passion in her darkened eyes, rimmed pink with grief, and in all her flushed, wet face.

'Why should it have been choked out like that? It's—it's so brutal!'

Cecilia slid an arm round her.

'I'm so distressed you saw it, dear,' she said.

'And grandfather *was* so——' A long sobbing quiver choked her utterance.

'Yes, yes,' said Cecilia; 'I'm sure he was.'

Clasping her hands together in her lap, Thyme muttered: 'He called him "Little Brother".'

A tear trickled down Cecilia's cheek, and dropped on her daughter's wrist. Feeling that it was not her own tear, Thyme started up.

'It's weak and ridiculous,' she said. 'I won't! Oh, go away,

Mother, please. I'm only making you feel bad, too. You'd better go and see to grandfather.'

Cecilia saw that she would cry no more, and since it was the sight of tears which had so disturbed her, she gave the girl a little hesitating stroke, and went away. Outside she thought: 'How dreadfully unlucky and pathetic; and there's father in the drawing-room!' Then she hurried down to Mr Stone.

He was sitting where he had first placed himself, motionless. It struck her suddenly how frail and white he looked. In the shadowy light of her drawing-room, he was almost like a spirit sitting there in his grey tweed—silvery from head to foot. Her conscience smote her. It is written of the very old that they shall pass, by virtue of their long travel, out of the country of the understanding of the young, till the natural affections are blurred by creeping mists such as steal across the moors when the sun is going down. Cecilia's heart ached with a little ache for all the times she had thought: 'If father were only not quite so——'; for all the times she had shunned asking him to come to them, because he was so——; for all the silences she and Stephen had maintained after he had spoken; for all the little smiles she had smiled. She longed to go and kiss his brow, and make him feel that she was aching. But she did not dare; he seemed so far away; it would be ridiculous.

Coming down the room, and putting her slim foot on the fender with a noise, so that if possible he might both see and hear her, she turned her anxious face towards him, and said: 'Father!'

Mr Stone looked up, and seeing somebody who seemed to be his elder daughter, answered: 'Yes, my dear?'

'Are you sure you're feeling quite the thing? Thyme said she thought seeing that poor baby had upset you.'

Mr Stone felt his body with his hand.

'I am not conscious of any pain,' he said.

'Then you'll stay to dinner, dear, won't you?'

Mr Stone's brow contracted as though he were trying to recall his past.

'I have had no tea,' he said. Then, with a sudden, anxious look at his daughter: 'The little girl has not come to me. I miss her. Where is she?'

The ache within Cecilia became more poignant.

'It is now two days,' said Mr Stone, 'and she has left her room in that house—in that street.'

Cecilia, at her wits' end, answered: 'Do you really miss her, Father?'

'Yes,' said Mr Stone. 'She is like——' His eyes wandered round the room as though seeking something that would help him to express himself. They fixed themselves on the far wall. Cecilia, following their gaze, saw a little solitary patch of sunlight dancing and trembling there. It had escaped the screen of trees and houses, and, creeping through some chink, had quivered in. 'She is like that,' said Mr Stone, pointing with his finger. 'It is gone!' His finger dropped; he uttered a deep sigh.

'How dreadful this is!' Cecilia thought. 'I never expected him to feel it, and yet I can do nothing!' Hastily she asked: 'Would it do if you had Thyme to copy for you? I'm sure she'd love to come.'

'She is my grand-daughter,' Mr Stone said simply. 'It would not be the same.'

Cecilia could think of nothing now to say but: 'Would you like to wash your hands, dear?'

'Yes,' said Mr Stone.

'Then will you go up to Stephen's dressing-room for hot water, or will you wash them in the lavatory?'

'In the lavatory,' said Mr Stone. 'I shall be freer there.'

When he had gone Cecilia thought: 'Oh dear, how shall I get through the evening? Poor darling, he is so single-minded!'

At the sounding of the dinner-gong they all assembled—Thyme from her bedroom with cheeks and eyes still pink, Stephen with veiled inquiry in his glance, Mr Stone from freedom in the lavatory—and sat down, screened, but so very little, from each other by sprays of white lilac. Looking round her table, Cecilia felt rather like one watching a dew-belled cobweb, most delicate of all things in the world, menaced by the tongue of a browsing cow.

Both soup and fish had been achieved, however, before a word was spoken. It was Stephen who, after taking a mouthful of dry sherry, broke the silence.

'How are you getting on with your book, sir?' he said.

Cecilia heard that question with something like dismay. It was so bald; for, however inconvenient Mr Stone's absorption in his manuscript might be, her delicacy told her how precious beyond life itself that book was to him. To her relief, however, her father was eating spinach.

'You must be getting near the end, I should think,' proceeded Stephen.

Cecilia spoke hastily: 'Isn't this white lilac lovely, Dad?'

Mr Stone looked up.

'It is not white; it is really pink. The test is simple.' He paused with his eyes fixed on the lilac.

'Ah!' thought Cecilia, 'now, if I can only keep him on natural science—he used to be so interesting.'

'All flowers are one!' said Mr Stone. His voice had changed.

'Oh!' thought Cecilia, 'he is gone!'

'They have but a single soul. In those days men divided, and subdivided them, oblivious of the one pale spirit that underlay those seemingly separate forms.'

Cecilia's glance passed swiftly from the man-servant to Stephen. She saw one of her husband's eyes rise visibly. Stephen did so hate one thing to be confounded with another.

'Oh, come sir,' she heard him say; 'you don't surely tell us that dandelions and roses have the same pale spirit!'

Mr Stone looked at him wistfully.

'Did I say that?' he said. 'I had no wish to be dogmatic.'

'Not at all, sir, not at all,' murmured Stephen.

Thyme, leaning over to her mother, whispered: 'Oh, Mother, don't let grandfather be queer; I can't bear it to-night!'

Cecilia, at her wits' end, said hurriedly:

'Dad, will you tell us what sort of character you think that little girl who comes to you has?'

Mr Stone paused in the act of drinking water; his attention had evidently been riveted; he did not, however, speak. And Cecilia, seeing that the butler, out of the perversity which she found so conspicuous in her servants, was about to hand him beef, made a desperate movement with her lips. 'No, Charles, not there, not there!'

The butler, tightening his lips, passed on. Mr Stone spoke:

'I had not considered that. She is rather of a Celtic than an Anglo-Saxon type; the cheek-bones are prominent; the jaw is not massive; the head is broad—if I can remember I will measure it; the eyes are of a peculiar blue, resembling chicory flowers; the mouth——' Mr Stone paused.

Cecilia thought: 'What a lucky find! Now perhaps he will go on all right!'

'I do not know,' Mr Stone resumed, speaking in a far-off voice, 'whether she would be virtuous.'

Cecilia heard Stephen drinking sherry; Thyme, too, was drinking something; she herself drank nothing, but, pink and quiet, for she was a well-bred woman, said:

'You have no new potatoes, dear. Charles, give Mr Stone some new potatoes.'

By the almost vindictive expression on Stephen's face she saw, however, that her failure had decided him to resume command of the situation. 'Talking of brotherhood, sir,' he said dryly, 'would you go so far as to say that a new potato is the brother of a bean?'

Mr Stone, on whose plate these two vegetables reposed, looked almost painfully confused.

'I do not perceive,' he stammered, 'any difference between them.'

'It's true,' said Stephen; 'the same pale spirit can be extracted from them both.'

Mr Stone looked up at him.

'You laugh at me,' he said. 'I cannot help it; but you must not laugh at life—that is blasphemy.'

Before the piercing wistfulness of that sudden gaze Stephen was abashed. Cecilia saw him bite his lower lip.

'We're talking too much,' he said; 'we really must let your father eat!' And the rest of the dinner was achieved in silence.

When Mr Stone, refusing to be accompanied, had taken his departure, and Thyme had gone to bed, Stephen withdrew to his study. This room, which had a different air from any other portion of the house, was sacred to his private life. Here, in specially designed compartments, he kept his golf clubs, pipes, and papers. Nothing was touched by anyone except himself, and twice a week by one peculiar housemaid. Here was no bust of Socrates, no books in deerskin bindings, but a bookcase filled with treatises on law, Blue Books, reviews, and the novels of Sir Walter Scott; two black oak cabinets stood side by side against the wall filled with small drawers. When these cabinets were opened and the drawers drawn forward there emerged a scent of metal polish. If the green-baize covers of the drawers were lifted, there were seen coins, carefully arranged with labels—as one may see plants growing in rows, each with its little name tied on. To these tidy rows of shining metal discs Stephen turned in moments when his spirit was fatigued. To add to them, touch them, read their names, gave him the sweet, secret feeling which comes to a man who rubs one hand against the other. Like a dram-drinker, Stephen drank—in little doses—of the feeling these coins gave him. They were his creative work, his history of the world. To them he gave that side of him which refused to find its full expression in summarising law, playing golf, or reading the reviews; that side of a man which aches, he knows not wherefore, to construct something ere he die. From Rameses to

George IV the coins lay within those drawers—links of the long unbroken chain of authority.

Putting on an old black velvet jacket laid out for him across a chair, and lighting the pipe that he could never bring himself to smoke in his formal dinner clothes, he went to the right-hand cabinet, and opened it. He stood with a smile, taking up coins one by one. In this particular drawer they were of the best Byzantine dynasty, very rare. He did not see that Cecilia had stolen in, and was silently regarding him. Her eyes seemed doubting at that moment whether or no she loved him who stood there touching that other mistress of his thoughts—that other mistress with whom he spent so many evening hours. The little green-baize cover fell. Cecilia said suddenly:

'Stephen, I feel as if I must tell father where that girl is!'

Stephen turned.

'My dear child,' he answered in his special voice, which, like champagne, seemed to have been dried by artifice, 'you don't want to reopen the whole thing?'

'But I can see he really is upset about it; he's looking so awfully white and thin.'

'He ought to give up that bathing in the Serpentine. At his age it's monstrous. And surely any other girl will do just as well?'

'He seems to set store by reading to her specially.'

Stephen shrugged his shoulders. It had happened to him on one occasion to be present when Mr Stone was declaiming some pages of his manuscript. He had never forgotten the discomfort of the experience. 'That crazy stuff,' as he had called it to Cecilia afterwards, had remained on his mind, heavy and damp, like a cold linseed poultice. His wife's father was a crank, and perhaps even a little more than a crank, a wee bit 'touched'—that *she* couldn't help, poor girl; but any allusion to his cranky produce gave Stephen pain. Nor had he forgotten his experience at dinner.

'He seems to have grown fond of her,' murmured Cecilia.

'But it's absurd at his time of life!'

'Perhaps that makes him feel it more; people do miss things when they are old!'

Stephen slid the drawer back into its socket. There was dry decision in that gesture.

'Look here! Let's exercise a little common sense; it's been sacrificed to sentiment all through this wretched business. One wants to be kind, of course; but one's got to draw the line.'

'Ah!' said Cecilia; 'where?'

'The thing,' went on Stephen, 'has been a mistake from first to last. It's all very well up to a certain point, but after that it becomes destructive of all comfort. It doesn't do to let these people come into personal contact with you. There are the proper channels for that sort of thing.'

Cecilia's eyes were lowered, as though she did not dare to let him see her thoughts.

'It seems so horrid,' she said; 'and father is not like other people.'

'He is not,' said Stephen dryly; 'we had a pretty good instance of that this evening. But Hilary and your sister are. There's something most distasteful to me, too, about Thyme's going about slumming. You see what she's been let in for this afternoon. The notion of that baby being killed through the man's treatment of his wife, and that, no doubt, arising from the girl's leaving them, is most repulsive!'

To these words Cecilia answered with a sound almost like a gasp. 'I hadn't thought of that. Then we're responsible; it was we who advised Hilary to make her change her lodging.'

Stephen stared; he regretted sincerely that his legal habit of mind had made him put the case so clearly.

'I can't imagine,' he said, almost violently, 'what possesses everybody! We—responsible! Good gracious! Because we gave Hilary some sound advice! What next?'

Cecilia turned to the empty hearth.

'Thyme has been telling me about that poor little thing. It seems so dreadful, and I can't get rid of the feeling that we're—we're all mixed up with it!'

'Mixed up with what?'

'I don't know; it's just a feeling like—like being haunted.'

Stephen took her quietly by the arm.

'My dear old girl,' he said, 'I'd no idea that you were run down like this. To-morrow's Thursday, and I can get away at three. We'll motor down to Richmond, and have a round or two!'

Cecilia quivered; for a moment it seemed that she was about to burst out crying. Stephen stroked her shoulder steadily. Cecilia must have felt his dread; she struggled loyally with her emotion.

'That will be very jolly,' she said at last.

Stephen drew a deep breath.

'And don't you worry, dear,' he said, 'about your dad; he'll have forgotten the whole thing in a day or two; he's far too wrapped up in his book. Now trot along to bed; I'll be up directly.'

Before going out Cecilia looked back at him. How wonderful was that look, which Stephen did not—perhaps intentionally—

see. Mocking, almost hating, and yet thanking him for having refused to let her be emotional and yield herself up for once to what she felt, showing him too how clearly she saw through his own masculine refusal to be made to feel, and how she half-admired it—all this was in that look, and more. Then she went out.

Stephen glanced quickly at the door, and, pursing up his lips, frowned. He threw the window open, and inhaled the night air. 'If I don't look out,' he thought, 'I shall be having her mixed up with this. I was an ass ever to have spoken to old Hilary. I ought to have ignored the matter altogether. It's a lesson not to meddle with people in those places. I hope to God she'll be herself to-morrow!'

Outside, under the soft black foliage of the Square, beneath the slim sickle of the moon, two cats were hunting after happiness; their savage cries of passion rang in the blossom-scented air like a cry of dark humanity in the jungle of dim streets. Stephen, with a shiver of disgust, for his nerves were on edge, shut the window with a slam.

Chapter 28

HILARY HEARS THE CUCKOO SING

IT was not left to Cecilia alone to remark how very white Mr Stone looked in these days.

The wild force which every year visits the world, driving with its soft violence snowy clouds and their dark shadows, breaking through all crusts and sheaths, covering the earth in a fierce embrace; the wild force which turns form to form, and with its million leapings, swift as the flight of swallows and the arrow-darts of the rain, hurries everything on to sweet mingling—this great, wild force of universal life, so-called the Spring, had come to Mr Stone, like new wine to some old bottle. And Hilary, to whom it had come, too, watching him every morning setting forth with a rough towel across his arm, wondered whether the old man would not this time leave his spirit swimming in the chill waters of the Serpentine—so near that spirit seemed to breaking through its fragile shell.

Four days had gone by since the interview at which he had sent away the little model, and life in his household—that quiet backwater choked with lilies—seemed to have resumed the tranquillity enjoyed before this intrusion of rude life. The paper whiteness of Mr Stone was the only patent evidence that anything disturbing had occurred—that and certain feelings about which the strictest silence was preserved.

On the morning of the fifth day, seeing the old man stumble on the level flagstones of the garden, Hilary finished dressing hastily, and followed. He overtook him walking forward feebly beneath the candelabra of flowering chestnut-trees, with a hail-shower striking white on his high shoulders; and, placing himself alongside, without greeting—for forms were all one to Mr Stone—he said:

'Surely you don't mean to bathe during a hail-storm, sir! Make an exception this once. You're not looking quite yourself.'

Mr Stone shook his head; then, evidently following out a thought which Hilary had interrupted, he remarked:

'The sentiment that men call honour is of doubtful value. I have not as yet succeeded in relating it to universal brotherhood.'

'How is that, sir?'

'In so far,' said Mr Stone, 'as it consists in fidelity to principle, one might assume it worthy of conjunction. The difficulty arises when we consider the nature of the principle. . . . There is a family of young thrushes in the garden. If one of them finds a worm, I notice that his devotion to that principle of self-preservation which prevails in all low forms of life forbids his sharing it with any of the other little thrushes.'

Mr Stone had fixed his eyes on distance.

'So it is, I fear,' he said, 'with "honour". In those days men looked on women as thrushes look on worms——'

He paused, evidently searching for a word; and Hilary, with a faint smile, said:

'And how did women look on men, sir?'

Mr Stone observed him with surprise. 'I did not perceive that it was you,' he said. 'I have to avoid brain action before bathing.'

They had crossed the road dividing the Gardens from the Park, and, seeing that Mr Stone had already seen the water where he was about to bathe, and would now see nothing else, Hilary stopped beside a little lonely birch-tree. This wild, small, graceful visitor, who had long bathed in winter, was already draping her bare limbs in a scarf of green. Hilary leaned against her cool, pearly body. Below were the chilly waters, now grey, now starch-blue, and the pale forms of fifteen or twenty bathers. While he stood shivering in the frozen wind, the sun, bursting through the hail-cloud, burned his cheeks and hands. And suddenly he heard, clear, but far off, the sound which, of all others, stirs the hearts of men: 'Cuckoo, cuckoo!'

Four times over came the unexpected call. Whence had that ill-advised, indelicate grey bird flown into this great haunt of men and shadows? Why had it come with its arrowy flight and mocking cry to pierce the heart and set it aching? There were trees enough outside the town, cloud-swept hollows, tangled brakes of furze just coming into bloom, where it could preside over the process of Spring. What solemn freak was this which made it come and sing to one who had no longer any business with the Spring?

With a real spasm in his heart Hilary turned away from that distant bird, and went down to the water's edge. Mr Stone was swimming, slower than man had ever swum before. His silver head and lean arms alone were visible, parting the water feebly; suddenly he disappeared. He was but a dozen yards from the shore; and Hilary, alarmed at not seeing him reappear, ran in. The water was not deep. Mr Stone, seated at the bottom, was doing all he could to rise. Hilary took him by his bathing-dress, raised him to the surface, and supported him towards the land. By the time they reached the shore he could just stand on his legs. With the assistance of a policeman, Hilary enveloped him in garments and got him to a cab. He had regained some of his vitality, but did not seem aware of what had happened.

'I was not in as long as usual,' he mused, as they passed out into the high road.

'Oh, I think so, sir.'

Mr Stone looked troubled.

'It is odd,' he said. 'I do not recollect leaving the water.'

He did not speak again till he was being assisted from the cab.

'I wish to recompense the man. I have half a crown indoors.'

'I will get it, sir,' said Hilary.

Mr Stone, who shivered violently now that he was on his feet, turned his face up to the cabman.

'Nothing is nobler than the horse,' he said; 'take care of him.'

The cabman removed his hat. 'I will, sir,' he answered.

Walking by himself, but closely watched by Hilary, Mr Stone reached his room. He groped about him as though not distinguishing objects too well through the crystal clearness of the fundamental flux.

'If I might advise you,' said Hilary, 'I would get back into bed for a few minutes. You seem a little chilly.'

Mr Stone, who was indeed shaking so that he could hardly

stand, allowed Hilary to assist him into bed and tuck the blankets round him.

'I must be at work by ten o'clock,' he said.

Hilary, who was also shivering, hastened to Bianca's room. She was just coming down, and exclaimed at seeing him all wet. When he had told her of the episode she touched his shoulder.

'What about you?'

'A hot bath and drink will set me right. You'd better go to *him*.'

He turned towards the bathroom, where Miranda stood, lifting a white foot. Compressing her lips, Bianca ran downstairs. Startled by his tale, she would have taken his wet body in her arms, if the ghosts of innumerable moments had not stood between. So this moment passed too, and itself became a ghost.

Mr Stone, greatly to his disgust, had not succeeded in resuming work at ten o'clock. Failing simply because he could not stand on his legs, he had announced his intention of waiting until half-past three, when he should get up, in preparation for the coming of the little girl. Having refused to see a doctor, or have his temperature taken, it was impossible to tell precisely what degree of fever he was in. In his cheeks, just visible over the blankets, there was more colour than there should have been; and his eyes, fixed on the ceiling, shone with suspicious brilliancy. To the dismay of Bianca—who sat as far out of sight as possible, lest he should see her, and fancy that she was doing him a service—he pursued his thoughts aloud:

'Words—words—they have taken away brotherhood!' Bianca shuddered, listening to that uncanny sound. '"In those days of words they called it death—*mors pallida*. They saw that word like a gigantic granite block suspended over them, and slowly coming down. Some, turning up their faces at the sight, trembled painfully, awaiting their obliteration. Others, unable, while they still lived, to face the thought of nothingness, inflated by some spiritual wind, and thinking always of their individual forms, called out unceasingly that those selves of theirs would and must survive this word—that in some fashion, which no man could understand, each self-conscious entity reaccumulated after distribution. Drunk with this thought, these, too, passed away. Some waited for it with grim, dry eyes, remarking that the process was molecular, and thus they also met their so-called death."'

His voice ceased, and in place of it rose the sound of his tongue moistening his palate. Bianca, from behind, placed a glass of barley-water to his lips. He drank it with a slow, clucking noise; then, seeing that a hand held the glass, said: 'Is that you? Are you ready for me? Follow. "In those days no one leaped up to meet pale riding Death; no one saw in her face that she was brotherhood incarnate; no one with a heart as light as gossamer kissed her feet, and, smiling, passed into the Universe."' His voice died away, and when next he spoke it was in a quick, husky whisper: 'I must—I must—I must——' There was silence; then he added: 'Give me my trousers.'

Bianca placed them by his bed. The sight seemed to reassure him. He was once more silent.

For more than an hour after this he was so absolutely still that Bianca rose continually to look at him. Each time, his eyes, wide open, were fixed on a little dark mark across the ceiling; his face had a look of the most singular determination, as though his spirit were slowly, relentlessly, regaining mastery over his fevered body. He spoke suddenly:

'Who is there?'

'Bianca.'

'Help me out of bed!'

The flush had left his face, the brilliance had faded from his eyes; he looked just like a ghost. With a sort of terror Bianca helped him out of bed. This weird display of mute white will-power was unearthly.

When he was dressed in his woollen gown and seated before the fire, she gave him a cup of strong beef-tea, with brandy. He swallowed it with great avidity.

'I should like some more of that,' he said, and fell asleep.

While he was asleep Cecilia came, and the two sisters watched his slumber, and, watching it, felt nearer to each other than they had for many years. Before she went away Cecilia whispered:

'B., if he seems to want that little girl while he's like this, don't you think she ought to come?'

Bianca answered: 'I don't know where she is.'

'I do.'

'Ah!' said Bianca; 'of course!' And she turned her head away.

Disconcerted by that sarcastic little speech, Cecilia was silent; then, summoning all her courage, she said:

'Here's the address, B. I've written it down for you;' and, with puckers of anxiety in her face, she left the room.

Bianca sat on in the old golden chair, watching the deep hollows beneath the sleeper's temples, the puffs of breath stirring the silver round his mouth. Her ears burned crimson. Carried out of herself by the sight of that old form, dearer to her than she had thought, fighting its great battle for the sake of its idea, her spirit grew all tremulous and soft within her. With eagerness she embraced the thought of self-effacement. It did not seem to matter whether she were first with Hilary. Her spirit should so manifest its capacity for sacrifice that she would be first with him through sheer nobility. At this moment she could almost have taken that common little girl into her arms and kissed her. So would all disquiet end! Some harmonious messenger had fluttered to her for a second—the gold-winged bird of peace. In this sensuous exaltation her nerves vibrated like the strings of a violin.

When Mr Stone woke it was past three o'clock, and Bianca at once handed him another cup of strong beef-tea.

He swallowed it, and said: 'What is this?'

'Beef-tea.'

Mr Stone looked at the empty cup.

'I must not drink it. The cow and the sheep are on the same plane as man.'

'But how do you feel, dear?'

'I feel,' said Mr Stone, 'able to dictate what I have already written—not more. Has she come?'

'Not yet; but I will go and find her if you like.'

Mr Stone looked at his daughter wistfully.

'That will be taking up your time,' he said.

Bianca answered: 'My time is of no consequence.'

Mr Stone stretched his hands out to the fire.

'I will not consent,' he said, evidently to himself, 'to be a drag on anyone. If that has come, then I must go!'

Bianca, placing herself beside him on her knees, pressed her hot cheek against his temple.

'But it has *not* come, Dad.'

'I hope not,' said Mr Stone. 'I wish to end my book first.'

The sudden grim coherence of his last two sayings terrified Bianca more than all his feverish utterances.

'I rely on your sitting quite still,' she said, 'while I go and find her.' And with a feeling in her heart as though two hands had seized and were pulling it asunder, she went out.

Some half-hour later Hilary slipped quietly in, and stood watching at the door. Mr Stone, seated on the very verge of his armchair, with his hands on its arms, was slowly rising to his feet, and slowly falling back again, not once, but many times, practising a standing posture. As Hilary came into his line of sight, he said:

'I have succeeded twice.'

'I am very glad,' said Hilary. 'Won't you rest now, sir?'

'It is my knees,' said Mr Stone. 'She has gone to find her.'

Hilary heard those words with bewilderment, and, sitting down on the other chair, waited.

'I have fancied,' said Mr Stone, looking at him wistfully, 'that when we pass away from life we may become the wind. Is that your opinion?'

'It is a new thought to me,' said Hilary.

'It is not tenable,' said Mr Stone. 'But it is restful. The wind is everywhere and nowhere, and nothing can be hidden from it. When I have missed that little girl, I have tried, in a sense, to become the wind; but I have found it difficult.'

His eyes left Hilary's face, whose mournful smile he had not noticed, and fixed themselves on the bright fire. '"In those days,"' he said '"men's relation to the eternal airs was the relation of a billion little separate draughts blowing against the south-west wind. They did not wish to merge themselves in that soft, moon-uttered sigh, but blew in its face through crevices, and cracks, and keyholes, and were borne away on the pellucid journey, whistling out their protests."'

He again tried to stand, evidently wishing to get to his desk to record this thought, but, failing, looked painfully at Hilary. He seemed about to ask for something, but checked himself.

'If I practise hard,' he murmured, 'I shall master it.'

Hilary rose and brought him paper and a pencil. In bending, he saw that Mr Stone's eyes were dim with moisture. This sight affected him so that he was glad to turn away and fetch a book to form a writing-pad.

When Mr Stone had finished, he sat back in his chair with closed eyes. A supreme silence reigned in the bare room above those two men of different generations and of such strange dissimilarity of character. Hilary broke that silence.

'I heard the cuckoo sing to-day,' he said, almost in a whisper, lest Mr Stone should be asleep.

'The cuckoo,' replied Mr Stone, 'has no sense of brotherhood.'

'I forgive him—for his song,' murmured Hilary.

'His song,' said Mr Stone, 'is alluring; it excites the sexual instinct.'

Then to himself he added:

'She has not come, as yet!'

Even as he spoke there was heard by Hilary a faint tapping on the door. He rose and opened it. The little model stood outside.

Chapter 29

RETURN OF THE LITTLE MODEL

THAT same afternoon in High Street, Kensington, 'Westminister', with his coat-collar raised against the inclement wind, his old hat spotted with rain, was drawing at a clay pipe and fixing his iron-rimmed gaze on those who passed him by. It had been a day when singularly few as yet had bought from him his faintly green-tinged journal, and the low class of fellow who sold the other evening prints had peculiarly exasperated him. His single mind, always torn to some extent between an ingrained loyalty to his employers and those politics of his which differed from his paper's, had vented itself twice since coming on his stand; once in these words to the seller of 'Pell Mells': 'I stupulated with you not to come beyond the lamp-post. Don't you never speak to me again—a-crowdin' of me off my stand'; and once to the younger vendors of the less expensive journals, thus: 'Oh, you boys! I'll make you regret of it—a-snappin' up my customers under my very nose! Wait until ye're old!' To which the boys had answered: 'All right, daddy; don't you have a fit. You'll be a deader soon enough without that, y'know!'

It was now his time for tea, but 'Pell Mell' having gone to partake of this refreshment, he waited on, hoping against hope to get a customer or two of that low fellow's. And while in blank insulation he stood there a timid voice said at his elbow:

'Mr Creed!'

The aged butler turned, and saw the little model.

'Oh,' he said dryly, 'it's you, is it?' His mind, with its incessant love of rank, knowing that she earned her living as a handmaid to that disorderly establishment, the House of Art, had from the first classed her as lower than a lady's-maid. Recent events had made him think of her unkindly. Her new clothes, which he had not been privileged to see before, while giving him a sense of Sunday, deepened his moral doubts.

'And where are you living now?' he said in tones incorporating these feelings.

'I'm not to tell you.'

'Oh, very well. Keep yourself to yourself.'

The little model's lower lip drooped more than ever. There were dark marks beneath her eyes; her face was altogether rather pinched and pitiful.

'Won't you tell me any news?' she said in her matter-of-fact voice.

The old butler gave a strange grunt.

'Ho!' he said. 'The baby's dead, and buried to-morrer.'

'Dead!' repeated the little model.

'I'm a-goin' to the funeral—Brompton Cemetery. Half-past nine I leave the door. And that's a-beginnin' at the end. The man's in prison, and the woman's gone a shadder of herself.'

The little model rubbed her hands against her skirt.

'What did he go to prison for?'

'For assaultin' of her; I was witness to his battery.'

'Why did he assault her?'

Creed looked at her, and, wagging his head, answered:

'That's best known to them as caused of it.'

The little model's face went the colour of carnations.

'I can't help what he does,' she said. 'What should *I* want him for—a man like that? It wouldn't be *him* I'd want!' The genuine contempt in that sharp burst of anger impressed the aged butler.

'I'm not a-sayin' anything,' he said; 'it's all a-one to me. I never mixes up with no other people's business. But it's very ill-convenient. I don't get my proper breakfast. That poor woman—she's half off her head. When the baby's buried I'll have to go and look out for another room before he gets a-comin' out.'

'I hope they'll keep him there,' muttered the little model suddenly.

'They give him a month,' said Creed.

'Only a month!'

The old butler looked at her. 'There's more stuff in you,' he seemed to say, 'than ever I had thought.'

'Because of his servin' of his country,' he remarked aloud.

'I'm sorry about the poor little baby,' said the little model in her stolid voice.

'Westminister' shook his head. 'I never suspected *him* of goin' to live,' he said.

The girl, biting the finger-tip of her white cotton glove, was staring out at the traffic. Like a pale ray of light entering the now dim cavern of the old man's mind, the thought came to Creed that he did not quite understand her. He had in his time had occasion to class many young persons, and the feeling that he did not quite know her class of person was like the sensation a bat might have, surprised by daylight.

Suddenly, without saying good-bye to him, she walked away.

'Well,' he thought, looking after her, 'your manners ain't improved by where you're living, nor your apperiance neither, for all your new clothes.' And for some time he stood thinking of the stare in her eyes and that abrupt departure.

Through the crystal clearness of the fundamental flux the mind could see at the same moment Bianca leaving her front gate.

Her sensuous exaltation, her tremulous longing after harmony, had passed away; in her heart, strangely mingled, were these two thoughts: 'If only she were a lady!' and, 'I am glad she is not a lady!'

Of all the dark and tortuous places of this life the human heart is the most dark and tortuous; and of all human hearts none are less clear, more intricate, than the hearts of all that class of people among whom Bianca had her being. Pride was a simple quality when joined with a simple view of life, based on the plain philosophy of property; pride was no simple quality when the hundred paralysing doubts and aspirations of a social conscience also hedged it round. In thus going forth with the full intention of restoring the little model to her position in the household, her pride fought against her pride, and her woman's sense of ownership in the man whom she had married wrestled with the acquired sentiments of freedom, liberality, equality, good taste. With her spirit thus confused, and her mind so at variance with itself, she was really acting on the simple instinct of compassion.

She had run upstairs from Mr Stone's room, and now walked fast, lest that instinct, the most physical, perhaps, of all—awakened by sights and sounds, and requiring constant nourishment—should lose its force.

Rapidly, then, she made her way to the grey street in Bayswater where Cecilia had told her that the girl now lived.

The tall, gaunt landlady admitted her.

'Have you a Miss Barton lodging here?' Bianca asked.

'Yes,' said the landlady, 'but I think she's out.'

She looked into the little model's room.

'Yes,' she said, 'she's out; but if you'd like to leave a note you could write in here. If you're looking for a model, she wants work, I believe.'

That modern faculty of pressing on an aching nerve was

assuredly not lacking to Bianca. To enter the girl's room was jabbing at the nerve indeed.

She looked round her. The mental vacuity of that little room! There was not one single thing—with the exception of a torn copy of *Tit-Bits*—which suggested that a mind of any sort lived there. For all that, perhaps because of that, it was neat enough.

'Yes,' said the landlady, 'she keeps her room tidy. Of course, she's a country girl—comes from down my way.' She said this with a dry twist of her grim, but not unkindly, features. 'If it weren't for that,' she went on, 'I don't think I should care to let to one of her profession.'

Her hungry eyes, gazing at Bianca, had in them the aspirations of all Nonconformity.

Bianca pencilled on her card:

'If you can come to my father to-day or to-morrow, please do.'

'Will you give her this, please? It will be quite enough.'

'I'll give it her,' the landlady said; 'she'll be glad of it, I daresay. I see her sitting here. Girls like that, if they've got nothing to do—see, she's been moping on her bed. . . .'

The impress of a form was, indeed, clearly visible on the red and yellow tasselled tapestry of the bed.

Bianca cast a look at it.

'Thank you,' she said; 'good day.'

With the jabbed nerve aching badly she came slowly homewards.

Before the garden gate the little model herself was gazing at the house, as if she had been there some time. Approaching from across the road, Bianca had an admirable view of that young figure, now very trim and neat, yet with something in its lines—more graceful, perhaps, but less refined—which proclaimed her not a lady; a something fundamentally undisciplined or disciplined by the material facts of life alone, rather than by a secret creed of voluntary rules. It showed here and there in ways women alone could understand; above all, in the way her eyes looked out on that house which she was clearly longing to enter. Not 'Shall I go in?' was in that look, but 'Dare I go in?'

Suddenly she saw Bianca. The meeting of these two was very like the ordinary meeting of a mistress and her maid. Bianca's face had no expression, except the faint, distant curiosity which seems to say: 'You are a sealed book to me; I have always found you so. What you really think and do I shall never know.'

The little model's face wore a half-caught-out, half-stolid look.

'Please go in,' Bianca said; 'my father will be glad to see you.'

She held the garden gate open for the girl to pass through. Her feeling at that moment was one of slight amusement at the futility of her journey. Not even this small piece of generosity was permitted her, it seemed.

'How are you getting on?'

The little model made an impulsive movement at such an unexpected question. Checking it at once, she answered:

'Very well, thank you; that is, not very——'

'You will find my father tired to-day; he has caught a chill. Don't let him read too much, please.'

The little model seemed to try and nerve herself to make some statement, but failing, passed into the house.

Bianca did not follow, but stole back into the garden, where the sun was still falling on a bed of wallflowers at the far end. She bent down over these flowers till her veil touched them. Two wild bees were busy there, buzzing with smoky wings, clutching with their black, tiny legs at the orange petals, plunging their black, tiny tongues far down into the honeyed centres. The flowers quivered beneath the weight of their small dark bodies. Bianca's face quivered too, bending close to them, nor making the slightest difference to their hunt.

Hilary, who, as it has been seen, lived in thoughts about events rather than in events themselves, and to whom crude acts and words had little meaning save in relation to what philosophy could make of them, greeted the girl's appearance in the corridor outside Mr Stone's apartment with a startled face. But the little model, who mentally lived very much from hand to mouth, and had only the philosophy of wants, acted differently. She knew that for the last five days, like a spaniel dog shut away from where it feels it ought to be, she had wanted to be where she was now standing; she knew that, in her new room with its rust-red doors, she had bitten her lips and fingers till blood came, and, as newly caged birds will flutter, had beaten her wings against those walls with blue roses on a yellow ground. She remembered how she had lain, brooding, on that piece of red and yellow tapestry, twisting its tassels, staring through half-closed eyes at nothing.

There was something different in her look at Hilary. It had lost some of its childish devotion; it was bolder, as if she had lived and felt, and brushed a good deal more down off her wings during those few days.

'Mrs Dallison told me to come,' she said. 'I thought I might. Mr Creed told me about *him* being in prison.'

Hilary made way for her, and, following her into Mr Stone's presence, shut the door.

'The truant has returned,' he said.

Hearing herself called so unjustly by that name, the little model flushed deeply, and tried to speak. She stopped at the smile on Hilary's face, and gazed from him to Mr Stone and back again, the victim of mingled feelings.

Mr Stone was seen to have risen to his feet, and to be very slowly moving towards his desk. He leaned both arms on his papers for support, and, seeming to gather strength, began sorting out his manuscript.

Through the open window the distant music of a barrel-organ came drifting in. Faint, and much too slow, was the sound of the waltz it played, but there was invitation, allurement, in that tune. The little model turned towards it, and Hilary looked hard at her. The girl and that sound together—there, quite plain, was the music he had heard for many days, like a man lying with the touch of fever on him.

'Are you ready?' said Mr Stone.

The little model dipped her pen in ink. Her eyes crept towards the door, where Hilary was still standing with the same expression on his face. He avoided her eyes, and went up to Mr Stone.

'Must you read to-day, sir?'

Mr Stone looked at him with anger.

'Why not?' he said.

'You are hardly strong enough.'

Mr Stone raised his manuscript.

'We are three days behind;' and very slowly he began dictating: ' "Bar-ba-rous ha-bits in those days, such as the custom known as War——" ' His voice died away; it was apparent that his elbows, leaning on the desk, alone prevented his collapse.

Hilary moved the chair, and, taking him beneath the arms, lowered him gently into it.

Noticing that he was seated, Mr Stone raised his manuscript and read on: ' "—were pursued regardless of fraternity. It was as though a herd of horn-èd cattle driven through green pastures to that Gate, where they must meet with certain dissolution, had set about to prematurely gore and disembowel each other, out of a passionate devotion to those individual shapes which they were so soon to lose. So men—tribe against tribe, and country against country—glared across the valleys with their ensanguined eyes; they could not see the moonlit wings, or feel the embalming airs of brotherhood." '

Slower and slower came his sentences, and as the last word died away he was heard to be asleep, breathing through a tiny hole left beneath the eave of his moustache. Hilary, who had waited for that moment, gently put the manuscript on the desk, and beckoned to the girl. He did not ask her to his study, but spoke to her in the hall.

'While Mr Stone is like this he misses you. You will come, then, at present, please, so long as Hughs is in prison. How do you like your room?'

The little model answered simply: 'Not very much.'

'Why not?'

'It's lonely there. I shan't mind, now I'm coming here again.'

'Only for the present,' was all Hilary could find to say.

The little model's eyes were lowered.

'Mrs Hughs' baby's to be buried to-morrow,' she said suddenly.

'Where?'

'In Brompton Cemetery. Mr Creed's going.

'What time is the funeral?'

The girl looked up stealthily.

'Mr Creed's going to start at half-past nine.'

'I should like to go myself,' said Hilary.

A gleam of pleasure passing across her face was instantly obscured behind the cloud of her stolidity. Then, as she saw Hilary move nearer to the door, her lip began to droop.

'Well, good-bye,' he said.

The little model flushed and quivered. 'You don't even look at me,' she seemed to say: 'you haven't spoken kindly to me once.' And suddenly she said in a hard voice:

'Now I shan't go to Mr Lennard's any more.'

'Oh, then you have been to him!'

Triumph at attracting his attention, fear of what she had admitted, supplication, and a half-defiant shame—all this was in her face.

'Yes,' she said.

Hilary did not speak.

'I didn't care any more when you told me I wasn't to come here.'

Still Hilary did not speak.

'I haven't done anything wrong,' she said, with tears in her voice.

'No no,' said Hilary; 'of course not!'

The little model choked.

'It's my profession.'

'Yes, yes,' said Hilary; 'it's all right.'

'I don't care what he thinks; I won't go again so long as I can come here.'

Hilary touched her shoulder.

'Well, well,' he said, and opened the front door.

The little model, tremulous, like a flower kissed by the sun after rain, went out with a light in her eyes.

The master of the house returned to Mr Stone. Long he sat looking at the old man's slumber. 'A thinker meditating upon action!' So might Hilary's figure, with its thin face resting on its hand, a furrow between the brows, and that painful smile, have been entitled in any catalogue of statues.

Chapter 30

FUNERAL OF A BABY

FOLLOWING out the instinct planted so deeply in human nature for treating with the utmost care and at great expense when dead those, who, when alive, have been served with careless parsimony, there started from the door of No. I in Hound Street a funeral procession of three four-wheeled cabs.

The first bore the little coffin, on which lay a great white wreath (gift of Cecilia and Thyme). The second bore Mrs Hughs, her son Stanley, and Joshua Creed. The third bore Martin Stone.

In the first cab Silence was presiding with the scent of lilies over him who in his short life had made so little noise, the small grey shadow that had crept so quietly into being, and, taking his chance when he was not noticed, had crept so quietly out again. Never had he felt so restful, so much at home, as in that little common coffin, washed as he was to an unnatural whiteness, and wrapped in his mother's only spare sheet. Away from all the strife of men he was journeying to a greater peace. His little aloe-plant had flowered; and, between the open windows of the only carriage he had ever been inside, the wind—which, who knows? he had perhaps become—stirred the fronds of fern and the flowers of his funeral wreath. Thus he was going from that world where all men were his brothers.

From the second cab the same wind was rigidly excluded, and

there was silence, broken by the aged butler's breathing. Dressed in his Newmarket coat, he was recalling with a certain sense of luxury past journeys in four-wheeled cabs—occasions when, seated beside a box corded and secured with sealing-wax, he had taken his master's plate for safety to the bank; occasions when, under a roof piled up with guns and boxes, he had sat holding the 'Honorable Bateson's' dog; occasions when, with some young person by his side, he had driven at the tail of a baptismal, nuptial or funeral cortège. These memories of past grandeur came back to him with curious poignancy, and for some reason the words kept rising in his mind: 'For richer for poorer, for better for worser, in health and in sick places, till death do us part.' But in the midst of the exaltation of these recollections the old heart beneath his old red flannel chest-protector—that companion of his exile—twittering faintly at short intervals, made him look at the woman by his side. He longed to convey to her some little of the satisfaction he felt in the fact that this was by no means the low class of funeral it might have been. He doubted whether, with her woman's mind, she was getting all the comfort she could out of three four-wheeled cabs and a wreath of lilies. The seamstress's thin face, with its pinched, passive look, was indeed thinner, quieter, than ever. What she was thinking of he could not tell. There were so many things she might be thinking of. She, too, no doubt, had seen her grandeur, if but in the solitary drive away from the church where, eight years ago, she and Hughs had listened to the words now haunting Creed. Was she thinking of that; of her lost youth and comeliness, and her man's dead love; of the long descent to shadowland; of the other children she had buried; of Hughs in prison; of the girl that had 'put a spell on him'; or only of the last precious tugs the tiny lips at rest in the first four-wheeled cab had given at her breast? Or was she, with a nicer feeling for proportion, reflecting that, had not people been so kind, she might have had to walk behind a funeral provided by the parish?

The old butler could not tell, but he—whose one desire now, coupled with the wish to die outside a workhouse, was to save enough to bury his own body without the interference of other people—was inclined to think she must be dwelling on the brighter side of things; and, designing to encourage her, he said: 'Wonderful improvement in these 'ere four-wheel cabs! Oh dear, yes! I remember of them when they were the shadders of what they are at the present time of speakin'.'

The seamstress answered in her quiet voice: 'Very comfortable this is. Sit still, Stanley!' Her little son, whose feet did not reach the floor, was drumming his heels against the seat. He stopped and looked at her, and the old butler addressed him.

'You'll a-remember of this occasion,' he said, 'when you gets older.'

The little boy turned his black eyes from his mother to him who had spoken last.

'It's a beautiful wreath,' continued Creed. 'I could smell of it all the way up the stairs. There's been no expense spared; there's white laylock in it—that's a class of flower that's very extravagant.'

A train of thought having been roused too strong for his discretion, he added: 'I saw that young girl yesterday. She came interrogatin' of me in the street.'

On Mrs Hughs' face, where till now expression had been buried, came such a look as one may see on the face of an owl—hard, watchful, cruel; harder, more cruel, for the softness of the big dark eyes.

'She'd show a better feeling,' she said, 'to keep a quiet tongue. Sit still, Stanley!'

Once more the little boy stopped drumming his heels, and shifted his stare from the old butler back to her who spoke. The cab, which had seemed to hesitate and start, as though jibbing at something in the road, resumed its ambling pace. Creed looked through the well-closed window. There before him, so long that it seemed to have no end, like a building in a nightmare, stretched that place where he did not mean to end his days. He faced towards the horse again. The colour had deepened in his nose. He spoke:

'If they'd a-give me my last edition earlier, 'stead of sending of it down after that low-class feller's taken all my customers, that'd make a difference to me o' two shillin's at the utmost in the week, and all clear savin's.' To these words, dark with hidden meaning, he received no answer save the drumming of the small boy's heels; and, reverting to the subject he had been distracted from, he murmured: 'She was a-wearin' of new clothes.'

He was startled by the fierce tone of a voice he hardly knew. 'I don't want to hear about her; she's not for decent folk to talk of.'

The old butler looked round askance. The seamstress was trembling violently. Her fierceness at such a moment shocked him. 'Dust to dust,' he thought.

'Don't you be considerate of it,' he said at last, summoning all his knowledge of the world; 'she'll come to her own place.' And at the sight of a slow tear trickling over her burning cheek, he added hurriedly: 'Think of your baby—I'll see yer through. Sit still, little boy—sit still! Ye're disturbin' of your mother.'

Once more the little boy stayed the drumming of his heels to look at him who spoke; and the closed cab rolled on with its slow, jingling sound.

In the third four-wheeled cab, where the windows again were wide open, Martin Stone, with his hands thrust deep into the pockets of his coat, and his long legs crossed, sat staring at the roof, with a sort of twisted scorn on his pale face.

Just inside the gate, through which had passed in their time so many dead and living shadows, Hilary stood waiting. He could probably not have explained why he had come to see this tiny shade committed to the earth—in memory, perhaps, of those two minutes when the baby's eyes had held parley with his own, or in the wish to pay a mute respect to her on whom life had weighed so hard of late. For whatever reason he had come, he was keeping quietly to one side. And unobserved, he, too, had his watcher—the little model, sheltering behind a tall grave.

Two men in rusty black bore the little coffin; then came the white-robed chaplain; then Mrs Hughs and her little son; close behind, his head thrust forward with trembling movements from side to side, old Creed; and, last of all, young Martin Stone. Hilary joined the young doctor. So the five mourners walked.

Before a small dark hole in a corner of the cemetery they stopped. On this forest of unflowered graves the sun was falling; the east wind, with its faint reek, touched the old butler's plastered hair, and brought moisture to the corners of his eyes, fixed with absorption on the chaplain. Words and thoughts hunted in his mind.

'He's gettin' Christian burial. Who gives this woman away? I do. Ashes to ashes. I never suspected him of livin'.' The conning of the burial service, shortened to fit the passing of that tiny shade, gave him pleasurable sensation; films came down on his eyes; he listened like some old parrot on its perch, his head a little to one side.

'Them as dies young,' he thought, 'goes straight to heaven. We trusts in God—all mortial men; his godfathers and his godmothers in his baptism. Well, so it is! *I'm* not afeared o' death!'

Seeing the little coffin tremble above the hole, he craned his head still further forward. It sank; a smothered sobbing rose. The old butler touched the arm in front of him with shaking fingers.

'Don't 'e,' he whispered; 'he's a-gone to glory.'

But, hearing the dry rattle of the earth, he took out his own handkerchief and put it to his nose.

'Yes, he's a-gone,' he thought; 'another little baby. Old men an' maidens, young men an' little children; it's a-goin' on all the time. Where 'e is now there'll be no marryin', no, nor givin' out in marriage; till death do us part.'

The wind, sweeping across the filled-in hole, carried the rustle of his husky breathing, the dry, smothered sobbing of the seamstress, out across the shadows' graves, to those places, to those streets. . . .

From the baby's funeral Hilary and Martin walked away together, and far behind them, across the road, the little model followed. For some time neither spoke; then Hilary, stretching out his hand towards a squalid alley, said:

'They haunt us and drag us down. A long, dark passage. Is there a light at the far end, Martin?'

'Yes,' said Martin gruffly.

'I don't see it.'

Martin looked at him.

'Hamlet!'

Hilary did not reply.

The young man watched him sideways. 'It's a disease to smile like that!'

Hilary ceased to smile. 'Cure me, then,' he said, with sudden anger, 'you man of health!'

The young 'Sanitist's' sallow cheeks flushed. 'Atrophy of the nerve of action,' he muttered; 'there's no cure for that!'

'Ah!' said Hilary: 'All kinds of us want social progress in our different ways. You, your grandfather, my brother, myself; there are four types for you. Will you tell me any one of us is the right man for the job? For instance, action's not natural to me.'

'Any act,' answered Martin, 'is better than no act.'

'And myopia is natural to you, Martin. Your prescription in this case has not been too successful, has it?'

'I can't help it if people will be d—d fools.'

'There you hit it. But answer me this question: Isn't a social conscience, broadly speaking, the result of comfort and security?'

Martin shrugged his shoulders.

'And doesn't comfort also destroy the power of action?'

Again Martin shrugged.

'Then, if those who have the social conscience and can see what is wrong have lost their power of action, how can you say there is any light at the end of this dark passage?'

Martin took his pipe out, filled it, and pressed the filling with his thumb.

'There *is* light,' he said at last, 'in spite of all invertebrates. Good-bye! I've wasted enough time,' and he abruptly strode away.

'And in spite of myopia?' muttered Hilary.

A few minutes later, coming out from Messrs Rose and Thorn's, where he had gone to buy tobacco, he came suddenly on the little model, evidently waiting.

'I was at the funeral,' she said; and her face added plainly: 'I've followed you.' Uninvited, she walked on at his side.

'This is not the same girl,' he thought, 'that I sent away five days ago. She has lost something, gained something. I don't know her.'

There seemed such a stubborn purpose in her face and manner. It was like the look in a dog's eyes that says: 'Master, you thought to shut me away from you; I know now what that is like. Do what you will, I mean in future to be near you.'

This look, by its simplicity, frightened one to whom the primitive was strange. Desiring to free himself of his companion, yet not knowing how, Hilary sat down in Kensington Gardens on the first bench they came to. The little model sat down beside him. The quiet siege laid to him by this girl was quite uncanny. It was as though someone were binding him with toy threads, swelling slowly into rope before his eyes. In this fear of Hilary's there was at first much irritation. His fastidiousness and sense of the ridiculous were roused. What did this little creature with whom he had no thoughts and no ideas in common, whose spirit and his could never hope to meet, think that she could get from him? Was she trying to weave a spell over him too, with her mute, stubborn adoration? Was she trying to change his protective weakness for her to another sort of weakness? He turned and looked; she dropped her eyes at once, and sat still as a stone figure.

As in her spirit, so in her body, she was different; her limbs looked freer, rounder; her breath seemed stirring her more deeply; like a flower of early June she was opening before his very eyes. This, though it gave him pleasure, also added to his fear. The strange silence, in its utter naturalness—for what could he talk about with her?—brought home to him more vividly than anything before, the barriers of class. All he thought of was how not to be ridiculous! She was inviting him in some strange, unconscious, subtle way to treat her as a woman, as though in spirit she had linked her round young arms about his neck, and through her half-closed lips were whispering the eternal call of sex to sex. And he, a middle-aged and cultivated man, conscious of everything, could not even speak for fear of breaking through his shell of delicacy. He hardly breathed, disturbed to his very depths by the young figure sitting by his side, and by the dread of showing that disturbance.

Beside the cultivated plant the self-sown poppy rears itself; round the stem of a smooth tree the honeysuckle twines; to a trim wall the ivy clings.

In her new-found form and purpose this girl had gained a strange, still power; she no longer felt it mattered whether he spoke or looked at her; her instinct, piercing through his shell, was certain of the throbbing of his pulses, the sweet poison in his blood.

The perception of this still power, more than all else, brought fear to Hilary. He need not speak; she would not care! He need not even look at her; she had but to sit there silent, motionless, with the breath of youth coming through her parted lips, and the light of youth stealing through her half-closed eyes.

And abruptly he got up and walked away.

Chapter 31

SWAN SONG

THE new wine, if it does not break the old bottle, after fierce effervescence seethes and bubbles quietly.

It was so in Mr Stone's old bottle, hour by hour and day by day, throughout the month. A pinker, robuster look came back to his cheeks; his blue eyes, fixed on distance, had in them more light; his knees regained their powers; he bathed, and, all unknown to him, for he only saw the waters he cleaved with his ineffably slow stroke, Hilary and Martin, on alternate weeks, and keeping at a proper distance, for fear he should see them doing him a service, attended at that function in case Mr Stone should again remain too long seated at the bottom of the Serpentine. Each morning after his cocoa and porridge he could be heard sweeping out his room with extraordinary vigour, and as ten o'clock came near anyone who listened would remark a sound of air escaping, as he moved up and down on his toes in preparation for the labours of the day. No letters, of course, nor any newspapers disturbed the supreme and perfect self-containment of this life devoted to Fraternity—no letters, partly because he lacked a known address, partly because for years he had not answered them; and with regard to newspapers, once a month he went to a Public Library, and could be seen with the last four numbers of two weekly reviews before him, making himself acquainted with the habits of those days, and moving his lips as though in prayer. At ten each morning anyone in the corridor outside his room was startled by the whirr of an alarum clock; perfect silence followed; then rose a sound of shuffling, whistling, rustling, broken by sharply muttered words; soon from this turbid lake of sound the articulate, thin fluting of an old man's voice streamed forth. This, alternating with the squeak of a quill pen, went on till the alarum clock once more went off. Then he who stood outside could smell that Mr Stone would shortly eat; if, stimulated by that scent, he entered, he might see the author of the 'Book of Universal Brotherhood' with a baked potato in one hand and a cup of hot milk in the other; on the table, too, the ruined forms of eggs, tomatoes, oranges, bananas, figs, prunes, cheese, and honeycomb, which had passed into other forms already, together with a loaf of wholemeal bread. Mr Stone would presently emerge in his cottage-woven tweeds, and old hat of green-black felt; or, if wet, in a long coat of yellow gaberdine, and sou'-wester cap of the same material; but always with a little osier fruit-bag in his hand. Thus equipped, he walked down to Rose and Thorn's, entered, and to the first man he saw handed the osier fruit-bag, some coins, and a little book containing seven leaves, headed 'Food: Monday, Tuesday, Wednesday', and so forth. He then stood looking through the pickles in some jar or other at things beyond, with one hand held out, fingers upwards, awaiting the return of his little osier fruit-bag. Feeling presently that it had been restored to him, he would turn and walk out of the shop. Behind his back, on the face of the department, the same protecting smile always rose. Long habit had perfected it. All now felt that, though so very different from themselves, this aged customer was dependent on them. By not one single farthing or one pale slip of cheese would they have defrauded him for all the treasures of the moon, and any new salesman who laughed at that old client was promptly told to 'shut his head'.

Mr Stone's frail form, bent somewhat to one side by the increased gravamen of the osier bag, was now seen moving homewards. He arrived perhaps ten minutes before the three o'clock alarum, and soon passing through preliminary chaos, the articulate, thin fluting of his voice streamed forth again, broken by the squeaking and spluttering of his quill.

But towards four o'clock signs of cerebral excitement became visible; his lips would cease to utter sounds, his pen to squeak. His face, with a flushed forehead, would appear at the open window. As soon as the little model came in sight—her eyes fixed, not on his window, but on Hilary's—he turned his back, evidently waiting for her to enter by the door. His first words were uttered in a tranquil voice: 'I have several pages. I have placed your chair. Are you ready? Follow!'

Except for that strange tranquillity of voice and the disappearance of the flush on his brow, there was no sign of the rejuvenescence that she brought, of such refreshment as steals on the traveller who sits down beneath a lime-tree towards the end of a long day's journey; no sign of the mysterious comfort distilled into his veins by the sight of her moody young face, her young, soft limbs. So from some stimulant men very near their end will draw energy, watching, as it were, a shape beckoning them forward, till suddenly it disappears in darkness.

In the quarter of an hour sacred to their tea and conversation he never noticed that she was always listening for sounds beyond; it was enough that in her presence he felt singleness of purpose strong within him.

When she had gone, moving languidly, moodily away, her eyes darting about for signs of Hilary, Mr Stone would sit down rather suddenly and fall asleep, to dream, perhaps, of Youth—Youth with its scent of sap, its close beckonings; Youth with its hopes and fears; Youth that hovers round us so long after it is dead! His spirit would smile behind its covering—that thin china of his face; and, as dogs hunting in their sleep work their feet, so he worked the fingers resting on his woollen knees.

The seven o'clock alarum woke him to the preparation of the evening meal. This eaten, he began once more to pace up and down, to pour words out into the silence, and to drive his squeaking quill.

So was being written a book such as the world had never seen!

But the girl who came so moodily to bring him refreshment, and went so moodily away, never in these days caught a glimpse of that which she was seeking.

Since the morning when he had left her abruptly, Hilary had made a point of being out in the afternoons and not returning till past six o'clock. By this device he put off facing her and himself, for he could no longer refuse to see that he had himself to face. In the few minutes of utter silence when the girl sat beside him, magnetic, quivering with awakening force, he had found that the male in him was far from dead. It was no longer vague, sensuous feeling; it was warm, definite desire. The more she was in his thoughts, the less spiritual his feeling for this girl of the people had become.

In those days he seemed much changed to such as knew him well. Instead of the delicate, detached, slightly humorous suavity which he had accustomed people to expect from him, the dry kindliness which seemed at once to check confidence and yet to say, 'If you choose to tell me anything, I should never think of passing judgment on you, whatever you have done'—instead of that rather abstracted, faintly quizzical air, his manner had become absorbed and gloomy. He seemed to jib away from his friends. His manner at the 'Pen and Ink' was wholly unsatisfying to men who liked to talk. He was known to be writing a new book; they suspected him of having 'got into a hat'—this Victorian expression, found by Mr Balladyce in some chronicle of post-Thackerayan manners, and revived by him in his incomparable way, as who should say, 'What delicious expressions those good bourgeois had!' now flourished in second childhood.

In truth, Hilary's difficulty with his new book was merely the one of not being able to work at it at all. Even the housemaid who 'did' his study noticed that day after day she was confronted by Chapter XXIV, in spite of her master's staying in, as usual, every morning.

The change in his manner and face, which had grown strained and harassed, had been noticed by Bianca, though she would have died sooner than admit she had noticed anything about him. It was one of those periods in the lives of households like an hour of a late summer's day—brooding, electric, as yet quiescent, but charged with the currents of coming storms.

Twice only in those weeks while Hughs was in prison did Hilary see the girl. Once he met her when he was driving home; she blushed crimson and her eyes lighted up. And one morning, too, he passed her on the bench where they had sat together. She was staring straight before her, the corners of her mouth drooping discontentedly. She did not see him.

To a man like Hilary—for whom running after women had been about the last occupation in the world, who had, in fact, always fought shy of them and imagined that they would always fight shy of him—there was an unusual enticement and dismay in the feeling that a young girl really was pursuing him. It was at once too good, too unlikely, and too embarrassing to be true. His sudden feeling for her was the painful sensation of one who sees a ripe nectarine hanging within reach. He dreamed continually of stretching out his hand, and so he did not dare, or thought he did not dare, to pass that way. All this did not favour the tenor of a studious, introspective life; it also brought a sense of unreality that made him avoid his best friends.

This, partly, was why Stephen came to see him one Sunday, his other reason for the visit being the calculation that Hughs would be released on the following Wednesday.

'This girl,' he thought, 'is going to the house still, and Hilary will let things drift till he can't stop them, and there'll be a real mess.'

The fact of the man's having been in prison gave a sinister turn to an affair regarded hitherto as merely sordid by Stephen's orderly and careful mind.

Crossing the garden, he heard Mr Stone's voice issuing through the open window.

'Can't the old crank stop even on Sundays?' he thought.

He found Hilary in his study, reading a book on the civilisation of the Maccabees, in preparation for a review. He gave Stephen but a dubious welcome.

Stephen broke ground gently.

'We haven't seen you for an age. I hear our old friend at it. Is he working double tides to finish his *magnum opus*? I thought he observed the day of rest.'

'He does as a rule,' said Hilary.

'Well, he's got the girl there now dictating.'

Hilary winced. Stephen continued with greater circumspection.

'You couldn't get the old boy to finish by Wednesday, I suppose? He must be quite near the end by now.'

The notion of Mr Stone's finishing his book by Wednesday procured a pale smile from Hilary.

'Could you get your Law Courts,' he said, 'to settle up the affairs of mankind for good and all by Wednesday?'

'By Jove! Is it as bad as that? I thought, at any rate, he must be meaning to finish some day.'

'When men are brothers,' said Hilary, 'he will finish.'

Stephen whistled.

'Look here, dear boy!' he said, 'that ruffian comes out on Wednesday. The whole thing will begin over again.'

Hilary rose and paced the room. 'I refuse,' he said, 'to consider Hughs a ruffian. What do we know about him, or any of them?'

'Precisely! What do we know of this girl?'

'I am not going to discuss that,' Hilary said shortly.

For a moment the faces of the two brothers wore a hard, hostile look, as though the deep difference between their characters had at last got the better of their loyalty. They both seemed to recognise this, for they turned their heads away.

'I just wanted to remind you,' Stephen said, 'though you know your own business best, of course.' And at Hilary's nod he thought: 'That's just exactly what he doesn't!'

He soon left, conscious of an unwonted awkwardness in his brother's presence. Hilary watched him out through the wicket gate, then sat down on the solitary garden bench.

Stephen's visit had merely awakened perverse desires in him.

Strong sunlight was falling on that little London garden, disclosing its native shadowiness; streaks, and smudges such as Life smears over the faces of those who live too consciously. Hilary, beneath the acacia-tree not yet in bloom, marked an early butterfly flitting over the geraniums blossoming round an old sundial. Blackbirds were holding evensong; the late perfume of the lilac came stealing forth into air faintly smeethed with chimney smoke. There was brightness, but no glory, in that little garden; scent, but no strong air blown across golden lakes of buttercups, from seas of springing clover, or the wind-silver of young wheat; music, but no full choir of sound, no hum. Like the face and figure of its master, so was this little garden, whose sundial the sun seldom reached—refined, self-conscious, introspective, obviously a creature of the town. At that moment, however, Hilary was not looking quite himself; his face was flushed, his eyes angry, almost as if he had been a man of action.

The voice of Mr Stone was still audible, fitfully quavering out into the air, and the old man himself could now and then be seen holding up his manuscript, his profile clear-cut against the darkness of the room. A sentence travelled out across the garden:

'"Amidst the tur-bu-lent dis-cov-eries of those days, which, like cross-currented and multi-billowed seas, lapped and hollowed every rock——"'

A motor-car dashing past drowned the rest, and when the voice rose again it was evidently dictating another paragraph.

'"In those places, in those streets, the shadows swarmed, whispering and droning like a hive of dying bees, who, their honey eaten, wander through the winter day seeking flowers that are frozen and dead."'

A great bee that had been busy with the lilac began to circle, booming, round his hair. Suddenly Hilary saw him raise both his arms.

'"In huge congeries, crowded, devoid of light and air, they were assembled, these bloodless imprints from forms of higher caste. They lay, like the reflection of leaves which, fluttering free in the sweet winds, let fall to the earth wan resemblances. Imponderous, dark ghosts, wandering ones chained to the ground, they had no hope of any Lovely City, nor knew whence they had come. Men cast them on the pavements and marched on. They did not in Universal Brotherhood clasp their shadows to sleep within their hearts—for the sun was not then at noon, when no man has a shadow."'

As those words of swan song died away he swayed and trembled, and suddenly disappeared below the sight-line, as if he had sat down. The little model took his place in the open window. She started at seeing Hilary; then, motionless, stood gazing at him. Out of the gloom of the opening her eyes were all pupil, two spots of the surrounding darkness imprisoned in a face as pale as any flower. As rigid as the girl herself, Hilary looked up at her.

A voice behind him said: 'How are you? I thought I'd give my car a run.' Mr Purcey was coming from the gate, his eyes fixed on the window where the girl stood. 'How is your wife?' he added.

The bathos of this visit roused an acid fury in Hilary. He surveyed Mr Purcey's figure from his cloth-topped boots to his tall hat, and said: 'Shall we go in and find her?'

As they went along Mr Purcey said: 'That's the young—the—er—model I met in your wife's studio, isn't it? Pretty girl!'

Hilary compressed his lips.

'Now, what sort of living do those girls make?' pursued Mr Purcey. 'I suppose they've most of them other resources. Eh, what?'

'They make the living God will let them, I suppose, as other people do.'

Mr Purcey gave him a sharp look. It was almost as if Dallison had meant to snub him.

'Oh, exactly! I should think this girl would have no difficulty.' And suddenly he saw a curious change come over 'that writing fellow', as he always afterwards described Hilary. Instead of a mild, pleasant-looking chap enough, he had become a regular cold devil.

'My wife appears to be out,' Hilary said. 'I also have an engagement.'

In his surprise and anger Mr Purcey said with great simplicity, 'Sorry I'm *de trop*!' and soon his car could be heard bearing him away with some unnecessary noise.

Chapter 32

BEHIND BIANCA'S VEIL

BUT Bianca was not out. She had been a witness of Hilary's long look at the little model. Coming from her studio through the glass passage to the house, she could not, of course, see what he was gazing at, but she knew as well as if the girl had stood before her in the dark opening of the window. Hating herself for having seen, she went to her room and lay on her bed with her hands pressed to her eyes. She was used to loneliness—that necessary lot of natures such as hers; but the bitter isolation of this hour was such as to drive even her lonely nature to despair.

She rose at last, and repaired the ravages made in her face and dress, lest anyone should see that she was suffering. Then, first making sure that Hilary had left the garden, she stole out.

She wandered towards Hyde Park. It was Whitsuntide, a time of fear to the cultivated Londoner. The town seemed all arid jollity and paper bags whirled on a dusty wind. People swarmed everywhere in clothes which did not suit them; desultory, dead-tired creatures who, in these few green hours of leisure out of the sandy eternity of their toil, were not suffered to rest, but were whipped on by starved instincts to hunt pleasures which they longed for too dreadfully to overtake.

Bianca passed an old tramp asleep beneath a tree. His clothes had clung to him so long and lovingly that they were falling off, but his face was calm as though masked with the finest wax. Forgotten were his sores and sorrows; he was in the blessed fields of sleep.

Bianca hastened away from the sight of such utter peace. She wandered into a grove of trees that had almost eluded the notice of the crowd. They were limes, guarding still within them their honey bloom. Their branches of light, broad leaves, near heart-shaped, were spread out like wide skirts. The tallest of these trees, a beautiful, gay creature, stood tremulous, like a mistress waiting for her tardy lover. What joy she seemed to promise, what delicate enticement, with every veined quivering leaf! And suddenly the sun caught hold of her, raised her up to him, kissed her all over; she gave forth a sigh of happiness, as though her very spirit had travelled through her lips up to her lover's heart.

A woman in a lilac frock came stealing through the trees towards

Bianca, and sitting down not far off, kept looking quickly round under her sunshade.

Presently Bianca saw what she was looking for. A young man in black coat and shining hat came swiftly up and touched her shoulder. Half hidden by the foliage they sat, leaning forward, prodding gently at the ground with stick and parasol; the stealthy murmur of their talk, so soft and intimate that no word was audible, stole across the grass; and secretly he touched her hand and arm. They were not of the holiday crowd, and had evidently chosen out this vulgar afternoon for a stolen meeting.

Bianca rose and hurried on amongst the trees. She left the Park. In the streets many couples, not so careful to conceal their intimacy, were parading arm-in-arm. The sight of them did not sting her like the sight of those lovers in the Park; they were not of her own order. But presently she saw a little boy and girl asleep on the door-step of a mansion, with their cheeks pressed close together and their arms round each other, and again she hurried on. In the course of that long wandering she passed the building which 'Westminister' was so anxious to avoid. In its gateway an old couple were just about to separate, one to the men's, the other to the women's quarters. Their toothless mouths were close together. 'Well, good-night, mother!' 'Good-night, father, good-night—take care o' your-self!'

Once more Bianca hurried on.

It was past nine when she turned into the Old Square, and rang the bell of her sister's house with the sheer physical desire to rest—somewhere that was not her home.

At one end of the long, low drawing-room Stephen, in evening dress, was reading aloud from a review. Cecilia was looking dubiously at his sock, where she seemed to see a tiny speck of white that might be Stephen. In the window at the far end Thyme and Martin were exchanging speeches at short intervals; they made no move at Bianca's entrance; and their faces said: 'We have no use for that handshaking nonsense!'

Receiving Cecilia's little, warm, doubting kiss and Stephen's polite, dry handshake, Bianca motioned to him not to stop reading. He resumed. Cecilia, too, resumed her scrutiny of Stephen's sock.

'Oh dear!' she thought. 'I know B.'s come here because she's unhappy. Poor thing! Poor Hilary! It's that wretched business again, I suppose.'

Skilled in every tone of Stephen's voice, she knew that Bianca's entry had provoked the same train of thought in him; to her he seemed reading out these words: 'I disapprove—I disapprove. She's Cis's sister. But if it wasn't for old Hilary I wouldn't have the subject in the house!'

Bianca, whose subtlety recorded every shade of feeling, could see that she was not welcome. Leaning back with veil raised, she seemed listening to Stephen's reading, but in fact she was quivering at the sight of those two couples.

Couples, couples—for all but her! What crime had she committed? Why was the china of her cup flawed so that no one could drink from it? Why had she been made so that nobody could love her? This, the most bitter of all thoughts, the most tragic of all questionings, haunted her.

The article which Stephen read—explaining exactly how to deal with people so that from one sort of human being they might become another, and going on to prove that if, after this conversion, they showed signs of a reversion, it would then be necessary to know the reason why—fell dryly on ears listening to that eternal question: Why is it with me as it is? It is not fair!—listening to the constant murmuring of her pride: I am not wanted here or anywhere. Better to efface myself!

From their end of the room Thyme and Martin scarcely looked at her. To them she was Aunt B., an amateur, the mockery of whose eyes sometimes penetrated their youthful armour; they were besides too interested in their conversation to perceive that she was suffering. The skirmish of that conversation had lasted now for many days—ever since the death of the Hughs' baby.

'Well,' Martin was saying, 'what are you going to do? It's no good to base it on the baby; you must know your own mind all round. You can't go rushing into real work on mere sentiment.'

'*You* went to the funeral, Martin. It's bosh to say you didn't feel it too!'

Martin deigned no answer to this insinuation.

'We've gone past the need for sentiment,' he said: 'it's exploded; so is Justice, administered by an upper class with a patch over one eye and a squint in the other. When you see a dying donkey in a field, you don't want to refer the case to a society, as your dad would; you don't want an essay of Hilary's, full of sympathy with everybody, on "Walking in a field: with reflections on the end of donkeys"—you want to put a bullet in the donkey.'

'You're always down on Uncle Hilary,' said Thyme.

'I don't mind Hilary himself; I object to his type.'

'Well, he objects to yours,' said Thyme.

'I'm not so sure of that,' said Martin slowly; 'he hasn't got character enough.'

Thyme raised her chin, and, looking at him through half-closed eyes, said: 'Well, I do think, of all the conceited persons I ever met you're the worst.'

Martin's nostril curled.

'Are you prepared,' he said, 'to put a bullet in the donkey, or are you not?'

'I only see one donkey, and not a dying one!'

Martin stretched out his hand and gripped her arm below the elbow. Retaining it luxuriously, he said: 'Don't wander!'

Thyme tried to free her arm. 'Let go!'

Martin was looking straight into her eyes. A flush had risen in his cheeks.

Thyme, too, went the colour of the old-rose curtain behind which she sat.

'Let go!'

'I won't! I'll *make* you know your mind. What do you mean to do? Are you coming in a fit of sentiment, or do you mean business?'

Suddenly, half-hypnotised, the young girl ceased to struggle. Her face had the strangest expression of submission and defiance—a sort of pain, a sort of delight. So they sat full half a minute staring at each other's eyes. Hearing a rustling sound, they looked, and saw Bianca moving to the door. Cecilia, too, had risen.

'What is it, B.?'

Bianca, opening the door, went out. Cecilia followed swiftly, too late to catch even a glimpse of her sister's face behind the veil. . . .

In Mr Stone's room the green lamp burned dimly, and he who worked by it was sitting on the edge of his camp-bed, attired in his old brown woollen gown and slippers.

And suddenly it seemed to him that he was not alone.

'I have finished for to-night,' he said. 'I am waiting for the moon to rise. She is nearly full; I shall see her face from here.'

A form sat down by him on the bed, and a voice said softly: 'Like a woman's.'

Mr Stone saw his younger daughter. 'You have your hat on. Are you going out, my dear?'

'I saw your light as I came in.'

'The moon,' said Mr Stone, 'is an arid desert. Love is unknown there.'

'How can your bear to look at her, then?' Bianca whispered.

Mr Stone raised his finger. 'She has risen.'

The wan moon had slipped out into the darkness. Her light stole across the garden and through the open window to the bed where they were sitting.

'Where there is no love, Dad,' Bianca said, 'there can be no life, can there?'

Mr Stone's eyes seemed to drink the moonlight.

'That,' he said, 'is the great truth. The bed is shaking!'

With her arms pressed tight across her breast, Bianca was struggling with violent, noiseless sobbing. That desperate struggle seemed to be tearing her to death before his eyes, and Mr Stone sat silent, trembling. He knew not what to do. From his frosted heart years of Universal Brotherhood had taken all knowledge of how to help his daughter. He could only sit touching her tremulously with thin fingers.

The form beside him, whose warmth he felt against his arm, grew stiller, as though, in spite of its own loneliness, his helplessness had made it feel that he, too, was lonely. It pressed a little closer to him. The moonlight, gaining pale mastery over the flickering lamp, filled the whole room.

Mr Stone said: 'I want her mother!'

The form beside him ceased to struggle.

Finding out an old, forgotten way, Mr Stone's arm slid round that quivering body.

'I do not know what to say to her,' he muttered, and slowly he began to rock himself.

'Motion,' he said, 'is soothing.'

The moon passed on. The form beside him sat so still that Mr Stone ceased moving. His daughter was no longer sobbing. Suddenly her lips seared his forehead.

Trembling from that desperate caress, he raised his fingers to the spot and looked round.

She was gone.

Chapter 33

HILARY DEALS WITH THE SITUATION

TO understand the conduct of Hilary and Bianca at what 'Westminister' would have called this 'crisax', not only their feelings as sentient human beings, but their matrimonial philosophy, must be taken into account. By education and environment they belonged to a section of society which had 'in those days' abandoned the more old-fashioned views of marriage. Such as composed this section, finding themselves in opposition, not only to the orthodox proprietary creed, but even to their own legal rights, had been driven to an attitude of almost blatant freedom. Like all folk in opposition, they were bound, as a simple matter of principle, to disagree with those in power, to view with a contemptuous resentment that majority which said, 'I believe the thing is mine, and mine it shall remain'—a majority which by force of numbers made this creed the law. Unable legally to be other than the proprietors of wife or husband, as the case might be, they were obliged, even in the most happy unions, to be very careful not to become disgusted with their own position. Their legal status was, as it were, a goad, spurring them on to show their horror of it. They were like children sent to school with trousers that barely reached their knees, aware that they could neither reduce their stature to the proportions of their breeches nor make their breeches grow. They were furnishing an instance of that immemorial 'change of form to form' to which Mr Stone had given the name of Life. In a past age thinkers and dreamers and 'artistic pigs', rejecting the forms they found, had given unconscious shape to this marriage law, which, after they had become the wind, had formed itself out of their exiled pictures and thoughts and dreams. And now this particular law in turn was the dried rind, devoid of pips or speculation; and the thinkers and dreamers and 'artistic pigs' were again rejecting it, and again themselves in exile.

This exiled faith, this honour amongst thieves, animated a little conversation between Hilary and Bianca on the Tuesday following the night when Mr Stone sat on his bed to watch the rising moon.

Quietly Bianca said: 'I think I shall be going away for a time.'

'Wouldn't you rather that I went instead?'

'You are wanted; I am not.'

That ice-cold, ice-clear remark contained the pith of the whole matter; and Hilary said:

'You are not going at once?'

'At the end of the week, I think.'

Noting his eyes fixed on her, she added:

'Yes; we're neither of us looking quite our best.'

'I am sorry.'

'I know you are.'

This had been all. It had been sufficient to bring Hilary once more face to face with the situation.

Its constituent elements remained the same; relative values had much changed. The temptations of St Anthony were becoming more poignant every hour. He had no 'principles' to pit against them: he had merely the inveterate distaste for hurting anybody, and a feeling that if he yielded to his inclination he would be faced ultimately with a worse situation than ever. It was not possible for him to look at the position as Mr Purcey might have done, if *his* wife had withdrawn from him and a girl had put herself in his way. Neither hesitation because of the defenceless position of the girl, nor hesitation because of his own future with her, would have troubled Mr Purcey. He—good man—in his straightforward way, would have only thought about the present—not, indeed, intending to have a future with a young person of that class. Consideration for a wife who had withdrawn from the society of Mr Purcey would also naturally have been absent from the equation. That Hilary worried over all these questions was the mark of his 'fin de siècleism'. And in the meantime the facts demanded a decision.

He had not spoken to this girl since the day of the baby's funeral, but in that long look from the garden he had in effect said: 'You are drawing me to the only sort of union possible to us!' And she in effect had answered: 'Do what you like with me!'

There were other facts, too, to be reckoned with. Hughs would be released to-morrow; the little model would not stop her visits unless forced to; Mr Stone could not well do without her; Bianca had in effect declared that she was being driven out of her own house. It was this situation which Hilary, seated beneath the bust of Socrates, turned over and over in his mind. Long and painful reflection brought him back continually to the thought that he himself, and not Bianca, had better go away. He was extremely bitter and contemptuous towards himself that he had not done so long ago. He made use of the names Martin had given him. 'Hamlet', 'Amateur', 'Invertebrate'. They gave him, unfortunately, little comfort.

In the afternoon he received a visit. Mr Stone came in with his osier fruit-bag in his hand. He remained standing, and spoke at once.

'Is my daughter happy?'

At this unexpected question Hilary walked over to the fireplace.

'No,' he said at last; 'I am afraid she is not.'

'Why?'

Hilary was silent; then, facing the old man, he said:

'I think she will be glad, for certain reasons, if I go away for a time.'

'When are you going?' asked Mr Stone.

'As soon as I can.'

Mr Stone's eyes, wistfully bright, seemed trying to see through heavy fog.

'She came to me, I think,' he said; 'I seem to recollect her crying. You are good to her?'

'I have tried to be,' said Hilary.

Mr Stone's face was discoloured by a flush. 'You have no children,' he said painfully; 'do you live together?'

Hilary shook his head.

'You are estranged?' said Mr Stone.

Hilary bowed. There was a long silence. Mr Stone's eyes had travelled to the window.

'Without love there cannot be life,' he said at last; and fixing his wistful gaze on Hilary, asked: 'Does she love another?'

Again Hilary shook his head.

When Mr Stone next spoke it was clearly to himself.

'I do not know why I am glad. Do you love another?'

At this question Hilary's eyebrows settled in a frown. 'What do you mean by love?' he said.

Mr Stone did not reply; it was evident that he was reflecting deeply. His lips began to move: 'By love I mean the forgetfulness of self. Unions are frequent in which only the sexual instincts, or the remembrance of self, are roused——'

'That is true,' muttered Hilary.

Mr Stone looked up; painful traces of confusion showed in his face. 'We were discussing something.'

'I was telling you,' said Hilary, 'that it would be better for your daughter if I go away for a time.'

'Yes,' said Mr Stone; 'you are estranged.'

Hilary went back to his stand before the empty fireplace.

'There is one thing, sir,' he said, 'on my conscience to say before I go, and I must leave it to you to decide. The little girl who comes to you no longer lives where she used to live.'

'In that street . . .' said Mr Stone.

Hilary went on quickly. 'She was obliged to leave because the husband of the woman with whom she used to lodge became infatuated with her. He has been in prison, and comes out to-morrow. If she continues to come here he will, of course, be able to find her. I'm afraid he will pursue her again. Have I made it clear to you?'

'No,' said Mr Stone.

'The man,' resumed Hilary patiently, 'is a poor, violent creature, who has been wounded in the head; he is not quite responsible. He may do the girl an injury.'

'What injury?'

'He has stabbed his wife already.'

'I will speak to him,' said Mr Stone.

Hilary smiled. 'I am afraid that words will hardly meet the case. She ought to disappear.'

There was silence.

'My book!' said Mr Stone.

It smote Hilary to see how white his face had become. 'It's better,' he thought, 'to bring his will-power into play; she will never come here, anyway, after I'm gone.'

But, unable to bear the tragedy in the old man's eyes, he touched him on the arm.

'Perhaps she will take the risk, sir, if you ask her.'

Mr Stone did not answer, and, not knowing what more to say, Hilary went back to the window. Miranda was slumbering lightly out there in the speckled shade, where it was not too warm and not too cold, her cheek resting on her paw and white teeth showing.

Mr Stone's voice rose again. 'You are right; I cannot ask her to run a risk like that!'

'She is just coming up the garden,' Hilary said huskily. 'Shall I tell her to come in?'

'Yes,' said Mr Stone.

Hilary beckoned.

The girl came in, carrying a tiny bunch of lilies of the valley; her face fell at sight of Mr Stone; she stood still, raising the lilies to her breast. Nothing could have been more striking than the change from her look of fluttered expectancy to a sort of hard dismay. A spot of red came into both her cheeks. She gazed from Mr Stone to Hilary and back again. Both were staring at her. No one spoke. The little model's bosom began heaving as though she had been running; she said faintly, 'Look; I brought you this, Mr Stone!' and held out to him the bunch of lilies. But Mr Stone made no sign. 'Don't you like them?'

Mr Stone's eyes remained fastened on her face.

To Hilary this suspense was, evidently, most distressing. 'Come, will you tell her, sir,' he said, 'or shall I?'

Mr Stone spoke.

'I shall try and write my book without you. You must not run this risk. I cannot allow it.'

The little model turned her eyes from side to side. 'But I *like* to copy out your book,' she said.

'The man will injure you,' said Mr Stone.

The little model looked at Hilary.

'I don't care if he does; I'm not afraid of him. I can look after myself; I'm used to it.'

'*I* am going away,' said Hilary quietly.

After a desperate look, that seemed to ask, 'Am I going, too?' the little model stood as though frozen.

Wishing to end the painful scene, Hilary went up to Mr Stone.

'Do you want to dictate to her this afternoon, sir?'

'No,' said Mr Stone.

'Nor to-morrow?'

'No.'

'Will you come a little walk with me?'

Mr Stone bowed.

Hilary turned to the little model. 'It is good-bye, then,' he said.

She did not take his hand. Her eyes, turned sideways, glinted; her teeth were fastened on her lower lip. She dropped the lilies, suddenly looked up at him, gulped, and slunk away. In passing she had smeared the lilies with her foot.

Hilary picked up the fragments of the flowers, and dropped them into the grate. The fragrance of the bruised blossoms remained clinging to the air.

'Shall we get ready for our walk?' he said.

Mr Stone moved feebly to the door, and very soon they were walking silently towards the Gardens.

Chapter 34

THYME'S ADVENTURE

THIS same afternoon Thyme, wheeling a bicycle and carrying a light valise, was slipping into a back street out of the Old Square. Putting her burden down at the pavement's edge, she blew a whistle. A hansom-cab appeared, and a man in ragged clothes, who seemed to spring out of the pavement, took hold of her valise. His lean, unshaven face was full of wolfish misery.

'Get off with you!' the cabman said.

'Let him do it!' murmured Thyme.

The cab-runner hoisted up the trunk, then waited motionless beside the cab.

Thyme handed him two coppers. He looked at them in silence, and went away.

'Poor man,' she thought; 'that's one of the things we've got to do away with!'

The cab now proceeded in the direction of the Park, Thyme following on her bicycle, and trying to stare about her calmly.

'This,' she thought, 'is the end of the old life. I won't be romantic, and imagine I'm doing anything special; I must take it all as a matter of course.' She thought of Mr Purcey's face—'that person!'—if he could have seen her at this moment turning her back on comfort. 'The moment I get there,' she mused, 'I shall let mother know; she can come out to-morrow, and see for herself. I can't have hysterics about my disappearance, and all that. They must get used to the idea that I mean to be in touch with things. I can't be stopped by what anybody thinks!'

An approaching motor-car brought a startled frown across her brow. Was it 'that person'? But though it was not Mr Purcey and his A.1. Damyer, it was somebody so like him as made no difference. Thyme uttered a little laugh.

In the Park a cool light danced and glittered on the trees and water, and the same cool, dancing glitter seemed lighting the girl's eyes.

The cabman, unseen, took an admiring look at her. 'Nice little bit, this!' it said.

'Grandfather bathes here,' thought Thyme. 'Poor darling! I pity everyone that's old.'

The cab passed on under the shade of trees out into the road.

'I wonder if we have only one self in us,' thought Thyme. 'I sometimes feel that I have two—Uncle Hilary would understand what I mean. The pavements are beginning to smell horrid already, and it's only June to-morrow. Will mother feel my going very much? How glorious if one didn't feel!'

The cab turned into a narrow street of little shops.

'It must be dreadful to have to serve in a small shop. What millions of people there are in the world! Can anything be of any use? Martin says what matters is to do one's job; but what *is* one's job?'

The cab emerged into a broad, quiet square.

'But I'm not going to think of anything,' thought Thyme; 'that's fatal. Suppose father stops my allowance; I should have to earn my living as a typist, or something of that sort; but he won't, when he sees I mean it. Besides, mother wouldn't let him.'

The cab entered the Euston Road, and again the cabman's broad face was turned towards Thyme with an inquiring stare.

'What a hateful road!' Thyme thought. 'What dull, ugly, common-looking faces all the people seem to have in London! as if they didn't care for anything but just to get through their day somehow. I've only seen two really pretty faces!'

The cab stopped before a small tobacconist's on the south side of the road.

'Have I got to live here?' thought Thyme.

Through the open door a narrow passage led to a narrow staircase covered with oilcloth. She raised her bicycle and wheeled it in. A Jewish-looking youth emerging from the shop accosted her.

'Your gentleman friend says you are to stay in your rooms, please, until he comes.'

His warm red-brown eyes dwelt on her lovingly. 'Shall I take your luggage up, miss?'

'Thank you; I can manage.'

'It's the first floor,' said the young man.

The little rooms which Thyme entered were stuffy, clean, and neat. Putting her trunk down in her bedroom, which looked out on a bare yard, she went into the sitting-room and threw the window up. Down below the cabman and tobacconist were engaged in conversation. Thyme caught the expression on their faces—a sort of leering curiosity.

'How disgusting and horrible men are!' she thought, moodily staring at the traffic. All seemed so grim, so inextricable, and vast, out there in the grey heat and hurry, as though some monstrous devil were sporting with a monstrous ant-heap. The reek of petrol and of dung rose to her nostrils. It was so terribly big and hopeless; it was so *ugly*! 'I shall never do anything,' thought Thyme—'never—never! Why doesn't Martin come?'

She went into her bedroom and opened her valise. With the scent of lavender that came from it, there sprang up a vision of her white bedroom at home, and the trees of the green garden and the blackbirds on the grass.

The sound of footsteps on the stairs brought her back into the sitting-room. Martin was standing in the doorway.

Thyme ran towards him, but stopped abruptly. 'I've come, you see. What made you choose this place?'

'I'm next door but two; and there's a girl here—one of us. She'll show you the ropes.'

'Is she a lady?'

Martin raised his shoulders. 'She *is* what is called a lady,' he said; 'but she's the right sort, all the same. Nothing will stop her.'

At this proclamation of supreme virtue, the look on Thyme's face was very queer. 'You don't trust me,' it seemed to say, 'and you trust that girl. You put me here for her to watch over me! . . .'

'I want to send this telegram,' she said aloud.

Martin read the telegram. 'You oughtn't to have funked telling your mother what you meant to do.'

Thyme crimsoned. 'I'm not cold-blooded, like you.'

'This is a big matter,' said Martin. 'I told you that you had no business to come at all if you couldn't look it squarely in the face.'

'If you want me to stay you had better be more decent to me, Martin.'

'It must be your own affair,' said Martin.

Thyme stood at the window, biting her lips to keep the tears back from her eyes. A very pleasant voice behind her said: 'I do think it's so splendid of you to come!'

A girl in grey was standing there—thin, delicate, rather plain, with a nose ever so little to one side, lips faintly smiling, and large, shining, greenish eyes.

'I am Mary Daunt. I live above you. Have you had some tea?'

In the gentle question of this girl with the faintly smiling lips and shining eyes Thyme fancied that she detected mockery.

'Yes, thanks. I want to be shown what my work's to be, at once, please.'

The grey girl looked at Martin.

'Oh! Won't to-morrow do for all that sort of thing? I'm sure you must be tired. Mr Stone, do make her rest!'

Martin's glance seemed to say: 'Please leave your femininities!'

'If you mean business, your work will be the same as hers,' he said; 'you're not qualified. All you can do will be visiting, noting the state of the houses and the condition of the children.'

The girl in grey said gently: 'You see, we only deal with sanitation and the children. It seems hard on the grown people and the old to leave them out; but there's sure to be so much less money than we want, so that it *must* all go towards the future.'

There was a silence. The girl with the shining eyes added softly: '1950!'

'1950!' repeated Martin. It seemed to be some formula of faith.

'I must send this telegram!' muttered Thyme.

Martin took it from her and went out.

Left alone in the little room, the two girls did not at first speak. The girl in grey was watching Thyme half timidly, as if she could not tell what to make of this young creature who looked so charming, and kept shooting such distrustful glances.

'I think it's so awfully sweet of you to come,' she said at last. 'I know what a good time you have at home; your cousin's often told me. Don't you think he's splendid?'

To that question Thyme made no answer.

'Isn't this work horrid,' she said—'prying into people's houses?'

The grey girl smiled. 'It *is* rather awful sometimes. I've been at it six months now. You get used to it. I've had all the worst things said to me by now, I should think.'

Thyme shuddered.

'You see,' said the grey girl's faintly smiling lips, 'you soon get the feeling of having to go through with it. We all realise it's got to be done, of course. Your cousin's one of the best of us: nothing seems to put him out. He has such a nice sort of scornful kindness. I'd rather work with him than anyone.'

She looked past her new associate into that world outside, where the sky seemed all wires and yellow heat-dust. She did not notice Thyme appraising her from head to foot, with a stare hostile and jealous, but pathetic, too, as though confessing that this girl was her superior.

'I'm sure I can't do that work!' she said suddenly.

The grey girl smiled. 'Oh, *I* thought that at first.' Then, with an admiring look: 'But I do think it's rather a shame for you, you're so pretty. Perhaps they'd put you on to tabulation work, though that's awfully dull. We'll ask your cousin.'

'No; I'll do the whole or nothing.'

'Well,' said the grey girl, 'I've got one house left to-day. Would you like to come and see the sort of thing?'

She took a small notebook from a side pocket in her skirt.

'I can't get on without a pocket. You must have something that you can't leave behind. I left four little bags and two dozen handkerchiefs in five weeks before I came back to pockets. It's rather a horrid house, I'm afraid!'

'*I* shall be all right,' said Thyme shortly.

In the shop doorway the young tobacconist was taking the evening air. He greeted them with his polite but constitutionally leering smile.

'Good-evening, mith,' he said; 'nithe evening!'

'He's rather an awful little man,' the grey girl said when they had achieved the crossing of the street; 'but he's got quite a nice sense of humour.'

'Ah!' said Thyme.

They had turned into a by-street, and stopped before a house which had obviously seen better days. Its windows were cracked, its doors unpainted, and down in the basement could be seen a pile of rags, an evil-looking man seated by it, and a blazing fire. Thyme felt a little gulping sensation. There was a putrid scent as of burning refuse. She looked at her companion. The grey girl was consulting her notebook, with a faint smile on her lips. And in Thyme's heart rose a feeling that was almost hatred for this girl, who was so business-like in the presence of such sights and scents.

The door was opened by a young red-faced woman, who looked as if she had been asleep.

The grey girl screwed up her shining eyes. 'Oh, do you mind if we come in a minute?' she said. 'It would be so good of you. We're making a report.'

'There's nothing to report here,' the young woman answered. But the grey girl had slipped as gently past as though she had been the very spirit of adventure.

'Of course, I see that, but just as a matter of form, you know.'

'I've parted with most of my things,' the young woman said defensively, 'since my husband died. It's a hard life.'

'Yes, yes, but not worse than mine—always poking my nose into other people's houses.'

The young woman was silent, evidently surprised.

'The landlord ought to keep you in better repair,' said the grey girl. 'He owns next door, too, doesn't he?'

The young woman nodded. 'He's a bad landlord. All down the street 'ere it's the same. Can't get nothing done.'

The grey girl had gone over to a dirty bassinette where a half-naked child sprawled. An ugly little girl with fat red cheeks was sitting on a stool beside it, close to an open locker wherein could be seen a number of old meat bones.

'Your chickabiddies?' said the grey girl. 'Aren't they sweet?'

The young woman's face became illumined by a smile.

'They're healthy,' she said.

'That's more than can be said for all the children in the house, I expect,' murmured the grey girl.

The young woman replied emphatically, as though voicing an old grievance: 'The three on the first floor's not so bad, but I don't let 'em 'ave anything to do with that lot at the top.'

Thyme saw her new friend's hand hover over the child's head like some pale dove. In answer to that gesture, the mother nodded. 'Just that; you've got to clean 'em every time they go near them children at the top.'

The grey girl looked at Thyme. 'That's where we've got to go, evidently,' she seemed to say.

'A dirty lot!' muttered the young woman.

'It's very hard on you.'

'It is. I'm workin' at the laundry all day when I can get it. I can't look after the children—they get everywhere.'

'Very hard,' murmured the grey girl. 'I'll make a note of that.'

Together with the little book, in which she was writing furiously, she had pulled out her handkerchief, and the sight of this handkerchief reposing on the floor gave Thyme a queer satisfaction, such as comes when one remarks in superior people the absence of a virtue existing in oneself.

'Well, we mustn't keep you, Mrs—Mrs——?'

'Cleary.'

'Cleary. How old's this little one? Four? And the other? Two? They *are* ducks. Good-bye!'

In the corridor outside the grey girl whispered: 'I do like the way we all pride ourselves on being better than someone else. I think it's so hopeful and jolly. Shall we go up and see the abyss at the top?'

Chapter 35

A YOUNG GIRL'S MIND

A YOUNG girl's mind is like a wood in Spring—now a rising mist of bluebells and flakes of dappled sunlight; now a world of still, wan, tender saplings, weeping they know not why. Through the curling twigs of boughs just green, its wings fly towards the stars; but the next moment they have drooped to mope beneath the damp bushes. It is ever yearning for and trembling at the future; in its secret places all the countless shapes of things that are to be are taking stealthy counsel of how to grow up without letting their gown of mystery fall. They rustle, whisper, shriek suddenly, and as suddenly fall into a delicious silence. From the first hazel-bush to the last may-tree it is an unending meeting-place of young solemn things eager to find out what they are, eager to rush forth to greet the kisses of the wind and sun, and for ever trembling back and hiding their faces. The spirit of that wood seems to lie with her ear close to the ground, a pale petal of a hand curved like a shell behind it, listening for the whisper of her own life. There she lies, white and supple, with dewy, wistful eyes, sighing: 'What is my meaning? Ah, I am everything! Is there in all the world a thing so wonderful as I? . . . Oh, I am nothing —my wings are heavy; I faint, I die!'

When Thyme, attended by the grey girl, emerged from the abyss at the top, her cheeks were flushed and her hands clenched. She said nothing. The grey girl, too, was silent, with a look such as a spirit divested of its body by long bathing in the river of reality might bend on one who has just come to dip her head. Thyme's quick eyes saw that look, and her colour deepened. She saw, too, the glance of the Jewish youth when Martin joined them in the doorway.

'Two girls now,' he seemed to say. 'He goes it, this young man!'

Supper was laid in her new friend's room—pressed beef, potato salad, stewed prunes, and ginger ale. Martin and the grey girl talked. Thyme ate in silence, but though her eyes seemed fastened on her plate, she saw every glance that passed between them, heard every word they said. Those glances were not remarkable, nor were those words particularly important, but they were spoken in tones that seemed important to Thyme. 'He never talks to me like that,' she thought.

When supper was over they went out into the streets to walk, but at the door the grey girl gave Thyme's arm a squeeze, her cheek a swift kiss, and turned back up the stairs.

'Aren't you coming?' shouted Martin.

Her voice was heard answering from above: 'No, not to-night.'

With the back of her hand Thyme rubbed off the kiss. The two cousins walked out amongst the traffic.

The evening was very warm and close; no breeze fanned the reeking town. Speaking little, they wandered among endless darkening streets, whence to return to the light and traffic of the Euston Road seemed like coming back to Heaven. At last, close again to her new home, Thyme said: 'Why should one bother? It's all a horrible great machine, trying to blot us out; people are like insects when you put your thumb on them and smear them on a book. I hate—I loathe it!'

'They might as well be healthy insects while they last,' answered Martin.

Thyme faced round at him. 'I shan't sleep to-night, Martin; get out my bicycle for me.'

Martin scrutinised her by the light of the street lamp. 'All right,' he said; 'I'll come too.'

There are, say moralists, roads that lead to Hell, but it was on a road that leads to Hampstead that the two young cyclists set forth towards eleven o'clock. The difference between the character of the two destinations was soon apparent, for whereas man taken in bulk had perhaps made Hell, Hampstead had obviously been made by the upper classes. There were trees and gardens, and instead of dark canals of sky banked by the roofs of houses and hazed with the yellow scum of London lights, the heavens spread out in a wide trembling pool. From that rampart of the town, the Spaniard's Road, two plains lay exposed to left and right; the scent of may-tree blossom had stolen up the hill; the rising moon clung to a fir-tree bough. Over the country the far stars presided, and sleep's dark wings were spread above the fields—silent, scarce breathing, lay the body of the land. But to the south, where the town, that restless head, was lying, the stars seemed to have fallen and were sown in the thousand furrows of its great grey marsh, and from the dark miasma of those streets there travelled up a rustle, a whisper, the far allurement of some deathless dancer, dragging men to watch the swirl of her black, spangled drapery, the gleam of her writhing limbs. Like the song of the sea in a shell was the murmur of that witch of motion, clasping to her the souls of men, drawing them down into a soul whom none had ever seen at rest.

Above the two young cousins, scudding along that ridge between the country and the town, three thin white clouds trailed slowly towards the west—like tired sea-birds drifting exhausted far out from land on a sea blue to blackness with unfathomable depth.

For an hour those two rode silently into the country.

'Have we come far enough?' Martin said at last.

Thyme shook her head. A long, steep hill beyond a little sleeping village had brought them to a standstill. Across the shadowy fields a pale sheet of water gleamed out in moonlight. Thyme turned down towards it.

'I'm hot,' she said; 'I want to bathe my face. Stay here. Don't come with me.'

She left her bicycle, and, passing through a gate, vanished among the trees.

Martin stayed leaning against the gate. The village clock struck one. The distant call of a hunting owl, 'Qu-wheek, qu-wheek!' sounded through the grave stillness of this last night of May. The moon at her curve's summit floated at peace on the blue surface of the sky, a great closed water-lily. And Martin saw through the trees scimitar-shaped reeds clustering black along the pool's shore. All about him the may-flowers were alight. It was such a night as makes dreams real and turns reality to dreams.

'All moonlit nonsense!' thought the young man, for the night had disturbed his heart.

But Thyme did not come back. He called to her, and in the death-like silence following his shouts he could hear his own heart beat. He passed in through the gate. She was nowhere to be seen. Why was she playing him this trick?

He turned up from the water among the trees, where the incense of the may-flowers hung heavy in the air.

'Never look for a thing!' he thought, and stopped to listen. It was so breathless that the leaves of a low bough against his cheek did not stir while he stood there. Presently he heard faint sounds, and stole towards them. Under a beech-tree he almost stumbled over Thyme, lying with her face pressed to the ground. The young doctor's heart gave a sickening leap; he quickly knelt down beside her. The girl's body, pressed close to the dry beech-mat, was being shaken by long sobs. From head to foot it quivered; her hat had been torn off, and the fragrance of her hair mingled with the fragrance of the night. In Martin's heart something seemed to turn over and over, as when a boy he had watched a rabbit caught in a snare. He touched her. She sat up, and, dashing her hand across her eyes, cried: 'Go away! Oh, go away!'

He put his arm round her and waited. Five minutes passed. The air was trembling with a sort of pale vibration, for the moonlight had found a hole in the dark foliage and flooded on to the ground beside them, whitening the black beech-husks. Some tiny bird, disturbed by these unwonted visitors, began chirruping and fluttering, but was soon still again. To Martin, so strangely close to this young creature in the night, there came a sense of utter disturbance.

'Poor little thing!' he thought; 'be careful of her, comfort her!'

Hardness seemed so broken out of her, and the night so wonderful! And there came into the young man's heart a throb of the knowledge—very rare with him, for he was not, like Hilary, a philosophising person—that she was as real as himself—suffering, hoping, feeling, not his hopes and feelings, but her own. His fingers kept pressing her shoulder through her thin blouse. And the touch of those fingers was worth more than any words, as this night, all moonlit dreams, was worth more than a thousand nights of sane reality.

Thyme twisted herself away from him at last.

'I can't,' she sobbed. 'I'm not what you thought me—I'm not made for it!'

A scornful little smile curled Martin's lip. So that was it! But the smile soon died away. One did not hit what was already down!

Thyme's voice wailed through the silence. 'I thought I could—but I want beautiful things. I can't bear it all so grey and horrible. I'm not like *that girl*. I'm—an—amateur!'

'If I kissed her——' Martin thought.

She sank down again, burying her face in the dark beech-mat. The moonlight had passed on. Her voice came faint and stifled, as out of the tomb of faith. 'I'm no good. I never shall be. I'm as bad as mother!'

But to Martin there was only the scent of her hair.

'No,' murmured Thyme's voice, 'I'm only fit for miserable Art. . . . I'm only fit for—nothing!'

They were so close together on the dark beech-mat that their bodies touched, and a longing to clasp her in his arms came over him.

'I'm a selfish beast!' moaned the smothered voice. 'I don't really care for all these people—I only care because they're ugly for me to see!'

Martin reached his hand out to her hair. If she had shrunk away he would have seized her, but as though by instinct she let it rest there. And at her sudden stillness, strange and touching, Martin's quick passion left him. He slipped his arm round her and raised her up, as if she had been a child, and for a long time sat listening with a queer twisted smile to the moanings of her lost illusions.

The dawn found them still sitting there against the bole of the beech-tree. Her lips were parted; the tears had dried on her sleeping face, pillowed against his shoulder, while he still watched her sideways with the ghost of that twisted smile.

And beyond the grey water, like some tired wanton, the moon in an orange hood was stealing down to her rest between the trees.

Chapter 36
STEPHEN SIGNS CHEQUES

WHEN Cecilia received the mystic document containing these words: 'Am quite all right. Address, 598, Euston Road, three doors off Martin. Letter follows explaining.—Thyme,' she had not even realised her little daughter's departure. She went up to Thyme's room at once, and opening all the drawers and cupboards, stared into them one by one. The many things she saw there allayed the first pangs of her disquiet.

'She has only taken one little trunk,' she thought, 'and left all her evening frocks.'

This act of independence alarmed rather than surprised her, such had been her sense of the unrest in the domestic atmosphere during the last month. Since the evening when she had found Thyme in floods of tears because of the Hughs' baby, her maternal eyes had not failed to notice something new in the child's demeanour—a moodiness, an air almost of conspiracy, together with an emphatic increase of youthful sarcasm. Fearful of probing deep, she had sought no confidence, nor had she divulged her doubts to Stephen.

Amongst the blouses a sheet of blue ruled paper, which had evidently escaped from a notebook, caught her eye. Sentences were scrawled on it in pencil. Cecilia read: 'That poor little dead thing was so grey and pinched, and I seemed to realise all of a sudden how awful it is for them. I must—I must—I *will* do something!'

Cecilia dropped the sheet of paper; her hand was trembling. There was no mystery in that departure now, and Stephen's words came into her mind: 'It's all very well up to a certain point, and nobody sympathises with them more than I do; but after that it becomes destructive of all comfort, and that does no good to anyone.'

The sound sense of those words had made her feel queer when they were spoken; they were even more sensible than she had thought. Did her little daughter, so young and pretty, seriously mean to plunge into the rescue work of dismal slums, to cut herself adrift from sweet sounds and scents and colours, from music and art, from dancing, flowers, and all that made life beautiful? The secret forces of fastidiousness, an inborn dread of the fanatical, and all her real ignorance of what such a life was like, rose in Cecilia with a force that made her feel quite sick. Better that she herself should do this thing than that her own child should be deprived of air and light and all the just environment of her youth and beauty. 'She must come back—she must listen to me!' she thought. 'We will begin together; we will start a nice little *crèche* of our own, or perhaps Mrs Tallents Smallpeace could find us some regular work on one of her committees.'

Then suddenly she conceived a thought which made her blood run positively cold. What if it were a matter of heredity? What if Thyme had inherited her grandfather's single-mindedness? Martin was giving proof of it. Things, she knew, often skipped a generation and then set in again. Surely, surely, it could not have done that! With longing, yet with dread, she waited for the sound of Stephen's latchkey. It came at its appointed time.

Even in her agitation Cecilia did not forget to spare him, all she could. She began by giving him a kiss, and then said casually: 'Thyme has got a whim into her head.'

'What whim?'

'It's rather what you might expect,' faltered Cecilia, 'from her going about so much with Martin.'

Stephen's face assumed at once an air of dry derision; there was no love lost between him and his young nephew-in-law.

'The Sanitist?' he said; 'ah! Well?'

'She has gone off to do work to some place in the Euston Road. I've had a telegram. Oh, and I found this, Stephen.'

She held out to him half-heartedly the two bits of paper, one pinkish-brown, the other blue. Stephen saw that she was trembling. He took them from her, read them, and looked at her again. He had a real affection for his wife, and the tradition of consideration for other people's feelings was bred in him, so that at this moment, so vitally disturbing, the first thing he did was to put his hand on her shoulder and give it a reassuring squeeze. But there was also in Stephen a certain primitive virility, pickled, it is true, at Cambridge, and in the Law Courts dried, but still preserving something of its possessive and assertive quality, and the second thing he did was to say, 'No, I'm damned!'

In that little sentence lay the whole psychology of his attitude towards this situation and all the difference between two classes of the population. Mr Purcey would undoubtedly have said: '*Well*, I'm damned!' Stephen, by saying '*No*, I'm damned!' betrayed that before he could be damned he had been obliged to wrestle and contend with something, and Cecilia, who was always wrestling too, knew this something to be that queer new thing, a Social Conscience, the dim bogey stalking pale about the houses of those who, through the accidents of leisure or of culture, had once left the door open to the suspicion: Is it possible that there is a class of people besides my own, or am I dreaming? Happy the millions, poor or rich, not yet condemned to watch the wistful visiting or hear the husky mutter of that ghost, happy in their homes, blessed by a less disquieting god. Such were Cecilia's inner feelings.

Even now she did not quite plumb the depths of Stephen's; she felt his struggle with the ghost, she felt and admired his victory. What she did not, could not, perhaps, realise, was the precise nature of the outrage inflicted on him by Thyme's action. With her —being a woman—the matter was more practical; she did not grasp, had never grasped, the architectural nature of Stephen's mind —how really hurt he was by what did not seem to him in due and proper order.

He spoke: 'Why on earth, if she felt like that, couldn't she have gone to work in the ordinary way? She could have put herself in connection with some proper charitable society—I should never have objected to that. It's all that young Sanitary idiot!'

'I believe,' Cecilia faltered, 'that Martin's *is* a society. It's a kind of medical Socialism, or something of that sort. He has tremendous faith in it.'

Stephen's lip curled.

'He may have as much faith as he likes,' he said, with the restraint that was one of his best qualities, 'so long as he doesn't infect my daughter with it.'

Cecilia said suddenly: 'Oh! what are we to do, Stephen? Shall I go over there to-night?'

As one may see a shadow pass down on a cornfield, so came the cloud on Stephen's face. It was as though he had not realised till then the full extent of what this meant. For a minute he was silent.

'Better wait for her letter,' he said at last. 'He's her cousin, after all, and Mrs Grundy's dead—in the Euston Road, at all events.'

So, trying to spare each other all they could of anxiety, and careful to abstain from any hint of trouble before the servants, they dined and went to bed.

At that hour between the night and morning, when man's vitality is lowest, and the tremors of his spirit, like birds of ill omen, fly round and round him, beating their long plumes against his cheeks, Stephen awoke.

It was very still. A bar of pearly-grey dawn showed between the filmy curtains, which stirred with a regular, faint movement, like the puffing of a sleeper's lips. The tide of the wind, woven in Mr Stone's fancy of the souls of men, was at low ebb. Feebly it fanned the houses and hovels where the myriad forms of men lay sleeping, unconscious of its breath; so faint life's pulse, that men and shadows seemed for that brief moment mingled in the town's sleep. Over the million varied roofs, over the hundred million little different shapes of men and things, the wind's quiet, visiting wand had stilled all into the wonder state of nothingness, when life is passing into death, death into new life, and self is at its feeblest.

And Stephen's self, feeling the magnetic currents of that ebb-tide drawing it down into murmurous slumber, out beyond the sandbars of individuality and class, threw up its little hands and began to cry for help. The purple sea of self-forgetfulness, under the dim, impersonal sky, seemed to him so cold and terrible. It had no limit that he coud see, no rules but such as hung too far away, written in the hieroglyphics of paling stars. He could feel no order in the lift and lap of the wan waters round his limbs. Where would those waters carry him? To what depth of still green silence? Was his own little daughter to go down into this sea that knew no creed but that of self-forgetfulness, that respected neither class nor person—this sea where a few wandering streaks seemed all the evidence of the precious differences between mankind? God forbid it!

And, turning on his elbow, he looked at her who had given him this daughter. In the mystery of his wife's sleeping face—the face of her most near and dear to him—he tried hard not to see a likeness to Mr Stone. He fell back somewhat comforted with the thought: 'That old chap has his one idea—his Universal Brotherhood. He's absolutely absorbed in it. I don't see it in Cis's face a bit. Quite the contrary.'

But suddenly a flash of clear, hard cynicism amounting to inspiration utterly disturbed him: The old chap, indeed, was so wrapped up in himself and his precious book as to be quite unconscious that anyone else was alive. Could one be everybody's brother if one were blind to their existence? But this freak of Thyme's was an actual try to be everybody's sister. For that, he supposed, one *must* forget oneself. Why, it was really even a worse case than that of Mr Stone! And to Stephen there was something awful in this thought.

The first small bird of morning, close to the open window, uttered a feeble chirrup. Into Stephen's mind there leaped without reason recollection of the morning after his first term at school, when, awakened by the birds, he had started up and fished out from under his pillow his catapult and the box of shot he had brought home and taken to sleep with him. He seemed to see again those leaden shot with their bluish sheen, and to feel them, round, and soft, and heavy, rolling about his palm. He seemed to hear Hilary's surprised voice saying: 'Hallo, Stevie! you awake?'

No one had ever had a better brother than old Hilary. His only fault was that he had always been too kind. It was his kindness that had done for him, and made his married life a failure. He had never asserted himself enough with that woman, his wife. Stephen turned over on his other side. 'All this confounded business,' he thought, 'comes from over-sympathising. That's what's the matter with Thyme, too.' Long he lay thus, while the light grew stronger, listening to Cecilia's gentle breathing, disturbed to his very marrow by these thoughts.

The first post brought no letter from Thyme, and the announcement soon after, that Mr Hilary had come to breakfast, was received by both Stephen and Cecilia with a welcome such as the anxious give to anything which shows promise of distracting them.

Stephen made haste down. Hilary, with a very grave and harassed face, was in the dining-room. It was he, however, who, after one look at Stephen, said:

'What's the matter, Stevie?'

Stephen took up the *Standard*. In spite of his self-control, his hand shook a little.

'It's a ridiculous business,' he said. 'That precious young Sanitist has so worked his confounded theories into Thyme that she has gone off to the Euston Road to put them into practice, of all things!'

At the half-concerned amusement on Hilary's face his quick and rather narrow eyes glinted.

'It's not exactly for you to laugh, Hilary,' he said. 'It's all of a piece with your cursed sentimentality about those Hughs, and that girl. I knew it would end in a mess.'

Hilary answered this unjust and unexpected outburst by a look, and Stephen, with the strange feeling of inferiority which would come to him in Hilary's presence against his better judgment, lowered his own glance.

'My dear boy,' said Hilary, 'if any bit of my character has crept into Thyme, I'm truly sorry.'

Stephen took his brother's hand and gave it a good grip; and, Cecilia coming in, they all sat down.

Cecilia at once noted what Stephen in his preoccupation had not—that Hilary had come to tell them something. But she did not like to ask him what it was, though she knew that in the presence of their trouble Hilary was too delicate to obtrude his own. She did not like, either, to talk of her trouble in the presence of his. They all talked, therefore, of indifferent things—what music they had heard, what plays they had seen—eating but little, and drinking tea. In the middle of a remark about the opera, Stephen, looking up, saw Martin himself standing in the doorway. The young Sanitist looked pale, dusty, and dishevelled. He advanced towards Cecilia, and said with his usual cool determination:

'I've brought her back, Aunt Cis.'

At that moment, fraught with such relief, such pure joy, such desire to say a thousand things, Cecilia could only murmur: 'Oh, Martin!'

Stephen, who had jumped up, asked: 'Where is she?'

'Gone to her room.'

'Then perhaps,' said Stephen, regaining at once his dry composure, 'you will give us some explanation of this folly.'

'She's no use to us at present.'

'Indeed!'

'None.'

'Then,' said Stephen, 'kindly understand that we have no use for *you* in future, or any of your sort.'

Martin looked round the table, resting his eyes on each in turn.

'You're right,' he said. 'Good-bye!'

Hilary and Cecilia had risen, too. There was silence. Stephen crossed to the door.

'You seem to me,' he said suddenly, in his driest voice, 'with your new manners and ideas, quite a pernicious youth.'

Cecilia stretched her hands out towards Martin, and there was a faint tinkling, as of chains.

'You must know, dear,' she said, 'how anxious we've all been. Of course, your uncle doesn't mean that.'

The same scornful tenderness with which he was wont to look at Thyme passed into Martin's face.

'All right, Aunt Cis,' he said; 'if Stephen doesn't mean it, he ought to. To mean things is what matters.' He stooped and kissed her forehead. 'Give that to Thyme for me,' he said. 'I shan't see her for a bit.'

'You'll never see her, sir,' said Stephen dryly, 'if I can help it! The liquor of your Sanitism is too bright and effervescent.'

Martin's smile broadened. 'For old bottles,' he said, and with another slow look round went out.

Stephen's mouth assumed its driest twist. 'Bumptious young devil!' he said. 'If that is the new young man, defend us!'

Over the cool dining-room, with its faint scent of pinks, of melon, and of ham, came silence. Suddenly Cecilia glided from the room. Her light footsteps were heard hurrying, now that she was not visible, up to Thyme.

Hilary, too, had moved towards the door. In spite of his preoccupation, Stephen could not help noticing how very worn his brother looked.

'You look quite seedy, old boy,' he said. 'Will you have some brandy?'

Hilary shook his head.

'Now that you've got Thyme back,' he said, 'I'd better let you know my news. I'm going abroad to-morrow. I don't know whether I shall come back again to live with B.'

Stephen gave a low whistle; then, pressing Hilary's arm, he said: 'Anything you decide, old man, I'll always back you in, but——'

'I'm going alone.'

In his relief Stephen violated the laws of reticence.

'Thank Heaven for that! I was afraid you were beginning to lose your head about that girl.'

'I'm not quite fool enough,' said Hilary, 'to imagine that such a liaison would be anything but misery in the long-run. If I took the child I should have to stick to her; but I'm not proud of leaving her in the lurch, Stevie.'

The tone of his voice was so bitter that Stephen seized his hand.

'My dear old man, you're too kind. Why, she's no hold on you—not the smallest in the world!'

'Except the hold of this devotion I've roused in her, God knows how, and her destitution.'

'You let these people haunt you,' said Stephen. 'It's quite a mistake—it really is.'

'I had forgotten to mention that I am not an iceberg,' muttered Hilary.

Stephen looked into his face without speaking, then with the utmost earnestness he said:

'However much you may be attracted, it's simply unthinkable for a man like you to go outside his class.'

'Class! Yes!' muttered Hilary: 'Good-bye!' And with a long grip of his brother's hand he went away.

Stephen turned to the window. For all the care and contrivance bestowed on the view, far away to the left the back courts of an alley could be seen; and as though some gadfly had planted in him its small poisonous sting, he moved back from the sight at once.

'Confusion!' he thought. 'Are we never to get rid of these infernal people?'

His eyes lighted on the melon. A single slice lay by itself on a blue-green dish. Leaning over a plate, with a desperation quite unlike himself, he took an enormous bite. Again and again he bit the slice, then almost threw it from him, and dipped his fingers in a bowl.

'Thank God!' he thought, 'that's over! What an escape!'

Whether he meant Hilary's escape or Thyme's was doubtful, but there came on him a longing to rush up to his little daughter's room and hug her. He suppressed it, and sat down at the bureau; he was suddenly experiencing a sensation such as he had sometimes felt on a perfect day, or after physical danger, of too much benefit, of something that he would like to return thanks for, yet knew not how. His hand stole to the inner pocket of his black coat. It stole out again; there was a cheque-book in it. Before his mind's eye, starting up one after the other, he saw the names of the societies he supported, or meant sometime, if he could afford it, to support. He reached his hand out for a pen. The still, small noise of the nib travelling across the cheques mingled with the buzzing of a single fly.

These sounds Cecilia heard, when, from the open door, she saw the thin back of her husband's neck, with its softly graduated hair, bent forward above the bureau. She stole over to him, and pressed herself against his arm.

Stephen, staying the progress of his pen, looked up at her. Their eyes met, and, bending down, Cecilia put her cheek to his.

Chapter 37

THE FLOWERING OF THE ALOE

THIS same day, returning through Kensington Gardens, from his preparations for departure, Hilary came suddenly on Bianca standing by the shores of the Round Pond.

To the eyes of the frequenters of these Elysian fields, where so many men and shadows daily steal recreation, to the eyes of all drinking in those green gardens their honeyed draught of peace, this husband and wife appeared merely a distinguished-looking couple, animated by a leisured harmony. For the time was not yet when men were one, and could tell by instinct what was passing in each other's hearts.

In truth, there were not too many people in London who, in their situation, would have behaved with such seemliness—not too many so civilised as they!

Estranged, and soon to part, they retained the manner of accord up to the last. Not for them the matrimonial brawl, the solemn accusation and recrimination, the pathetic protestations of proprietary rights. For them no sacred view that at all costs they must make each other miserable—not even the belief that they had the right to do so. No, there was no relief for their sore hearts. They walked side by side, treating each other's feelings with respect, as if there had been no terrible heart-burnings throughout the eighteen years in which they had first loved, then, through mysterious disharmony, drifted apart; as if there were now between them no question of this girl.

Presently Hilary said:

'I've been into town and made my preparations; I'm starting to-morrow for the mountains. There will be no necessity for you to leave your father.'

'Are you taking her?'

It was beautifully uttered, without a trace of bias or curiosity, with an unforced accent, neither indifferent nor too interested—no one could have told whether it was meant for generosity or malice. Hilary took it for the former.

'Thank you,' he said; 'that comedy is finished.'

Close to the edge of the Round Pond a swan-like cutter was putting out to sea; in the wake of this fair creature a tiny scooped-out bit of wood, with three feathers for masts, bobbed and trembled; and the two small ragged boys who owned that little galley were stretching bits of branch out towards her over the bright waters.

Bianca looked, without seeing, at this proof of man's pride in his own property. A thin gold chain hung round her neck; suddenly she thrust it into the bosom of her dress. It had broken into two, between her fingers.

They reached home without another word.

At the door of Hilary's study sat Miranda. The little person answered his caress by a shiver of her sleek skin, then curled herself down again on the spot she had already warmed.

'Aren't you coming in with me?' he said.

Miranda did not move.

The reason for her refusal was apparent when Hilary had entered. Close to the long bookcase, behind the bust of Socrates, stood the little model. Very still, as if fearing to betray itself by sound or movement, was her figure in its blue-green frock, and a brimless toque of brown straw, with two purplish roses squashed together into a band of darker velvet. Beside those roses a tiny peacock's feather had been slipped in—unholy little visitor, slanting backward, trying, as it were, to draw all eyes, yet to escape notice. And, wedged between the grim white bust and the dark bookcase, the girl herself was like some unlawful spirit which had slid in there, and stood trembling and vibrating, ready to be shuttered out.

Before this apparition Hilary recoiled towards the door, hesitated, and returned.

'You should not have come here,' he muttered, 'after what we said to you yesterday.'

The little model answered quickly: 'But I've seen Hughs, Mr Dallison. He's found out where I live. Oh, he does look dreadful; he frightens me. I can't ever stay there now.'

She had come a little out of her hiding-place, and stood fidgeting her hands and looking down.

'She's not speaking the truth,' thought Hilary.

The little model gave him a furtive glance. 'I *did* see him,' she said. 'I must go right away now; it wouldn't be safe, would it?' Again she gave him that swift look.

Hilary thought suddenly: 'She is using my own weapon against me. If she *has* seen the man, he didn't frighten her. It serves me right!' With a dry laugh, he turned his back.

There was a rustling sound. The little model had moved out of her retreat, and stood between him and the door. At this stealthy action, Hilary felt once more the tremor which had come over him when he sat beside her in the Broad Walk after the baby's funeral. Outside in the garden a pigeon was pouring forth a continuous love-song; Hilary heard nothing of it, conscious only of the figure of the girl behind him—that young figure which had twined itself about his senses.

'Well, what is it you want?' he said at last.

The little model answered by another question. 'Are you really going away, Mr Dallison?'

'I am.'

She raised her hands to the level of her breast, as though she meant to clasp them together; without doing so, however, she dropped them to her sides. They were cased in very worn suède gloves, and in this dire moment of embarrassment Hilary's eyes fastened themselves on those slim hands moving against her skirt.

The little model tried at once to slip them away behind her. Suddenly she said in her matter-of-fact voice: 'I only wanted to ask—Can't I come too?'

At this question, whose simplicity might have made an angel smile, Hilary experienced a sensation as if his bones had been turned to water. It was strange—delicious—as though he had been suddenly offered all that he wanted of her, without all those things that he did not want. He stood regarding her silently. Her cheeks and neck were red; there was a red tinge, too, in her eyelids, deepening the 'chicory-flower' colour of her eyes. She began to speak, repeating a lesson evidently learned by heart.

'I wouldn't be in your way. I wouldn't cost much. I could do everything you wanted. I could learn typewriting. I needn't live too near, or that, if you didn't want me, because of people talking; I'm used to being alone. Oh, Mr Dallison, I could do everything for you. I wouldn't mind *anything*, and I'm not like some girls; I do know what I'm talking about.'

'Do you?'

The little model put her hands up, and, covering her face, said:

'If you'd try and see!'

Hilary's sensuous feeling almost vanished; a lump rose in his throat instead.

'My child,' he said, 'you are too generous!'

The little model seemed to know instinctively that by touching his spirit she had lost ground. Uncovering her face, she spoke breathlessly, growing very pale:

'Oh no, I'm not. I *want* to be let come; I don't want to stay here. I know I'll get into mischief if you don't take me—oh, I know I will!'

'If I were to let you come with me,' said Hilary, 'what then? What sort of companion should I be to you, or you to me? You know very well. Only one sort. It's no use pretending, child, that we've any interests in common.'

The little model came closer.

'I know what I am,' she said, 'and I don't want to be anything else. I can do what you tell me to, and I shan't ever complain. I'm not worth any more!'

'You're worth more,' muttered Hilary, 'than I can ever give you, and I'm worth more than you can ever give me.'

The little model tried to answer, but her words would not pass her throat; she threw her head back trying to free them, and stood, swaying. Seeing her like this before him, white as a sheet, with her eyes closed and her lips parted, as though about to faint, Hilary seized her by the shoulders. At the touch of those soft shoulders, his face became suffused with blood, his lips trembled. Suddenly her eyes opened ever so little between their lids, and looked at him. And the perception that she was not really going to faint, that it was a little desperate wile of this child Dalilah, made him wrench away his hands. The moment she felt that grasp relax she sank down and clasped his knees, pressing them to her bosom so that he could not stir. Closer and closer she pressed them to her, till it seemed as though she must be bruising her flesh. Her breath came in sobs; her eyes were closed; her lips quivered upwards. In the clutch of her clinging body there seemed suddenly the whole of woman's power of self-abandonment. It was just that, which, at this moment, so horribly painful to him, prevented Hilary from seizing her in his arms—just that queer seeming self-effacement, as though she were lost to knowledge of what she did. It seemed too brutal, too like taking advantage of a child.

From calm is born the wind, the ripple from the still pool, self out of nothingness—so all passes imperceptibly, no man knows how. The little model's moment of self-oblivion passed, and into her wet eyes her plain, twisting spirit suddenly writhed up again, for all the world as if she had said: 'I won't let you go; I'll keep you—I'll keep you.'

Hilary broke away from her, and she fell forward on her face.

'Get up, child,' he said—'get up; for God's sake, don't lie there!'

She rose obediently, choking down her sobs, mopping her face with a small, dirty handkerchief. Suddenly, taking a step towards him, she clenched both her hands and struck them downwards.

'I'll go to the bad,' she said—'I *will*—if you don't take me!' And, her breast heaving, her hair all loose, she stared straight into his face with her red-rimmed eyes. Hilary turned suddenly, took a book up from the writing-table, and opened it. His face was again suffused with blood; his hands and lips trembled; his eyes had a queer fixed stare.

'Not now, not now,' he muttered; 'go away now. I'll come to you to-morrow.'

The little model gave him the look a dog gives you when it asks if you are deceiving him. She made a sign on her breast, as a Catholic might make the sign of his religion, drawing her fingers together, and clutching at herself with them, then passed her little dirty handkerchief once more over her eyes, and, turning round, went out.

Hilary remained standing where he was, reading the open book without apprehending what it was.

There was a wistful sound, as of breath escaping hurriedly. Mr Stone was standing in the open doorway.

'She has been here,' he said. 'I saw her go away.'

Hilary dropped the book; his nerves were utterly unstrung. Then, pointing to a chair, he said: 'Won't you sit down, sir?'

Mr Stone came close up to his son-in-law.

'Is she in trouble?'

'Yes,' murmured Hilary.

'She is too young to be in trouble. Did you tell her that?'

Hilary shook his head.

'Has the man hurt her?'

Again Hilary shook his head.

'What is her trouble, then?' said Mr Stone.

The closeness of this catechism, the intent stare of the old man's eyes, were more than Hilary could bear. He turned away.

'You ask me something that I cannot answer.'

'Why?'

'It is a private matter.'

With the blood still beating in his temples, his lips still quivering, and the feeling of the girl's clasp round his knees, he almost hated this old man who stood there putting such blind questions.

Then suddenly in Mr Stone's eyes he saw a startling change, as in the face of a man who regains consciousness after days of vacancy. His whole countenance had become alive with a sort of jealous understanding. The warmth which the little model brought to his old spirit had licked up the fog of his Idea, and made him see what was going on before his eyes.

At that look Hilary braced himself against the wall.

A flush spread slowly over Mr Stone's face. He spoke with rare hesitation. In this sudden coming back to the world of men and things he seemed astray.

'I am not going,' he stammered, 'to ask you any more. I could not pry into a private matter. That would not be——' His voice failed; he looked down.

Hilary bowed, touched to the quick by the return to life of this old man, so long lost to facts, and by the delicacy in that old face.

'I will not intrude further on your trouble,' said Mr Stone, 'whatever it may be. I am sorry that you are unhappy, too.'

Very slowly, and without again looking up at his son-in-law, he went out.

Hilary remained standing where he had been left against the wall.

Chapter 38

THE HOME-COMING OF HUGHS

HILARY had evidently been right in thinking the little model was not speaking the truth when she said she had seen Hughs, for it was not until early on the following morning that three persons traversed the long winding road leading from Wormwood Scrubs to Kensington. They preserved silence, not because there was nothing in their hearts to be expressed, but because there was too much; and they walked in the giraffe-like formation peculiar to the lower classes—Hughs in front; Mrs Hughs to the left, a foot or two behind; and a yard behind her, to the left again, her son Stanley. They made no sign of noticing anyone in the road besides themselves, and no one in the road gave sign of noticing that they were there; but in their three minds, so differently fashioned, a verb was dumbly, and with varying emotion, being conjugated:

'I've been in prison.'
'You've been in prison.'
'He's been in prison.'

Beneath the seeming acquiescence of a man subject to domination from his birth up, those four words covered in Hughs such a whirlpool of surging sensation, such a ferocity of bitterness, and madness, and defiance, that no outpouring could have appreciably relieved its course. The same four words summed up in Mrs Hughs so strange a mingling of fear, commiseration, loyalty, shame, and trembling curiosity at the new factor which had come into the life of all this little family walking giraffe-like back to Kensington that to have gone beyond them would have been like plunging into a wintry river. To their son the four words were as a legend of romance, conjuring up no definite image, lighting merely the glow of wonder.

'Don't lag, Stanley. Keep up with your father.'

The little boy took three steps at an increased pace, then fell behind again. His black eyes seemed to answer: 'You say that because you don't know what else to say.' And without alteration in their giraffe-like formation, but again in silence, the three proceeded.

In the heart of the seamstress doubt and fear were being slowly knit into dread of the first sound to pass her husband's lips. What would he ask? How should she answer? Would he talk wild, or would he talk sensible? Would he have forgotten that young girl, or had he nursed and nourished his wicked fancy in the house of grief and silence? Would he ask where the baby was? Would he speak a kind word to her? But alongside her dread there was fluttering within her the undying resolution not to 'let him go from her, if it were ever so, to that young girl.'

'Don't lag, Stanley!'

At the reiteration of those words Hughs spoke.

'Let the boy alone; You'll be nagging at the baby next!'

Hoarse and grating, like sounds issuing from a damp vault, was this first speech.

The seamstress's eyes brimmed over.

'I won't get the chance,' she stammered out. 'He's gone!'

Hughs' teeth gleamed like those of a dog at bay.

'Who's taken him? You let me know the name.'

Tears rolled down the seamstress's cheeks; she could not answer. Her little son's thin voice rose instead:

'Baby's dead. We buried him in the ground. I saw it. Mr Creed came in the cab with me.'

White flecks appeared suddenly at the corners of Hughs' lips. He wiped the back of his hand across his mouth, and once more, giraffe-like, the little family marched on. . . .

'Westminister', in his threadbare summer jacket—for the day was warm—had been standing for some little time in Mrs Budgen's doorway on the ground floor at Hound Street. Knowing that Hughs was to be released that morning early, he had, with the circumspection and foresight of his character, reasoned thus: 'I shan't lie easy in my bed, I shan't hev no peace until I know that low feller's not a-goin' to misdemean himself with me. It's no good to go a-puttin' of it off. I don't want him comin' to my room attackin' of old men. I'll be previous with him in the passage. The lame woman 'll let me. I shan't trouble her. She'll be palliable between me and him, in case he goes for to attack me. *I* ain't afraid of him.'

But, as the minutes of waiting went by, his old tongue, like that of a dog expecting chastisement, appeared ever more frequently to moisten his twisted, discoloured lips. 'This comes of mixin' up with soldiers,' he thought, 'and a low-class o' man like that. I ought to ha' changed my lodgin's. He'll be askin' me where that young girl is, I shouldn't wonder, an' him lost his character and his job, and everything, and all because o' women!'

He watched the broad-faced woman, Mrs Budgen, in whose grey eyes the fighting light so fortunately never died, painfully doing out her rooms, and propping herself against the chest of drawers whereon clustered china cups and dogs as thick as toadstools on a bank.

'I've told my Charlie,' she said, 'to keep clear of Hughs a bit. They comes out as prickly as hedgehogs. Pick a quarrel as soon as look at you, they will.'

'Oh dear,' thought Creed, 'she's full o' cold comfort.' But, careful of his dignity, he answered: 'I'm a-waitin' here to engage the situation. You don't think he'll attack of me with definition at this time in the mornin'?'

The lame woman shrugged her shoulders. 'He'll have had a drop of something,' she said, 'before he comes home. They gets a cold feelin' in the stomach in them places, poor creatures!'

The old butler's heart quavered up into his mouth. He lifted his shaking hand, and put it to his lips, as though to readjust himself.

'Oh yes,' he said; 'I ought to ha' given notice, and took my things away; but there, poor woman, it seemed a-hittin' of her when she was down. And I don't *want* to make no move. I ain't got no one else that's interested in me. This woman's very good about mendin' of my clothes. Oh dear, yes; she don't grudge a little thing like that!'

The lame woman hobbled from her post of rest, and began to make the bed with the frown that always accompanied a task which strained the contracted muscles of her leg. 'If you don't help your neighbour, your neighbour don't help you,' she said sententiously.

Creed fixed his iron-rimmed gaze on her in silence. He was considering perhaps how he stood with regard to Hughs in the light of that remark.

'I attended of his baby's funeral,' he said. 'Oh dear, he's here a'ready!'

The family of Hughs, indeed, stood in the doorway. The spiritual process by which 'Westminister' had gone through life was displayed completely in the next few seconds. 'It's so important for me to keep alive and well,' his eyes seemed saying. 'I know the class of man you are, but now you're here it's not a bit o' use me bein' frightened. I'm bound to get up-sides with you. Ho! yes; keep yourself to yourself, and don't you let me hev any o' your nonsense, 'cause I won't stand it. Oh dear, no!'

Beads of perspiration stood thick on his patchily coloured forehead; with lips stiffening, and intently staring eyes, he waited for what the released prisoner would say.

Hughs, whose face had blanched in the prison to a sallow grey-white hue, and whose black eyes seemed to have sunk back into his head, slowly looked the old man up and down. At last he took his cap off, showing his cropped hair.

'*You* got me that, daddy,' he said, 'but I don't bear you malice. Come up and have a cup o' tea with us.'

And, turning on his heel, he began to mount the stairs, followed by his wife and child. Breathing hard, the old butler mounted too.

In the room on the second floor, where the baby no longer lived, a haddock on the table was endeavouring to be fresh; round it were slices of bread on plates, a piece of butter in a pie-dish, a teapot, brown sugar in a basin, and, side by side, a little blue jug of cold milk and a half-empty bottle of red vinegar. Close to one plate a bunch of stocks and gillyflowers reposed on the dirty tablecloth, as though dropped and forgotten by the God of Love. Their faint perfume stole through the other odours. The old butler fixed his eyes on it.

'The poor woman bought that,' he thought, 'hopin' for to remind him of old days. She had them flowers on her weddin'-day, I shouldn't wonder!' This poetical conception surprising him, he turned towards the little boy, and said: 'This'll be a memorial to you, as you gets older.' And without another word all sat down.

They ate in silence, and the old butler thought: 'That 'addick ain't what it was; but a beautiful cup o' tea. He don't eat nothing; he's more ameniable to reason than I expected. There's no one won't be too pleased to see him now!'

His eyes, travelling to the spot from which the bayonet had been removed, rested on the print of the Nativity. '"Suffer little children to come unto *Me*,"' he thought, '"and forbid them not". He'll be glad to hear there was two carriages followed him home.'

And, taking his time, he cleared his throat in preparation for speech. But before the singular muteness of this family sounds would not come. Finishing his tea, he tremblingly arose. Things that he might have said jostled in his mind. 'Very pleased to 'a seen you. Hope you're in good health at the present time of speaking. Don't let me intrude on you. We've all a-got to die some time or other!' They remained unuttered. Making a vague movement of his skinny hand, he walked feebly but quickly to the door. When he stood but half-way within the room, he made his final effort.

'I'm not a-goin' to say nothing,' he said;—'*that'd* be superlative! I wish you a good-morning.'

Outside he waited a second, then grasped the banister.

'For all he sets so quiet, they've done him no good in that place,' he thought. 'Them eyes of his!' And slowly he descended, full of a sort of very deep surprise. 'I misjudged of him,' he was thinking; 'he never was nothing but a 'armless human being. We all has our predijuices—I misjudged of him. They've broke his 'eart between 'em—that they have.'

The silence in the room continued after his departure. But when the little boy had gone to school, Hughs rose and lay down on the bed. He rested there, unmoving, with his face towards the wall, his arms clasped round his head to comfort it. The seamstress, stealing about her avocations, paused now and then to look at him. If he had raged at her, if he had raged at everything, it would not have been so terrifying as this utter silence, which passed her comprehension—this silence as of a man flung by the sea against a rock, and pinned there with the life crushed out of him. All her inarticulate longing, now that her baby was gone, to be close to something in her grey life, to pass the unfranchisable barrier dividing her from the world, seemed to well up, to flow against this wall of silence and recoil.

Twice or three times she addressed him timidly by name, or made some trivial remark. He did not answer, as though in very truth he had been the shadow of a man lying there. And the injustice of this silence seemed to her so terrible. Was she not his wife? Had she not borne him five, and toiled to keep him from that girl? Was it her fault if she had made his life a hell with her jealousy, as he had cried out that morning before he went for her, and was 'put away'? He was her 'man'. It had been her right—nay, more, her duty!

And still he lay there silent. From the narrow street where no traffic passed, the cries of a coster and distant whistlings mounted through the unwholesome air. Some sparrows in the eave were chirruping incessantly. The little sandy house-cat had stolen in, and, crouched against the door-post, was fastening her eyes on the plate which held the remnants of the fish. The seamstress bowed her forehead to the flowers on the table; unable any longer to bear the mystery of this silence, she wept. But the dark figure on the bed only pressed his arms closer round his head, as though there were within him a living death passing the speech of men.

The little sandy cat, creeping across the floor, fixed its claws in the backbone of the fish, and drew it beneath the bed.

Chapter 39

THE DUEL

BIANCA did not see her husband after their return together from the Round Pond. She dined out that evening, and in the morning avoided any interview. When Hilary's luggage was brought down and the cab summoned, she slipped up to take shelter in her room. Presently the sound of his footsteps coming along the passage stopped outside her door. He tapped. She did not answer.

Good-bye would be a mockery! Let him go with the words unsaid! And as though the thought had found its way through the closed door, she heard his footsteps recede again. She saw him presently go out to the cab with his head bent down, saw him stoop and pat Miranda. Hot tears sprang into her eyes. She heard the cab-wheels roll away.

The heart is like the face of an Eastern woman—warm and glowing, behind swathe on swathe of fabric. At each fresh touch from the fingers of Life, some new corner, some hidden curve or angle, comes into view, to be seen last of all—perhaps never to be seen—by the one who owns them.

When the cab had driven away there came into Bianca's heart a sense of the irreparable, and, mysteriously entwined with that arid ache, a sort of bitter pity. What would happen to this wretched girl now that he was gone? Would she go completely to the bad—till she became one of those poor creatures like the figure in 'The Shadow', who stood beneath lamp-posts in the streets? Out of this speculation, which was bitter as the taste of aloes, there came to her a craving for some palliative, some sweetness, some expression of that instinct of fellow-feeling deep in each human breast, however disharmonic. But even with that craving was mingled the itch to justify herself, and prove that she could rise above jealousy.

She made her way to the little model's lodging.

A child admitted her into the bleak passage that served for hall. The strange medley of emotions passing through Bianca's breast while she stood outside the girl's door did not show in her face, which wore its customary restrained, half-mocking look.

The little model's voice faintly said: 'Come in.'

The room was in disorder, as though soon to be deserted. A closed and corded trunk stood in the centre of the floor; the bed, stripped of clothing, lay disclosed in all the barrenness of discoloured ticking. The china utensils of the washstand were turned head downwards. Beside that washstand the little model, with her hat on—the hat with the purplish-pink roses and the little peacock's feather—stood in the struck, shrinking attitude of one who, coming forward in the expectation of a kiss, has received a blow.

'You are leaving here, then?' Bianca said quietly.

'Yes,' the girl murmured.

'Don't you like this part? Is it too far from your work?'

Again the little model whispered: 'Yes.'

Bianca's eyes travelled slowly over the blue beflowered walls and rust-red doors; through the dusty closeness of this dismantled room a rank scent of musk and violets rose, as though a cheap essence had been scattered as libation. A small empty scent-bottle stood on the shabby looking-glass.

'Have you found new lodgings?'

The little model edged closer to the window. A stealthy watchfulness was creeping into her shrinking, dazed face.

She shook her head.

'I don't know where I'm going.'

Obeying a sudden impulse to see more clearly, Bianca lifted her veil. 'I came to tell you,' she said, 'that I shall always be ready to help you.'

The girl did not answer, but suddenly through her black lashes she stole a look upward at her visitor. 'Can *you*,' it seemed to say, '*you*—help me? Oh no; I think not!' And as though she had been stung by that glance, Bianca said with deadly slowness:

'It is my business, of course, entirely, now that Mr Dallison has gone abroad.'

The little model received this saying with a quivering jerk. It might have been an arrow transfixing her white throat. For a moment she seemed almost about to fall, but gripping the window-sill, held herself erect. Her eyes, like an animal's in pain darted here, there, everywhere, then rested on her visitor's breast, quite motionless. This stare, which seemed to see nothing, but to be doing, as it were, some mortal calculation, was uncanny. Colour came gradually back into her lips and eyes and cheeks; she seemed to have succeeded in her calculation, to be reviving from that stab.

And suddenly Bianca understood. This was the meaning of the packed trunk, the dismantled room. He was going to take her, after all!

In the turmoil of this discovery two words alone escaped her: 'I see!'

They were enough. The girl's face at once lost all trace of its look of mortal calculation, brightened, became guilty, and from guilty sullen.

The antagonism of all the long past months was now declared between these two—Bianca's pride could no longer conceal, the girl's submissiveness no longer obscure it. They stood like duellists, one on each side of the trunk—that common, brown-japanned, tin trunk, corded with rope. Bianca looked at it.

'You,' she said, 'and he? Ha, ha; ha, ha! Ha, ha, ha!'

Against that cruel laughter—more poignant than a hundred homilies on caste, a thousand scornful words—the little model literally could not stand; she sat down in the low chair where she had evidently been sitting to watch the street. But as a taste of blood will infuriate a hound, so her own laughter seemed to bereave Bianca of all restraint.

'What do you imagine he's taking you for, girl? Only out of pity! It's not exactly the emotion to live on in exile. In exile—but that you do not understand!'

The little model staggered to her feet again. Her face had grown painfully red.

'He wants me!' she said.

'Wants you? As he wants his dinner. And when he's eaten it—what then? No, of course he'll never abandon you; his conscience is too tender. But you'll be round his neck—like this!' Bianca raised her arms, looped, and dragged them slowly down, as a mermaid's arms drag at a drowning sailor.

The little model stammered: 'I'll do what he tells me! I'll do what he tells me!'

Bianca stood silent, looking at the girl, whose heaving breast and little peacock's feather, whose small round hands twisting in front of her, and scent about her clothes, all seemed an offence.

'And do you suppose that he'll tell you what he wants? Do you imagine *he'll* have the necessary brutality to get rid of you? He'll think himself bound to keep you till you leave him, as I suppose you will some day!'

The girl dropped her hands. 'I'll never leave him—never!' she cried out passionately.

'Then Heaven help him!' said Bianca.

The little model's eyes seemed to lose all pupil, like two chicory flowers that have no dark centres. Through them, all that she was feeling struggled to find an outlet; but, too deep for words, those things would not pass her lips, utterly unused to express emotion. She could only stammer:

'I'm not—I'm not—I will——' and press her hands again to her breast.

Bianca's lip curled.

'I see; you imagine yourself capable of sacrifice. Well, you have your chance. Take it!' She pointed to the corded trunk. 'Now's your time; you have only to disappear!'

The little model shrank back against the window-sill. 'He wants me!' she muttered. 'I *know* he wants me.'

Bianca bit her lips till the blood came.

'Your idea of sacrifice,' she said, 'is perfect! If you went now, in a month's time he'd never think of you again.'

The girl gulped. There was something so pitiful in the movements of her hands that Bianca turned away. She stood for several seconds staring at the door, then, turning round again, said:

'Well?'

But the girl's whole face had changed. All tear-stained, indeed, she had already masked it with a sort of immovable stolidity.

Bianca went swiftly up to the trunk.

'You *shall*!' she said. 'Take that thing and go!'

The little model did not move.

'So you won't?'

The girl trembled violently all over. She moistened her lips, tried to speak, failed, again moistened them, and this time murmured: 'I'll only—I'll only—if *he* tells me!'

'So you still imagine he will tell you!'

The little model merely repeated: 'I won't—I won't do anything without *he* tells me!'

Bianca laughed. 'Why, it's like a dog!' she said.

But the girl had turned abruptly to the window. Her lips were parted. She was shrinking, fluttering, trembling at what she saw. She was indeed like a spaniel dog who sees her master coming. Bianca had no need of being told that Hilary was outside. She went into the passage and opened the front door.

He was coming up the steps, his face worn like that of a man in fever, and at the sight of his wife he stood quite still, looking into her face.

Without the quiver of an eyelid, without the faintest trace of emotion, or the slightest sign that she knew him to be there, Bianca passed and slowly walked away.

Chapter 40

FINISH OF THE COMEDY

THOSE who may have seen Hilary driving towards the little model's lodgings saw one who, by a fixed red spot in either cheek, and the over-compression of his quivering lips, betrayed the presence of that animality which underlies even the most cultivated men.

After eighteen hours of the purgatory of indecision, he had not so much decided to pay that promised visit on which hung the future of two lives, as allowed himself to be borne towards the girl.

There was no one in the passage to see him after he had passed Bianca in the doorway, but it was with a face darkened by the peculiar stabbing look of wounded egoism that he entered the little model's room.

The sight of it coming so closely on the struggle she had just been through was too much for the girl's self-control.

Instead of going up to him, she sat down on the corded trunk and began to sob. It was the sobbing of a child whose school-treat has been cancelled, of a girl whose ball-dress has not come home in time. It only irritated Hilary, whose nerves had already borne all they could bear. He stood literally trembling, as though each one of these common little sobs were a blow falling on the drumskin of his spirit, and through every fibre he took in the features of the dusty, scent-besprinkled room—the brown tin trunk, the dismantled bed, the rust-red doors.

And he realised that she had burned her boats to make it impossible for a man of sensibility to disappoint her!

The little model raised her face and looked at him. What she saw must have been less reassuring even than the first sight had been, for it stopped her sobbing. She rose and turned to the window, evidently trying with handkerchief and powder-puff to repair the ravages caused by her tears; and when she had finished she still stood there with her back to him. Her deep breathing made her young form quiver from her waist up to the little peacock's feather in her hat; and with each supple movement it seemed offering itself to Hilary.

In the street a barrel-organ had begun to play the very waltz it had played the afternoon when Mr Stone had been so ill. Those two were neither of them conscious of that tune, too absorbed in their emotions; and yet, quietly, it was bringing something to the girl's figure—like the dowering of scent that the sun brings to a flower. It was bringing the compression back to Hilary's lips, the flush to his ears and cheeks, as a draught of wind will blow to redness a fire that has been choked. Without knowing it, without sound, inch by inch he moved nearer to her; and as though, for all there was no sign of his advance, she knew of it, she stayed utterly unmoving except for the deep breathing that so stirred the warm youth in her. In that stealthy progress was the history of life and the mystery of sex. Inch by inch he neared her; and she swayed, mesmerising his arms to fold round her thus poised, as if she must fall backward; mesmerising him to forget that there was anything there, anything in all the world, but just her young form waiting for him—nothing but that!

The barrel-organ stopped; the spell had broken! She turned round to him. As a wind obscures with grey wrinkles the still green waters of enchantment wherein some mortal has been gazing, so Hilary's reason suddenly swept across the situation, and showed it once more as it was. Quick to mark every shade that passed across his face, the girl made as though she would again burst into tears; then, since tears had been so useless, she pressed her hand over her eyes.

Hilary looked at that round, not too cleanly hand. He could see her watching him between her fingers. It was uncanny, almost horrible, like the sight of a cat watching a bird; and he stood appalled at the terrible reality of his position, at the sight of his own future with this girl, with her traditions, customs, life, the thousand and one things that he did not know about her, that he would have to live with if he once took her. A minute passed, which seemed eternity, for into it was condensed every force of her long pursuit, her instinctive clutching at something that she felt to be security, her reaching upwards, her twining round him.

Conscious of all this, held back by that vision of his future, yet whipped towards her by his senses, Hilary swayed like a drunken man. And suddenly she sprang at him, wreathed her arms round his neck, and fastened her mouth to his. The touch of her lips was moist and hot. The scent of stale violet powder came from her, warmed by her humanity. It penetrated to Hilary's heart. He started back in sheer physical revolt.

Thus repulsed, the girl stood rigid, her breast heaving, her eyes unnaturally dilated, her mouth still loosened by the kiss. Snatching from his pocket a roll of notes, Hilary flung them on the bed.

'I can't take you!' he almost groaned. 'It's madness! it's impossible!' And he went out into the passage. He ran down the steps and got into his cab. An immense time seemed to pass before it began to move. It started at last, and Hilary sat back in it, his hands clenched, as still as a dead man.

His mortified face was recognised by the landlady, returning from her morning's visit to the shops. The gentleman looked, she thought, as if he had received bad news! She not unnaturally connected his appearance with her lodger. Tapping on the girl's door, and receiving no answer, she went in.

The little model was lying on the dismantled bed, pressing her face into the blue and white ticking of the bolster. Her shoulders shook, and a sound of smothered sobbing came from her. The landlady stood staring silently.

Coming of Cornish chapel-going stock, she had never liked this girl, her instinct telling her that she was one for whom life had already been to much. Those for whom life had so early been too much, she knew, were always 'ones for pleasure'! Her experience of village life had enabled her to construct the little model's story—that very simple, very frequent little story. Sometimes, indeed, trouble of that sort was soon over and forgotten; but sometimes, if the young man didn't do the right thing by her, and the girl's folk took it hardly, well, then——! So had run the reasoning of this good woman. Being of the same class, she had looked at her lodger from the first without obliquity of vision.

But seeing her now apparently so overwhelmed, and having something soft and warm down beneath her granitic face and hungry eyes, she touched her on the back.

'Come, now!' she said; 'you mustn't take on! What is it?'

The little model shook off the hand as a passionate child shakes itself free of consolation. 'Let me alone!' she muttered.

The landlady drew back. 'Has anyone done you a harm?' she said.

The little model shook her head.

Baffled by this dumb grief, the landlady was silent; then, with the stolidity of those whose lives are one long wrestling with fortune, she muttered:

'I don't like to see *anyone* cry like that!'

And finding that the girl remained obstinately withdrawn from sight or sympathy, she moved towards the door.

'Well,' she said, with ironical compassion, 'if you want me, I'll be in the kitchen.'

The little model remained lying on her bed. Every now and then she gulped, like a child flung down on the grass apart from its comrades, trying to swallow down its rage, trying to bury in the earth its little black moment of despair. Slowly those gulps grew fewer, feebler, and at last died away. She sat up, sweeping Hilary's bundle of notes, on which she had been lying, to the floor.

At sight of that bundle she broke out afresh, flinging herself down sideways with her cheek on the wet bolster; and, for some time after her sobs had ceased again, still lay there. At last she rose and dragged herself over to the looking-glass, scrutinising her streaked, discoloured face, the stains in the cheeks, the swollen eyelids, the marks beneath her eyes; and listlessly she tidied herself. Then, sitting down on the brown tin trunk, she picked the bundle of notes off the floor. They gave forth a dry peculiar crackle. Fifteen ten-pound notes—all Hilary's travelling money. Her eyes opened wider and wider as she counted; and tears, quite suddenly, rolled down on to those thin slips of paper.

Then slowly she undid her dress, and forced them down till they rested, with nothing but her vest between them and the quivering warm flesh which hid her heart.

Chapter 41

THE HOUSE OF HARMONY

AT half-past ten that evening Stephen walked up the stone-flagged pathway of his brother's house.

'Can I see Mrs Hilary?'

'Mr Hilary went abroad this morning, sir, and Mrs Hilary has not yet come in.'

'Will you give her this letter? No, I'll wait, I suppose I can wait for her in the garden?'

'Oh yes, sir!'

'Very well.'

'I'll leave the door open, sir, in case you want to come in.'

Stephen walked across to the rustic bench and sat down. He stared gloomily through the dusk at his patent-leather boots, and every now and then he flicked his evening trousers with the letter Across the dark garden, where the boughs hung soft, unmoved by wind, the light from Mr Stone's open window flowed out in a pale river; moths, born of the sudden heat, were fluttering up this river to its source.

Stephen looked irritably at the figure of Mr Stone, which could be seen, bowed, and utterly still, beside his desk; so, by lifting the spy-hole thatch, one may see a convict in his cell stand gazing at his work, without movement, numb with solitude.

'He's getting awfully broken up,' thought Stephen. 'Poor old chap! His ideas are killing him. They're not human nature, never will be.' Again he flicked his trousers with the letter, as though that document emphasised the fact. 'I can't help being sorry for the sublime old idiot!'

He rose, the better to see his father-in-law's unconscious figure. It looked as lifeless and as cold as though Mr Stone had followed some thought below the ground, and left his body standing there to await his return. Its appearance oppressed Stephen.

'You might set the house on fire,' he thought; 'he'd never notice.'

Mr Stone's figure moved; the sound of a long sigh came out to Stephen in the windless garden. He turned his eyes away, with the sudden feeling that it was not the thing to watch the old chap like this; then, getting up, he went indoors. In his brother's study he stood turning over the knick-knacks on the writing-table.

'I warned Hilary that he was burning his fingers,' he thought.

At the sound of the latchkey he went back to the hall.

However much he had secretly disapproved of her from the beginning, because she had always seemed to him such an uncomfortable and tantalising person, Stephen was impressed that night by the haunting unhappiness of Bianca's face; as if it had been suddenly disclosed to him that she could not help herself. This was disconcerting, being, in a sense, a disorderly way of seeing things.

'You look tired, B.,' he said. 'I'm sorry, but I thought it better to bring this round to-night.'

Bianca glanced at the letter.

'It is to you,' she said. 'I don't wish to read it, thank you.'

Stephen compressed his lips.

'But I wish you to hear it, please,' he said. 'I'll read it out, if you'll allow me.

"CHARING CROSS STATION.

"DEAR STEVIE,

"I told you yesterday morning that I was going abroad alone. Afterwards I changed my mind—I meant to take her. I went to her lodgings for the purpose. I have lived too long amongst sentiments for such a piece of reality as that. Class has saved me; it has triumphed over my most primitive instincts.

"I am going alone—back to my sentiments. No slight has been placed on Bianca—but my married life having become a mockery, I shall not return to it. The following address will find me, and I shall ask you presently to send on my household gods.

"Please let Bianca know the substance of this letter.

"Ever your affectionate brother,

"HILARY DALLISON." '

With a frown Stephen folded up the letter, and restored it to his breast pocket.

'It's more bitter than I thought,' he reflected; 'and yet he's done the only possible thing!'

Bianca was leaning her elbow on the mantelpiece with her face turned to the wall. Her silence irritated Stephen, whose loyalty to his brother longed to find a vent.

'I'm very much relieved, of course,' he said at last. 'It would have been fatal.'

She did not move, and Stephen became increasingly aware that this was a most awkward matter to touch on.

'Of course,' he began again. 'But, B., I don't think you—rather—

I mean——' And again he stopped before her utter silence, her utter immobility. Then unable to go away without having in some sort expressed his loyalty to Hilary, he tried once more: 'Hilary is the kindest man I know. It's not his fault if he's out of touch with life—if he's not fit to deal with things. He's *negative*!'

And having thus in a single word, somewhat to his own astonishmen, described his brother, he held out his hand.

The hand which Bianca placed in it was feverishly hot. Stephen felt suddenly compunctious.

'I'm awfully sorry,' he stammered, 'about the whole thing. I'm awfully sorry for you——'

Bianca drew back her hand.

With a little shrug Stephen turned away.

'What are you to do with women like that?' was his thought, and saying dryly, 'Good-night, B.,' he went.

For some time Bianca sat in Hilary's chair. Then, by the faint glimmer coming through the half-open door, she began to wander round the room, touching the walls, the books, the prints, all the familar things among which he had lived so many years.

In that dim continual journey she was like a disharmonic spirit traversing the air above where its body lies.

The door creaked behind her. A voice said sharply:

'What are you doing in this house?'

Mr Stone was standing beside the bust of Socrates. Bianca went up to him.

'Father!'

Mr Stone stared. 'It is you! I thought it was a thief! Where is Hilary?'

'Gone away.'

'Alone?'

Bianca bowed her head. 'It is very late, Dad,' she whispered.

Mr Stone's hand moved as though he would have stroked her.

'The human heart,' he murmured, 'is the tomb of many feelings.'

Bianca put her arm round him.

'You must go to bed, Dad,' she said, trying to get him to the door, for in her heart something seemed giving way.

Mr Stone stumbled; the door swung to; the room was plunged in darkness. A hánd, cold as ice, brushed her cheek. With all her force she stifled a scream.

'I am here,' Mr Stone said.

His hand, wandering downwards, touched her shoulder, and

she seized it with her own burning hand. Thus linked, they groped their way out into the passage towards his room.

'Good-night, dear,' Bianca murmured.

By the light of his now open door Mr Stone seemed to try and see her face, but she would not show it him. Closing the door gently, she stole upstairs.

Sitting down in her bedroom by the open window, it seemed to her that the room was full of people—her nerves were so unstrung. It was as if walls had not the power this night to exclude human presences. Moving, or motionless, now distinct, then covered suddenly by the thick veil of some material object, they circled round her quiet figure, lying back in the chair with shut eyes. These disharmonic shadows flitting in the room made a stir like the rubbing of dry straw or the hum of bees among clover stalks. When she sat up they vanished, and the sounds became the distant din of homing traffic; but the moment she closed her eyes, her visitors again began to steal round her with that dry, mysterious hum.

She fell asleep presently, and woke with a start. There, in a glimmer of pale light, stood the little model, as in the fatal picture Bianca had painted of her. Her face was powder white, with shadows beneath the eyes. Breath seemed coming through her parted lips, just touched with colour. In her hat lay the tiny peacock's feather beside the two purplish-pink roses. A scent came from her, too—but faint, as ever was the scent of chicory flower. How long had she been standing there? Bianca started to her feet, and as she rose the vision vanished.

She went towards the spot. There was nothing in that corner but moonlight; the scent she had perceived was merely that of the trees drifting in.

But so vivid had that vision been that she stood at the window, panting for air, passing her hand again and again across her eyes.

Outside, over the dark gardens, the moon hung full and almost golden. Its honey-pale light filtered down on every little shape of tree, and leaf, and sleeping flower. That soft, vibrating radiance seemed to have woven all into one mysterious whole, stilling disharmony, so that each little separate shape had no meaning to itself.

Bianca looked long at the rain of moonlight falling on the earth's carpet, like a covering shower of blossom which bees have sucked and spilled. Then, below her, out through candescent space, she saw a shadow dart forth along the grass, and to her fright a voice rose, tremulous and clear, seeming to seek enfranchisement beyond the barrier of the dark trees: 'My brain is clouded. Great Universe! I cannot write! I can no longer discover to my brothers that they are one. I am not worthy to stay here. Let me pass into You, and die!'

Bianca saw her father's fragile arms stretch out into the night through the sleeves of his white garment, as though expecting to be received at once into the Universal Brotherhood of the thin air.

There ensued a moment, when, by magic, every little dissonance in all the town seemed blended into a harmony of silence, as it might be the very death of self upon the earth.

Then, breaking that trance, Mr Stone's voice rose again, trembling out into the night, as though blown through a reed.

'Brothers!' he said.

Behind the screen of lilac bushes at the gate Bianca saw the dark helmet of a policeman. He stood there staring steadily in the direction of that voice. Raising his lantern, he flashed it into every corner of the garden, searching for those who had been addressed. Satisfied, apparently, that no one was there, he moved it to right and left, lowered it to the level of his breast, and walked slowly on.